FULL RATCHET

ALSO BY MIKE COOPER

Clawback

MIKE COOPER
FULL RATCHET

VIKING

VIKING

Published by the Penguin Group

Penguin Group (USA) Inc., 375 Hudson Street,

New York, New York 10014, USA

USA | Canada | UK | Ireland | Australia | New Zealand | India | South Africa | China

Penguin Books Ltd, Registered Offices: 80 Strand, London WC2R 0RL, England

For more information about the Penguin Group visit penguin.com

Library of Congress Cataloging-in-Publication Data

Cooper, Mike.

 Full ratchet / Mike Cooper.

    pages cm

 ISBN 978-0-670-02579-4

 1. Auditors—Pennsylvania—Pittsburgh—Fiction.   2. Financial crises—Fiction.
 3. Avarice—Fiction.   4. Pennsylvania—Fiction.   I. Title.

 PS3603.O58284F85 2013

 813'.6—dc23   2013001603

Printed in the United States of America

1   3   5   7   9   10   8   6   4   2

Set in Walbaum MT Std

Book design by Alissa Amell

This is a work of fiction. Names, characters, places, and incidents either are the product of the author's imagination or are used fictitiously, and any resemblance to actual persons, living or dead, businesses, companies, events, or locales is entirely coincidental.

For Sonia and Elliot

ACKNOWLEDGMENTS

I'm enormously grateful to the many people who helped me write this story. Advice, fact-checking and all kinds of support came from Yuri Berkovich, Samantha Cameron, Lynne Heitman, Ross Hoham, Joel Johnson, Josh Kendall, Sophie Littlefield, Claudia Ramirez, Vladimir Simine, Kyle Steele and Kim Ablon Whitney.

Linda Landrigan published Silas Cade's first short stories.

Julie Miesionczek is the best kind of editor: thoughtful, enthusiastic, funny. She and the team at Viking took a rough manuscript and turned it into a book.

Heide Lange, agent extraordinaire, along with Rachael Dillon Fried, Jen Linnan and Stephanie Delman saw the potential in Silas and brought him to the wide world.

Finally, my wife and children provide the encouragement that makes everything both possible and worthwhile.

FULL RATCHET

Hey Little Brother—

You're surprised, right?

Because if you already heard, for sure you would of tracked me down. I know it.

The state split us up when we were babies. Least you were a baby—I was one or two. Of course I don't remember, but my family told me later. I ended up staying with them the whole way through. I guess that wasn't how it went for you. New Hampshire DHHS gave me a little information—I had to hire a lawyer and file all these papers but they came through with the basics. I wrote to your last parents, and they gave me this address.

Also they told me a little about you. CPA—how about that! And in Vegas, too. Guess I know what kind of accountant that makes you, huh? Working for the casinos. I was out there, few years back. But not too long. Back east is home for me.

I fix cars, do a little welding, that kind of thing. Racing sometimes, on the weekend—dirt track, kind of like you got out there. Not the Speedway of course, more like Battle Mountain. I do all right. Got two alimonys to pay though, you know how that goes.

You and me should talk sometime. Catch up. We don't have any other blood relatives, not that I heard about anyway. It's just you and me.

I looked for you on the google, I don't know, computers aren't my thing. You call me instead. I got some ideas.

Your big brother,
Dave Ellins

CHAPTER ONE

What the big accounting firms forget is, if someone's rigging the books, they're *already* lying to you. And the longer they've gotten away with it, the better they're going to be.

A good audit isn't a playdate with calculators.

It's a hostile interrogation.

The Clay Micro offices were on the second floor of a converted industrial building. Pittsburgh's local rust belt was right outside but state development funds had paid for a nice rehab, all exposed brick and granite columns. Across a range of cubicles I could see interior glass overlooking the line floor.

"Sir? Sir?" A young woman behind the chrome reception desk, wireless earpiece blinking, tried to wave me down. "Do you have—?"

"Here to see the chief." I smiled and finished removing my cap—I'd stretched it out an extra two seconds. Long enough to keep my hand, and the hat itself, in front of my face while I crossed the ceiling camera's field.

"Is he expecting you?"

"Sure." I kept moving.

"Because I don't——"

"Thank you, Sharon." And I was in, headed for the executive suites at the end of the wing.

Hearing her name puzzled the receptionist an extra moment, even though I'd simply read it off the nameplate on her desk. But she was fast enough to dial up help. Two young guys in suits arrived at the CEO's office the same time I did. Not security but willing to pitch in. One had a coffee cup in hand, and it spilled down his shirt as I shoved past and banged open the door.

The CEO twisted around in his leather chair, reading glasses falling off his nose, staring in pasty surprise. "Wha——?"

I slammed the door in the face of my pursuers and said, rather loudly, "False invoices for ten point one million in Q4. Your boss sent me, Brinker."

Then I opened the door again, stepped to the side and waited.

I'll give him this, Brinker was quick. He gestured at the two eager beavers bursting in and said without hesitation, "It's okay. I need to talk to him. Back to work."

And five seconds later we were alone. That told me something about his style. He confirmed that our conversation was going to be harder than necessary when his next words to me were, "You're full of crap. The audit committee passed on those statements, and I've got signatures. Understand?"

I sighed.

"You think I'm an accountant," I said. "Here to cross-check invoices, review the bank recs, that sort of thing. Right?"

Brinker picked up his glasses and laid them on the gleaming hardwood desk, perhaps comforted by its vast size and weight. The office had that hushed, opulent feel of a hundred-grand interior design contract. Thin gray light filtered through the windows, which must have created a glare problem on his plasma monitor, but which lit the room pleasantly.

"You can pound sand," he said. "That's what I think."

I drew my Sig Sauer P226 from its around-the-back holster. It's a nice workaday handgun, pricey to be sure, but heavy, reliable and intimidating. The suppressor made it look like something out of *Hitman*. Brinker, showing nice reflexes, immediately dove under the desk. Without really aiming I shot out the monitor, his telephone console and for good measure the framed Harvard diploma on the wall.

Destroying the phone must have triggered an intercom or something. The door flew open as Brinker pulled his way back up from the floor, glaring. The two young men outside peered in suspiciously, but between the suppressor and the high-class soundproofing I doubt they'd heard anything. The Sig was already back under my jacket.

"Sorry, private meeting." I pushed the door shut again.

"All right." Brinker brushed broken plastic from the desk. "You're *not* an accountant."

"Actually—well, never mind. Ready to talk about revenue recognition?"

He was a tough nut. After several fruitless minutes, I opened the door and called out, "Where's the supply closet? We need a paper cutter."

The two men were still in the hallway, along with the receptionist. The three of them stared back at me, uncertain.

I looked at Brinker. "You want them to hear what we're talking about?"

He frowned and said past me, "Just do what he says. Sharon, you."

"Uh, sir, are you sure—?"

"Don't worry." The son of a gun was getting confident again, which began to annoy me. When Sharon brought up the paper cutter—a nice big one, a grid-marked platform with a two-foot swivel blade—I locked the door and dumped it on Brinker's desk.

"Drop your pants," I said, and opened the blade.

———

When I left Brinker's office, it was clear that little work was going on. Brinker had yelled some, even though we compromised on his finger instead—and I let him jerk it away at the last instant, so he lost only the tip, not even any bone. The soundproofing had muffled that noise, too. Still, his employees kept their distance. They knew *something* was up, but they couldn't be sure who I was, why I was there or what they ought to do in response. Small clusters of them peeked over cubicle walls, falling silent when I passed.

"Just routine," I said with a big smile. "Nice day, huh?" Spreading cheer everywhere I went.

I wasn't having fun. This was just getting the job done, as efficiently as possible. I arrived at the CFO's office.

His name was Nabors, and he was waiting for me. Brinker must have called to warn him. "It wasn't my fault," he said, the moment I walked through his door, talking fast. "He told me to do it. I didn't want anything to do with the entry. I knew it was wrong. I wanted to take the writedown, show it just as generally accepted accounting principles require, but he said we couldn't hit the bottom line like that all at once."

"Slow down." Nabors was a weasel, with slicked-back hair and a crisp white-over-blue shirt. His office was smaller than Brinker's, of course, and his desk and paneling were light colored—ash, maybe, or birch. "Tell me what I need to know and I'll let you live." I thought that was funny, but he didn't.

"The board reviewed the financials." Excuses continued to tumble out. "I was sick and couldn't check all the subledgers—"

"That's enough." He finally shut up and I watched him for a minute in silence, frowning. When the strain of keeping the words in became unbearable, he opened his mouth and I immediately said, "Don't talk, listen."

He stared at me, quivering a bit.

I nodded. "You drive a Porsche Cayenne Turbo, right? License plate says S-8. That's cute." SEC Form S-8 reports a company officer's exercise of stock options. "Before I came in this afternoon, I wired an M67 fragmentation grenade into the front axle linkage." He looked confused, so I continued. "It's simple. You can start the car and even drive it, but the first time you make a left-hand turn, the tie rod pulls the detonator, and . . . boom."

"But—"

"So here's what you can do. Calling the cops seems like a bad idea because they'll have some questions you really don't want to get into." I paused, and after a moment he nodded hastily. "Maybe you could disarm it yourself. Of course you only get one try . . . or maybe you know someone you could call, has some expertise? No?"

"All right, all right," he said. "Just let me tell it, okay?" And it was that easy.

The problem I'd been hired to solve was right out of Fraud 101. Clayco was a big, privately held manufacturing company. A few billion in sales, plus or minus. This division, Clay Micro, made some sort of computer-controlled hardware and contributed maybe a tenth of that.

Every quarter they'd send in their numbers, to be consolidated companywide. Recently central-office accounting staff had noticed some odd trends in the division's reporting: receivables up 120 percent, even though revenue was flat, along with negative cash flow and a sudden writedown of inventory.

In other words, the division was almost certainly booking nonexistent sales.

Companies do this all the time, of course. Usually they're just puffing up results to meet their targets, and the fake sales are simply reversed early in the next period. Not exactly legal, but tolerated.

The cash flow and inventory issues suggested worse, however: that someone inside the division was actively stealing. *That* Clayco's top management could not accept—but they sure didn't want it to come out publicly, say in an external auditor's annual report.

That's why they hired me instead.

Brinker had already admitted that the false invoicing was necessary to prop up net income, because they'd found millions of dollars of worthless silicon in the work-in-process inventory. Some kind of problem at the fabrication plant they'd contracted to make the chips, undiscovered until too late. According to Nabors, he'd documented the problem, all the way through a journal entry, when Brinker decided to cover it up instead.

"The chips were made by someone else?" I asked. "Why wasn't it their problem?"

"We'd already accepted the stock and built the machines. Contractual obligation."

"How much was the writedown?"

"Seven million or so." He looked defensive. "They were the core processors, and Manufacturing lost hundreds. Not cheap."

I thought about it. "The false sales were more than ten. Why'd you overcompensate?"

"We didn't want it to be too obvious."

I shook my head. "I don't know how you thought you'd get away with it," I said.

"It was just . . . smoothing the earnings, see? We knew we could journal it out over the next five or six months. We just didn't want to take the bad news all at once. The market hates surprises."

"Not so much as your boss." We went round a few more times, and Nabors's story didn't change. When I got up to leave he started to relax, tension draining from his shoulders.

"What about my car?" he asked.

He'd helped me out, but he was also a liar, a cheat and a coward. And rich, not coincidentally.

"You've got GPS on your phone, don't you?" I said.

"Huh?"

"So figure out how to get home with only right-hand turns." I walked out.

———

Sometimes, investigating something like this, you work the chain of command: start with a specific event, and each revelation takes you one step up the ladder, closer to Mr. Big. But today I seemed to be going in the opposite direction. Based on Nabors's account, the problem started on the production line.

I found the director of manufacturing downstairs, in a design lab off the manufacturing floor. He was standing with several technicians at a bench cluttered with blinking equipment and discarded circuit boards. When I came in, he jerked his head toward an office in the corner—no windows, just cheap partitions separating him from the lab. His gunmetal desk overflowed with paper.

Like he'd been expecting me. Everyone was gossipy today, talking behind my back.

"The chips," I said. "Seven million dollars of bad inventory."

"No." He crossed his arms, closed his mouth firmly and waited.

Finally I said, "No what?"

"No, it wasn't seven million. Only five point three." He grimaced. "No wonder you're here, they get the numbers wrong like that."

"Hmm." I might have scratched my head, but something about this guy made me not want to move my hand too far from my weapons. "So . . . why do you think I'm here?"

"Uh-uh." He shook his head. "I'm not saying anything else."

"Why not?"

"I heard what you did upstairs."

"And?"

"Let me tell you something, okay?" He spat into his wastebasket. Now that I noticed, the small office smelled of chewing tobacco. "I like this job, but I started out in the rough. Worked my way up from the shop floor, except for three years I spent on the docks, putting automation into the cranes. Putting crane operators out of work, that meant." He looked back at me. "Putting longshoremen out of work."

"So?"

He shrugged. "So you don't scare me. Go ahead and try."

I'd done some background research on all the division's managers. Just for situations like this.

"I know where you live," I said. "And that means I know where your wife lives, too."

He grunted. "Hah. You can save me the lawyer's bill. We're getting divorced."

"And your son? Working for A-1 Parking downtown . . . I could find him easy."

"That junkie?" This time the grunt was half laughter. "I threw him out of the house last year after I caught him selling my power tools to buy drugs."

Some days, I tell you. I couldn't try the car thing, either—I knew he drove a twelve-year-old Cavalier. The man stood waiting, and I could see that his hands were large and scarred and evidently used to pounding on more than desktops.

He looked like he really, really wanted me to try him.

Finally I nodded. "Okay," I said, and reached into my back pocket.

He barely moved, but enough—his weight suddenly on the balls of his feet, one hand forward, a slight turn sideways—and we were a split second from a lethal escalation of the discussion.

"Relax." I pulled out my wallet.

He looked puzzled.

"No need to do this the hard way," I said. "How about five hundred?"

———

One more rung down the ladder: the Quality Assurance lab. According to the manufacturing director—who'd chiseled me out of a grand in the end, can you believe it—the bad silicon was QA's fault because they'd accepted two full runs from the chip fabricator without completely testing the samples. Somehow the design specs had been corrupted by the fab, one or two transistors out of a zillion were backward or something. I didn't understand the explanation. But QA had been sloppy and passed the shipments, so the company got stuck with payment even after Manufacturing realized their automation controllers, built with the problem chipsets, were failing.

Lunchtime had come and gone and I was still walking back the cat—that's a little counterintelligence jargon, just to show I really was in the business. Still looking for the prime culprit. The current suspect, the QA manager, appeared unpromising. He was young enough to have tattoos and a shaved head, and dumb enough to think that both were cool. But his ecru shirt was stained with sweat, and he stuttered a pathetic greeting when I loomed over the opening to his cubicle. He was flat-out terrified, for which I was grateful, after the parade of rockheads so far.

"Wh-what can I d-d-do for you?" he asked. He had three computer monitors on his desk, all of them dirty and festooned with Post-it notes.

I pointed at the middle screen. "What's that?" It showed a pair of boxes, numbers flashing and disappearing, with long strings of gibberish slowly scrolling past.

"Uh?" He twisted around. "That's, uh, a test run on the CDU processors racked in over there . . . ah, why do you . . . ?" His voice trailed away.

"Just making conversation." I waited, but he didn't pick up the ball. "Look, I'm here from headquarters, checking some accounts. That's all."

"Yes sir." His eyes were fixed about three feet to my left.

"The manufacturing director, he says you destroyed more than five million dollars of chips by accident."

"What?" His voice cracked, but suddenly he was looking directly at me, with more than simple fear. "He said five million?"

Aha, I thought. "It wasn't?"

"It wasn't near that much. Maybe a million, and that's only at the transfer price, not wholesale."

"So he overreported the bad inventory by a factor of five." I glared at the boy. "Why would he do that?"

"He must have . . ."

"What?"

The QA manager continued to hesitate. "I don't want to get anybody in trouble."

I had to laugh. "Look, kid, you can safely assume that right now every person here is in trouble. The question is, how are you going to get yourself out?"

You could see smoke coming from the gears, but he spilled it after another minute. The manufacturing director must have taken the useless chips and set aside another four million dollars' worth, then sold the good chips on the sly. There's a gray market for stolen chips, which I'd heard about—during the bubble, Vietnamese gangs with AK-47s would sometimes burst into Silicon Valley office parks. But illegal channels always mean a steep discount.

"What do you think he cleared?" I asked.

The manager shook his head, no longer so much afraid of me as worrying about being blamed. Or more likely, angered by his own failure to think of it first. "Maybe five percent," he muttered. "Ten, tops."

I thought about going back and shooting the manufacturing director, but that could wait. I was more and more impressed by the utter venality of the company. Was every single employee crooked?

You hear a lot about fostering a good corporate culture: respect your workers, your customers and your goals, and business will take care of itself. Clay Micro seemed to be a case study in the opposite.

"Back up a moment," I said. "Maybe he took advantage, but you still dustbinned quite a few of these chips on your own. How did that happen?"

"That jerk who runs our network, it was his fault. Said it was a mistake." He scowled. "Like any idiot could confuse an ethernet switch with a base-10 cable hub!"

Well. "The kindergarten version, please."

"Mistake, my ass." The manager spoke bitterly. "He was too cheap to buy the right equipment, is all. Probably kept the switch for himself and swapped in a no-name hub he found for ten dollars on eBay. When I racked in the chips and started the diagnostics, the routines ran fine for five minutes—just long enough for me to go for a coffee. When I came back, the whole frame was on fire. On fire! Flames, smoke—lucky they got rid of the halon last year, after the OSHA inspection, or we'd all be dead now."

He started to rant. To sober him up, I reminded him that being dead now was certainly something I could arrange.

"It was his fault," the QA manager repeated, sullenly. "I do as good as I can, with the equipment they give me."

"I'll make sure you get a gold star in your performance review," I said. "Now, this computer guy—where do I find him?"

———

"I'm a Microsoft-certified network engineer," the man said prissily. He was bald and short, feet barely touching the ground below his stool. "Not to mention my degree from PTI, and I've passed more than half the courses for a master's. That's with no tuition reimbursement, mind you."

14

"Fine. Let me ask—"

"Not that these ingrates would even notice. Most of them are so lazy they can't even unjam their lousy printers. If I had a nickel for every time I've said, 'Turn it off, then turn it on again,' well, I'd have a lot of nickels, I tell you what."

The network administrator—excuse me, network engineer—had his own nook in an isolated room next to the loading dock, with cinderblock walls and crowded racks of computers and cables everywhere. Half the overhead lights were out, making the man look even more molelike behind his thick, plastic-framed glasses. The air smelled of ozone and warm plastic.

"And don't get me started on those nitwits in engineering. Think they're all hotshots, just because they have some worthless options from the last dot-com flameout they worked at. Could any of them even punch down a wall jack, I ask you? But as soon as they forget their password, well, *then* I get a polite message on my voicemail."

"Let's try to stay focused here, okay?" I thought about pulling out the Sig, but the mole was so wrapped up in his own bitterness I'd have to fire a few rounds to get his attention, and unlike Brinker's office, down here I'd probably hit something that would explode. I reached out, put one hand on top of his head and one under his jaw and squeezed his face.

Forced to stop talking, he glared at me.

"The QA manager says you gave him a bad stub," I said. "Or something like that." I eased up on his jaw.

"It wasn't me—I didn't do it!"

The company motto, apparently. "Yeah, yeah. Who did?"

"The co-op. I wasn't even here that day."

"Huh? Co-op?" Hippies and organic tofu?

"His name is Timmy. He's a co-op student from Pitt. Like an intern, helps out three days a week, part of his degree program."

I looked at him. "There's someone lower on the totem pole than you?"

He unconsciously stroked the humming computer alongside his chair, for comfort, I guess. "I was letting him do basic network maintenance, load software, handle simple complaints. When that QA knucklehead said he needed a few more ports, Timmy just plugged in another hub, but he didn't check with me first. Over-loaded the entire frame! If he had asked me, of course, I would have said—"

You get the drift. This case started out like MF Global, but it was finishing like a two-bill slip-and-fall.

The network engineer sputtered to a stop after another minute of buck-passing, and he looked sideways at me. "So . . . who are you, anyway?" For the first time he sounded unsure.

"An accountant," I said. "Where's Timmy?"

CHAPTER TWO

By the time I finished with Timmy, Brinker must have given everyone the rest of the afternoon off. Mental health day, maybe. The parking lot was almost empty.

Just one lonely Porsche Cayenne sitting by itself in the executive row.

The day had warmed up—a little too warm for late spring in western Pennsylvania—and I stood in the pleasant breeze for a minute.

Lawrenceville was a scruffy neighborhood even by Pittsburgh standards. Clay Micro's long brick factory, a hundred years old, looked over at the backside of a food wholesaler. Its blank, corrugated steel walls were stained and rusty at the joints. Potholed asphalt filled the space between them—half parking lot, half roadway. The street dead-ended at a narrow canal.

I didn't want to leave immediately. If Brinker was going to call in a reaction team, better it happen here, while I was ready, instead of on the road somewhere. I walked to the canal's edge and admired the cut granite blocks descending to waterline, perfectly fitted a century ago by masons who'd probably been working with hand tools. Just to the left a box trestle crossed the canal—a railroad bridge, long fallen into disuse. Its classic trapezoid of iron girders was stark against the sky, black and rusty red in the late-afternoon sun.

I kicked some gravel into the canal. There was a sort of *gloop* instead of a splash, the water viscous with grime and oil. On the other side of the bridge the old rails disappeared into brush. More brick remnants of industry were slowly crumbling into ruin over there—windows gaping, scarred plywood across the dock doors.

A boat horn sounded. The Allegheny was only a few hundred yards farther, though invisible behind the structures. Upriver I could see the 40th Street Bridge overhead, homeward commuter traffic starting to thicken at rush hour.

Nothing happened. No one came out of the Clay Micro offices. I walked back to my rental car, a Chevy Malibu—I'd wanted something reliable, but that's what they had—plugged my phone in to charge and drove away.

———

The tail picked me up after a quarter mile.

Lawrenceville wasn't just abandoned industry and cheap warehouses. Compact two- and three-story row houses butted right up against the factories—worker housing, from back when. People had fixed some of them up. Wooden trim had been painted, cars were parked on the street, here and there a barbecue grill sat on a stoop.

A pair of boys were flicking a lacrosse ball back and forth, sticks swinging. They stopped as I passed. I looked in the rearview, wondering if they were watching me.

And by chance I saw a car turn onto the street behind me, two blocks back.

Downtown then onto I-376 would have been a quicker way to leave the city. Instead I turned onto Butler, then Penn, meandering east toward city neighborhoods that most people tended to avoid—according to police statistics and local news, anyhow. Google can tell remarkably detailed stories if you ask. I'd never been here before.

The car was newish and had four doors. What can I say? I live in New York City, I don't drive much, I just don't know much about them. It kind of looked Japanese, but they all do nowadays.

I turned left, it turned left. I turned right, it kept going . . . then reappeared a minute later, turning onto the street fifty yards in front of me. They must have taken a shortcut, accelerating through some alley to take the lead. A pretty good move for single-car surveillance.

I never would have noticed if I hadn't been looking for it.

We drove through Homewood. Residential and not a lot of money: weedy lots behind waist-high chain-link, foreclosures, scrawny men talking to themselves on the street. The dark car—metallic royal blue—stayed nearby.

But that was all. Just followed, and watched. Anything else was going to happen later.

Finally I turned south, went through Edgewood and took an on-ramp onto 376 going east. A few miles later I saw a sign, smaller than a billboard—the Hiway Rest Motel. I signaled, took the exit at a reasonable speed, and led the dark car onto a four-lane avenue.

The motel was close to the highway, a plain concrete two-story with red doors every ten feet, top and bottom. FREE HBO IN EVERY

ROOM! the sign said, like it was 1985. I pulled in several spaces away from the front entrance—no need for the clerk to see my car—and walked in.

"Just one night," I said. "Cash all right?"

"Certainly. Ninety-seven dollars plus tax."

I filled out the card with imaginary details, reversing two digits on the license plate, and handed over my twenties.

"Continental breakfast, six to nine," the clerk said. "Coffee all day."

"Can't wait."

Outside I strolled to the car, drove it to the end of the building and reparked. Room 14 was on the first floor. I turned the key—no fancy card entry here—went inside and closed the door.

I waited thirty minutes, lights out and gun drawn, sitting on a chair in the corner opposite the door.

Nothing happened.

I thought about Clay Micro. Rotten from top to bottom was not so common, even among my sort of clients. The division had to be making money somehow, to avoid attention from Clayco corporate for so long. Brinker might have been doing something right.

But he wouldn't be doing it much longer.

I assumed that he'd called the cavalry. Brinker looked like a Rotary Club businessman, but he ran a thoroughly corrupt shop, and grimy environments attract more germs. All the same, it was surprising he had friends with pursuit and intimidation skills— friends who could show up with less than an hour's notice.

After half an hour I stood up, pausing to let the blood recirculate. It was still light outside, not even five o'clock. The window drape was heavy but not fully drawn, so I peeked around the edge.

The blue car was still with me, parked in a restaurant lot across the broad street. It sat off to one side, late sunlight glinting off the windshield so I couldn't see inside. They had a good position, with a clear view of my room and a straight shot to the lot's exit.

A rifle aimed at me from inside the vehicle seemed unlikely— someone would notice, and a sniper would have to fire through tempered auto glass. I could probably walk over to the restaurant without being shot.

Why not? If they attacked me on the way, we could all improvise. I felt a frisson of adrenaline at the thought.

Enough fucking around. I'd whacked the hornet's nest, and now it was time to shoo them away.

I took off my jacket and let it fall over my right hand; the pistol was concealed, and I could drop the jacket in an instant if necessary. I left the key on the nightstand.

I waited until the lights turned, up the road, so traffic dropped to nothing—what I could see from the room, at least. Then I opened the door, let it close behind me and walked directly across the motel's parking lot.

No reaction from the car. I wasn't going toward them, but toward the front of the restaurant. I hopped the grassy ditch between the motel and the road, jogged across its four lanes and fell in behind two couples, older folks, probably here for an AARP discount.

A warm Fryalator smell drifted from the rear of the building. My shoes scuffed pebbles and grit on the asphalt. The senior citizens shielded me from my pursuers' sight lines until we approached the door, and then the car was blocked completely by the corner of the restaurant.

I immediately took off, going right, along the front window glass. Diners inside glanced up from their booths as I passed, so I kept the pistol low down, still covered by my jacket. Around the corner, moving faster now, then across the back of the building. A busboy in dirty whites stood at a dumpster, tossing plastic bags of garbage over the lip. He looked at me running past, started to say something.

Around the last corner, and the rear of the dark car was dead in front of me. I dodged a Lincoln and an SUV. Two people, front seat. No brake lights, no exhaust visible. The driver's window was rolled down—that was convenient, I wouldn't have to smash it out.

"Don't move. Don't *move*." I stopped four feet from the vehicle, outside the door's radius, with the pistol raised but only the barrel end visible. The jacket was still draped over my forearm.

"Put your hands behind your neck." I kept my voice just loud enough to carry, quiet enough not to attract attention. "Do it. Now."

Both glared at me, motionless. About my age. One was huge—his seat was all the way back, and his head brushed the car's roof. He had sunglasses on, the other was stubbly, both had very short hair and broad shoulders. I couldn't see much else.

"The early bird ends at five-thirty," I said. "What are you waiting for?"

The giant driver slowly shook his head. He muttered something I couldn't catch.

"Open your door. Just you—driver's side." I gestured with the pistol.

A long moment, and then he put one hand down, pulled the latch, and pushed the door halfway open. I stepped up, standing just behind the roof pillar on his side, gun at my side.

Now he couldn't hit me with the door. Trying to reach back and grab the pistol would be awkward. It was a risk, coming in this close, but the situation was as much in my favor as I could expect. Main thing, I wasn't presenting an OK Corral tableau to all the elderly busybodies in the restaurant.

The car was a Nissan—I could see a logo. I smelled exhaust, and now that I was next to it, I could hear the faint thrum of the car's engine. They'd left it running after all.

"Who are you?" I said, trying to watch both heads and all four hands.

"You make a mistake." Strong accent there, something from Eastern Europe.

"That's my line."

"Go away."

"Shit, that's my line *too*."

"Fuck you."

"Okay, I was holding that one back—"

He stamped the accelerator and the engine roared, wheels suddenly screaming on the pavement. The Nissan surged forward. I jumped out of the way. The open door swung wildly as the vehicle banged over the lot's curb and into the street. The driver fought the wheel, hand over hand. He kept his foot on the gas, though. The skid was out of control—one eighty, then all the way around. Horns blared as two passing cars veered out of the way, almost hitting each other.

Another slew to the left, then right, and the door finally swung shut. The driver got himself straightened out, the wheels caught, and they shot off down the road about three times the speed limit.

I watched them disappear. The burnt-rubber smell was strong and acrid.

"What was *that* all about?"

A guy in a ball cap had come up behind me, staring at the tire marks, then at the street. I lowered my hand, ruffling the jacket to make sure the Sig was covered.

"Skipping out on his bill, maybe? I got no idea."

"Assholes."

"No kidding." I shook my head. "I'm leaving."

"Yeah." He kept peering down the road. I went back around the restaurant—better that no one saw me go directly back to the motel—reholstering the pistol on the way. The busboy had finished up and lit a cigarette, sitting on a pile of wooden produce crates. I nodded at him, but this time he didn't say anything.

I waited for a pause in traffic, crossed back over and went straight to my own car, keys in hand. I slid in, shifting around as the Sig jammed into my lower back, and started up.

The first stoplight was a hundred yards down the street, green when I got there. I picked up speed going through.

A hundred bucks blown. I wouldn't be sleeping *there* tonight.

CHAPTER THREE

I felt uncomfortable and out of place.

Pittsburgh was better than I expected. A lot better than, say, East St. Louis. People still lived here, went to work, kept the streets clean. The industrial collapse had happened, manufacturing jobs evaporated, then somehow the city picked itself up and moved on. Some of the architecture was beautifully preserved, and the rivers looked like you could swim in them even without a tetanus shot.

But it was . . . *empty*.

Streets were wide and barely occupied, with parking anywhere. The industrial districts—Lawrenceville, the Strip, areas down the Monongahela—looked like vast metal sheds had been dropped into scraggly open fields, with just enough truck traffic to keep the weeds from completely taking over.

I missed New York, with all its bustle and noise and people in your face. I missed decent food and coffee shops on every corner. I missed the comforting anonymity of the crowds, the squealing rush of the subways, the constant nonstop chatter of the streets.

Which is funny, considering I grew up in rural New Hampshire. I joined the service before high school even ended, a week before graduation, right to Fort Benning. Then I spent several years in remote parts of the world, mostly living in shipping containers and dugouts and bivvy sacks. Pittsburgh was Paris compared to that.

Maybe I'd been too long in the city, gotten too used to life in Manhattan. Maybe I needed to get outside the loop, spend time in real America.

Maybe I needed to finish this damn job and go home.

I pulled into an empty lot a few miles later. A sagging fence at its edge surrounded an abandoned construction site—excavation had started, one curtain wall poured, then nothing. Weeds grew in the piles of dirt, and a pool of black water had accumulated in the bottom of the hole. In the dusk I couldn't read the fading sign wired to the chain-link.

Parked by the fence, facing the road, I had a nice view in either direction. Plenty of time to see someone coming. I started to switch off the engine, then changed my mind.

My crummy phone was still plugged into the dash. A twenty-dollar disposable, but it worked fine. I pick them up two or three at a time. This one came from a bodega on 108th that still hadn't installed security cameras. I stretched the power cord, leaning back, and dialed a 917 number.

It rang five times and clicked into silence. No invitation to leave a message.

Not good. Ryan *always* answered his calls.

See, I wasn't actually the principal on this Clayco job. When the board of directors—or whoever—decided they needed the swamp drained at Clay Micro, they'd hired a different guy. Ryan had the same sort of line I did, and like all independent contractors he couldn't say no to any offer of work. But maybe he was busy, or just didn't feel like leaving New York for a few days. Instead, he asked around and subbed it out to me.

Normally I wouldn't step a foot from the city either, if I could avoid it. But I had personal business in Pittsburgh, business I'd been avoiding for months, and when Ryan called, it felt like the universe had decided enough was enough. So I said yes, and here I was, dodging eurotrash muscle in the fallen wastelands of western Pennsylvania.

I dialed again, and again got no answer.

In the middle of heavy traffic, all four lanes filled, a city bus appeared. The electronic sign over the driver had a pleasant LED glow, but the lighted interior carried only a few passengers, slumped in the plastic seats. It trundled past, groaning with effort on the incline, doubtless irritating drivers behind it.

I dialed another, more familiar, number. This one picked up after one ring.

"What?"

"It's Silas."

"Uh-huh."

Zeke's an actual friend, and another specialty contractor. "You in the clear there?"

"Call you back." Click.

He wasn't necessarily in a bad mood, though it could be hard to tell. Zeke tends to be economical with his words. The army calls what he did for them MOUT—"military operations in urban terrain"—or even better, "kinetic response." He never talks about it. Clients basically hire him when fucking-around time is *over.*

We knew each other back when we were both in uniform. Well, Zeke never wore a uniform, but you know what I mean—running into each other on the sort of ad hoc, deep-black missions that policy makers love.

Zeke has some issues, but so do we all.

The phone in my hand buzzed. Zeke hadn't dialed it direct, of course I couldn't be updating my entire contact list every week or two when I switched to a new disposable. Instead he called my permanent number. I use an electronic forwarding service to switch incoming calls to Canada, where an anonymizing server scrubs the metadata and forwards it again, to whatever phone I happen to be using. Canada, because for now they have real, enforceable data-privacy laws.

Zeke would have switched to a more secure line, perhaps his own prepaid disposable. Kind of a pain in the ass, like most op-sec procedures, but neither of us wanted someone listening in, however remote the possibility. I suppose the NSA wouldn't have any trouble, but local law enforcement is generally stymied by cross-border wiretapping.

Or so the theory goes. So far it's worked.

"What's going on?"

"Not much. Seen Ryan lately?"

"No."

"He's not answering his phone," I said.

"Uh-oh."

Like I said, abnormal behavior. It's a small world, our little corner of the informal economy, and we all know one another.

"Don't suppose you've heard anything," I said.

"Nope. Why do you need to reach him?"

I gave a brief and elliptical explanation. "And now someone's following me."

"They a problem?"

"Nah."

"I'll ask around."

"Thanks."

"What do you want me to do if I find him?"

"Tell him to answer his damn calls."

"I'll see what I can do. Sure you're good?"

"Yeah."

"Pittsburgh." Like it was Ulan Bator. "Didn't know people still lived there."

"It's not so bad."

"I'll get back to you." He hung up.

I sat another five minutes, studying a paper map I'd picked up at the AAA office on 62nd Street in Manhattan before coming on this bumfuck jaunt. The rental car had GPS, but I'd turned it off the moment I got in—as bad as a telephone, for privacy.

I had a half-dozen other maps, too, including Ohio, Buffalo and Washington, D.C. If some suspicious meddler found them, I didn't want to give the center of my interest away.

The route looked easy enough. I folded the map, checked the road once more and eased the Malibu back into traffic.

———

Clabbton was a three-block downtown, surrounded by houses that looked like they'd been built from Sears Roebuck kits in 1925. Beyond them, the usual sprawl of gas stations, fast-food and big-box stores outside town limits. It lay in Fayette County, an hour southeast of Pittsburgh and halfway to the West Virginia border, where the hills began to rise gradually into mountains. I arrived with the last of the daylight, shadows falling, streetlights coming on. I drove through town at twenty miles an hour, careful to follow local speed limits.

The only attractive section was a row of old stores on Main

Street, built of quarry stone and granite, and the town hall facing them across a small green. A war monument—man on a horse, so it must have been the Civil War—was floodlit from a single lamp below. I crossed a railroad bridge, catching a glimpse of a darkened mainline stretching into the woods on either side, then drove down the commercial strip. Rite Aid, convenience stores, a Super Duper supermarket—the usual.

I turned around and went back, taking one of the side streets, then another. Fifteen minutes was enough to cover most of the town—really, it wasn't much more than the intersection of two state roads, plus a square mile of settlement.

Finally, back out on the strip, I stopped at a motor court with a VACANCY sign. It was old-fashioned, the tiny bungalows in a neat row. The Scotch pines overhanging them had probably been planted when the place was built, fifty or sixty years ago.

Half the cabins had lit windows, and the white-gravel circle drive held seven or eight pickup trucks. Workingmen's vehicles: older, dented, most with metal tool cases mounted behind the cab or along the bed walls.

In the office I tapped a counter bell, and a woman came from the back of the house. I could hear television behind her.

"You're in luck," she said, putting on a pair of reading glasses from around her neck. "Had a man leave just this morning, so one unit's open."

"You're that busy?"

"Folks are always coming and going, of course, so you'd probably get something somewhere. But I had someone tell me just last week they drove all the way from Erlenton before they found a room." She pushed over a registration card and a pen. "You're with the drillers, aren't you?"

I had to think about what I was writing, so as not to repeat the made-up information I'd used at the last place. "Um, no, just some family business."

"Oh, I'm sorry. So many big men have come in lately, I assume they're all working on the rigs."

I realized what she was talking about. "The fracking, is it?"

"Yes." She nodded, waiting while I finished the card. "Wells and test bores and people selling their land leases like they won the lottery—I tell you, life sure is different around here."

"Uh-huh."

"Not that I'm complaining. Some folks, they don't like all the commotion and new faces and crowds. But Clabbton needs the business, and that's good, no matter where they're coming from."

I returned the card, along with a night's payment in cash.

"If they all go to work at five A.M.," I said, "they're probably in bed and quiet at nine."

She laughed. "Oh, yes, every one of them. Like an empty church here at night."

"Excellent."

"If there's any problem with the cabin, you let me know." She handed over my key—also old-fashioned, with a brass chain connecting it to a small painted diamond of hardboard. "I had my girl redd it up after lunch, but she was in a hurry to see her boyfriend . . . you know how it goes."

The cabin's walls were about as well soundproofed as a sheet of newspaper. Someone was playing a video game in the bungalow to my left, and I could hear every burst of weapon fire, every explosion, every grunt. To the right, someone had talk radio on, sports and politics, the entire discussion irritating. A minute later gravel crunched in front as a vehicle drove in, tinny music blasting.

I looked at my phone. Even in the din, if I could hear all my neighbors, there was a chance they could hear me. I was dog tired, but I put my boots back on and went back to the Malibu.

I turned left, away from Clabbton center. The road narrowed to two lanes, then climbed some hills into deep forest. Houses thinned. Every now and then there'd be a farmstead or a liquor store or a gas station, each with a gravel parking lot and a few pickups, none closer than a quarter mile to the next. Twice I drove under massive sets of power lines, draped from huge pylons marching across the hills, a clear-cut track like a ski run following underneath.

It was dark, and I couldn't see anyone behind me. I suppose they could have turned off their headlights, but that would be awfully dumb on this road. I accelerated, swung through a series of curves, and pulled into the first dirt turnoff I saw. I slowed but not much, bumping and scraping and banging on the rough path, then slammed to a halt and killed the engine as soon as I was out of sight of the road.

Silence.

I considered the dome light above my head—I couldn't tell which way the switch turned it off, so I rammed my elbow up into the plastic cover instead. It cracked. I felt around to make sure the bulb was broken, then quietly opened my door and slipped out.

No cars passed. I waited a few minutes. Someone approached from the other direction, but it was a jacked-up Mustang, and from my hiding spot near the verge, I saw a teenager behind the wheel. An SUV drove by towing a horse trailer. A few more cars, none likely.

It was impossible I'd had a surveillance team on me all the way from Pittsburgh. But if by some scant chance there *had* been, they were long gone now. A small weight lifted.

The woods were cool, the night air smelling of fern and dirt and berries. I discovered I still had phone service.

This time, Ryan answered on the first ring.

"Silas!"

"Ryan?" I was relieved. "Where've you been?"

"What?"

"I called twice already, you didn't answer."

"Shit, yeah, sorry." There was a pause, as he apparently took the phone away from his ear long enough to check the display. "Oops, fuck, looks like I missed like five calls. It's the job, man—they keep calling me. What're you *doing*? They're so pissed, they're hinting around they want me to take a *contract* on you."

Great. "You hired me, I did what you said."

"Dude, you were supposed to do a fucking *audit*. What the hell happened out there?"

New Yorkers. That was what I'd been missing.

"I fast-tracked it," I said.

"Is anyone still alive?"

"What?"

"Because, what I'm hearing—and when I say 'hearing,' that's like I'm getting calls every fucking ten *minutes*—is you showed up with, fuck, a chainsaw and a machete or shit like that."

"They were all still standing when I left." Those that I saw, anyway. Brinker had probably gone to get his finger sewn up, and everyone else had disappeared.

"Seriously, the man's not happy."

"Come on, Ryan." I closed my eyes, leaning against a tree. The cellphone's lousy voice quality hurt my head as much as Ryan's complaining. "They came to you first, didn't they? What did they expect?"

"I dunno, maybe not the cutting-off-thumbs part. Did you really do that?"

"Of course not."

"Or blow up some VP's sports car?"

"Not that either. Jesus."

"Good. Okay."

I frowned. "You *told* them I wouldn't have done shit like that, didn't you?"

"Well, fuck, I'm not there. I've been on jobs—um, never mind."

"Remind me not to use you as a reference."

Ryan laughed. "You know, they probably would have paid a per diem. You didn't have to, like, superexpedite the discovery phase."

"Right. Think they're unhappy *now?*—all I can say is, good thing you didn't handle it yourself." Ryan tended to be more physical than me, believe it or not. "The building's still there, and nothing's on fire."

"Whatever. Anyway, it's been ten minutes, I'm about due for another fucking call. Give me the executive summary."

So I explained Clay Micro's little comedy of errors, starting with Timmy the Slacker's careless infrastructure maintenance, proceeding through opportunistic skimming and fraud at every level, and finishing with Brinker, the depantsed CEO. When I was done, Ryan didn't say anything for a moment.

"Dude." He started laughing again. "That's an awesome story. Like, I mean, truly *awesome*. Only what the fuck am I going to tell them? Send everyone to jail and shut the place down? Didn't you ever study client management?"

Ryan had gone to business school. "How about, I dunno, the truth?" I said.

"That's the last thing they want to hear." His chuckling died away. "Jesus, this is fucked up. Let me get some details, okay?"

We ran over it again, Ryan taking notes this time. He stopped messing around, too—asked brief, relevant questions, listened, didn't crack any more jokes.

"Okay," he said when I finished. "Good enough for now. I'll see if they want something written."

I breathed the forest air. "One more thing," I said.

"Yeah?"

"I was followed on the way out." I described the dark blue car.

"You sure?"

Sometimes Ryan could be stupid, but that's okay. "Yeah, I'm sure."

"How long were you inside?"

"Forty-seven minutes." Yes, of course I checked.

"So the CEO . . . um, Brinker?—he had plenty of time to call someone. Probably just wants to know who you are. Can't really blame him, right?"

Like I said, Ryan was good on the physical side. Maybe not so good on the thinking-it-through part.

"Nothing in the background material suggested Brinker is anything but an overpaid company executive," I said. "It turns out he's crooked, but there's no mention of gambling or brushes with the law or a bad reputation or whatever."

"So?"

"So how did he *know* who to call?"

"Oh."

Projection bias. For people like Ryan and me, being followed by shady characters probably carrying guns, that's just part of the working day. We get used to it.

If you're not careful, though, you can forget that the rest of the world doesn't live that way.

"Not to mention," I said, "that the A-Team must have gotten on site in about forty-five minutes."

"Maybe they're really efficient."

"Uh-huh. Or maybe they were already on call." If they'd been there from the beginning, of course, I wouldn't have had so easy a time of it inside. "Either way, there might be more going on here than they told you."

"I'll be sure to—wait, hang on."

I heard another phone ring in the background.

"It's . . . yeah, it's them again," Ryan said. "Gotta go."

"Remember, even if they stiff you, I still get paid."

"Next round at Volchak's is on me." He clicked off.

I'd been standing in the trees long enough to start to get cold. Still nothing suspicious on the road. Something cracked in the woods, but it was probably just a big dumb animal wandering around.

I dialed another number, again from memory.

"Clara Dawson." No caller ID, so she'd assume it was a professional call. "What can I do for you?"

"Hi, Clara."

"Silas!" She laughed. "It's been . . . hell, it's been days!"

Clara's career had well and truly taken off last year. We'd both gotten tangled up in a series of high-profile killings on Wall Street. As the banksters went down, one by one, most of America seemed happy to cheer on the assassin. Clara figured out what really happened—predictably, a massive pile of money was at root—and her reporting vaulted her from hardscrabble blogger to distinguished journalist and pundit, all in one go.

I'd had something to do with the investigation as well, but Clara left me out of it. Not many journos can actually keep a secret. Even more remarkably, after our relationship first went decidedly non-professional and then, unfortunately, back to just friends, we'd managed to remain, well, *friends.*

Sometimes I wondered. Paths not taken. Choices not made, possibilities not pursued. But my gray-zone existence didn't exactly mesh with high-profile journalism. It's just as well we didn't try harder to make it work—jail for me and disgrace for her would have been the inevitable outcome.

As it is, we talk, have dinner occasionally, sometimes go running together. She doesn't use me for a source too often, and I don't ask for favors. Much. Mostly, it works.

"You know," I said. "This job and that. It never ends."

"Tell me about it. Or rather, don't, not now—I'm expecting another call."

"I'll save the social graces, then. What do you know about a company called Clayco? Or one of their divisions, Clay Micro?"

"Nothing. What *should* I know?"

I heard a faint clatter in the background—her keyboard.

"Not much," I said. "A little assignment I'm about to wrap up."

"Mostly defense. Military-grade avionics, telemetry . . . founded in the sixties, still private." She was reading from some online profile. "Sensor integration, large-scale data analysis. Fairly high-tech."

"I got that." Standard background, right off the internet.

"They seem to have focused on missile technology—guidance systems and so forth. Can that be right? That sort of technology is dominated by the majors. Raytheon. Lockheed."

"It's where they started, back in the seventies." I'd read the same material she must have been looking at. "Now they've got some sort of niche in tactical guided arms. Like a soldier fires a rocket from a shoulder launcher—they're not wire guided anymore, the nosecones are smart enough to make their own decisions. Sounds all Skynet to me, but Clayco's on the cutting edge of this sort of thing."

"And you're working on Clay Micro?" Pause. "It's small, relative to the parent. One of six or eight divisions. They make seismic sensors. Tracking earthquakes, maybe, that kind of thing."

"Underground nuclear tests, I think, but nowadays more useful for geological surveys—the kind they use looking for oil, for example."

"Fine. That's Clay Micro. So what?"

"How do the financials look?"

"Dunno. They're private. Give me a minute."

I waited, leaning against the rental car. My eyes had gradually adjusted to the dark forest, but it was still difficult to see anything. The moon either hadn't risen or was behind clouds. I couldn't see through the tree cover.

"Clay Micro's initial investors snuck in some strong antidilution provisions," Clara said.

"Hmm." The way it works is, the first guys bringing cash to the table usually end up with a big piece of ownership. Fair enough. But when later investors buy in—and *nobody* makes it on just one round of financing—the first team can see its stake diluted. "That's common enough."

"They got full ratchet."

"Oh." Not so common after all. Full ratchet meant a guaranteed-percent piece of the pie. Company founders desperate for financing certainly had worse options—death-spiral convertible bonds, anyone?—but full ratchet was usually great for those first investors and lousy for everyone else. "How'd that work out?"

"What you'd expect, it looks like. The founder got squeezed out a few years later, around when they were acquired by Clayco. It wasn't called Clay Micro until then, of course."

And in the end the founder might well have lost his entire stake, even though the company itself apparently did well. Another happy Wall Street story. "When was that?"

"Late nineties. There was some press on it. But that's about it . . . No other significant acquisitions. Clayco's gone to the debt markets a few times since then. Borrowings are what you'd expect for their size. Nothing's jumping out here."

About what I thought. "Okay."

"Oh, wait!"

"What?"

"They're part owned by Sweetwater Institutional Investors."

"Sweetwater . . . *Wilbur Markson?*"

"Exactly. The Buddha himself."

Good God.

You've heard of Wilbur Markson. You've probably seen his folksy, down-to-earth op-eds or heard him on TV or—if you were very, very lucky—bought a few shares of Sweetwater when it was the counterculture's first, early foray into ethical investing. After graduating from Oberlin, Markson ran a food co-op in the 1970s before getting interested in the stock market. From the very beginning he stuck by several principles: *no* to toxic chemicals, tobacco, children's cereal; *yes* to sustainable energy, organic foods, animal-safe health and beauty products. He popularized responsible, guilt-free capitalism, rode a wave of rising markets and became a billionaire.

He's now beaten Wall Street by double digits for more than thirty years. Sweetwater's annual meetings are like tent revivals, with fans swooning and begging pictures. And for all that, Markson lives a modest, mid-American life: married to his college sweetheart, still in the same Ohio farmhouse he grew up in, cheerful and decent. If guys like Dick Fuld and Lloyd Blankfein are the dark *ober-leutnants* of capitalism, Markson is Main Street personified, the everyman investor made good.

Everybody loves Wilbur Markson.

"Markson owns Clayco?" I'd been working for the most honest and well-respected figure of American capitalism and didn't even know it. "What the hell's he doing in the missile business?"

"That's where the money is." Clara took a jaded view. "Smart weapons are better than dumb ones—they don't kill so many people. Or something like that. I assume that average annual revenue growth of eighteen percent was the real draw."

"That's not bad." I thought about it. "Was Markson in from the beginning?"

"Like, was he in on the squeeze-out? Let me see—"

"It'd be out of character," I said. "And then some."

"And it looks like Markson didn't start buying until a few years ago, long after. He's clean."

An operation as shady as Brinker's would have no place in an upright, ethically pure empire like Markson's. He'd shutter them immediately, or sell out and call the police. And not everyone would like that—for example, the many people who'd lose their bonuses, their jobs or their freedom.

That could certainly explain why I'd been hired—or Ryan, but to the same effect. If a faction on the board learned before Markson that Clay Micro was a cesspool, they'd have a strong reason to clean it up ASAP.

Very strong.

"That's interesting," I said.

"Really?"

"Yup."

"Want to tell me about it?"

"Not now." Probably not ever, but it depended on how things went from here. "I told you, it's a little job. Nothing your readers would care about."

Clara laughed again. "I *know* you, Silas."

"No, really."

"All of your jobs are interesting to someone."

"Tell you what, when I'm done, we'll have a drink. I'll outline the story, you decide if it's worth running down." She'd never source me directly, so anything for print would have to be backstopped by redundant reporting. Often that meant more effort than could be justified, which Clara understood better than anyone.

"I'll take it."

"And if you hear anything . . ."

"I'll look into Clayco, see if anyone's talking about them."

"I appreciate it."

We chatted another minute, then Clara's call came in and she hung up on me. I stood in the woods, staring into the murk, wondering what I'd stepped into.

Wilbur *Markson*?

I got back in the car, plugged the phone into the dash to top off its charge and bumpity-bumped back to the blacktop. Dinnertime had come and gone hours ago, but I had some personal reconnaissance to finish up.

Back through Clabbton and out the other side. Again, the woods closed in quickly. I turned onto a county road, which twisted and turned as it rose toward state forest. By now the moon was up and I could see the countryside fairly well.

I crossed a four-way intersection under a blinking yellow, no cars coming from any direction. A diner appeared on the right, closed and empty. A small field contained big dark lumps—cows, maybe, hard to tell.

And a mile later I found Barktree Welding.

The shop could have been built in the 1940s: ancient layers of white paint flaking from concrete brick. It sat close to the road, the way they were placed when most traffic was Model A's on unimproved dirt. A battered pickup slumped by the side of the garage. All three bays were dark, their doors pulled shut, but a blue light glowed behind a window on the second story. It looked like an addition, a room or two built atop one end of the shop.

Someone was watching television. The business seemed buttoned up for the day. The owner might have an apartment up there.

I slowed and stopped by the side of the road, just where it began to curve around the hillside. Peering back I could see a machine in the small field beside the garage—an old diesel tractor, with that boxy hood that looked like 1950. In the moonlight it appeared that half the field had been mowed, then the job and tractor abandoned in the middle.

I waited a few minutes. When I saw a headlight glow coming through the trees on the road below, I started up again and drove quietly away.

Barktree Welding was owned by Dave Ellins.

CHAPTER FOUR

The pictures I'd found—a dirt-track fan website, some Facebook tags—they hadn't lied.

He looked just like me.

I'd woken early, after a surprisingly restful night. The roughnecks in the other cabins really did shut down at a reasonable hour—by eleven the music had stopped and the gamers were quiet, and at midnight I could even hear crickets in the trees, dodging bats.

Before dawn boots were clumping on wooden floorboards. Toilets flushed, sinks ran. Quiet greetings as the men walked outside. Truck doors slammed, cab radios came on, vehicles rumbled out the drive and accelerated onto the road.

It was Saturday, but the drillers must have been on a frontier schedule. I wondered if they took Sunday off.

I felt like a sleepyhead layabout when I finally emerged, yawning. Clouds in the east banded yellow to pink to white. Trees dripped, dew or overnight rain I couldn't tell.

The Chamber of Commerce couldn't have ordered up a better morning.

Breakfast was fried eggs and pancakes in a diner across the road—I didn't even have to drive, it was less than a hundred yards away. Some old guys in a booth, wearing seed caps and canvas jackets, drank coffee and talked about the Penguins. A few pipeline workers were scraping up the last of their lumberjack specials. A television mounted in a ceiling corner above the cash register was on but silent, the morning-show talking heads showing teeth and yammering mutely away.

"Six-twenty?" I wasn't sure I correctly read the scrawl on the tab the waitress dropped off. "Is that right?"

"No charge for the refills," she said.

"Thanks." I put down a ten. The food was indifferent, but for that I would have gotten a small OJ in Manhattan.

On the other hand, no newspapers. Yeah, yeah, everyone makes fun, but I can't use a smartphone or a tablet—everything you do online is tracked, and I'm neither skilled nor diligent enough to reliably circumvent the relentless data hoover. One basic cellphone and a wad of cash is the most I'll carry on a job. Security through obscurity.

So I stared out the plate glass instead. The motel cabins were almost empty now; one SUV and my rental were the only vehicles still parked out front. Traffic passed, back and forth, down toward Clabbton and up toward the hills.

"You just hire on?" said the waitress, taking my plates away. "Saw you walking over from Annie's just now."

In the city, wearing a suit, people assumed I was a businessman. Out here everyone looked at me and saw an Okie well digger. Context is all.

"Family business," I said, same as at the motel. Simple, consistent lies are the best.

"Nice day for it."

"Couldn't be better."

Back at the cabin I collected my toothbrush, dropped a couple bucks on the bed, and ran a damp washcloth over the door handle, sink taps, table edge—it took only a few minutes to clean the room, and basic precautions make good habits.

But when I found myself wiping down the masonite key fob, I realized I was stalling.

Second thoughts, now that I was so close.

There was no reason I *had* to follow through and see Dave El-lins in person. He'd reached me through my Vegas mail drop—a guy out there does me a favor, forwarding the occasional letter, but he thinks I'm New Jersey mob, and he doesn't have anything but an uptown PO box number. Anyway, the whole story was ludicrous: long-lost brothers, given up at birth to different families? A tabloid fairy tale. Dave, whoever he was, might have duped my last set of foster parents, good-hearted and rather dim as they are. That didn't mean I had to go along.

I walked out, closing the door with my hip, and walked around back, under the pines. I stared through the trees, thinking.

The problem was, if he found me once, maybe he could find me again.

And if he could, so could someone else.

Fine. Best get it over with—find out who Dave really was and what he wanted. I walked quickly to the Malibu, settled the Sig's holster as comfortably as I could in the driver's seat, turned on my phone and got going.

My mood improved. Making a decision always makes a difference.

The route went by quicker the second time, daylight and famil-iarity bringing everything closer. As the hills closed in, dark patches appeared on the road, then puddles—it must have rained harder farther up. Mist drifted among the trees, rising from damp ground. The morning sun would dry it all out, but the hollows were still half in shadow, the night cool lingering. The last bits of town dwindled away. Occasional barbwire and fading NO TRESPASSING signs were nailed to the trees; gravel pullouts had broken gates or nothing at all.

It felt like leaving civilization. I'd really become a New York urbanite, my natural environment no longer the woods and back-lands of my youth.

Dave had company.

Three men stood in the muddy lot in front of Barktree Welding.

The discussion was exuberant, or maybe an argument. Hard to tell as I drove past. Hands thrust and pointed and gestured. I didn't catch the words, and it was hard to say how serious they were. One might have been laughing.

I didn't slow down, looked over once and then returned my face to the road ahead.

A few hundred yards farther I pulled over. Overcast hung so low it hid the tops of the steep, wooded hills rising all around. I'd stopped at what looked like a building site; the ground had been roughly prepared, raw dirt graded more or less flat. A muddy flat-bed carrying a large stack of cinderblock was parked in the middle. Steel bands securing the bricks to pallets were cut and hanging loose, and a few of the bricks had been unloaded onto the ground.

But no one was around. The truck's wheels were sunk a few inches into the dirt. They might have started the job yesterday or a week ago, impossible to tell.

I closed my eyes and reviewed the mental video.

One younger man, two older. Barktree Welding looked even shabbier in daylight, the paint peeling and stained. The pickup was still there, not moved from last night—it was a Ford, hard used, shocks done in. Split wood tumbled into a heap near the back of the building. The three bays were open now, doors pulled up, but shadowed inside and I didn't see much.

A canvas-top Jeep was new, parked square in the middle of the lot. The Jeep pulled an odd trailer: an open, rusty iron box about twenty feet long.

Two customers and the shop's owner, talking about a job. They'd driven out. Maybe it wasn't ready. Maybe, like Ryan's employer, they weren't happy with the result. Who knows?

Dave was the young one, the owner.

I waited five minutes. Only one vehicle passed the whole time. I kept my head turned away, pretending to stare pensively into the woods, though I'd twisted the rearview mirror so I could watch its passage. Finally I put the gear into drive and turned back.

I had the window halfway down, so I could hear the yelling as I came up and into the lot, bouncing on the rocky gravel.

"I'll fix it right now." Dave Ellins flipped an aluminum hose running from a pair of red welding tanks, apparently rolled from the garage. It was connected to a torch in his other hand, and he wore heavy leather gloves. "Not my fault you ran it over the rocks at the park, and it wouldn't have broken at all if you didn't leave it out to rust all summer. Look at that—the spar just pulled right away from the old weld. That's crap work."

"That's *your* work." One of the older guys, in overalls and crusty boots. All three glanced over at me, then turned back to the trailer.

They had business. I was nobody they knew. Fair enough.

"Nuh-uh. I fixed the axle, not that panel." He picked a face shield up from the ground and slipped it on, then fired the torch. Both other men stepped back from the loud, hissing flame.

"I'll patch it, but that's all." The welder's voice was muffled behind the mask. "Take it back to—who built this piece of shit anyway? Bale?"

"Naw, it was Charley. Ten, fifteen years ago now."

"Figures." He bent over the trailer, studying the break.

"Shouldn't you clean it up first?"

"You ain't never cleaned this in fifteen years, why bother now?"

The older man shrugged. "It's a barbecue trailer, that's all. Lots of grease dripped down there over time."

Now that he said it, I could see the grills, folded down to one side. They must tow the thing to festivals and picnics, cook hundreds of hamburgers or chickens at once.

All three continued to ignore me.

"Two minutes," said the man from his mask. "Then you haul it away and I never see it again."

He tapped a length of welding rod inside the trailer, considered a moment longer, then aimed the torch. Sparks showered out.

WHOOOSH!

The entire base of the trailer burst into flame, flaring out yellow and black. Smoke billowed. The welder was knocked backward and the two old guys about fell over themselves from laughing.

"Haw, Dave, you dumb cluck!"

"Look at *that* shit."

Dave got to his feet, flipping up the mask and shaking his head.

"Okay, I wasn't *going* to charge you," he said. "But that's extra work I done there."

"Extra work? What're you talking about?"

"Cleaned out the pan. Fifteen years of grease, wasn't that you said?"

"Haw."

"Anyways, that's it for me. Tell Charley to fix his own damn fuckups."

It was strange, watching him move. Like seeing yourself on video—close, but not quite right.

The fire burned down quickly. Smoke drifted my way, smelling of burned meat and barbecue sauce. I coughed.

"You racing Saturday?" asked the man in overalls.

"Might be." Dave started coiling the hose. "Car's fixed up."

"You decide to run, you let me know. I'll put some money down with Van."

The other man shook his head. "Van thinks you pulled that race," he said. "Two weeks ago."

"That's bullshit and you know it."

A shrug. "Sure. Just saying. They were talking about it, down at the VFW."

"They got something to say, they come say it to me." Dave jammed the hose coil onto the tank's handle. "Assholes."

"We know you wouldn't do anything like that."

When the Jeep drove off, Dave muttered, watching them go, then walked over to me.

"They're gonna burn out the Rotary one of these years," he said. "Hell of a barbecue though. What can I—?"

He stopped dead, staring.

I shrugged.

"Yeah," I said.

"It's you!" He grabbed me in a bear hug, the blackened leather gloves ruining my shirt. "I'll be goddamned! It's *you*!"

CHAPTER FIVE

A in't you never looked in a mirror? Plain as the nose on my face." He laughed. "Hell, it kind of *is* the nose on my face, right? Not just twins, we're like *identical* twins."

"I don't know." Close up our differences seemed stronger—different lines in the face, different hair, different habits of movement. "Didn't you say you were born two years later?"

"Yeah, I guess. But anyway I got the records, and the state don't lie. I mean, not about shit like that. Paper going back twenty, thirty years. Want to see the copies?"

"Maybe later."

"Sure." Dave drank off half a Rolling Rock and clanked the bottle onto the toolbox by his stool. "You should of told me you were coming."

"I travel around," I said. "Work. I had a job nearby and I thought I'd look you up."

"Travel, huh? That accounting business, I figured you sat in an office all day. Keeping the books."

"It's just as boring as you think."

His hair was on the long side. I'd been in Kentucky a few years ago, chasing a penny-stock fraudster who liked the horses, and back then every guy in the region seemed to have his head shaved down to stubble. It looked like boot camp. Now the style pendulum was apparently drifting back to the 1970s.

Besides that: my height, maybe no surprise, but ten or twenty pounds more muscle and most of that in the belly. In the country men carried their weight with pride. When we shook hands, his felt hard and calloused—from manual labor, not the *makiwara*.

"You ain't drinking. Want coffee or something?"

"It's a little early." I put my own beer on the workbench. The shop was crowded inside, tools and mysterious engine parts dark with grease cluttering every horizontal surface. That distinctive smell of gasoline and differential lube was cut with an ozone tang— the welding equipment, I assumed. An inexplicable frame of steel pipe sat half assembled on the concrete floor.

Beyond it, just inside the bay door, a decades-old muscle car gleamed black. Unlike the rest of the garage, a two-foot space was cleared all the way around—no junk, no tools, even the floor swept perfectly clean. The hood was up, with a cloth draped over the side panel and into the engine compartment, so you could lean in without marring the finish.

Dave saw me looking. "1969 Charger."

"You keep it in good shape."

"Grandpa's axe, right? Rebuilt from the pistons out, and more than once." He smiled, his eyes on the vehicle. "That's a work of beauty in a world of sin."

Through the open doors I could see the clumpy field with the old tractor, between the road and the hill behind Dave's shop. In daylight it was even clearer the mower had been abandoned halfway into the job: half the field was cut down to turf, and half had wild grass and weeds two feet high.

Dave seemed to have trouble keeping up with everything except his car.

"You race it?"

"On occasion. Dirt track, on the weekends. I told you that, didn't I? In the letter?"

"You any good?"

"Yeah."

I waited, but he didn't say more, just drank the rest of his beer and tossed the bottle toward the back of the shop. It landed in a wooden box of empties, somehow not breaking.

"Silas?"

"Yes?"

"Is that your real name?"

"Sure it is." Which wasn't quite lying. That's what people called me.

"Because I asked around. Some of the answers . . ."

"Around?"

"You know." He waved one hand vaguely, then reached over to retrieve another Rock from the stained refrigerator alongside the bench. "Don't know if I mentioned, I did a stretch some time back. Eleven months at Houtzdale."

"Why?"

"Why? Bad fucking lawyers, that's why." But he laughed and popped open the beer. "Criminal conversion of a motor vehicle, if you have to ask."

"Borrow the wrong car?"

"Nope. Stole it myself." Once again not boasting, just stating a fact. "I admit, kind of a dumbshit thing to do. You been inside?"

"No." Not really. Not counting an MP holding cell in, well, let's just say, a major American military facility in another country.

A very dusty country. They told me I can't ever discuss what I did in the service.

"Nothing to do all day but lift weights and talk shit. You think *accounting*'s boring . . . anyway, some of the guys, I see them now and then. In the city." Pittsburgh, I assumed. "Silas Cade has a reputation."

"Some other Silas."

"Like, some company's got a problem with the numbers, cash disappearing from bank accounts, bent accountants and all that—you're the go-to. Mr. Fix-It." He stared me in the eye. "CPA with a bullet."

"Huh." Not a bad description, actually.

"So." His grin was gone. "True?"

Outside a light rain began to fall, pocking the dirt, pattering on the shop's metal roof. So much for the beautiful day we were supposed to have. The interior was dim and dank, the only other sound a hum from the refrigerator's compressor. I sat still in the wooden chair, hands on my knees, staring back.

"What do you want?" I said.

"You're my *brother*, Silas." He leaned forward. "My whole life thinking I'm alone in the world, and then I find out I have a brother. Ain't that something to celebrate?"

"Why did you track me down?"

"You're here, right?"

I shook my head. "I'm leaving."

"You and me—we can do stuff. We can get some shit *done*."

Great. *I got some ideas*, he'd written.

"What are you talking about, exactly?"

"Let me tell you." He leaned back, grinned again, and picked up the beer. "I got *plans*."

And what plans they were.

"It's just lying on the ground, most of these places. I can show you seven steel mills, all shut down in the eighties, all no more'n twenty miles from here. Every one of them, the pipe is sitting there like, like, I dunno, apples on the tree. Or ground. Whatever—we just got to drive a truck in and pick it up. Copper and steel and iron. Tons of it! You know what that kind of metal's selling for? China wants it, they'll pay anything."

I looked at him. "Let me get this straight—you want to steal *scrap* metal?" I thought about the scavengers you see in the Bronx, rolling shopping carts piled with plumbing and doorknobs ripped out of abandoned houses, off to trade at the recyclers for ten or fifteen bucks.

"It's an idea. Something, you know, I work out here all day, sometimes nobody comes by. I got time to think."

"Uh-huh."

"Whatever. It's just a start. Capital formation. Right? I saw a show on the cable about that."

It only got better. Once the initial investment was assembled, Dave figured we could finance the guns and cars and maybe some helpers . . . and start knocking over casinos.

"They're everywhere, you notice that? Over in Chester, or the Meadows, even right on the river in downtown Pittsburgh. Everyone goes in with their wallet full up, comes out flat. All that cash money, piling up."

"Um."

"They drive it over to the bank in the morning. Or maybe in the middle of the night. It's not like, I mean, those places don't *ever* close. But in between, it just sits there. Waiting."

"Dave—"

"Easy, right? And we're a perfect team. I got the connections around here—set it all up, no problem. You, we can trust each other, see? So we don't need nobody else."

Trust?

I didn't know where to start. "Look, they expect—there are thousands of idiots thinking exactly the same thing. Hey, let's go get some of that free money there! And the smart guys running the casinos? They *know* that."

"Course they do. Don't mean they don't get stuck in their ruts, though. Know how many times they been robbed, ever? Since they started putting in tables and slot machines, I mean—not the race-tracks." He raised a hand when I started to answer. "Zero. Never. Not one single once."

"Doesn't that kind of prove my point?"

"Proves they're fat and happy and lazy. Like the Steelers."

Jesus. "Maybe, but they're not stupid. There's basically a private army of rent-a-cops and security and fucking *assault* forces, not to mention the entire law-enforcement apparatus of the state, ready to protect its tax base. You might as well try to steal the gold out of the Federal Reserve vaults."

"Yeah, yeah. We can figure it out." He waved a hand dismissively. "That's all just, I dunno, *logistics*."

I felt very tired. "You never saw *Ocean's Eleven*, huh?"

"Look. You know why people get caught? When they try something like this?"

"Because they trip about twenty alarms and then heavily armed guards converge from everywhere and shoot them dead."

"No, no." He shook his head, grinning. "Afterwards, I mean. It's the money. Most guys, they can't think any further than grabbing the cash and running away. Maybe they planned ahead and rented a storage locker, but most of them don't even do that. The bags of hundred-dollar bills, that's like the goal line." He drained his bottle and set it next to the first. "When really, it ain't no more'n the opening kickoff."

All that talking in the pen, I guess Dave thought he'd learned something. "Football doesn't send you to jail for thirty years."

"But that's where *you* come in! See? It's your *business*. I figure you know exactly how to take a few hundred pounds of twenty-dollar bills and turn it into a nice, safe, boring bank account that the IRS and the FBI will never ever notice."

I stood up and turned to look out the bay at the falling rain. Mud spattered gently in the dirt lot, dirtying the welding tanks that Dave had left outside. A fresh, wet smell drifted in.

Dave's plan was the stupidest, most wrongheaded, misguided, moronic idea I'd ever heard.

"Your plan," I said, "is the stupidest, most wrongheaded, mis-guided . . ." I stopped.

Dave was chuckling behind me. I turned back, and he started laughing, then harder, then so hard he wheezed and bent over with his hands on his knees.

Usually I get the jokes tossed my way. Brothers or whatever, Dave and I didn't seem to be very well synchronized.

"What?" I said. He just shook his head, still laughing, and swiped at the corner of one eye. "What's so funny?"

"Had you *going*, Silas!"

Oh, for Christ's sake. "Are you—?"

"You're right, that's all bullshit. I wouldn't do none of that."

I grunted, didn't say anything.

"I mean, scrap steel's like three hundred dollars a ton now. You can make more money chopping firewood. And sticking up The Rivers, hell, only an idiot'd even *think* of that."

I stared at him. "So why are we talking about it?"

"'Cause maybe you'd have said yes." He got off the chair and gave me another bear hug. "Fortunately, you actually ain't that dumb."

I disengaged myself. Hugging's not my thing.

"Fine."

"Some people'll do *anything,* you know?"

"Glad I passed the test." I was still irritated.

"Relax, man. Like I said, I got lots of time to think out here. Maybe I think too much."

Yeah, maybe so. I shook my head.

Dave picked up the three bottles and dropped them in a crate already overflowing with empties, then checked his pockets. "I got something I got to do. Helping some guys up in Glassville. You want to come along?"

"I don't know—"

"You didn't tell me you were coming, right?"

"Huh?"

"So I promised. But it's all right. I know they'd be happy, have someone else."

I crossed my arms. "Stealing cars? Bank robbery?"

"I *told* you I was kidding." He didn't seem bothered. "A little demolition work. Half a day, eight hundred bucks. You'll get a fair cut."

"Demolition." I felt pulled along, but what the hell.

My brother.

"It'll be fun." He walked over to pull down the first of the bay doors, which screeched and rattled and slammed onto the concrete floor. "What else you gonna do today?"

CHAPTER SIX

We took my car.

"The pickup ain't registered," Dave said, gesturing at the brokeback Ford. "And I left my other truck up the road, kinda in the middle of something."

"Up the road?"

"Yeah, you see it?"

"Might have."

"Tumbug, he owns that land, and he wants to build a little cabin. I said I'd help start the foundation. We got a deal on the cinderblock from the concrete plant over in Connellsdale. I drove it here, but as soon as we started unloading, Bug's all like, shit, my back hurts! It's killing me!" Dave went back into the shop, came back a moment later with a five-gallon plastic bucket holding a pair of sledgehammers, a corded hammer drill, gloves and some other tools. "You ask me, I think he was just worried about missing the start of the Panthers game."

"Why don't you drive that?" I pointed at the bay that held the Charger.

"Oh, no." For the first time he seemed completely serious. "She's just for *racing*."

When all the bay doors were closed, Dave went inside the office once more. "Too much beer. I'll be right back."

The rain had eased, hardly more than a drizzle. It felt like it was going to be that kind of weather—on and off, clouds heavy overhead. I wondered what I was doing here, whether I should just get in the Malibu and leave, right now.

Instead, I took out my crummy phone and dialed Ryan.

Ten rings.

No answer.

He hadn't picked up earlier in the morning, either—I'd tried twice, once when I got up and once on the way to Dave's shop.

When he didn't answer his phone yesterday, it was five rings then *click*. Now it was just ring-ring-no-answer.

If that meant something, I didn't know what. I tried another number.

Zeke picked up right away.

"Silas? Shit. Wait."

My phone rang fifteen seconds later—he had to call me back through the Canadian anonymizer.

"What the fuck's going on?" Zeke demanded.

"Nothing. I lost the tail and they never came back."

"You sure?"

Dave was still inside. I put my back to the shop and watched the road.

"What do you mean?" I said.

"At least you're alive."

"Um . . . you thought I might not be?"

"You talked to anyone else yet? Since yesterday?"

This was not making me feel better. "Just tell it."

"There's a team looking for you," he said. "They came into Volchak's last night, around eleven—direct to the bar, then around the tables. A thousand bucks for an address or a phone number. They had your name. Said it right out loud." He paused. "They had your *name.*"

Shit. "Anyone give me up?"

"Sure. The guys are like, I know him! Silas, yeah, that asshole!"

"*What?*"

"Well, everyone tried—fake information, of course. For a grand? But the men in black didn't actually pay out, so I guess it's all fair."

"Were you there?"

"No. I got three calls right after they left."

"Who were they?"

"No one knows."

Thin sunshine brightened, filtering through the overcast, then faded away again.

"But one of them was a woman," he added.

"I thought you didn't see them."

"Not at Volchak's."

I don't think he was doing it deliberately, so I suppressed an urge to yell into the phone. Speaking slowly: "Did you encounter them someplace *else?*"

"After I heard, I went up to your place. They were coming out when I got there."

Worse and worse.

So far, I've always been able to keep my public and work lives completely separate—my home is Manhattan, for God's sake, not a cave in the mountains. To most people, I'm a guy they see around, something in finance or insurance, a face at the gym. Not *hiding*, in other words. But when I'm on the job, I disappear. Completely. No connection to the real me whatsoever.

Until now.

"Recognize them?"

"No. A woman, like I said, and two men." He gave me a useless description. Unless someone's albino or missing an arm or something, eyewitness testimony is pointless. Five ten, fit, short hair—we all look like that, Zeke and me included.

Which Zeke knew, of course. "The girl, though—reminded me of someone. Maybe it was the hair. Stylish."

"Stylish?"

"A blonde. Light colored. Too dark on your street to see much." Which is one reason I chose the place. "Good cut."

Maybe he'd started reading *Vogue*. "So?"

"So she was in charge."

"How could you tell?"

"She got into the front passenger seat. Plus the body language. I was down the block, by the laundromat. Couldn't hear anything, and they drove away before I could get close."

"How'd you know they were coming out of my apartment, then?"

"Because the lock was broke when I went up. They'd drilled it out and punched the deadbolt. Metal bits on the floor, they didn't even try to clean up."

He didn't bother describing the car. It would have been a rental or stolen or a throwaway.

"Ryan's still not answering," I said. "I talked to him once, twenty-one hundred last night or so, but now nothing."

"I've been calling him too. Nothing."

"You check out his place?"

"Don't know where he lives. You?"

"No." Ryan might have had a life somewhere, but he kept it secret, which is good practice until you need someone like Zeke to come help you out.

"No one else cares about Ryan. They're all talking about you. And your new friends."

Suddenly I had new friends everywhere.

"It's two teams," I said. "Guys in a car, following me out of Pittsburgh, and a separate group at my apartment in New York."

"Working together, though."

"That's not an unreasonable assumption." Given the timeframe. "But it's hard to believe Brinker has enough sway to whistle up a nationwide manhunt."

"How much do you think he's skimming?"

"I don't know."

"Millions?"

"Maybe."

"So there's your juice." Zeke had a simple view of the world.

What made it complicated was Markson. Brinker had obvious reasons to want me out of the picture. Someone at Clayco corporate, worried that Markson might find out about Clay Micro's spectacular malfeasance, might also want me out of the picture. Nothing made sense otherwise; companies following Markson's business ethics just don't hire people like me or my pursuers.

But still: *two* teams?

A door banged. I glanced back to see Dave coming out of the office.

"I have to go," I said.

"You want my advice, stay out of the city for a while."

"You serious?"

"They didn't toss it."

I didn't follow. "Toss what?"

"Your place. I looked in, and everything was in order. The way they treated the lock, if they'd done a search it would have been totally ransacked."

"Well, fuck." More bad news.

"That's right." Zeke got the final word. "They're not after information, or clues, or whatever. They want *you.*"

CHAPTER SEVEN

The drive took thirty minutes, west and back toward Pittsburgh, roughly following the Monongahela. I had the wipers on, then off, then on again—the clouds just wouldn't make up their mind.

I wasn't saying much, distracted by Zeke's news. I don't mind the usual riffraff populating my line of work, but another team of professionals was different. Intimidating white-collar executives is one thing; shooting it out with high-powered mercenaries quite another.

Dave leaned his seat back.

"I tried to find our mother," he said.

"Uh." I looked over at him.

The change of topic was abrupt. Or maybe hearing it like that—*our* mother—threw me.

Of course I'd thought about doing the same when I was young. The middle years were rough. I got a new family every year or two—some of it my fault, but mostly it was the adults' bad luck and money problems. I imagined the same thing I figure all foster kids do, the ones who were put up as infants: *They're European royalty. Or supersecret spies. Or Bill Gates!—he wants me to grow up normal before he gives me a billion dollars.*

My last folks were okay, though. They stuck with me all through high school. After that I was in the world, and my origins were ancient history. The desire to go back faded away, not worth it.

"That's what got me started, right?" Dave looked out his window. "Never imagined I'd find a brother. I just wanted to know who my mother and father were."

"Yeah."

"Or really just mother. My family, as I got older they said things once or twice—not meaning to, just little things that slipped out. But you know how it is. You pay attention."

Yes, you *do* pay attention. Growing up like Dave or me, you're never on sure ground. Every clue, every hint matters, trying to figure it out.

If you don't know where you came from, it's so much harder to know where you're going.

"They didn't like our father. Or had heard bad things about him. I don't know what, exactly, but I just picked up the idea he was worthless."

"He gave us away," I said.

Surprising myself. Some buried emotion had surfaced there, just for a moment.

"That's right." Dave was silent. "Anyway, I thought maybe I could find Mother. The adoption registries, sometimes they'll let you send a letter or something. But it didn't work."

A small puzzle. "This was all in New Hampshire?"

"Only a year. My adoption family moved here when I was two.

The old man was following steel work, can you believe it? I don't know what he was thinking, like they were knocking down all the mills just so they could put up new ones."

"I thought everybody went bankrupt in the eighties."

"A few hung on." Dave yawned. "Not forever, though. In fact, that's what we're doing today."

"What?"

"Helping take down the last blast furnace in Pittsburgh." He laughed. "In *America*, for all I know. Some shit, huh?"

The mill was a small one. That's what Dave said, but it was hard to believe, looking at the huge complex of towers and ironwork and massive buildings. A bright sign at the entrance had a swoosh logo and "FerroCorp" in a modern, purple font, but everything else looked like 1935. Rusty train tracks switched in amid heaps of clinker and slag. A vast parking lot, mostly deserted, just a handful of vehicles up by the main gate.

The gloomy drizzle didn't help.

I parked next to a Ford 350 with a bed hitch and an empty gun rack in the cab window. Dave was on his phone—"Yeah, sorry, got held up this morning, where are you?" He clicked off and pointed at the largest tower. "Over there. We have to walk in."

He carried the bucket of tools. A guard in a dark blue jacket nodded us past the gate.

"Sad day," he said.

"Guess so," Dave said. "You work here long?"

"Ten years." He looked beyond retirement age. "In the cast house mostly. That furnace was hot for eighty years, until just a month ago."

"Bet it's *still* hot."

The man grimaced. "Damn sure."

Inside, the natural world disappeared. No trees, no hills visible, no birds, just cracked paving in a landscape of rust and broken metal.

Like every postapocalyptic video game brought to life.

We found a half-dozen men in flannel and Carhartt standing at the base of the cylindrical furnace. It was a broad chimney, fifty feet high, made of oversized, black-glazed refractory brick. A low, dark building grew from one side; a conveyor slanted up the other, and various pipework and scaffolding seemed to run everywhere.

At five points around the base, crude platforms had been set up: a pallet on a pair of sawhorses, two fifty-five-gallon drums placed together, a stack of wooden crates. On one a man stood precariously, swinging a sledgehammer to drive a long pipe into the heart of the furnace.

"Yo, Dave."

"Hey, man."

The guy with the sledge hammered the pipe end flush with the brick. Holes had been drilled above each platform, and the others had their pipe already installed. He admired his work, then hopped down, hammer on one shoulder like John Henry. His Tractor Supply boots slipped a bit on the damp ground.

"That's it. Ready to go." He had two missing teeth in front but long mutton chops to make up for it.

"All right then."

"Where's the dynamite?"

Dynamite?

So here's how their mad plan was going to work. The furnace was full of slag and waste, topped off from decades of use. Even a month after the last steel had been poured, the huge thermal mass of the tower kept the heat trapped—as much as five hundred degrees at the core. If they knocked the tower down in a conventional way, the white hot remnants would scatter everywhere, damaging equipment and injuring workers.

Explosive demolition, done professionally, could handle it: set charges, establish a perimeter, get the right paperwork and inspections done, on and on. But that would cost more money than Ferro-Corp wanted to spend.

Instead, Dave's friends had offered a simple alternative. They put a stick of dynamite in each pipe, sticking halfway out. Five guys were going to take position, standing on the platforms with sledgehammers ready. On the count of three, they'd slam the dynamite into the core, drop the hammers and run like hell. A few moments later heat would detonate the charges, the base would blow out and the furnace would come down.

"That's insane." I couldn't believe they were serious. "What if somebody trips or something? What if the dynamite goes off two seconds early?"

"Naw, we done it before." The evident leader had several inches and maybe fifty pounds on me. "OSHA ain't in favor, but hell, this is how the flatheads been doing it for a hundred years."

"Blowing up furnaces?"

"Clearing the scrag inside."

I didn't think anyone even used actual dynamite anymore. Water-gel explosives like Tovex are easier, less toxic and so much safer that only a moron would do so.

The U.S. military gave me as thorough an education in small explosives as you can get anywhere, and we never *once* detonated a stick of dynamite.

This argument met with complete indifference. "You got a hammer?" the chief asked Dave.

"Two."

"Two? Don't sound like he's interested." Looking at me. "But that's all right, we're good."

Dave shrugged, an odd expression on his face. Embarrassment? I felt an unfamiliar emotion ripple through me.

It took a moment: I was letting him down.

"Sorry," I said. "I've never seen anything like this before."

"No problem. Brendt, we ready?"

They were like a bunch of third-graders.

"Don't you fuck up and hit it *early*."

"Yo, Brendt, on three or five?"

"Three. Can you count that high?"

"Who's got the video?"

I backed away, not taking my time. Out in the parking lot seemed like a minimum safe distance. A sixth guy, who I hadn't noticed before, stood behind a slag car on one of the railroad sidings, holding a camera at ready, and he called as I passed.

"You can stand here. Best view."

I looked over. "That's not even two hundred yards. Wouldn't you be happier farther away?"

"Better shot from here. We're gonna put it on YouTube."

The slag car had a massive, bell-shaped iron tureen suspended between two pivots. It probably weighed several tons. Maybe the videographer was more cautious than I thought.

Still.

"Don't take this the wrong way, but we should call 911 right now. Give them a head start."

"Don't worry about it. Brendt knows what he's doing."

"I don't see any company bosses standing around."

"It's Saturday."

Oh, yeah, I'd lost track. No doubt a weekend was all the better for slipshod, regulation-violating, totally illegal demolition jobs.

"I'm going to watch from over there."

"Okay." He shrugged and raised the camera to his eye, shielding the lens from a gust of light rain. "Won't be more'n another few seconds though."

Sure enough, a loud shout came from the base of the furnace.

"Go!"

I looked over in time to see the hammers all swing simultaneously. They struck the furnace walls in silence—the sharp cracks arrived a second later, while the five men were leaping and stumbling and sprinting away.

Fuck. I jumped to land behind the slag car, covering my head with both arms and crouching in the shelter of the iron vat.

BO-O-O-O-M-M-MMM!

The explosion was a deep, roaring blast. I glanced out, peering past the railcar's frame, to see the base of the tower balloon outward in a cloud of dust and smoke.

The chimney swayed and collapsed in on itself. The noise deafened, a long thundering crash of masonry and metal. Our view was cut off as a debris cloud engulfed the entire area. Before everything disappeared into the maelstrom I saw the very top of the furnace fall and the conveyor's heavy scaffold start to collapse.

I hunched down again, trying to press my ears shut with my fingers while keeping my forearms crossed over my face. Video Guy laughed and shouted, barely audible over the roar. Standing unprotected, his video might end up like one of those avalanche films, a sudden rushing tumble then black.

It was over in a minute, maybe more. The noise eased and the smoke began to clear. I stood slowly, blinking at the sharp dust in my eyes.

"Whoo-*hoooo!*" The other lunatics emerged from different places around the furnace. Or where the furnace used to be, rather. Now it was a huge smoking pile of rubble.

Dave came over. "How about *that*, little brother!" Everyone seemed overadrenalized, slapping each other on the arms, pointing, laughing. Video Guy had his camera on review, watching the screen. They all looked grimier than five minutes ago, dust in their hair and black dirt on their clothes. In the mist the smudges turned to muddy smears.

"Everyone lived," I said, surprised.

"Well, yeah."

"Now what happens?"

"Now?"

"If the idea was to clear the site, you actually haven't made much progress."

Brendt walked up. "Now the slag can cool, that's all," he said. "Stopped up inside, it would of taken months. This way they start hauling it away next week."

Cleaning up and collecting tools shouldn't have taken long, but somehow they stretched it out an hour. Three sledgehammers were lost, abandoned and buried under the falling masonry. Dave still had his bucket, though. When we finally finished up, he dropped his gloves in.

"Here, take these," said Brendt. He held out two more sticks of dynamite. They looked just like the cartoons—not much shorter than a paper-towel tube, wrapped in red paper. Splotches on the paper suggested that nitroglycerine had begun to destabilize and leak out. I stepped back.

"You don't need them?"

"Naw. You can use them to take out that stump you was talking about."

"Thanks." Dave added them to the bucket.

"When we gonna get paid?" Vidco Guy asked.

"Monday." Brendt brushed grit from his beard. "I'll collect from the office."

"Hope they don't decide to fuck around—sixty-day terms, that kinda bullshit." All of them had probably done 1099 work and knew how slow big companies could be.

"Nuh-uh." He flipped his sledgehammer in his left hand, like it was a juggling club. "They'll see right here what we can do. I don't think they'll want us *angry* with them."

He threw the hammer twice more, then tried to catch it in the other hand. He missed and it flew out of control, bouncing onto the ground inches from my foot.

"Oops, sorry." He picked it up. "Hey, Dave, I forgot—might have another job next week. You interested?"

"What is it?" I said. "Blowing up a dam? Setting the national forest on fire?"

He laughed like I was kidding. "Construction. Temporary structure for a party or something. Easy."

"Maybe." Dave picked up his bucket. "Give me a call."

We walked out to the parking lot. The guard saluted us. "Nice clean job, fellas."

"Thanks."

"Glad to see everyone coming out what went *in*."

"You got that right."

At the car, I popped the door locks with the remote. Dave pointed at the trunk. "Can you open that up?"

I looked at his bucket, with the two sticks of explosive poking out. "No way."

"It's safe enough."

"Not for me." Maybe I'd just seen too many vehicles demolished when I was in the service.

"Okay, no problem. Listen, we thought we might go out," he said. "Get a beer. You want to come?"

"I'll pass." I closed the trunk. "Some things to do."

"Sure. I'll go with Brendt, then. He'll drop me off at the shop later." Dave hesitated, oddly reticent. "You, uh, you want to come over tomorrow?"

"Yeah." I realized it was true, and not just because New York was apparently a no-go-home zone at the moment.

My brother. I felt a pull.

"Yeah, I'd like that."

"Awesome." He grinned, grabbed my hand for a moment, then jogged off to Brendt's car. The other guys were already moving, trucks turning and squealing tires and barreling out to the exit. By the time I got my car started, only one other vehicle was left—probably the guard's.

I couldn't see the top of the rubble pile from here, but a thick plume of smoke rose and bent east with the wind. I wondered what FerroCorp planned to do with the site.

CHAPTER EIGHT

drove all the way back to Pittsburgh. Coming in on I-376—the Parkway, apparently everyone called it—from the east. Late in the day the sun had finally come out and now it was setting, red and orange behind the city skyline.

Not *much* of a skyline, compared to back home. But pretty all the same.

Clay Micro was dark. No surprise, on Saturday night. I got out and walked around again, down to the trestle bridge over the canal, along the road, all the way to the front of the grocery wholesaler and back. Not sure what I was looking for. Some sort of clue about the mystery Nissan that had followed me last night. In the falling dusk I couldn't see much.

I didn't find anything.

Leaving, I followed the same route I'd taken yesterday. The lacrosse players were gone, but the street was livelier, families home and together on the weekend. I backtracked a block to where the tail had appeared—just another street. They could have been waiting there, or come from anywhere.

I got some takeout at a Foodland supermarket: something green from the salad bar and a container of rice pilaf. Farther down the highway, across the river, I found another roadside motel. This one had several long-haul rigs in the lot. The desk clerk was incurious, the room shabby, the television small. I ate my solitary dinner, then carried the trash out to a garbage can in the parking lot.

While I was out there I took another walk, circling the motel for a block in all directions, checking likely surveillance points and routes in and out. It felt like a lonely edge of the city—sparse traffic, a warehouse type of operation down the road one way and some shuttered stores the other. One of the truckers had left his diesel running, light seeping from the sleeping area behind the cab seats. Maybe he had better television in there.

I finished my paranoid patrol, slipped back inside and brushed my teeth. For a while I sat in the dark, doing nothing. At nine I went to bed.

The life of an itinerant accountant is far too glamorous for most.

———

In the morning, a phone call.

I was halfway into my usual routine of push-ups, crunches and open-hand kata. Pilates for leg breakers, Zeke calls it, but he does yoga himself. The room's dark, synthetic carpet was unpleasant and dirty close up. Last night I'd found only one set of outlets, behind the television, and I had to scramble to recover my phone from where it was charging back there.

"Hello?"

"Silas, yo."

"Johnny!" I dropped into the room's single chair. "What are you doing up? It's Sunday."

"The markets run twenty-four hours now."

"Sunday *morning?*"

"It's a perfect time. Everyone's hung over on this side of the Atlantic and out watching cricket or whatever the fuck on the other side. Thin participation—lots of opportunity."

"If you say so."

Johnny and I go way back—all the way to New Hampshire, in fact—and after separate paths we both arrived in the financial world. He landed on the slightly more legitimate side, running an incremental fund downtown. Three billion of alternative-asset money. Big enough to ride the waves, small enough to catch them in the first place. His style is distinctly out of fashion, relying as it does on short-term technical trading. A little rumormongering, good contacts around the Street, fundamental instinct. Now that the high-frequency shops have largely taken over—behemoths with ultrafast pipes and computers that place millions of orders on nanosecond latency—traders like Johnny are going extinct. They're like the old pit traders: almost entirely gone, just a few blue jackets left for show on the floor of the NYSE.

Johnny has managed to stay ahead, partly through intellectual brilliance but mostly by obsessive, nonstop immersion in real-time data every waking moment. He wakes up, he turns on twenty flat-screen terminals, he goes to work.

"I still can't believe you're sitting in the office at dawn on Sunday."

"I don't sleep much." Which I knew was true. "Anyway, that's not why I'm calling. You okay?"

"Well, shit. Zeke asked the same thing yesterday. I'm fine."

"Good."

"What's going on?"

"I don't want to worry you—"

Too late for that. "What *happened?*"

"Visitors. They just waylaid me."

"What, at home?" Johnny had a big, renovated loft in Soho, the sort of thing an investment banker buys with one year's bonus and then sells during the divorce. Johnny got the place in foreclosure—yup, happens all the time among the one percent, too—because it was walking distance to work. But the building had a lobby with permanent staff and a private elevator. I couldn't figure where he might be accosted.

"No, here at the office. They talked their way past security downstairs—you know, ID cards in little leather cases—and banged on my door until I let them in."

He had a dozen traders and some administrative staff on one floor of a hundred-year-old building on Beaver Street, but none of them worked Sunday. Of course.

I stood up, suddenly feeling confined by the drab little motel room. "Which agency?"

"What?"

"Were they from Justice? SEC? What the hell, has the Consumer Fraud Protection Bureau started fielding agents?"

"They weren't government."

"But I thought you said—"

"That was downstairs. Give a little credit here, I think I'm smarter than a rent-a-cop."

"So . . . ?"

"I don't know. One man, one woman. She did most of the talking."

A woman? "What'd she look like?"

"Nice. Blond hair, expensive cut. Some kind of dark jacket, soft pants. I dunno. The guy was just, you know, a guy. Blue suit. His head was shaved."

Like I said, eyewitnesses are pretty much useless. Still—"Zeke might have seen her, too," I said.

"Yeah, she seemed more like his part of the economy than mine."

"What did she want?"

"You."

I walked to the window, stood to the side and pushed the drape open a few inches. Daylight, momentarily dazzling.

Johnny keeps a little money of mine in a beneficiary account. We talk, now and then, usually on the phone. Once a month maybe we have dinner, often in the middle of the night when Johnny finally leaves his trading room. We don't have many friends in common.

What I mean is, it's not an *obvious* connection. Not the sort of lead you'd run down after canvassing friends and neighbors. But given Johnny's profession, it might seem like an important one to someone worried about my involvement in top-drawer corporate finance.

Say, some shady, multimillion-dollar improprieties at a Pennsylvania manufacturer.

"What'd you give them?"

"Nothing. We haven't talked for weeks, I have no idea where you are or what you're doing."

"Were they happy?"

"Didn't seem to care much, actually. She asked a lot of questions but never reacted particularly."

The motel's parking lot was emptier now, the tractor trailers all gone, maybe a fourth of the spaces still occupied by other vehicles. Nothing seemed out of place.

"I have to ask, why did they . . . why did you talk to them at all?"

"I don't know." He paused. "They didn't threaten me or anything. They were just kind of implacable. Like we were absolutely going to have a discussion no matter what, so don't even bother objecting."

"Uh-huh."

"Also, the woman—" He stopped.

"What?"

"I'd say . . . she's *really* good-looking."

I had to laugh. "Sounds like she ought to be on the floor. If she can turn *your* head, she can probably roll traders all over the market."

A door slammed outside. A man walked past my window, coming from another room, and got into a silver two-door parked down the row. He sat for a moment, then the brake and running lights came on, and the car backed out.

"What else?" I asked.

"Nothing. They left."

"Did anyone else see them?"

"I suppose, but you know how it is—they were paying attention to their screens, not some visitors they didn't recognize. You want to tell me what's going on?"

"I'm not sure. I did a job this week at a company division in Pittsburgh called Clay Micro." I gave him the thirty-thousand-foot overview. "So it looks like simple housecleaning, though the management here might have a few more dirty diapers than most. It might not even be related. The kind of people visiting you and Zeke are just . . . disproportionate."

"Clay Micro is part of Clayco?"

"Yeah."

"They're majority owned by Sweetwater Investments."

Figures he'd know that. "Yeah," I said again.

"So in effect, you're on the clock for Wilbur Markson." Johnny laughed. "What'd you do, cheat on the preemployment personality test?"

"Apparently, someone really doesn't want Markson finding out how deep into the swamp Clay Micro is."

"But they *hired* you."

"I know. Could be the Clay Micro CEO instead, trying to clean things up . . . it's confusing."

We went round at it another minute, until Johnny got bored. I didn't have any new ideas.

"You're there now?" he said. "In Pittsburgh?"

"Yeah."

"Maybe you should stay a little longer."

First Zeke, now Johnny. "Why?"

"I said they didn't threaten me." He paused. "But the woman did threaten *you*."

"How?"

"Like they weren't going to stop looking. The sooner they found you, the better. But all unemotional, like she was talking about grocery shopping. That made it almost . . . scary, you know? 'We're going to tear this city apart, there's nowhere he can hide'—as a simple statement of fact."

"Hmm."

I heard some clacking at Johnny's end. He was probably getting back to work, drawn by the irresistible pull of the screens.

"Let me know if you hear anything about Clayco," I said.

"I'll ask around."

"And Johnny? I'm taking you serious and all."

"What?"

"If you think they're dangerous, they're dangerous. Don't fuck around."

"Sure. I already told the beezers downstairs, and called the management company, too. They won't get inside again."

"No, that's fine, but what I mean is, this isn't a trading opportunity, okay? At least not now. You find something out about Clayco, call me first. I'm feeling a little exposed."

"Sure, okay."

"I mean it." I didn't think Johnny would sell me out for a few points of alpha.

Probably.

"Take a vacation," he said. "Tour the sites. See the Liberty Bell."

"It's *Pittsburgh*, not Philly."

"Whatever. I'm just saying, maybe you don't want to meet this woman in person."

"Really good-looking, huh? You just want the field to yourself."

"Never." He laughed. "I'd sooner sleep with a pit bull."

"I thought you already did."

"So I know what I'm talking about."

After we hung up I tried to finish the kata, but I was too distracted. Shotokan is mostly about mental focus, and the conversation with Johnny had ruined mine.

I thought about the woman in New York. She was making fast progress, hardly slowed by all the chaff and evasion in my background. Zeke said she had a reputation.

Dave said Silas Cade had a reputation.

I wondered what she was doing, right then. Arriving in Pittsburgh, this hotel's address in hand? Eating breakfast? Finishing a two-hour combatives workout?

Whatever, she was probably being more productive than me. I sighed and got up.

CHAPTER NINE

I t was time to leave. Fuck the threats. Stop in and say goodbye to Dave, then back to New York.

Johnny and Zeke were well meaning, but I needed to be back on home turf. If Catwoman was looking for me in the city, I'd damn well meet her there. The hills and forests and decaying steel mills out here were unfamiliar, and you make mistakes when things are unfamiliar.

Some long driving, then, later today. I hadn't flown into Pittsburgh, and I wouldn't fly out. As far as possible, I never fly. Depending on your viewpoint, you could regard that as a success story for the TSA.

See, all the ID checking and scanners and take-your-shoes-off and the pat downs and shampoo confiscation—none of that's going to catch a terrorist. Because the thing is, a terrorist who blows up airplanes, he does that *once* only. By definition. Nobody knows who the next terrorist is going to be—certainly not the TSA, which is always fighting the last scenario.

So the watch lists are pointless if you're worried about Al Qaeda or Timothy McVeigh. But they're great for screwing with citizens who just like to travel without the whole world knowing. False IDs work if they're good enough, sure, but they cost real money—and even then, you still have to go through that damned endless line, with cameras and inspectors and full-body radiation. It's a risk.

I hate risk.

Instead, I'd driven here three days ago. Six hours on the turnpike, a long drive. In my own car, which was registered to a legitimately incorporated limited liability company in White Plains, all excise fees paid up, license plates shiny, the inspection current. I put it in the Pittsburgh airport's central parking—long-term is always too far away from the terminals, and no one cares if a vehicle's been left for a week or two—and walked over to the Alamo desk on the baggage floor.

True, I'd had to use a false license. But it didn't go into a federal database, and it wasn't actively cross-checked against anything except the credit card's payment history—which another PO box LLC was careful to keep fully paid. Now I'd return the rental, pretend I was getting a flight out, and no one would ever be the wiser.

I pulled into Barktree Welding midmorning. The welding tank Dave had used for the barbecue cart still stood abandoned in the middle of the gravel out front. The bay doors were all open again, perhaps for fresh air—the day had turned beautiful, clear and sunny, a light breeze bringing the smell of trees and moss down from the hills around us.

I parked to one side. Dave came out from the shop, a sponge in one hand.

"Hiya, Silas!"

"Hey."

Funny thing—he looked less like me every time I saw his face. Increasingly I saw the individual personality engraved there: the laugh lines and a crease above his nose and a faint scar on one cheekbone.

"Putting a shine on the Charger," he said. "Don't mind if I finish up, do you? I need to get the wax on."

"Want help?"

"No! No, that's okay."

The hood was closed today, whatever tuning he'd done yesterday complete. Swirls of light-colored wax covered most of the car's exterior, everything except the driver's-side panels. Dave knelt, dipped the sponge in a bucket of water, then the can, and gently wiped more on.

"I like the old-fashioned paint," he said. "There's a shop over in Uniontown did this for me. But it needs waxing regular."

I remembered buffing my folks' car in high school—Saturday afternoon, warm in the bright sun, baseball on the radio. For a year or two there I cared a lot about what I drove and how I looked in it.

Bouncing around in Humvees and MRAPs, the vehicles constantly getting shot and blown up and breaking down, somehow ended that simple pleasure. Cars were just dull machines to me now.

Not that I'd say so to Dave. "Looks real nice."

"Needs to sit an hour." He wrung the sponge out, put it to dry on a shelf and carried the bucket to spill out the water on the gravel. "Want a beer?"

"Nope. Too early."

"Beer's pretty much all I drink."

So much for a quick goodbye.

We sat in the same spot, next to a workbench in the first bay. The refrigerator was close to hand, a battered wooden chair and two stools were available and an old CRT television sat on a pass-through counter into the office. That room was smaller and just as cluttered as the shop, albeit more with stacks of grimy paper than metal parts and tools.

"I been thinking," he said.

"Uh-huh." I hadn't known Dave long, but he seemed to start a lot of conversations that way.

"What I was saying yesterday, about the scrap and the casinos and all, you know I was messing, right? All that petty-ass lawbreaking—only a fuckwad would do that." He drank some Rock Green Light. "I mean, more than once."

"Hard to disagree."

"Right. Because you go to jail, and listen—I know—jail's fucked up. You do not want to be there."

In my career I'd come to see that, no, some people *did* want to be in jail, but of course that only strengthened Dave's point.

"So why aren't the *bankers* behind bars?" he asked. "I figure you can explain this to me. Those assholes on Wall Street pretty much destroyed the world economy, right after they sent all our jobs to China. And what happens?—they keep getting, like, million-dollar bonuses at Christmas. And buying yachts and shit, going skiing in France."

It was almost poignant how limited Dave's imagination was. I've spent some time in the plutocracy. As a mere hired hand, of course, somewhere between the pool boy and the first footman, but I've seen some of the estates. Private islands, castles on the Rhine, Connecticut-sized cattle "ranches."

Not to mention that a million dollars was more or less cafeteria change. Real bonuses, the kind the managing directors hand themselves, can run ten or a hundred times that.

"It's not complicated," I said. "They run the game. The house always wins."

"And the politicians—?"

"Owned. Everyone knows that."

"Yeah." Dave tipped his chair back. "Well, that ain't right."

I almost laughed. "Who are you, Wyatt Earp?"

"No. But why not? Town needs a sheriff."

"Good luck with that."

"I guess it's not what you do, huh?"

"No." I felt a pang of . . . something. Embarrassment? Disappointment? "No, I can't say I'm righting wrongs."

"Does make you wonder why nobody's taken a rocket launcher into Goldman Sachs, though." He put his bottle down and looked over at me, kind of thoughtful. "Maybe you can help *me* out instead."

A shadow crossed the sun. Or maybe I just felt the first inkling of what *family* could mean.

"Well, I don't—"

"See, I owe some money."

"So does everyone else in America."

"It's a problem," he said. "A big problem."

But we never got to discuss it.

Engine noise outside. We both looked up, just as a familiar, dark blue car squealed off the road and bounced into the lot. Doors on both sides sprang open. Behind it, an older, beat-up vehicle roared in from the other direction, skidding to a halt so hard its nose practically scraped the dirt.

Three men came out of the cars holding assault rifles. One was very tall.

"Down!" I yelled, diving off the chair. "Down, down!"

Bullets slammed into the walls, the doors, the bench, smashing tools and ricocheting off loose metal everywhere. Auto parts crashed to the floor, adding to the din and dust and smoke. I crab crawled straight to the office, five feet away. Too much noise and adrenaline to hear anything, but I glimpsed Dave rolling the other direction, headed for the last bay.

The cinderblock walls were beautiful. Any other building material would have perforated like cardboard under the hail of firepower.

The office window blew in, shattered by a three-second burst. I ducked the shards, swept all the crap off Dave's metal desk, and peeked through the frame.

We were totally boxed. Two men remained at the blue Nissan, one crouched behind the hood and one behind the trunk, sweeping their weapons across the shop's front. Another guy sprinted for the adjacent field, holding his rifle like he'd done this many, many times before. In a few seconds he landed behind the tractor Dave had left out there—perfect sightlines across the shop's rear.

We wouldn't be leaving through the back door.

On the other hand, I now had my own weapon out. Ten rounds available, and one spare magazine. I ducked to the other side of the window frame, counted two, and raised up long enough to fire three times.

Nobody got hurt, but it kept them in place for a moment. Silence returned abruptly as everyone stopped shooting.

"Silas!" Dave called from the opposite end of the shop. "Silas!"

"I'm okay!" I yelled as loud as I could. "I found the M16. Where's the box of frag grenades?"

"*What?*" But our assailants began firing again, cutting him off.

Of course they'd figure out I was bluffing soon enough. Bullets slapped the wall behind me and the ceiling—the two at the Nissan were firing slightly upward from their position, through the window. Chunks of asbestos rained down from shredded ceiling tiles.

I moved to the side window, now also broken, and put a round into the hood cowling of the tractor in the field. Just to keep that asshole in place.

"Dave? You hurt?"

No answer. I returned to the front, and saw that we weren't going to settle in for a siege: the men had gotten back into their car, and the driver backed it into the road. I was pretty sure they were the same two I'd confronted at the restaurant.

I fired twice, starring the windshield, but they must have been hunched down below the dashboard.

Anyway, good riddance. I stood up and gave them the finger through the window. "Yeah, fuck *off,* motherfuc—"

Oops, that was a little premature. The driver was only aligning the vehicle, making sure he was pointed directly at the office so the engine block would remain between me and them. He started forward, and the other guy held his rifle outside the window— impossible to aim very well like that, but on full auto all he had to do was pull the trigger in my general direction. I ducked back down as bullets slammed all around.

They were going to drive their improvised APC right into the bay, and there wasn't a thing I could do about it.

Or—hang on. I went to the floor and looked around the frame of the door between the office and the bay. The Nissan was moving forward, halfway to the shop, and they didn't see me immediately.

I steadied the Sig in two hands, aimed, and shot the welding gas tank Dave had left out there.

KA-WHUUUUMP!

They were right alongside. The fireball engulfed the entire side of the car as the tank exploded. Both left-side tires blew, and metal shards tore across the car's panels. The driver yelled in pain.

At that exact instant, I heard an engine roar into life from the last bay. Tires screamed—and Dave's Charger leaped out of the garage so fast it actually went airborne coming off the concrete pad. The car hit the gravel, spun left, and went into a long skid that somehow ended with Dave exactly centered on the blacktop. He fishtailed about one degree, rammed the accelerator all the way to the floor, and left a smoking trail of rubber on the pavement. A second later he was gone, disappearing around the curve at warp five.

Okay, well, I couldn't really blame him.

The man in the field found his range and started putting rounds through the side window, irregularly spaced, keeping me on the floor. The Nissan wasn't moving, but I could see motion. The passenger door opened, apparently kicked from inside. The driver must not have been hurt that bad, because he reached up over the dash and pushed out the windshield glass, knocking it onto the hood. The rifle came up next, naturally, and he fired a long burst at the garage's concrete floor.

Which was smart, because the bullets hit and then traveled parallel to the ground, six inches above it. I'd already rolled back into the office, fortunately.

Options were diminishing rapidly. For nearly a minute I just lay there, curled up, listening to bullets crack over my head and into the walls. Plaster and furniture fell to pieces all around.

Then over the din, I heard a heavy truck on the road, downshifting with a *BLAAAT* from the airbrakes. The fusillade lightened, then stopped—and the truck's engine roared, apparently accelerating. I hunched up to peek through the window frame.

Dave was in the cab of the flatbed I'd parked by earlier. The truck swung off the road at, Jesus, fifty miles an hour? I had a half second to think *Fuck he's going to crash right into the fucking BUILDING!*—

—when Dave yanked the wheel around, throwing the entire truck out of control. It slewed left, but the momentum was far too much, and the vehicle went over on its side. Somehow this happened exactly alongside the Nissan. The stack of cinderblocks flew off the bed and hammered onto the car, pounding it into a pile of junk.

The truck continued to slide across the gravel, finally stopping when it smashed into my rented Malibu.

I couldn't see how anyone might still be alive under that rockslide of bricks, but a moment later one of the men was shoving his door open and trying to crawl out. When his arm was mostly outside I fired, aiming for the elbow, and he pulled back. The guy over by the tractor yelled, the words meaningless.

Dave pushed up his own door, opening it like a tank hatch, and looked cautiously out. I waved him back down just as Tractor Boy fired a few rounds.

Then . . . nothing. Silence finally settled over the scene. I waited.

Thirty seconds. A full minute.

Well. *That* was fun.

I breathed a few times, nice and slow.

"Silas?" Dave's voice came from inside the truck cab. "We good now?"

"Not yet," I hollered back. "Don't do anything stupid."

Anything *else*.

Tractor Boy was suddenly up and running, sprinting for the squashed Nissan. I followed him with the pistol, but didn't fire— I'm not good enough to hit a moving target with a handgun, and I had to think about conserving ammunition. He reached the door, yanked it all the way open, pulled out first one man and then the other. Out in the open, the big one must have been seven feet tall.

All three glanced my way, rifles more or less at ready, but no one moving to shoot.

Apparently we were tabling our discussion. More resistance than they'd expected, perhaps.

They were alive and not even limping much, which was something, considering their car looked like it had gone through a junkyard crusher. Still staring my way, they backed up to the other vehicle. Five seconds later it peeled onto the road and took off.

Dave hopped out and I met him halfway, stepping over the remnants of the welding tank. Diesel pooled and gasoline fumes drifted across the war zone.

"Thought you'd gone," I said.

"Come on." He had keys in his hand. "Car's up the road. We got to get out of here."

"Just a minute." The landslide of bricks had so deformed the Nissan's rear bumper that the license plate had sprung off. I picked it up.

I could run it later, maybe find out who we were dealing with.

"Let's go." Dave was impatient. "We got to *move*."

True enough. Traffic was awfully light, but civilians were sure to happen by any minute. My own car was trapped by the fallen truck. I nodded and we started to jog up the road.

"Why'd you come back?" I said as I holstered the Sig—a little awkward, while we ran.

Dave grinned over his shoulder. "Why? *Why?*" he said. "You're my *brother*, man."

CHAPTER TEN

Maybe I should drive," I said, clutching the roll bar at the side pillar so hard my hand hurt.

"Don't be stupid." Dave slowed, took the Charger through the blinking-light intersection at about sixty, double-clutched down and accelerated back up to eighty. "You don't know this car like I do."

"No." We passed a motorcycle, then feathered back into the lane just in front of an oncoming pickup. "But I know other things. For example, I know I'd like to live at least until—*look out!*"

Coming around an endless curve, trees down to the verge blocking all views, we were suddenly up the tail of a big brown UPS truck. Instead of steering left to pass, Dave yanked the wheel just enough right to throw the car into a skid—and we drifted into the passing lane anyway, tires screaming, all the way around and past the truck. At the last moment, before we exited the blacktop entirely, Dave touched the gas. The wheels bit again, and we were back in control, a hundred yards ahead of the stunned UPS man.

"You ain't one to talk," Dave said. "After getting my garage all shot to hell."

There was that. "Would you just keep your eyes on the damn road?"

As we approached Clabbton, traffic increased, vehicles every few hundred yards in both directions. Small houses sat back from the street, with wide scraggly yards. We shot past a roadhouse, dark windows under a low roof, a faux neon sign in the shape of a naked woman, three Harleys parked out front.

"Maybe we should figure out where we're going," I said.

Dave glanced sideways. "How much ammo you got left in that gun?"

"Dunno." Three rounds loaded and a spare magazine, but the very question made me not want to answer. "Why?"

"Didn't you recognize that car?"

"What?"

"The Saturn. Long scratch on the left panel, crack in the windshield? Brendt, hell, he's been driving that thing for years. I helped him overhaul the brakes a couple years ago."

"*Brendt?* Your improvised-explosives buddy?"

Maybe the car had looked a little familiar.

"He was driving it yesterday, up at the mill. I can't believe you didn't see it right off. Hell, for a moment I was afraid Brendt was gonna be inside it."

I tried to keep up. If Brendt was involved, the story changed completely. Much better this was some local hillbilly feud or something, rather than people looking for me.

Much, much better.

Though I couldn't see how the Nissan could chase me two days ago and not be connected. "You think this was, I don't know, a *prank?*"

"No, course not." He sounded offended. "I can't say about your friends, but mine? They don't generally try to blow the shit outta me."

"So what——?"

"So maybe he let somebody use his car. Loaned it out." Dave shook his head, not looking away from the road. "Brendt, well, he's a few feathers short of a duck, you know? If someone came up and told him a story, he'd go right ahead and believe it."

He accelerated again, the engine loud and road noise louder. We closed at frightening speed on more Sunday drivers ahead.

I decided I'd had enough.

"Pull over," I yelled above the Charger's roar.

"What?"

"Stop the car, damn it!"

Dave slowed abruptly, but only to avoid colliding with the pickup in front of us. The road rose into a long hill. Trees and dirt on one side, a long low school on the other. The parking lot was vast and empty.

"In there." I whacked Dave's shoulder and pointed. "We need to stop."

He started to say something, then jerked the wheel in an irritated way, engaged the hand brake briefly and took us through the lot's entrance in a long, graceful skid. He kept it going across half the acre of pavement, the car feeling completely out of control, rubber screaming. We finally slid to a stop dead in the middle, turned all the way around. After a moment Dave killed the engine.

Silence.

I breathed a few times.

"What's wrong?" Dave shifted in his seat, flexing his muscles, twisting restlessly.

Combat adrenaline stops being your friend as soon as any immediate danger's over. The worst mistakes in the field happen at the end of an engagement, when everyone's still totally jacked and can't stop shooting.

"At the moment, no one's trying to kill us," I said. "We need to take a break, calm down and think it through. No need to rush off. Last thing we want to do is stumble right into another assault."

"They fucking obliterated my shop!"

"Yes, they did."

"And almost killed me!"

"Me too, for that matter."

"Shit!"

It took a few minutes, but he finally settled. As we sat quietly, I studied our surroundings. The school was single story, brick and aluminum, the way they built them in the sixties. Illegible graffiti wound around the walls in the back, poorly scrubbed off. An old Dodge Sportsman was parked at the rear corner, a stylized wolf's head painted on its side—the team van, no doubt.

On the other side of an open field was another, smaller school, playground structures on woodchips alongside. The acres of empty parking felt like the old P1 lot at Shea on an off day.

"You okay now?" I said after a while.

"Sure." His breathing was normal.

Sunshine and faint birdsong. Life in the country.

"We're alive, we're in one piece, let's keep it that way." The veteran soldier's philosophy.

Dave looked around. "I went to school here," he said.

I blinked. "High school?"

"All the way through." He gestured at the elementary building. "Kindergarten on up."

"Like it?"

He shrugged. "My foster dad taught me to drive right here. Round and round the parking lot."

"Seems like a good place—nothing to run into."

"Nope, just stalled out like a hundred times."

"And look at you now."

Cars passed on the road. A few hundred yards down two orange trucks were parked at the side, along with an excavator—all locked up and empty, in the middle of some infrastructure project that would no doubt resume on Monday.

"I think we can rule you out as the target," I said.

"Huh?"

"I'm the one they were shooting at. You just happened to be there."

"Well, I . . . sure." He seemed flummoxed. "No one's got any reason to be gunning for *me*."

Since the attack on the garage we'd been riding momentum, but the forward velocity had burned out. Energy drained away, leaving me slumped in the roll cage.

The interior of Dave's car, I should mention, was barren. Not even a sound system. Just exposed metal—cleanly painted, to be sure, even around the welds and joints—two bucket seats in the front and a plain bench in the rear, and some serious safety equipment. Not only the bars, which bolstered the entire frame, but five-point harnesses and a fire extinguisher, clamped sideways under the dash.

Also, no speedometer. Just a big tachometer, and smaller dials I didn't recognize.

"Is this what you expected?" I asked. "When you wrote that letter?"

"Naw." Dave didn't say anything else for a moment, then laughed. "I mean, not exactly. It ain't like I had so much to lose, back there. I had the shop five years now. No—six? Six in November. But the mortgage is so far underwater, I wasn't looking at *ever* paying off. Fuck it."

Mortgage? For a convicted felon coming off real prison time?

The timing put it right before the bubble burst, which was just believable. Banks were lending to *anybody*, right up until the whole thing exploded. Pulse and a scrawled X—good enough!

"You need to call the police," I said. "Right now."

"But Brendt's car —"

"You're not a detective." I glanced over, then back out the windshield. "Neither am I. This isn't a fistfight behind the pool hall—those guys were using military full auto. Like it or not, law enforcement is going to be all over Clabbton."

"So what?"

"So you need to talk to them."

"What about you?"

"Ah." We'd come to the hard part of the conversation. "Well, I can't."

"Can't what?"

"Talk to them." I turned toward him again, and didn't take my gaze away this time. "I have a complicated life."

Dave half frowned, half rolled his eyes. "I *knew* it."

"It's not what you think."

"No? You're gonna take off, leave me standing here scratching my ass?"

"Um." That was about right, in fact.

"Like I said."

"I need to do three things," I said. "Number one is find out who's trying to kill me, and why. No way I can do that from inside a jail cell."

"Uh-huh. What's number two?"

"Then I'll . . . discourage them."

"Kill them." He said it without particular emphasis.

"No. Not unless I absolutely have to. That just attracts even more attention, which interferes with goal number three."

"Yes?"

"When it's over, I disappear."

A siren in the distance, but it faded away. I rolled my window all the way down—with a crank, no power assists in the Charger—and leaned one arm out.

"We've barely got to know each other," Dave said.

"I'll stay in touch."

"You're kinda missing the point."

I sighed. "Drop me off and call the cops, okay?"

"No." He smiled. "I'm going with you. We'll solve this together."

"That's a really bad idea."

"Nope."

A pause. Eventually I said, "Okay, tell me."

"First, like I told you, I got some history with the law. If I talk to Gator, he's gonna be thinking one thing—somehow, some way, it's my fault. Or at least I'm involved."

"Gator?"

"Police chief in Clabbton. He went to school here too, matter of fact. That history I mentioned—he's in it."

"Is that his real name?"

"Course it is." Dave hesitated. "I mean, it's what we always called him. I ain't never seen a birth certificate."

"Never mind."

"But more important is *you*." He reached over and kind of lightly slapped my head. "My brother."

What could I say?

"All right." I shook my head. "Okay. Let's do this—we'll try to chase down Brendt's car." Truth was, I needed Dave's help anyway. He was the local, and I didn't know *anything*. "But you're not going underground. First opportunity, you have a sit-down with, uh,

Gator. And if the bad guys show up with tanks and missiles again, you go straight to safety. I can take care of myself."

"Sure, that's fine. But meanwhile, if anyone asks . . . ?"

"Don't mention the shop. You weren't there, you don't know anything about it."

"Great!" His mood had swung back to cheerful, like some inconsequential spot of bother was now behind us.

I should work on being so resilient.

"So this little setback——?"

"I got the car." Dave slapped the dash. "I got a few hundred bucks in my pocket. They'll repossess everything else. So what?" He grinned. "I got *you*, Silas. It's all good."

"Uh . . ."

What we had, actually, was at least a dozen stone killers chasing us, a trail of destruction, and nowhere to run. That I could think of. "Yeah. All good." Christ.

Dave started the car and we drove out of the lot—slowly, this time. Only ten or twenty miles over the speed limit. The town was quiet. Everything seemed normal again.

We stopped at a light, the crossroads empty. A stone church at the corner was boarded up, even the clerestory windows nailed over. As we waited, another siren rose, then a blue light, and a big, red, shiny, double-cab pickup flashed past, whip antenna streaming behind it.

I didn't like that. "Unmarked police?"

"Naw, the volunteer firefighters. I think that was Dink—I heard he got a new truck. Someone must have seen the smoke and called it in."

The welding shop was not only a fire hazard, it was also a crime scene. The local PD wouldn't know what to do with it, so state detectives would jump in. Once they ran the ballistics and discovered that military-grade armament had been involved, they'd probably call the FBI. I groaned.

"You all right?"

"Great." Looking Dave up was starting to seem like the worst decision I'd made since punching out a first lieutenant one night in a Kabul bar. "Really great."

———

We stopped in front of a small, sagging bungalow. Dave parked directly on its gravel drive, blocking access onto the road. Clabbton didn't seem to go in for zoning: next door was another house only slightly less ramshackle, then a car wash and a feed store. Down the road the other way an empty, weedy lot surrounded a charred foundation.

"Maybe you should stay here." Dave studied the house. "Brendt, well, he don't always take well to strangers."

"I met him yesterday!"

"Not at his house. He gets kinda territorial."

"That's stupid."

"Just saying."

I looked hard at him. "Maybe I should come in."

"Maybe you shouldn't."

The staredown went on a few seconds too long.

"Fine." What was I going to do, shoot my own brother? "Keep it simple. Don't use my name."

"Course not."

"Five minutes, then I'm coming in."

"Why? I *told* you—"

"I need to hear the story myself."

"Whatever." He slammed the door on the way out.

Cars swooshed past. None slowed, but I felt every eye. The Charger was about as anonymous as a parade float. It even looked a little like one, covered in white smears of turtle wax.

Dave walked across the ill-kempt lawn, going opposite the drive, around the side of the house. Paper shades were pulled down two of the windows I could see, and the third was dark and crusted with dirt.

I checked my phone—still working. It might have cost twenty dollars but it seemed to be as reliable as any of that military-grade hardware the army loaded us down with. I called Zeke.

No answer.

Johnny—no answer.

Ryan—you get the picture.

I checked the Sig Sauer. It still smelled from the firefight. I didn't feel like disassembling it—who knows what Brendt was up to? I might need a weapon again real soon. The cleaning would have to wait. Instead, I took my one spare magazine, removed all the rounds and pushed them back in again, nice and careful. The used magazine still had three left, so I put it in an outside pocket.

The pistol itself I held down at seat level.

Two minutes went by. The sun reflected sharply off one of the windows in Brendt's shack, and I shifted my head away from the glare.

A door slammed, and Dave came running out.

CHAPTER ELEVEN

He opened the door, slid in and pulled it shut—not loudly—in about two seconds.

"His girlfriend took it." Dave rumbled the Charger's engine into life and stamped the accelerator. We squealed through a U-turn and roared back toward town center.

"The Saturn?"

"She works at the Super Duper, went in this morning at seven. He says."

"You believe him?"

"I think so." Dave looked over at me, checked all three mirrors automatically and thought for a moment. "He was just waking up. Brendt is kind of slow, like I said. He looked way too hung over to be making up stories. Elsie's moved in, and he's sharing the car with her."

"Elsie?"

"She's from Fairville," he said. "Next county over. No one I know."

A setup seemed impossible. "How long's she been with him?"

"Brendt said a few months."

"You didn't know about her?"

"He never mentioned."

"Hard to believe you never even *saw* her before."

"I ain't seen much of Brendt either lately—now I know why."

"Okay." The social mores seemed odd, but it wasn't my town.

Dave slowed behind an RV—some retiree out to see America, his home on his metaphorical back. The thing must have been forty feet long and fifteen wide.

"Maybe . . ." Dave hesitated. "Brendt and I have some history. You know, with women."

Ah. "Let me guess."

"Yeah." He grimaced. "I don't know how, he always seems to find the good ones first."

"And you're like, what, share and share alike? All's fair in love and war?"

"I can't help it." He shrugged without taking his hands from the wheel. "Some of them, they decide they'd rather step out with me."

"Jesus. And he's still friends with you?"

"Mostly." Dave abruptly accelerated. The Charger bounded forward, barely missing the corner of the RV. The oncoming lane was empty for a few hundred yards, but a trailer truck was approaching fast. We roared past the RV, engine screaming in high gear. Dave yanked the wheel, and we slipped back across the solid line—about ten feet in front of certain death on the truck's bumper.

"Oh. My. God." I tried to breathe again.

"Anyway, Brendt was real worried, thought this might fuck up the relationship or something."

Worried about Dave, or worried about his girlfriend handing his car over to a squad of terrorists? Maybe it didn't matter. "I could see that."

A mile down we slowed, entering a turn lane at a blinker. At the intersection Dave turned into the jammed parking lot, the Charger rumbling as he nosed slowly among the rows, looking for a space. Women pushed loaded shopping carts to their SUVs; men ambled along carrying 24-packs and sacks of charcoal. Sunday was Clabbton's big shopping day, apparently.

The Super Duper occupied one end of the strip mall. A Chinese restaurant, a gun shop and dollar store filled out the rest. Dave parked around the side, on top of the yellow zebra stripes. He pointed at the NO PARKING YOU WILL BE TOWED! sign.

"Better stay here," he said. "In case they're serious."

Again? "Now, wait a min—"

He raised his hands. "No, no, don't worry, I'll find Elsie and bring her out. You're right, we should both talk to her."

"All right." I gave in. "Fine."

He disappeared into the supermarket. I took a minute to study the lot, including the service drive that continued behind the car and around the back. The cab of an eighteen-wheeler was just visible in the rear, probably where it had backed up to the loading dock. Out front, the parking lot was a hive of cars coming and going.

The sun came out again, stronger this time.

Nothing looked out of place.

The attack had to be connected to Clayco. The other work I'd had lately was nothing—some collection work, sorting out a low-level abstraction of funds, and even a few tax returns, mostly as favors to friends. Glamorous, huh? Nothing that would draw a Call of Duty strike force.

Anyway, the timing made it certain: run my little audit one day, assault forces are parachuting in forty hours later.

The problem was, they *knew* me.

Or they knew Ryan, and they got my name from him. Actually,

that was more likely. But either way, it was an inside job. Only someone in the loop would be able to run the pingback so quickly.

So the job had either been a setup from the start—or there were some very big, very fast sharks swimming in the same pool.

Dave came back around the corner, a woman gesturing beside him, and I stopped worrying about Soap MacTavish.

Stunning. Drop-dead. Heartstopping. She should have been on a Brazilian runway, not schlumping frozen pizzas across a scanner. Willowy tall—too tall for the baggy yellow employee smock—hair flowing with streaks of gold and silver, eyes green and knowing. She was knocking a cigarette out of a box, Dave hastily checking his pockets.

I'll bet her checkout line was twenty deep. Guys buying one or two items—"Honey, can *I* do the grocery shopping today?"

I got out, closed the door, and met them in front of the hood.

"Silas? Elsie." Dave made the introduction, kind of grudging, getting his lighter into play.

"Hi, Silas." Her voice husky and low and tuned to that frequency that switches off men's cortexes. She got the cigarette going and looked me in the face. "Damn! What're you, twins?"

"Brothers."

"I *guess.*"

"I known Brendt since grade school," Dave said. "He must be doing all right in the world."

"He's really *nice* to me."

"Uh-huh," I said. "Lends you his car and all."

"Yeah, I had a little fender bumper last week." She exhaled smoke to the side like a forties movie queen. "I think Brendt mentioned your name, Dave. Thought you could fix it up for me."

"Sure, no problem!" He paused, his brain catching up. "Or, well, actually. Maybe I should swing by instead. Sometimes you can just knock the dents out with a mallet."

The attack, the destruction of his garage, our screaming high-speed drive through the county—Elsie seemed to have driven everything out of Dave's head.

Some teenagers walking from their car passed us, the boys' mouths hanging open as they stared. One of the girls elbowed her boyfriend, sharp, and he yelped. Aggrieved complaints and laughter from the others took them into the store.

Elsie didn't take any more notice than she would have a bumblebee.

"You parked here?" I tried to keep the conversation on point.

"Out at the edge." She lifted one finger, gracefully indicating the far side of the lot. "They don't like us to take spaces *closer* than that."

"Uh-huh. Is it still there?"

We all peered across the pavement.

"Sure." And indeed, I thought I recognized the same dull-colored car the gunmen had driven off in, not forty minutes earlier.

"Is it where you left it? In the same parking place, I mean?"

Elsie's gaze turned to me. "That's a funny question."

I shrugged.

"Maybe we should take a look."

We walked across the lot, zigzagging around parked cars. Shoppers watched us openly, sideways, subtle, blatant. I realized that Elsie was perhaps the most effective camouflage I'd ever used. No one had a microsecond glance for me.

Good thing I hate the smell of cigarettes—one thing about the city, the air's lousy but hardly anyone smokes in public anymore. Elsie might have distracted me utterly, otherwise.

Like Dave, who walked straight into the bed of a pickup, his head turned around to talk to her instead of watching where he was going.

"Fuck!" He picked himself up from the ground, rubbing his knee.

"Ouch," said Elsie.

"No, I'm fine. Fine!"

"It came out of *nowhere*, didn't it?"

I glanced over quickly, but her face was clear.

The Saturn's hood was warm. Dave nodded, already stooping to look closely at the driver's-side lock.

"Maybe scratched, maybe not," he said. "They could of just slim-jimmied it."

"I think I parked here," said Elsie. "This same spot. I usually do." She crossed her arms, the cigarette still held in perfect equipoise. "But you boys seem to be saying someone took it for a *ride* this morning. While I was working."

"Can you let me in?" I asked. She nodded. The keys were in a pocket deep in the smock's waist, and yes, I watched their extraction quite closely. Just like Dave.

"Here you go." Elsie swung the door open and made a slight, perfectly timed voilà gesture.

Almost ironic. There seemed to be some deep currents running under that Elite Models façade.

Inside we found french fry bags, empty cups, a dirty towel, loose shotgun shells, a videogame cartridge, three T-shirts—all dirty and one torn—and another armful or two of similar junk. It smelled of Elsie's cigarettes. If the attackers had left any clues behind, they were impossible to find in the heaps of Brendt's trash.

No blood on the seats.

But as I looked more closely at the stained cushions, I noticed something stuck in the gap between the seat and the hand brake. I worked it out from the crack.

"I got to get back," Elsie said when we emerged. "Manager's strict about breaks."

"You're smoking Virgina Slims?" I asked.

She paused. "Super Slims."

I looked at the cigarette in my hand. "Not this kind?"

Elsie leaned over to look and shook her head. "That one doesn't even have a *filter.* And what's that writing? Not English."

"Cyrillic, I think." I found a dollar bill in my pocket, the only paper I had on me, and carefully folded it around the cigarette. "A clue."

"Congratulations, Mr. Holmes." She nodded. "I really got to go."

"Yeah. Okay." Dave scratched his head. "Thanks."

"You want to tell me what's going on? Since I have to drive this home tonight?"

I looked at Dave and shook my head a little.

"Not rightly sure," Dave said. "Some visitors out to the shop, thought they might have been in this car."

"Why would they do *that?*"

Because they needed another car. It was clear enough. The three men couldn't have been local—Pittsburgh, just maybe, but the skills they demonstrated tended not to live in slow, rustic parts of the country. So they drove here, either direct or from the airport, almost certainly in one car. But for the assault they needed another. A backup. In case something went wrong—you know, like a ton of bricks falling onto your getaway vehicle.

Say you want a car for a quick in-and-out. Borrowing from someone on an eight-hour shift, from what was probably the busiest parking lot in the county?—that's how *I'd* do it. They might even have staked out the lot, waiting until an obvious employee arrived.

Just coincidence they picked a vehicle Dave knew? Believable enough, I suppose, considering Clabbton's small size—Dave probably had some connection to nine tenths of the people here.

Still.

"If the police come calling, don't bother hiding anything," I said. "Go ahead and tell them we were here."

"Why *wouldn't* I?" Elsie's wide gaze stayed on mine, this time.

"Uh, just, you know."

When she'd gone back into the Super Duper, the sunshine went with her. Literally—clouds closed over the sky again, the light dimmed, and a rising breeze blew some paper trash through weeds in the drainage ditch by the road.

"Brendt's a *loser*." Dave seemed in pain. "In high school, I seen the guy eat his own boogers."

"What, you didn't?"

"Not where anyone could watch me."

"How would you know?"

"He works in a fucking *muffler* shop." Apparently in the auto-repair world, you couldn't go much lower. "I'm not sure he knows how to open a bar of soap."

The drift wasn't hard to catch. "Just because *you* don't want to sleep with him doesn't mean she can't."

"Yeah, but . . . *why*?" His question plaintive, almost keening. "What could she possibly see in Brendt?"

"Don't go there." I looked across the lot. "Come on, I need to get something."

But as we walked to the row of stores, Dave stopped abruptly. "Hey, wait a minute."

"What?"

"The bad guys. They borrowed the Saturn, along with the blue car. Right? But they drove back here in just the Saturn."

"Right." I nodded. "I know what you're thinking."

"How did they *leave*?"

"They probably had another car waiting. The one they drove here in originally. One big shell game."

"Oh." He started walking again. "I thought they might still be here."

"Unlikely." I looked at the teeming lot. "But who knows? Keep your eye out."

CHAPTER TWELVE

The gun shop was typical: metal plates bolted over the windows, reinforced door, linoleum and exposed concrete inside. The interior was smaller than expected, because a heavy wall had been built crossways, to add an ammunition bunker in the rear. Only the psychotically fearless keep their crates of black powder out in the open.

"No blue laws?" I asked as we entered.

"Not for selling guns," Dave said. "But you can't *use* them—no hunting on Sunday in Pennsylvania."

A man stood behind the counter, catalog open on the glass case, marking annotations on the page. He looked up when we entered, then twitched a smile and slapped the pen down.

"Dave, bro." He came around to shake hands, rural-America style—a plain hearty grip, no fist bump or shoulder clasp or high punch. "How'ya?"

"Aw, you know."

The man looked at me. "Who's this, separated at birth?"

"My brother."

"Brother?!"

Would we have to endure this every single encounter? I nodded, let Dave run through the introductions. He still sounded a little amped, talking a bit too fast, laughing a half second too long, but the owner didn't seem to notice.

Meanwhile, I glanced over the stock. Hunting rifles, shotguns, a wide range of handguns, a few assault-style weapons locked to rings on the pegboard. Ammunition boxes lined one shelf. Cleaning kits, eye and ear protection, a rack of DVDs. Belts and camo.

I felt more secure already. Whoever had come gunning, if they returned, guns blazing, I'd be able to fire back more than just thirteen times.

"Heard you were up with Van," the owner said to Dave.

"Been talking to him, yeah." Dave shook his head. "Van, shit, I swear he's got a piece of every man, woman and child in Clabbton."

"I'm paying him."

"He's a good guy, but, you know."

"Yeah."

They caught up on other acquaintances. I remembered what it was like in New Hampshire growing up—small-town life, everyone in everyone else's business all the time.

It was one reason I'd been so ready to leave.

"Four boxes of nine millimeter," I said, when we finally got around to business. "Overpressure rounds."

"What weight?"

"One twenty-four, one twenty-seven. Whatever you have."

"Remington hollow point? That's one forty-seven."

"My experience, the heavier weights underperform."

"The Federal, then. One twenty-four."

"Sounds fine."

"That all for you?" He snapped open a brown paper sack from under the counter and placed the boxes inside.

I'd been eyeing the armament on the wall, but this guy was clearly a legitimate dealer. I didn't have the ID to pass a background check, and Dave was an ex-convict. Neither of us could buy anything more dangerous than bullets.

"I think so," I said. "But let me ask you, when's the next gun show around here?"

"Gun show?"

"Within, oh, a hundred miles?" No response. "Two hundred?"

He studied me, then looked at Dave. "What do you need?"

Dave raised his hands in a wide shrug. "You know me, I just do a little quail shooting in the fall."

"That's a real nice-looking bullpup," I said. "Is it really a TAR-21?"

A pause.

"Were you in the service?" he asked.

I nodded. "Yes."

"Didn't think the Pentagon was buying Tavors."

"Standard issue was M4, that's right. But once we were in the field, we kind of got to choose."

"That right?"

"A lot of the guys, they liked the carbine. Reliability, though—I heard too many stories about sand jamming them up. I got to know this Polish commando on some joint patrols, and he swore by the Tavor. After he let me try it out, I had to agree."

"Army doesn't let you choose your own weapon." His face was unreadable.

"Not the Marines, either. You're right."

"Special Forces, now . . . I heard the rules was looser for them."

"Could be."

"How long were you in?"

"Eight years. U.S. military the whole time." I'd noticed the tattoo on his forearm, long faded. "No two hundred grand a year for me, contractor bullshit, driving politicians around. Low pay and lieutenants yelling at me, all the way through."

"I hear that." Another pause, then back to Dave. "He's your brother, you say?"

"Yup."

"How come you never mentioned him before?"

"Just found each other. You knew I was a foster kid, right? Finally went through the records, and here we are." Dave grinned. "Just look at him. Of *course* we're related."

What I'd forgotten was, Dave had served only eleven months—which was the full sentence; nobody gets parole anymore. The Brady law rules you out if you've got a one-year record. Dave scraped in just under the wire, and his background check was already on file here.

I think the guy might even have discounted us. When we left I had a large paper bag in each hand, and they were sagging from the weight of a Beretta M9, the ammunition boxes, cleaning supplies—and a well-used MP5, chambered for 9mm, so both weapons could take the same rounds. I'd paid cash, nearly emptying my wallet.

Not the Tavor, though. It was display only—the shop owner had gotten around import rules by swapping out just enough parts with domestic replacements—and even if he'd been willing to sell, I sure didn't have another three thousand bucks for it.

"I was serious," Dave said as we walked down the cracked

pavement fronting the stores. "Skeet's about all I done my whole life. I couldn't handle that stuff you got there without a month of practice."

"I'm glad to hear you say that."

"Huh?"

I meant it. "Most people, they figure, how hard can it be? Then they shoot their best friend in the head by accident."

"No, I—"

"These things—" I hefted the sacks—"they make it too easy. Anyone can pick one up and start putting rounds into a twenty-five-yard target. They're probably the best engineered machines on the planet." I considered. "Apart from Toyotas, of course."

"*Toyotas?*"

"It's good to recognize your limitations, that's all." I tipped my head. "Mine are cars, by the way."

When we turned the corner, Dave stopped short with a grunt, and I almost ran into him.

A police cruiser was pulled alongside the Charger, and a tall officer stood in front of it, arms crossed, waiting for us.

"Dave." The officer's uniform was tucked and neat, the Sam Browne belt worn from use but polished clean. His sidearm—a 1911 maybe, the holster flap covered it over—draped a leather lanyard in a neat loop. "Been looking for you."

"What's up, Chief?" Dave didn't sound the least bit surprised or nervous.

Had to say I was impressed.

"Who's this?" Looking at me.

"My brother. Never knew I had one!—tracked him down through the registry, and he came to visit. Silas, this is Gator."

Of course. Who else? I shifted the paper bags and we shook hands.

"Gator and I, we used to run into each other on the football field," Dave said.

He seemed to know everyone. Memory lane lasted another minute, which was good, because it allowed me to study the chief of police—but not good, because it allowed him to study me.

Satisfying neither of us, naturally.

"Bad news," the chief said. "You had an explosion out at your shop."

"What? No way!" Dave's act was actually convincing. "What happened?"

"Where have you been the last hour or so?"

"Around town. Silas came up this morning, we, you know, sat around a while, talking." He hesitated. "I had a beer, but you know me—only one. Then I wanted to show him around, and we ended up here to pick up a few things."

He indicated the paper bags in my hands with a slight wave of one hand. Incredible.

Gator looked at the Charger. "Seems like you stopped right in the middle of a waxing job."

"Just letting it cure before buffing." Dave made a face. "I won't deny it looks like shit. But the coating stays on better."

"Uh-huh." He switched to me. "You help with that? Putting on the turtle wax?"

It felt like a trick question. "Uh, no. I just watched."

He didn't respond, just waited. We stood in silence long enough it started to feel uncomfortable.

"Someone called in a fire," the chief said finally. "But that was the least of it. Looks like a truck crashed into two cars, and some-thing blew up. I'm sorry, Dave—the place is a goner."

"Blew *up?*"

I decided I'd better step in before Dave went for an Oscar. "I left my rental car there. Parked right out front. A Malibu. You said there was an accident?"

"I hope you bought the insurance." He pronounced it with an accent on the first syllable: *in*-surance.

"Aw, shoot."

"You mind if I look at your license, Silas?"

Another long moment.

As I mentioned, half my life is on the grid, perfectly normal, perfectly correct. The other half . . . not so much. "Silas" is the first half, and he's got a whole legitimate paper trail: ID, bank account, tax returns, rent checks, you name it. Even a few credit cards. Hell, the government has my fingerprints and DNA—and the Pen-tagon, for all its wasteful incompetence in so many areas, might not have lost them yet.

But according to Zeke, the firewall had been compromised. Bad guys were at my apartment—*Silas's* apartment. The dam was breached.

I didn't want to give the chief a foothold. I was within my rights—you never *have* to tell the cops anything. But of course I couldn't refuse.

He studied the license briefly, then pulled out his cellphone and took a picture of it.

"New York City, huh?"

"Yes."

"Like it?" He smiled, sort of. "Too crowded and noisy for me."

"No one's ever blown up my car there."

"Good point."

The discussion ran aground. Obviously, the chief wasn't telling us everything he must have seen, hoping for a slip. But it would be remarkably stupid for Dave to destroy his shop, his livelihood, and several other vehicles—and then go shopping at the Super Duper. So we weren't exactly suspects, either. He just didn't know what was going on, and he really didn't like that.

"Call your insurance agent," he said to Dave when we were done. "And you might have to find another place to stay."

Driving away, I looked back and saw him still standing there, arms crossed again, watching us go. Dave demonstrated an uncharacteristic respect for traffic law, stopping to signal his turn at the parking lot exit, waiting for a long break in traffic, and turning slowly into the road before moving off at about twenty miles an hour.

"You're going the wrong way," I said.

"Huh?"

"What would a normal person do, if the police just told them their house was destroyed?"

"Go to a bar?"

"They'd head right over to see for themselves."

"Oh. Sure. But do we really want to do that?"

I twisted around to look back—hard to see much, with the roll bars and the rather small rear-window glass. The Super Duper had already disappeared, sunk behind a Lukoil gas station and a bend in the road.

"Your pal Officer Friendly was surely paying attention. Now he's curious why you're *not* driving straight back to the shop."

Dave gave the car some rein, picking up speed. "Maybe we're taking Furnace Creek Road, around Bass Lake."

I thought for a moment. "That doesn't make sense. You'd end up in Connellsdale. It's at least ten extra miles."

He glanced over. "I thought you never been here before."

"That's right."

"Then how—?"

"I'm good with maps."

Because I have to be. In ten years GPS smartphones have basically obliterated the human race's sense of direction. But I can't use them, because it's a two-way data flow—if Google tells me where I am, then Google knows too. And what Google knows, anyone can find out. Usually without a subpoena, or even a warrant.

Which means that I have to rely on paper maps and memory. Conveniently, Uncle Sam provided lots of training in that area—topos and artillery grids mostly, but it carries over.

Always study the terrain beforehand.

"Well, it's too late now."

"Yeah." I found the license plate that had come from the attackers' Nissan on the floor of the car and added it to one of the paper sacks, then started unpacking our Christmas presents. "Where *are* you going anyway?"

"What I was thinking was . . . I thought I'd circle around for ten minutes, give Gator time to clear out, and go back to the supermarket."

"Oh, for—that's stupid." I pulled the Beretta out of its box, the cool comforting weight of metal in my hand. With a gun cloth spread on my lap I started to strip it down.

"What?"

"She's Brendt's girlfriend. She's been living with him for months. Brendt's your friend too, for that matter."

"Naw. She's just with him for his car."

"What?"

"You saw her. Hell, a woman like that? And Brendt? There's no way she'd—I mean, for her to voluntarily, like, it'd be motherfucking *end* times. The earth cracking open and flaming swords and hordes of angels cleansing the earth."

I paused, putting down the brass rod and brush I'd been screwing together, and looked at him. "Are you out of your mind?"

"Her and Brendt—that's just *wrong*."

Okay, here's what I was struggling with. On the one hand, it was clear that the attackers were after me—Dave was just a bystander, standing in the way when the Legion of Doom decided my time was up. So his shop, the police, God knows what other trouble down the road, it was all my fault. My responsibility. I couldn't just toss him to the wolves.

On the other hand, Dave's approach to the world was, well, "oblivious" comes to mind, and what was I supposed to do? Fix every broken-winged bird in the world? Anyway, he'd probably be safer once I was gone, trailing the hounds in some opposite direction.

The car bumped over a railroad crossing, Dave doing exactly what he was supposed to: stop, look both ways, continue.

"Okay." I finished reassembling the pistol and began loading its magazine. "Fine. Go make your play. You probably don't want me hanging around though, right?"

He grinned. "Yeah, maybe not."

"Because if I'm there, she's not even going to *look* at you . . . how about you drop me somewhere?"

"Where? The Alamo office?"

I paused. "How'd you know I rented from them?"

"Saw the key chain when you were driving yesterday. Big old plastic thing, it was hard to miss."

"Oh." He was right, I did have to do something about the destroyed car, but not now. "No. I'll just call them."

"Jake's Breakfast, over by the tracks—they do a good sit-down lunch."

"Actually, how about downtown? Pittsburgh, I mean."

Dave frowned. "That's like half an hour, each direction."

"The way you drive?" I set the Beretta aside and took the MP5 from the other sack. It had come off the pegboard and looked clean already. But I started breaking it down. "She's on shift until four, she said. You have plenty of time."

"Yeah. Yeah, you're right." He was cheerful again. "Better to show up right when she's clocking out, got the whole evening ahead."

Traffic was heavier now on commuter arteries aimed at the city: rural blacktop replaced by four lanes across a median, more and more businesses, tract developments dropped in here and there. Dave kept his speed reasonable, maybe because we'd left Clabbton.

Two hours ago his life had been turned upside down—long-lost brother, house and business blown to rubble, armed attackers doing their damnedest to kill him and probably soon to try again. But all Dave could think about was a pretty girl he'd just met, and driving his car fast, and maybe getting a beer later.

Zen Buddhists can spend their entire lives trying to release the burden of knowing, to achieve a pure and undistracted mindfulness, to live purely in the moment.

Dave was already there. I kind of envied him.

CHAPTER THIRTEEN

Dave dropped me at Market Square in downtown Pittsburgh and I stood on the corner, watching him go. A street performer had set up on a raised, stage-like area in the middle of the brick plaza, stepping onto a slackrope he'd tied between a light pole and an iron fence. As a small crowd assembled, he tossed a machete in the air, then another, then was suddenly juggling three.

I knew how he felt.

I was glad to be out of the Charger, which was basically the Elsie of the roadways—every sentient being for ten miles around noticed it. When the juggler was done, I put a few dollars into his bag and walked five blocks to the Intercontinental.

Nice hotel for a city I'd thought was no better than Detroit-on-the-Allegheny. But like I said, Pittsburgh seemed to be doing okay—clean streets, if a little empty, new buildings, parkland along the rivers.

In the lobby I sat in an inconspicuous chair, half hidden by a low-glow lamp on an end table. A family with toddlers tossed coins into the atrium fountain. Businessmen strode through, not a single one wearing a tie, tapping at their cellphones. Some sort of convention going on in the mezzanine levels—people with tags hung around their necks flocked and chattered among the couches artfully arranged throughout the lobby.

Nothing out of the ordinary.

First things first. I found a floor phone that allowed local calls—800 numbers are almost always included—and rang the toll-free directory. I'd memorized the number as a matter of habit, but going through a 411 service instead and having them connect the call would sever the telco's record back to this particular phone.

"Thank you for calling Alamo, my name is Gina, how may I help you today?"

When I explained that the car had been destroyed by terrorists, she didn't seem at all surprised, just took down Chief Gator's information and Dave's address and about twenty other items, half of which I had to make up. Fortunately, I really had bought every single insurance option—it adds a few hundred dollars to the tally, but paperwork minimization is how I live. It all gets billed to the client anyway.

Which made me think of Ryan. I'd left my phone on, but no calls, no messages, no texts.

Not good.

After the family left, I sat next to the fountain—nice sightlines across both the front entrance and the hallway behind the desk, and a pleasant rushing noise of falling water that would defeat most remote mikes—and called Zeke.

"Her name's Harmony." To the point, as always.

"What? Who?"

"No bells?"

"That name, I'd remember. Why?"

"West Coast, apparently. Some guys heard of her in LA. Hard reputation."

Oh. "The team leader," I said.

"Right, coming out of your apartment."

"Harmony. That's quite a name. What is she, the fifteenth Avenger?"

"An alias?"

"Sure sounds like it. So what's her story?"

"Some kind of military background, but who knows? That's what everyone says. No bullshit, never fucks up, cold as ice—she sounds perfect."

"I'll try to get you a date."

"That's the thing about women—they have to be twice as good to get half the respect. She sounds . . . serious."

High praise, from Zeke. "And she's what, trying to kill me?"

"No idea. She matches the description, that's all. But what they told me, her specialty is extractions."

"Well, fuck." I felt my face grimace. "That's just great."

"Yeah."

Because it was one thing if someone wanted me dead—it happens, right? The kind of work I do, solving problems, sometimes they decide *I'm* the problem. It's all very unsubtle. But an extraction, shit, that meant they wanted to talk.

No *possible* good can come from talking.

"You need some help." Zeke didn't make it a question.

"Thanks, but nah. She's looking for me in New York, not here."

"So stay there."

"Things just got complicated." I told him about the attack on Dave's garage.

"Shit, I'm sorry I missed that."

"I have to figure out what's going on."

"What's to figure? The Alpha Team didn't find you here, the Beta Team tracked you down there."

"Maybe."

"At the garage—they saw you, right?"

I thought about the siege. Ten thousand bullets. "I hope so."

"Huh?"

"If it was random, this country's in worse shape than I thought."

"There you go. They report in, Harmony and her professionals will be there on the next flight."

"They seemed pro to me, this morning."

"Three, you said? And you're walking around?"

Ha-ha. "I picked up a plate number. Can you run it down?"

"Yeah."

I peeked in the paper sack that held the plate from the Nissan and read off the number.

"Where's the car now?"

"In the junkyard. Or the police lot. Either way they're done using it."

"I'll see what I can find out."

I told Zeke about Dave—the short version. He knew about the letter already because I'd been sitting on it for so long.

"Your brother." He grunted. "I still can't believe it."

"He drives very, very fast and very, very dangerously. He doesn't seem to care that his shop was just blown to shit by armored assault. And at the moment he's entirely focused on stealing away his best friend's girl."

"Okay, I take it back."

"He's on his own for now. I need to do some detecting, learn why the Anti-Justice League is suddenly all over my ass."

"I've got something going today," Zeke said. "Another twenty, twenty-four hours. But as soon as that's done, I'm coming out."

"You don't have to." Though it might be nice to have him around. I don't like being completely on my own outside the wire.

"I'd be there sooner, but you know."

"Yeah." The kind of jobs Zeke does, he generally can't drop things in the middle.

"Where're you staying?"

"No idea. I'll let you know."

"Try not to shoot anyone before I get there."

We hung up. Foot traffic through the lobby still seemed innocuous—tourists, expense accounts, staff in dark polyester uniforms. I bought a leather shoulder bag from the accessories shop next to the restaurant. In a bathroom stall I transferred the guns into it, wrapping them loosely in the paper bags so they wouldn't rattle. Now I looked like a business traveler myself. A little tired, wanting to get home. Like they say, the best deceptions are the true ones.

The Sig I reloaded and left in my belt.

The concierge desk had a single staffer, and he was overwhelmed by a mob of the conference attendees—they all wore blue T-shirts, for some reason, waving tour brochures and chattering. The front desk had a clerk standing idle, though, so I went over there.

"My flight got moved up," I told the woman. "When's the next airport shuttle?"

She checked a sheet. "Fifty minutes. Would you like a ticket?"

"Sure."

I sorted through the small amount of cash left in my wallet. Before I could hand it over, a man stalked up next to me, holding his plastic room card out to the desk clerk.

"I need a new keycard," he said, annoyance clear in his tone. He wore a pressed, open-collar oxford shirt untucked over blue jeans, with shined square-toe shoes. "This is the third one that's stopped working."

"I'll be with you in a moment, sir."

"The *third* time!"

"I'm sorry—" She reached for the money I was holding out, but the man actually pushed my arm aside and slapped his card into her hand.

"You have to take care of this now," he said.

I could have snapped his elbow, thrown him to the floor and kicked him in the head. But confrontation would only attract attention, which I certainly didn't need more of. Let the desk clerk remember the asshole, not me. I politely stepped aside.

She looked at the card in her hand for a moment, then set it on the counter.

"We've had some trouble with these," she said. "They seem to be more sensitive to electronics." Like the guy's smartphone, I guessed, which he held in his other hand. "I'll run a new one." She looked him directly in the eye. "After I finish with the other gentleman."

He didn't even glance my way. "Room four seventeen, and you need to do it right *now*. I'm late."

"It's fine," I said.

The woman hesitated, but she was smart enough not to escalate— Mr. 417's fuse was obviously burning down fast. She smiled apologetically at me, took the card and clacked her keyboard.

"Ingerson?"

"That's right."

"Let's see . . . there's a charge for eighteen dollars and fifteen cents from last night. *Three* in-room movies?"

Oh, that was well done. Ingerson glared. "Just give me a new card!"

"Thank you." She dropped the bad card in a drawer, swiped a new one through a reader connected to her computer and held it out. "Perhaps you'd like a spare as well?"

"No." He grabbed it and walked away.

"Sorry about that," she said to me.

"No problem. Where's the shuttle?"

She handed me a card-stock ticket. "Should be here in about forty-five minutes, right out the front door. Have you already checked out?"

"Yes, thanks."

"Have a good day, then."

"What movies were they?"

She laughed. "I think we can guess."

I returned to the lobby and looked for a discreet place to wait.

I wasn't leaving Pittsburgh, of course. Not now. Had the job gone normally, I would have returned the rental car, walked away and never thought twice.

This job could no longer be described as normal.

Staying in town meant that transportation was a problem. Back home, we have the subway and buses. Taxis. On-call limos. Illegal dollar vans. Bicycle rickshaws. Horse-drawn carriages! And most places, if you have to, you can just walk.

But out in real America, you need a car. I didn't want to rent a new one downtown, where the offices are small and customers few. Better to go back to the airport and again pretend I was an arriving air passenger.

Which reminded me. I went back to the bathroom stall and studied the license and credit card I'd used for the Malibu. I admired the pair for a moment. Beautiful work: the holograms just right, nice crisp imprinting, and the photo of my face perfectly photoshopped, recognizable but just distorted enough to fool a facial-recognition scan.

Walter had done them—he's retired, but we're old friends. Retired, I'm sorry to say, in part because of the same series of Wall Street killings that Clara had ridden to glory. When the bodies stopped falling, I was still standing, but not everyone I knew could say the same. Walter didn't hold a grudge, though.

And he really seemed to enjoy the bonefishing down in the Keys.

I sighed, got out my Leatherman—another reason not to fly, because even the ¾-inch-blade micro models are usually confiscated— and cut the cards into plastic strips. After washing my hands, I dropped them into three different trash receptacles around the lobby. What a waste.

And now I was going to have to blow *another* false identity to rent another damn car. But what could I do, ride a bicycle? Having Dave chauffer me around was an even worse option. Nope, nothing for it but to—

Wait.

I stopped and stood in the middle of the lobby. Brainstorm.

I found the business center two flights up, next to the fitness room. Like I said, the Intercontinental was downtown Pittsburgh's nicest hotel, and the center was overseen by a real person, not a series of automated card swipes.

"My laptop broke," I told her, trying to look like a harried long-haul salesman. "Can you set me up with some basic internet here?"

"Certainly, sir. Would you like to charge it to your room?"

"Please. Four-seventeen."

She tapped her computer. "Your name?"

"Ingerson."

"Thank you." More tapping. "I've activated station number two, on the left." She pointed at a glass-fronted cubicle.

"Is there a phone in there, by any chance? I hate making important calls on my cellphone—the voice quality's terrible."

"Of course. Remember that long-distance is billed at hotel rates."

I smiled. "No problem, the company pays."

"Indeed." She smiled back, and I let myself into my new office.

I had my own phone, sure. And the hotel's wifi was free. But for some tasks you just don't want an electronic trail. The data aggregators keep track of *everything* nowadays—every keystroke, every site you visit, every interaction is captured and stored and analyzed.

That sort of record keeping is detrimental to my lifestyle.

Carpet, real-wood desk and credenza, a computer still smelling of fresh plastic—nice. It might even have been soundproofed, because a total hush descended as I closed the door. The woman was visible through the glass, her back to me, but I couldn't hear a thing.

A thirty-second search to see what Pittsburgh's largest employers were. Alcoa, Heinz, 84 Lumber, USX—geez, it was like a hundred years ago, all these companies that *made* things—University of Pittsburgh . . . ah, here we go, Morgan Bancorp. Perfect. Lots of employees traveling on business, a nice large internal bureaucracy, and best of all, thanks to all those bank bailouts, lots and lots of money floating around.

Another couple minutes got me some names of Morgan's mid-ranked executives. Not board members or C-level officers—too stratospheric. It helped that everyone and their cubicle mate was a vice president—that's typical in financial services, if you didn't know. Like an A- at Harvard.

I dialed Morgan's main number. "I'm trying to reach Jim Howell?"

"One moment please." Muzak while she switched me through.

A man's voice. "Jim Howell."

I hung up, and went to the next name on the list. Voicemail. I tried another.

And so on. Finally, about the sixth call, I got a secretary.

"I'm sorry, Mr. Welch is out today. May I forward a message to him?"

"Oh, it's not that important—this is Jim Howell down in Compliance." That was to make sure she didn't blow me off. "I'm working from home myself today . . . listen, could you just forward me to Ginny Yao's office?"

Ginny Yao was Morgan's assistant controller, which I'd learned from an article in *CFO Online*. The combination of "Compliance" and "Accounting" was, as I'd hoped, intimidating enough that the secretary just said, "Why yes, of course," instead of wondering why I couldn't dial the number myself.

Thus, when Ginny Yao's assistant answered the phone, she saw the call coming from an internal number.

"Hi, this is Bill Unfelder," I said. "I'm trying to make some travel reservations for next week." Plausible. Bill Unfelder wasn't senior enough for his own secretary, and nowadays all firms, even flush, well-paying banks, usually had their employees save a few bucks with DIY travel planning. Thanks, internet. "I lost my Gold Club card—I mean, I didn't *lose* it, I'm sure the darn thing's in this file cabinet somewhere, but I can't find it right this second. Anyway, can you remind me the company account number?"

Naturally it wasn't that easy. She followed procedure, told me to ask my department's administrator, information like that couldn't be conveyed without authorization, really sorry Mr. Unfelder. I thanked her politely, hung up, and . . . went through the whole rigmarole again with new names and new numbers.

It took fifteen minutes, but eventually I reached someone cheerfully, sufficiently careless of the rules that she just read off the number, told me to be more careful in the future and let me go.

While I was looking up Hertz reservations, my cellphone rang. "Yes?"

"Got a match for you." Zeke's voice.

"That was fast."

"Not really. It doesn't exist."

"What?"

"It's a ghost plate."

"Uh-oh."

Certain government agencies realized long ago that they needed anonymous license plates—otherwise their officers would be visible to anyone with access to state DMV records. Everyone in the world, in other words. When you come across one of these numbers, they'll either redirect to something totally innocuous, or—less commonly—they simply don't exist in the system at all.

"Could be a plain old data error," Zeke said. "That's what my guy said. Every now and then a perfectly legitimate plate gets screwed up."

"I think we have to apply Occam's razor here. Is it a total dead end?"

"There has to be a record *somewhere*."

But nowhere a regular person, or even Zeke, could get at. "Okay, thanks."

"Kind of makes you wonder which side you ended up on, doesn't it?"

"The wrong one, as usual."

I hung up and stared at the wall. The government certainly has teams of assassins on the payroll—well, lately they've moved off the payroll, to the contractors, but the idea's the same. They generally operate in war zones, though, not rural America.

Not that I could do anything about it.

I shook my head and found Hertz's 800 number.

Fortunately Morgan Bancorp didn't use Alamo, which might have been a little awkward. I gave them Welch's name and the corporate account, and reserved a car at Pittsburgh International for Gold account pickup.

"It's kind of last minute, I'm actually calling from the airplane," I said. "I thought my colleague was driving, but he has to go to a different office. Can you have it ready in an hour?"

"That should be no problem." The man paused, and I heard clacking in the background as he typed. "Yes, we have a Toyota Corolla available. You can go directly to our area in the central parking garage—check the electronic notice board for your stall number."

"I don't need to check in at the desk, do I? I'm kind of in a hurry—they moved the meeting up."

"Not at all. The paperwork will be on the dash. Just show it to the gate attendant when you exit."

"Thanks a million. That's a lifesaver." I hung up the phone, cleared all history from the browser I'd used and shut down the computer. On the way out the woman was helping someone figure out the fax machine—people still *use* those things?—so I just waved and left.

Isn't America great?

CHAPTER FOURTEEN

It was late afternoon when I got back to Pittsburgh.

Picking up my new vehicle—a Lincoln Town Car, I think there was some sort of automatic upgrade on the Morgan account—was as easy as I could have hoped. I'd been prepared to hand over my license, which of course didn't have Welch's name on it, and tell some story about how corporate must have screwed up the reservation again, this was *always* happening to me, did I have to go back to the counter? But the gate attendant just took the printed reservation sheets, checked the plate number, yawned, gave me back my copy and waved me through.

It wasn't a flawless situation. If I was stopped by the police, they would be far more curious about the mismatch of names. But considering that only a few hours ago I was on foot, this had to be considered an accomplishment.

I was also a little worried about Dave, but he should be safe now. Safe from shoot-to-kill mercenaries anyway. Brendt would surely be pissed that Dave was going all big-game hunter on Elsie, but that wasn't my problem.

My problem was Clayco.

Let's walk it through: Someone at headquarters discovers an irregularity in the books. They're worried about Markson finding out, because Clay Micro is so far over the line that heads will certainly roll if it isn't cleaned up immediately. Thus Ryan. Of course his hiring is an irregularity in itself. But when the water heater bursts in the middle of the night you don't go back to sleep, right?— you call a twenty-four-hour plumber.

Anyway Ryan's lazy, so he subcontracts it to me. I conduct my usual polite but thorough investigation and solve the mystery.

A few hours later Ryan's gone. *Gone* gone. Meanwhile, one team follows me from Clay Micro until I lose them, and another goes looking for me in Manhattan. Which, come to think of it, suggests they might not have been coordinated after all. The guys in the Nissan knew exactly where I was Friday evening—two car lengths ahead of them—and so there would have been no reason for Harmony and her crew to be asking around at Volchak's.

Sitting in traffic at yet another light, I thought about that. Hard.

Two teams, *not* working together. The gameboard had just gotten more crowded.

A day later the Pittsburgh posse comes for me, guns blazing. They either work for Brinker or he called them into play—they were the same as those who had followed me from Clay Micro, and no one but Brinker could have activated them so quickly.

Ryan's disappearance, though—that had to be Harmony. Brinker knew who I was, but I never mentioned Ryan to him. And Ryan disappeared from New York, where Harmony had been housebreaking and offering bribes at bars.

Unless there was a *third* team involved. My head started to hurt.

The people who knew about Ryan were the same ones who hired him—and they wouldn't turn around and disappear him, would they?

The only explanation I could see involved board-level, factional infighting at Clayco. Or deepwater Hollywood-style conspiracies. Or really, really, *really* bad luck.

None of these options was cheering.

One fact was clear: very dangerous men—and at least one woman—were trying to kill me. To get them off my back, I had to know why they'd been dispatched in the first place.

And that meant following the only bread crumb on the trail.

Brinker himself.

———

He liked horses.

Not in a big flashy way—the countryside here, rolling hills and forest, wasn't Kentucky Derby land. But Brinker's house was one of those mock southern plantations, albeit on a smaller scale: two stories with broad verandas on both floors, running the entire length of the front and sides, held up by wide Doric columns. A long circle drive led from the county road, through an arching gate marked DUNNEWELL FARM. The sweeping lawn and paddock were enclosed by that horse-country white fencing, glowing in the late dusk.

I guess he'd been skimming from Clayco for a while.

When I drove up, it became clear the big house was just another recent McMansion, its period detail revealed as flimsy trim. But the barn, fifty yards down the rear slope, was a hundred years old easy—weathered timbers that had settled into a comfortable skew, wooden shingles and a second-level set of doors opening onto nothing, with that cantilevered beam hook for hauling hay up to the loft by pulley. Two small rings were fenced in close by, one for jumping, one for riding.

It was almost dark. The front of the house was illuminated by small spotlights in the yard. Light glowed in the barn, too.

And there was Brinker himself, walking a saddled horse from the paddock.

I eased the Lincoln down the drive. Passing the house, I noticed a white panel van, some sort of contractor's vehicle, parked behind it. In the dusk I couldn't see much—a roof rack with a ladder or something, unreadable lettering on the side. But it sat silent and dark, and no one else seemed to be around.

Brinker glanced up as my car crunched over the gravel, then disappeared inside.

Maybe he recognized me, maybe not—the day was fading fast. I shouldered my new luggage, drew the Sig, held it down at my side and walked down.

He stood waiting, legs apart on the ancient, planked floor, one hand on his horse's neck. A second was behind him, a chestnut warmblood also tacked up. The barn was lit by a single unshaded bulb hanging from a wooden ceiling beam. Another, older man was in front of the stalls, but he wore torn jeans and a cotton shirt buttoned to the neck, holding a pitchfork and the chestnut's bridle—clearly the groom.

"I've got nothing more to say to you." Brinker crossed his arms. I noticed a white bandage on one of his fingers. When he took his hand away the horse turned to look at him, then at me.

"I think you do." I kept the pistol out of the groom's line of sight, not exactly hiding it but not wanting to scare him, either.

Not to mention the horses. Most would tolerate strangers well enough, but seeing a weapon might set them off.

"Send in your report, I don't care. It doesn't matter. The acquisition's totally fucked now."

"Acquisition?"

He shook his head. "You did your job, asshole. Fuck off."

The groom had leaned his pitchfork out of the way, led the chestnut into a stall, then taken Brinker's horse and begun securing him to the crossties for brushing. He made a quiet cough to catch Brinker's eye. "*¿Ya me puedo retirar, señor?*" he said.

"*Sí, por favor acabe despues de que este imbécil se vaya.*"

The man finished tying the horse in the grooming stall and faded away out the back. I could see an open trapdoor in the next stall—he'd been mucking it out into a manure pit below the barn. Old-fashioned.

"Your life is rotten from stem to stern," I said. "Or at least your company is. Honestly, I don't think I've ever seen every single employee show up crooked. Truly impressive."

"We're making money."

"Yeah, like a mafia bust-out makes money. You're blaming the wrong guy—I'm just the accountant. I don't think you could have held it together for even one more quarter."

"Whatever."

I raised the Sig. "Tell me about this acquisition."

"You can go fuck yourself." Brinker glanced past me, and a harsh smile appeared on his face. "No, really, fuck you."

At the same time I heard tires spitting gravel on the drive above the barn. I spun and saw the white van skidding to a halt behind the Town Car. Doors opened but no interior lights came on, and shadowy figures went to ground.

I guess someone had been waiting there after all.

BAANNG!

A bullet smacked the wall near my head. I dropped immediately as several more shots cracked. Brinker went down, clutching his arm.

"What the hell did you do that for?" he screamed.

I'd already hit the floor with him, rolling away from the open doors. "Shut up—it wasn't me!"

More shots. The two horses reared, anxious, turning in the stalls.

Squinting into the darkness outside I saw muzzle flash from two points near the van. Just to even things up, I twisted onto my back and shot out the light bulb.

The shattered bits fell onto Brinker, who yelled again, but maybe he'd taken another hit.

The shooting stopped. Something was pressing my back—an iron hoof pick, lying on the floor planks. I shifted and picked it up with my free hand.

"Okay!" one of the gunmen shouted. "All is okay now!"

I recognized that accent. And given how free they'd been with the firepower at Dave's garage, Brinker's barn probably wouldn't be standing much longer either.

"What took you so long?" Brinker yelled to them.

"We are here."

"No shit. You *shot* me, you fuckhead."

I aimed where half the rounds had come from and fired once, hoping to keep them down and fend off a rush. A few moments passed.

"If these are your friends," I said into the lull, "I'd hate to be your enemy."

"You *are* my enemy." Pain in Brinker's voice, but anger, too. He was tougher than I'd thought. He raised his voice, shouting toward the van. "He's all yours!"

"You!" The heavy accent again. "Silas Cade!"

No doubt about it. I glimpsed him in the moonlight, standing long enough to move a few yards. He was positioned some way to the left of his gunmen, setting up a defilade.

It was the seven-foot giant.

I hunched lower behind the stall's corner beams. "What do you want?"

"We need talk to you." His voice was lower. No need to holler.

"I've got nothing to say."

I heard a grunt from Brinker. Yes, yes, very funny, having the tables turned like this. After a moment I stuck my arm out and fired three more times. Gunfire erupted in return. I hunched as bullets splintered wood and slammed into the floor all around me. Dust and wood chips filled the air.

The shooting stopped. For a few moments I heard nothing but the ringing in my ears.

"*Nikogo ne ranilo?*"

"*Net, my v poryadke.*"

"*Nikto ne vidit etogo mudaka?*"

Shit, that was Russian.

I didn't understand any of it, but the sound was unmistakable. I'd once spent a few months at a Defense Language Institute immersion class in Monterey—Arabic, if you must know—and the other half of our floor was doing the post-Soviet thing. I heard enough to get familiar with basic phrases.

I peered behind me at the muck door in the stall's floor. Scoot over, drop through and be gone . . . it was tempting, except for the part where I fell headfirst into a ton of horseshit.

"You are *difficult*," the Russian called back, in English.

I wished he was visible. The disembodied voice was disconcerting. Not to mention the rustling I thought I could hear from the other side of the yard. His shooters were probably repositioning themselves.

I couldn't see any way out. They had superior firepower, higher terrain, greater numbers and—I had to admit—a better strategy.

The leather bag was still over my shoulder, but even the MP5 wouldn't make enough difference. I holstered the pistol and pulled out one of my cellphones.

"See this?" I held it up slightly. Of course we were in the dark but I assumed at least some of them had IR goggles on. "I'm dialing . . . nine. One. One."

The Russian made a sort of roaring noise. After a moment I recognized it as laughter.

"Yes, sure," he said. "You have service?"

What? I glanced quickly at the display, not wanting to lose what little night vision I'd developed, and—oh, shit, he was right. No bars.

"We turned on jammer," he said.

A long pause.

"All right," I said. "I'm open to negotiations."

"First, Brinker—out."

"I'm not going anywhere!"

I looked back out the door, opened my mouth and—wait. Was that a light on the road?

"He's wounded," I yelled, squinting hard up the hill.

"That is tough shit." The Russian seemed to have moved, about five meters left. "He leaves now, or he dies with you."

And these were his allies? No wonder Brinker didn't want to move.

"Wait a minute, wait a minute!" I moved backward, toward the hatch. "I'm ready to come out myself. Don't shoot me. Don't shoot!"

"Yes, good. Throw the gun first."

"Okay." I hefted the hoof pick, then tossed it as far as I could through the door, aiming for a spot I thought was midpoint between the Russian and his crew. It clanked on the gravel.

"Now stand and mo—"

An engine roared from the road, and suddenly a truck was skidding down the drive, gravel spraying, headlights jouncing all over the place.

WHUMP!

It slammed into my Lincoln, knocking the sedan over—in the headlight glare, I had a flashing glimpse of the underside as it rolled onto its back.

Dammit, I hadn't even had that car half a *day*.

Rifle fire came from the Russian's soldiers, loud, some of it on auto, bullets tearing into both vehicles. The truck slewed sideways, came to a halt, and several dark figures leaped out, going to ground.

The horse nearest me kicked against the stalls again with a terrified whinny. The other joined in, breaking the crossties and almost trampling Brinker, who groaned and pushed himself across the floor.

Someone threw a flare, which tumbled onto the drive farther down. The magnesium fire was white bright even to my eyes—if anyone's night-vision scope had been pointed that way when it ignited, they were now blind.

Gunfire increased. The newcomers seemed more disciplined but rounds flew everywhere, raking the barn, into the fields, raising dust and spattering gravel in all directions across the drive.

"CE-E-E-EASE F-I-I-R-E!"

A *woman's* voice. Her side stopped shooting. The opposing fire trickled to a halt a half minute later.

"*Poshel na huy!*"

"Who the fuck are you?" the woman called.

I uncurled a bit and spat dust. "What do you want, Harmony?"

Silence. I hated giving that up so quickly, but I needed her off-balance.

"Yeah, we know who you are," I called. "All of you, drop your weapons and walk out *now*."

Brinker made a disgusted sound, but his arm apparently hurt too much for him to do much more.

"You think I'm an idiot?" Harmony said. "You're alone. There's nobody else for half a mile."

Which was probably true. Brinker's nearest neighbor wasn't even visible from the road where I'd turned into his drive.

"Now what?"

"First thing, send out the dumb motherfucker."

I glanced at Brinker. "I don't think she means the horse."

"Jesus fuck."

"What's up with your guys?"

"My guys?" He actually laughed.

"Yo!" I called. "Any legitimate law enforcement out there?"

Silence, except for the stamping and trembling of the horses. Neither seemed to be hit, astonishingly, but there was a strong smell of manure. Both had crapped all over the planks—I seemed to be lying in a puddle.

Could this get any worse?

Up at the road, no traffic. The moon was just at the horizon. The truck's headlights had gone off or been shot out. Gunsmoke drifted through the air.

"*Kto ona?*" the Russian called.

"*Hooy yeyo znayet.*"

I scraped through my memory, then shouted as loud as I could, "*Gde, blyad pivo?*"

Brinker turned my way. "What?"

Okay, so I'd just called for more beer. "Trying to confuse things."

More Russian yammering. When they stopped, I answered.

"*Otyebis, pidoras!*" It was an insult, if I remembered right. A crude one.

Assault weapons suddenly opened up again, aimed entirely at me. Brinker and I tried to disappear into the floorboards. The horses kicked, their hooves hammering as loudly as the bullets on the walls.

The firing stopped more quickly this time. Probably had to reload.

"Hey!" Harmony's voice. "Who the fuck are you?"

The Russian responded, in English again. The accent seemed worse. "He is ours. Go away."

"Go *away*?"

"We will finish. You go."

"Walk out and show yourself."

"*Ne pizdi!*"

They started arguing. Possibly this was a good thing—everyone had stopped trying to kill me, for example—but there was now twice as much trigger-happy firepower out there.

I looked at the muck door, then at the horses.

"Hey," I said to Brinker, this time trying to keep quiet. "These horses—which one's stronger?"

"What?"

"They look like good animals. You like one better than the other?"

He stared at me. "Bandit cost forty thousand dollars. He's a great jumper—he'll go through anything I point him at."

"Hmm. Means he's all short-tempered and twitchy, right?"

"Of course not!"

"This one?" I gestured to the horse Brinker had walked in. It was a reasonable guess—he didn't seem like a guy who'd choose the cheaper nag for himself.

"Yes, but . . ."

Brinker was about my size, and that settled the question—his stirrups would be at the correct height.

"We're not done," I said. "Don't do anything stupid."

"Wha—?"

"*More* stupid, I mean. You can't answer questions if you're dead."

I rose to a crouch, keeping as much of my profile behind the structural post as possible, and Brinker finally caught on. "Hey," he shouted. "You can't *do* that!"

"I think I can," I said, and I stood, threw Bandit's reins over his head and patted his neck. You can't be timid with horses—they respect a firm hand. I got a foot into the stirrup and swung myself up. The shoulder bag swung around but stayed on my back.

Bandit sidestepped and skittered, making ready to throw me. I squeezed his sides with both legs and leaned forward, all the way down.

"We're leaving, Bandit," I murmured in his ear. "You and me."

Then I eased the reins and kicked him harder . . . and we rocketed out the barn's rear door like an Aqueduct thoroughbred leaving the gate.

I grew up in New Hampshire, and my last two foster families had farms, okay? I'd ridden bareback from age ten, done the 4H fairs in high school.

It's like riding a bike.

Bandit was a hero. He wasn't a combat horse, one of those hard scrappy beasts the SF guys had in Afghanistan, ride through mortar fire and never blink. He'd just suffered an assault of noise and terror worse than anything in his life, seen his owner fall and smelled his blood, and now a complete stranger had jumped on his back. But he was smart—smart enough to figure out where safety lay, smart enough to trust me—and strong.

We were a hundred yards into the fields before anyone realized.

"Sila-a-a-s!" Harmony's angry shout and a few scattered shots followed us, none coming close.

But it was dark. The moon had only begun its rise, dim and haloed through the damp overcast. I had a vague sense of terrain—hills that way? open field this way?—but kicking Bandit into anything more than a canter would be to seriously risk a stumble and a broken leg.

He deserved better than that.

I aimed for the hill and its treeline, hoping to get out of sight.

Shouting continued back at the barn, indistinct but audible. A few more rounds, then nothing. Bandit's breathing was loud but steady.

Thirty seconds later, nearing the trees, another shot cracked loudly. Much more loudly—and I heard the *thonk* as the bullet slapped into a trunk in front of us. I twisted around to look back.

A horse and rider in full gallop, gaining fast. The rider had one hand raised toward me, and I saw the flash at the same moment I heard the second shot.

"Halt!"

It was Harmony. Son of a bitch. She must have sprinted into the barn and taken the second horse.

This was like some lousy video game. Harmony and I were going to end up shooting it out at the edge of a chasm, volcanic lava below and everything on fire.

Bandit slowed, and suddenly we were among the trees. There might have been a path—he seemed to know where he was going—but I could see nothing in the dark woods. Twigs and branches slashed at my face and torso. I hunched down, one forearm in front of my head, urging him to keep going.

"Stop running, you motherfucker!" Her voice seemed a little hoarse now, but she was getting closer. She fired twice. I heard the rounds slapping leaves to my right. "Your Russian pals can't help you here."

My pals? I kept quiet, staring as hard as I could ahead of us. Was the ground rising or falling?

Bandit whinnied. Maybe he caught scent of his stablemate. He turned his head and I started to yank him back into line, fearing he'd decided enough was enough—but, no, the path curved. We went up a slight rise, then began to descend.

Good enough. With the thought, the deed: I dropped my stirrups, patted Bandit's neck once, and hopped off his back, landing right beside him. Without pausing I slapped his rump. "Go with God," I whispered, and ducked off the path.

Bandit leaned forward, confused. Harmony came crashing through the woods, fifty feet away—now that I was off Bandit, I could clearly hear all the noise *she* was making. I crouched behind a locust tree and froze.

Harmony must have seen my horse, but not clearly enough to realize I was no longer aboard. She fired once more, the gunshot close and loud.

Bandit lunged into the forest.

"Harmony!" I yelled, but with the tree trunk between her and my face, dispersing the sound a little. "Stop there or you're dead."

Only her head moved, tracking my voice. In the dark I was pretty sure she couldn't see me.

"Drop the weapon," I said.

"No."

It was in her right hand, which was on her side opposite me, so I couldn't see it. "I can shoot you off the horse if you don't," I said.

"Silas Cade." A normal tone, like we were at a dinner party. It was too shadowed to see much detail. "You *are* Silas Cade, right?"

"What do you want with me?"

"Some people want to talk."

"You're not working with those Russians, are you?"

"What do you think?" She laughed—and used the noise to cover up an arm motion.

"I said don't move!" I shifted to the other side of the tree and went lower down.

"I think I saved your life, you know," she said.

"From those guys? Nah. I was just getting ready to leave."

I couldn't see any percentage in starting another shootout. For one thing, I might very well lose. Harmony had the horse, her weapons—more than one, I was sure—and no doubt plenty of re-loads, while I was down to four rounds. If I'd counted correctly. And if by some unlikely chance I *did* come out on top, she might not be able to talk, and explain to me exactly what the hell was going on.

"Exactly what the hell is going on?" I said.

"I told you. Some people hired me. They want to talk to you."

"Sorry, booked up right now. What's their number?"

She didn't respond. Trees rustled invisibly in the dark. Bandit was still nearby, whuffling quietly somewhere.

"I think we'll have to finish up later," Harmony said.

"No, wait a sec—"

Too late. She yanked the reins, turned her horse and kicked him into a run, leaning down to present a minimal target. I stood and aimed, but didn't fire.

The sound of their progress through the woods faded, but not before Bandit took off after them. I suppose he wanted to go home, and figured they were his best bet.

Their crashing diminished, farther and farther away. After fifteen seconds it was gone completely. I slowly stood up.

The ground was damp, and I could walk without making too much noise. It was still dark, but my eyes had finally begun to adjust, and I could see most obstacles before I ran smack into them.

Most. Not all.

Fifteen minutes later, scratched and tired, I was back at the edge of the woods. I'd come out farther down, several hundred yards from the barn. It was hard to tell from a distance, but the truck seemed to be gone. Someone, perhaps Brinker, had turned on an exterior light mounted below the barn's eave, and I could see the vague lump that was the wreck of my Lincoln. The Russian's crew had either departed in their own vehicles, or they were parked too far away to see.

I pulled out my phone and pressed the keypad, illuminating the display. Four bars, this time. I dredged a number from my wobbly memory and dialed.

"Yello." Background noise—music, voices, crashing. A bar, maybe.

"Dave?"

"Yeah, who's this?"

"Silas." I sighed. "You think you could give me a ride?"

CHAPTER FIFTEEN

was getting somewhere," Dave said.

"Yeah, sorry."

"She was coming *around*."

"What was she even doing in a bar with you? And without Brendt?"

"No, he was there, too."

"He *was*?"

"I kept buying him pitchers."

Dave seemed to have been buying himself pitchers, too. He had that excessively careful enunciation of the self-aware drunk, and he wore only a T-shirt despite the evening's deepening chill.

But his driving was, as ever, totally controlled. I tightened the harness once more, against the sway of centripetal acceleration, as we took an S curve at some ungodly speed. The country road was dark, and the Charger's headlights lit up the trees flashing past.

"So let me get this straight. You were trying to get Brendt, your friend since grade school, drunk enough that he didn't notice you were hitting on his girlfriend?"

Dave laughed. "It doesn't sound good that way."

"I hate to ask, but where were you planning to sleep tonight? I'm sure there's still police tape at the shop." I paused. "And don't say in *her* bed."

"I don't know." His mood dropped. He was open as a six-year-old, you could read every emotion plain on his face: *Oh shit I forgot, my shop got blown to rubble and my life is totally fucked up. Damn.* "What about you?"

"I'd hoped to be leaving town."

"Yeah? Drop you at the bus station?"

"It's not working out that way."

When Dave found me at the side of the road, thirty minutes after I'd called, we drove past Brinker's gentleman farm. It was completely dark: no lights in the house, the yard or the barns. I hoped that Harmony hadn't crippled the horses, or killed them, galloping through the black forest. I hoped the groom had been able to leave, uninvolved—he seemed like someone who might have trouble with his documentation. I hoped Harmony and the mad Russians had cleaned up after themselves, so the police didn't hear anything.

The Lincoln, well, Morgan Bancorp would get a phone call eventually. I'd taken it out for an entire week, so Hertz shouldn't get concerned until long after I'd finished up here.

Assuming no one noticed the wreck.

"Look," I said. "I need a place to stay. So do you. There must be a truck stop or something. I'll pay for the room—I feel sort of responsible."

"Thanks, Silas." He reached over to clap my shoulder. "But it ain't that."

"What?"

"You're my brother. That's all that's necessary."

Closing in on midnight, I gave up on the pile of scratchy, filthy wool blankets, threaded the belt back through my pants and went outside. Dave snored on the floor by the fireplace, heedless of the damp and the cold, rolled up in what looked a lot like a nylon shower curtain.

Off the grid. Good for evading pursuit by heavily armed criminal gangs, but bad for comfort, sleep and decent food.

We weren't in a motel because Dave had remembered visiting this hunting cabin years ago—it belonged to a friend of a friend, but they never used it much and the son was at Houtzdale anyway, five months into a one-to-three. Something about meth, probably. Dave couldn't remember exactly. It didn't sound like a preferred option, just better than registering at some public establishment.

The drive into Monongahela National Forest, across the border into West Virginia, had taken forty-five minutes. Dinner was peanut butter crackers and beef jerky from the gas station we filled up at, off I-79. Dave insisted on a couple more six-packs, one of which was gone by the time we arrived at our upcountry hideaway.

Okay, I admit I was helping by then.

It felt like a hundred miles from civilization but phone reception was nice and clear. Away from the cabin, standing near the edge of the bluff it overlooked, I listened to the ringing.

"Hello?"

"Hey Clara. Didn't wake you, did I?"

"Of course you did."

"Sorry. Really?"

"Only by half an hour. What's going on?"

"I'm in the countryside," I said.

"Having a nice vacation?"

"Friendly people everywhere. Listen, you hear anything on Clayco?"

"Not much. I'll say this, the Pittsburgh division seems completely anomalous. The rest of the company's doing defense, but Clay Micro's product line is seismographic tracking equipment."

"Missile tracking, underground monitors—they're both remote sensors."

Clara sounded skeptical. "Sort of related. Maybe."

"No, you're right. It's a different field entirely. Different customers, different requirements, different economics. So it makes sense they'd be selling it. Clay Micro's not a core competency."

"Wait. Selling? They're on the block?"

"The CEO told me so himself a few hours ago." Brinker had said *acquisition,* and that made my own assignment a little clearer: if a deal was in the works, the last thing senior management needed was a restatement-level accounting issue. Ryan had been hired to sweep dirt under the rug just long enough to close the sale. "And here's the thing, I think the buyers might be Russian."

"Whoa." Clara perked up. The sale of a small division by a private company wasn't normally news—the only really interested parties were Clayco's immediate owners. But if a *foreign* buyer was involved, especially a frenemy like Russia, things got complicated. "Tell me about this."

"I can't say much."

"Hypothetical."

"No, really."

"Let me guess." She was off and running. "You don't know the buyers for sure, so you're working for the sellers. Right? If they hired *you*, they're worried Clayco's books are seriously fucked." Clara was no dummy. "Fraud? Or are the numbers just a little too shiny?"

"Like we said, Clayco's big. Clay Micro is one small part, run by a guy named Brinker, and they must have figured it would be easy to spin off. But headquarters seems not to have been paying enough attention to Brinker's numbers, and when they finally got around to due-diligence prep, they found some problems. Not big enough to kill the deal, I don't think, but big enough to change the terms substantially."

"Headquarters . . . ?"

"What?"

"You mean Markson?"

I'd been thinking about that. "No. I can't see it. If he knew about this, he'd probably be talking to a federal prosecutor, don't you think? They call him the Buddha, for Christ's sake."

"You sure?"

I couldn't see it. "Wilbur Markson would never stand for the kind of general lawlessness at Clay Micro."

"Fine. So whoever's trying to tidy up the mess, they've got double incentives. They can't let Markson *or* the buyer find out what's been going on."

"That's how it seems to play."

"Okay, makes sense. You've cleaned it up for them now?"

"Uh, yeah, right." The breeze coming up the bluff was cold. I could see a silver glint of the river below, nothing but dark forest everywhere else. "Except my last discussion with Brinker was interrupted by, well, I don't know, but they were carrying assault weapons and speaking Russian."

Clara laughed. "Why does that always happen to you?"

Good question. "Just follow up, will you? Maybe the seismo-graphic stuff is dual use or something, like they use it to monitor nuclear tests. If it's sensitive and export-controlled, that might explain a few things. In any event, if the business gets all geopolitical, I seriously need to bail."

"I'll see, but if it's private, that's tough. You don't need me, you need a contract in, I dunno, the Carlyle Group."

"I wouldn't trust anyone but you, Clara."

"If there's one buyer interested, there might be more." She was thinking aloud. "Which maybe means a competitive situation. And if the lead bidder is knocked out for some reason—like, say, they're working for Gazprom or some Russian oligarch—then the others might start scrambling."

"Yeah, so?"

"If no one's aware of these circumstances until I publish them . . . that's a hell of a scoop."

"Hold off a bit, will you? It's all guesswork. You go dropping bombs now, I might never solve it."

An animal screeched in the woods, loud and close. Bird? Wild-cat? Russian paramilitary? I crouched and twisted around and drew the Sig without even thinking, aiming it across the trees one-handed.

Nothing happened.

"Silas? You still there?" Clara's voice was tinny, the phone in my left hand, down at my side. After a long moment, I raised it back to my ear.

"Sorry. Got distracted."

"If I find anything out, I'll call you." She paused before adding, not too grudgingly, "Before I publish."

"I think you might want to steer clear of this one," I said. "Any business deal where the participants are this eager to kill each other seems like, you know, a red flag."

"How serious are they?"

"Live fire and lots of it. Check the newswires."

"And they're shooting at you?"

"Some of them. The Russians are. The other one, I'm not sure about—their leader, she's hard to read."

"She?"

"Harmony. Zeke couldn't find out a last name. I've only seen her firing a sidearm, but she was certainly good with it, and she apparently intimidates everyone she meets."

"Perfect name for her, then."

"She rides horses, too." I had an image of her, bareback and upright on the chestnut, galloping through the forest like a video-game warrior queen.

Clara paused, then laughed. "Uh-huh."

"What?"

"You're sweet on her, aren't you?"

"Get out. She tried to kill me."

"Are you sure? I can hear it in your voice."

"She's on the other team," I said. "And that's the entire story."

"Oka-a-y."

"Why don't we ever talk about *your* love life?"

"I don't have time for one."

I pocketed my phone, then moved into cover behind a fallen tree, twenty or thirty meters from the cabin. Dave's car reflected a bit of moonlight, but otherwise everything was just different degrees of blackness.

I waited thirty minutes. All was quiet. We were at the end of a few miles of dirt road, the river bluff to one side and tens of thousands of acres of national forest to the other. No one could sneak up here.

Eventually I went back inside, wrapped up in the blankets again, and wondered how long I really wanted to keep doing this kind of work.

―――――――

"I want to help."

"Don't be ridiculous."

"Why not?"

It was morning, eight or nine o'clock, the sun bright in a clear sky, dew still on shaded areas of the ground. Dave sat on the cabin's small porch, eating the last of the jerky. I studied the forest on the far side of the bluff through some binoculars that had been sitting on the cabin's mantelpiece. Dave had the shower curtain pulled around his shoulders. I wore a jacket, a fleece-lined nylon shell.

Despite the sun it must have been ten degrees cooler up in the mountains.

"You lost the shop and your house already. Whoever these people are, they're shooting to kill."

"What happened out at that farm last night?"

"Nothing you want to be a part of."

"You have no idea." Dave shook his head. "You really don't."

The light breeze carried smells of foliage and earth. I wished we'd remembered to buy water, not just beer, last night.

Dave stood up and tossed the shower curtain in through the door. He stretched, scratched, rubbed the stubble on his face.

"Those guys come after you in a car," he said, "you ought to have me there. To drive."

Some truth in that. "I'll manage."

"You know, when they were pounding the hell out of the garage, and I realized the only thing I could do was take the Charger right out, right *toward* them, that might have been the scariest thing I ever done." Dave looked at me.

"I believe that."

"But I wasn't frightened, exactly. More like, *hot damn, let's go!* You know what I mean? It was . . ." His voice trailed off. "I'd say it was the greatest feeling in the world."

Great. My brother, adrenaline junkie. "I get you."

"On the track, sometimes there's an act, the guy who jumps over speeding cars." Dave was off on another tangent. "You ever seen that?"

"Internet video, yeah."

"Like there's two or four or five cars driving straight toward him at ninety miles an hour, all lined up, and he has to jump straight up in the air at *exactly* the right moment, so they go right under him."

"The one I saw, he mistimed it. Landed in front of the last car."

"Well, that hardly ever happens."

I put the binoculars back into their case. "Look, when this is over and I have some free time, we can do some adventure stuff. A HALO parachute jump, maybe. Ski down an avalanche zone. Scuba dive with sharks."

"All I'm saying is, maybe the garage getting blown up, it's like a message. God's telling me I shouldn't be sitting around fixing barbecue grills."

"Instead you should be, what, engaging in personal warfare with overarmed Russian mercenaries?" I sighed. "Isn't the racing enough?"

"Plus you haven't told me a damn thing about why you're here, but I figure there's money involved."

"No—"

He cut me off. His mood had suddenly turned. "Has to be. You think you're gonna keep that all to yourself?"

"It's not about money."

"Oh, fuck it." Dave punched the post at the end of the porch, hard enough to shake the entire cabin. "And fuck you."

He stomped off around the corner.

I sat for a few minutes, then stood up and followed.

A rhododendron bush was in early bloom at the edge of the cabin's field, pink flowers against glossy, dark green foliage. The Charger sat beside them, at the end of parallel ruts leading through the muddy track from the road where we'd driven in last night. The driver's door was open, and Dave sat sideways on the seat, feet outside the car.

"Sorry," I said.

"You been talking down to me since you got here." His voice was flat, the usual exuberance gone.

"No, I—"

"You're the big-city guy. Where do you really live?"

Not a question I'd answer, normally, but here we were. "New York."

"Right. Park Avenue, whatever. Come out here like you're slumming. Visit the rednecks, see how they live."

"You think that's what I'm doing?"

"Brendt and Dink and them all? They're my *friends*."

Well, he had a point. I wasn't particularly happy to be here, and maybe I'd been taking it out on him.

Real America doesn't *need* irony.

I stood for a while, looking off over the bluff, where it fell away at the end of the field.

"Car looks good," I said. He'd finally buffed the wax, sometime late yesterday.

"Shit."

"Hey, it was the *other* guys flattened your house, not me."

"But—" He let it drop. "Fuck all."

"Look," I said. "I'll tell you what's going on."

And the thing was, I *did* have to explain the situation to him. Not only did I owe him—for the ride, for the shop, for basically keeping me alive recently—but he was probably a target, too, now. I couldn't walk away and let him be killed.

"Naw, forget it." He pulled himself out of the car. "I'm just cranky for missing breakfast."

"Let's find a diner or something." I held out my hand, and after a moment he took it. "And I'll explain exactly how little I know about who's trying to kill us."

CHAPTER SIXTEEN

The first task was to get another damn car.

"I don't mind driving," Dave said.

"Yes, I know." We were rattling down the mountain, jouncing along the dirt-and-chert fire road. For once Dave took it slow and easy, steering around the bigger rocks, trying to stay out of the deeper, muddier ruts. "But, and I mean no disrespect, your car is kind of . . . memorable. I need something anonymous and forgettable."

"So, what, a rental?"

"Maybe." But I didn't want to go back to the airport—the cameras were unavoidable, and eventually, too many appearances, someone would notice. "I was thinking Craigslist. Seems like every other house around here has a cleaned-up car in their front yard with a FOR SALE sign on it."

"Uh-huh. Plenty more than usual, too, these last couple of years. So you want to buy one?"

"Yes, but not from some old lady or laid-off millworker."

"Why not?"

The truth was an old lady would remember far too many details about me, but I didn't want to say that. "They're amateurs. Anyone selling their own vehicle has no idea of its value, so you have to bargain them down, which pisses them off. But I don't want to deal with a used-car lot, either. The best way to do this is find some guy who does it as a sideline, off the books. Buys a car every month or two from one of the old ladies, fixes it up, and then sells it himself for a little profit."

"Sure. I know what you mean."

"Of course they're like rug merchants in the bazaar—try every trick in the book. Worse than a used-car salesman."

"Oh, please." Dave shook his head. "You think they could put something over on *me*?"

Exactly. "So . . . you know anyone?"

"I might."

"Thought so." I shifted the harness enough to pull out my wallet and checked inside. "We need to stop at some cash machines first. I'm about out of money."

We finally reached a paved road, some state blacktop through the forest. Dave picked up speed. Wind whistled through the windows, engine noise waxed and waned, the wheels screeched and skidded through the turns.

"How is it you still have a license?" I asked.

"License?"

Super.

We made it to the interstate and had the eggs-pancakes-sausage-biscuits and grits special at a truck stop outside Morgantown. Dave filled the tank while I tried to clean up in the bathroom. They had shower stalls, but I didn't want to put bare feet on the floor in there.

Another twenty minutes took us back to Clabbton. We drove

past the town green, back out the east road. When the Super Duper came into view, I realized where Dave was going.

I didn't say a word, but he must have realized what I was thinking.

"She's off today," he said. "Told me last night."

"Really?"

"You said you wanted an ATM that wasn't in a bank, right? There's one in front. And I think we can find another at the Lukoil."

"Okay."

Cash is another of those persistently annoying problems for the privacy conscious. Usually I carry a few hundred dollars, sometimes more—enough for a day's work. I can always replenish from my legitimate, Silas-owned bank account, especially in the city, where bank machines are everywhere.

But not on the job.

I had two more false-identity credit cards left, but I didn't want to burn them. Not that a guy illegally selling cars out of his driveway would take one anyway.

Prepaid debit cards are the way to go. I buy them at check-cashing stores. Jesus would kick their ass over the fees, which are truly extortionate, but you can lie all you want on the application form and they don't care. I put nine thousand dollars on each one, to stay under the CTR reporting limit—and then I can draw what I need, anywhere in the country.

For more than that, you need to use the big-dog money-laundering channels. The people who set those up wear nicer suits, and usually draw $400-per-hour fees in their downtown tax-law offices, but the rake-off is pretty much the same.

Anyway, I had Dave park on the other side of the lot—"Look, we want to *minimize* people seeing me get in and out of your car, okay?"—and walked over to the ATM next to the takeout Chinese place. First thing, I stuck a Post-it note over the camera window. When I got the default opening screen, the suggested withdrawals topped out at fifty dollars, in ten-dollar increments.

I took out a thousand dollars, which was the limit. We'd be making several stops today.

When I emerged, Dave was nowhere to be seen.

I muttered and looked around. The Charger sat where we'd parked it, empty as far as I could tell from a distance. Elsie's spot was unoccupied. Midmorning, not much business—only the supermarket and the dollar store were open.

Dave finally wandered around from back, along the same truck alley we'd parked in yesterday.

"What?" he said, catching my look. "I had to piss."

"If Chief Gator catches you publicly urinating, it's a criminal offense." I shook my head. "You go on the sex offender registry. Can't step within half a mile of a school or a church ever again your whole life."

"School or church? That's no hardship."

"Come on, I need to buy a toothbrush." And some underwear. It looked like I might be on the lam for a few days yet.

"Ninety-five hundred," the guy said. "I tuned this engine like a motherfucker. I used to work a NASCAR pit. I know what I'm doing."

"Uh-huh." Dave was in the driver's seat. He started the engine, listened for a moment, turned it off. A moment later he switched it on again. "You hear that tapping?" he said. "Sounds like the valve lifters."

"I cleaned 'em."

"Could still be worn out." Dave looked up at him. "Like if whoever owned it before wasn't changing the oil regular."

"Not what I saw." The guy wasn't giving ground.

We were in the indeterminate exurbia between Clabbton and Pittsburgh—steady traffic on the four-lane state highway nearby, seed dealers and self-storage businesses, a few old farmhouses amid the sprawl. Pootie—that was how he'd introduced himself, honest to God—had one of these houses, along with a falling-down wooden garage. We stood in the shade of a grand elm, on the cracked drive, watching Dave's inspection.

He got out and started checking the outside of the car, studying the wheel wells, looking at the underside, peering down each side from the rear corner.

"Uh-oh," he said. "Looks like the frame's bent." He switched to the other side. "Yup. Got a little curve on the right, and you can see how the left is crooked the other way."

"Naw, that's bullshit."

It was a Chevy Aveo and looked fine to me, dumpy but clean, twenty-three thousand miles, six years old. No rust that I could see and decent tires. The engine compartment was spotless.

Dave shook his head at me. "It might be okay for driving down to the video store. Keep it under forty, forty-five, probably won't be too bad when the engine seizes up and you crash."

"Hey, fuck off. This ain't no shit heap."

"Look, Pootie. You know and I know you bought this car at the impound auction. Probably a repo, right? A fleet rental, the mileage would be two or three times as high. You did a good job, fixed it up as reasonable as anyone could. But the car's got *problems*, man."

Pootie shrugged.

"So here's the question," Dave said. "My brother and I, we do need a ride, and we'd be happy to pay a fair price. Three grand seems about right to me." He held up one hand as Pootie frowned and started to object. "That's cash, and we hand it over to you right here."

I pulled out the thick wad of twenties we'd accumulated that morning—six more ATMs after leaving the Super Duper—and riffled the stack.

"But you don't have to take it." Dave echoed Pootie's shrug back at him. "Some dumbass will pay your price. Someday. I mean, not *your* price, unless he's a total moron. But you might get a little more. Right?"

"Yeah . . ."

"So the question is, how long you want to wait around and hope that happens? Hoping to get lucky?" Dave lowered his voice. "Or do you want to take the money we're offering, right here, right now?"

Pootie grimaced, and scratched his forearm, and looked at the Charger where Dave had parked it on the street.

"That yours?" he asked.

"Yup."

"It's totally murdered out." He said it like a compliment. "Do the work yourself?"

"Sure." Dave grinned. "You come up to Lernerville sometime, you can see me race."

"I ain't bullshitting you. I worked hard on this car."

"I know you did. I can see it. Engine's running as smooth as anyone could get it without a new block and a total rebuild. Brakes are good. Could use a new tire, left rear, but we can afford that."

"Fifty-nine hundred," he said.

"Now we're *talking*," said Dave.

———

"What was it *really* worth?"

"About four grand, maybe four and a half."

"What? I thought you bargained him down to an honest price. I paid *five*!"

"Hey, he worked hard on it. Like he said." Dave laughed. "What's a few hundred bucks?"

Not that much, true, but I didn't have much left on the debit cards. Until this job wrapped up and I was back on familiar ground, cash flow was a concern.

"Anyway, just as well Pootie went away happy," Dave said. "Don't want him complaining about you to anyone, right? This way, it's all good."

"Yeah, yeah." I admit, he was right.

We were parked a half mile down the road, in front of a shuttered restaurant. I finished tightening the screws holding my new car's license plate—the one I'd taken from the attacker's Nissan two days ago.

They wouldn't return the number to circulation, not after the debacle at Barktree. Whoever supplied Harmony's team had to know that canceling the plate would only attract even more attention from Chief Gator. The best thing would be to let it lie, and trust that the ghost status would deflect further inquiry.

Now I had my *own* ghost vehicle.

I closed the Leatherman's screwdriver blade and stood up.

"Let's go detect some clues," I said.

CHAPTER SEVENTEEN

As we drove up the winding forest road out of Clabbton, approaching Dave's garage, a state police forensics van came down the other way. It was big enough we had to squeeze past each other, guardrails on either side, along a wooded ridge.

The driver nodded, but we were in the utterly forgettable Aveo, and didn't attract further attention. We'd left the Charger at Brendt's house, for lack of any better place.

The carryall full of weapons I kept with me.

"Wonder what they found?" Dave said. He had one elbow out the open window as he sat tipped back in his seat.

"A ton of brass." The Aveo's transmission had trouble with the grade, kicking back and forth between second and third gears. "And some wrecked cars. You should call one of those scrap metal companies, see what you can get."

"Police will take all the good stuff with them."

"If there's anyone there, even if they're *not* police, we'll drive on by and come back some other time."

But Barktree Welding was empty. Yellow tape sagged, and piles of debris here and there showed where the technicians had been sorting through the wreckage. It was midafternoon, shadows from the hills already falling across the field. Bullet holes pocked the brick walls everywhere.

"I'm supposed to see Gator sometime," Dave said.

"Not now."

"Think it's okay if I get some clothes out?"

There wasn't any mystery about what happened in the assault, so I couldn't see any purpose in maintaining crime-scene inviolability. "Sure, why not?"

Dave wandered in, stepping carefully. I saw him become immediately distracted inside the garage bay, stooping to pick up some tool or other, checking behind the bench.

Most of his shop equipment might be salvageable, and not just by him. "Close and lock the doors when you leave!" I called over. He waved an acknowledgment.

I walked through the field toward the tractor. State CSI would have done a good job scouring the building and the lot—no need to follow them around. But out in the weeds they might have missed something, especially because they probably didn't know for sure a third gunman had been out here.

The uncut grass near the tractor was trampled slightly, either by the shooter or someone later, but it had mostly bounced back since yesterday. I crouched behind the engine compartment and looked over. The office window was clearly visible. I pretended I was holding a rifle, pointed at the building.

The Russians had all been using similar weapons—short-barreled, extended stocks. The magazines might have been a little longer than typical. I guessed where the ejector port might have been, traced a trajectory with my eyes and looked in the grass.

A gleam of brass, exactly where it should have been. I bent to pick it up.

No head stamp, but the cartridge style was distinctive. There was another nearby, and a third farther away. I pocketed one and left the others in place.

Back at the car Dave had a bundle of clothes, a wrench set and a six-pack.

"My torque wrenches," he said. "That's a thousand bucks' worth of tools there."

"And the beer?"

"Aw, you know." He stood, looking at the damaged garage, then turned away. "What'd you find?"

"They were firing 9x39. It's a Russian subsonic round, high-powered."

"That don't mean much to me."

"Their special forces use them. I think the rifles were SR-3 Vikhrs."

"Is that good or bad?"

"I suppose it depends." I opened the Aveo's door. "Does anyone *want* spetsnaz commandos chasing after them?"

As we drove back to Clabbton, Dave untwisted the cap from one of his salvaged beers. The forest smell blowing through the car was stronger now.

"Seeing all that," he said. "Man."

"You can put it back together." A lot of damage, but the walls were thick, and nothing seemed to have collapsed.

"I thought maybe, but now I don't know." He seemed discouraged.

"Find something else, then?"

I slowed at the blinking light and coasted through. No traffic.

"It's the money," Dave said. He put his hands on his knees, straightening his posture. "You're right. There's nothing wrong there that couldn't be fixed up again. The problem—what I'm—well, I kinda owe some guys."

"Van?"

He didn't seem surprised. "Him and some others. Van's been around Clabbton for—like—ever. Old as my dad—my foster dad, I mean. Not ours."

"So . . . ?"

"When I got out." He hesitated. "You know how hard it is to get started again? Once you've got a record?"

"Sure." It's difficult enough as an honorably discharged veteran—everyone says we're heroes but just try to get a job. A résumé with prison time? Forget it.

"No one would hire me. Not even my buddies. Always had a good excuse, but, you know. I did all kinds of shit work there for a while—day labor on a jackhammer, that was probably the worst, but it weren't none of it fun."

The picture was clear enough. "Van helped you out."

"Yup. I saw the garage was for sale, even talked to the old guy selling it. But he wanted the cash to retire out to Alabama on, and no one would talk to me about a loan."

Maybe local underwriting hadn't been as lax as I'd thought. "How much?"

"Hundred and twenty thousand. I had six grand for a down payment—cash buried in an aluminum suitcase in Brendt's backyard, as a matter of fact. He didn't know about it. Nobody knew, not even my asshole lawyer."

"Uh-huh."

"Good thing, or he would have ended up with that too."

"You needed financing for ninety-five percent."

Dave nodded. "Van offered to put it up. No questions, no bullshit."

"And now you owe him."

"I keep paying off, every month, never missed a single payment. But somehow the nut don't ever get any smaller."

I took one hand off the wheel to scratch my other arm. Some welts there, red and itchy. The cabin blankets might have been hiding more than just dirt.

"What did you think I'd be able to do?" I said. "I don't have a hundred grand either."

"You're a numbers guy, right? Adding machine and a CPA? Only with guns." He smiled. "Perfect background to talk to Van with."

"Talk to him?"

"Uh, yeah. Could you?" He grinned. "I mean, I *know* you can get me a better deal."

Like life wasn't complicated enough. Two death-dealing mobs after me already, Dave wanted to add a third. "I think the shop could be rebuilt, but insurance adjusters tend to see things different. Van might be the same."

"Well, in fact, you know . . . no insurance."

"Van won't be happy to hear that. Not one iota."

"I guess I was a bad risk after all." Dave shrugged. "You're right, I got nothing. All the more reason Van ought to back off."

"Yeah, guys like Van *always* see it that way."

"Exactly." He stood up. "Let's go!"

What could I do?

"Right," I said. And we drove on into Clabbton.

Dave gave some directions—over the railroad bridge and then left, along the tracks. Just a few blocks away from the town green the streets got scruffy. Signs in low storefronts housed a pawnshop, two nail salons and FOR LEASE signs. Trash lay dirty and flattened in the gutter.

But when we arrived, it wasn't the warehouse or pool hall or razor-wire-encircled junkyard I thought might be Van's business office. Instead, we pulled into a blacktop lot beside a freestanding one-story with mirror windows and a drive-through. A patch of chemically controlled and neatly trimmed grass surrounded the front.

I stared.

"Don't need these!" Dave said cheerfully as he picked my carryall off the floor and dropped it behind the seat. "Best not be carrying inside."

Indeed not. We were about to enter the home office of Clabbton Savings and Loan—Clark Vanderalt, president and chief executive officer. I got out of the truck, bemused.

"David, come in, come in!" He shook hands and led us into his glass-fronted office behind the teller counter. Fifties, not much hair left on top, decent suit. "Thanks for stopping by."

"Hey, Van."

"And nice to meet you."

"Silas Cade," I said. "Dave's brother. I happened to be visiting."

Vanderalt looked like he was interested in that, but we let it drop. "Real sorry to hear about the shop," he said to Dave.

"Yeah, I know, right? Ain't nothing left but rubble."

"What in the world happened? Gator was here yesterday, asking to see all the loan paperwork. Said they were still picking bullets out of the walls, and everything else was blown to kingdom come."

"No idea." Dave put a serious, sober, completely sincere face on. "Might have been meth gangs. Don't know who else would be carrying around those kinds of guns and bombs. All I can think is they made some huge mistake, got the wrong address or something."

"I'm just glad no one was hurt."

And there you have it. Dave's last-resort loan shark was the president of the local bank. A pillar of the community. The wall behind his desk held a framed degree from Duquesne, a series of gold Kiwanis plaques and a display of softball team photos. Everyone wore blue and gold uniform shirts.

Clabbton S&L probably sponsored the Boy Scouts, too, and raised thousands of dollars at Christmas for homeless families.

No too-big-to-fail bank here. The financial apocalypse wasn't caused by local lenders like Vanderalt. No doubt he'd just kept doing business the way he always had: simple loans to people he saw on the street every day, uncomplicated deposit accounts, extremely conservative cash handling and investments. He sure wasn't getting rich, not by megabank standards, but he had standing in the community and people who respected him. He'd probably known Dave from childhood.

They didn't have to watch *It's a Wonderful Life,* they were *living* it.

"So what are you going to do now?" Vanderalt asked.

"Yeah." Dave kind of grimaced and looked down and nodded. "See, I know I should of—the thing is, well, I missed some payments on the insurance."

"Hmm."

"For maybe . . . let's see . . . I think, a while?"

Vanderalt turned stern but sympathetic. "When did the policy lapse?"

"Maybe two years ago?"

"I see."

We all looked at one another for a while, then the walls. Two customers were outside the glass, talking with the tellers, smiling. Vanderalt's computer hummed quietly.

"Your principal balance is one hundred ten thousand," he said. "I looked it up when Gator was here."

Dave nodded. "But you know I sure don't have *that*."

"Yes." He looked at me, one eyebrow raised. "Silas?"

I shook my head. "Sorry. I'd help out if I could."

"Well."

"You can foreclose," I said. "The building's maybe a loss, maybe not, but the land has to be worth something."

"Twenty thousand, maybe." Vanderalt's affect shifted again, subtly, to steel and business. "It's assessed separate from the construction. Of course demolition and site remediation will cut into that."

"Fifteen percent, then, with luck. Worse than a Greek government bond."

"Indeed."

"If it *was* a drug gang . . ." I glanced his way. "Dave certainly has grounds for a civil suit. Damages could cover the loss."

"Possibly, after years of litigation." He shook his head. "Years and years and years. And more years."

Sounded like the voice of experience. "Could be."

Dave perked up. "What about, like, the cops seize the gang's cars and boats and all?"

"Asset forfeiture?"

"I could get a piece of that, right?"

Vanderalt sighed.

The meeting struggled to a close, no one happy, least of all the banker. But what could he do? We shook hands again, walked back past the counters and sat in the Aveo outside.

"That didn't go great," Dave said.

"Yeah."

"Maybe I could declare bankrupt."

"That would get you out from under the mortgage. Of course, not even Van would lend you anything else for a decade."

"Well, fuck."

"Yeah."

I started the car and drove out of the parking lot. It was four-thirty, and three cars were stopped at the next corner—Clabbton's rush hour had begun.

"I need some money," Dave said.

CHAPTER EIGHTEEN

I dropped Dave at the police building, an unprepossessing block of 1960s public architecture. Not in front, but a hundred yards up the street—he had to do a second, formal interview with the chief, and I didn't feel like getting drawn in.

"I'm surprised he didn't have you in hours ago," I said. "Or yesterday."

"It's the fracking. All these drillers everywhere, pockets full of cash every weekend. Gator spends most of his time breaking up bar fights and arresting drunks."

"You ever think about doing that?"

"Drinking and bar fights?" He laughed. "On occasion."

"No. Working on the rigs."

The grin faded. "Naw. But I might have to now. The money's good."

He got out of the car and walked off. Back drooped a little, like he was tired. I knew the feeling, but I was sorry to see Dave that way.

Nothing I could do. After a moment I turned around, pointed the Aveo north and got back on the road to Pittsburgh.

Brinker and I hadn't been able to finish our conversation the previous night.

———

Clay Micro looked closed down when I arrived, a little before five P.M., and the small parking lot was not close to full. I drove around, scouting routes and exits, reminding myself of the layout. Yes, I'd been here twice already, but refreshers never hurt. The lot had only two entrances, both onto the street along the canal. The iron trestle spanning the waterway was illuminated in stark outline by the late-day sun behind it, two hundred yards down.

I couldn't wait in the lot itself—it would be too easy to get boxed, not to mention seen. The best surveillance location was clear—a driveway opposite the bridge, leading to a locked-down loading bay in the grocery wholesaler. It dead-ended against the building's dock, and a low wall concealed the Aveo from the Clay Micro lot.

I backed in, killed the engine.

I'd kept the binoculars from the forest cabin, and they brought the cars in the lot into sharp focus. I wasn't sure what Brinker was driving now, but the CFO's Cayenne was visible, still in the row of executive spots near the front door. I wondered if he'd ever driven it again.

Nothing but country and ranting on the radio—kind of like you get on AM, back home, but this was FM. Not so many stations. Maybe with all the industrial iron around, it was a broadcast dead zone.

Maybe it was because civilization's edge was three hundred miles east. I gave up and sat in silence—and ran out of patience after five minutes. I *hate* surveillance.

Time to move things along.

"Good afternoon, Clay Micro Technology. How may I help you?"

It sounded like Sharon. At least *someone* was working a full day. I shifted the phone away from my mouth and put some phlegm in my voice. "This is Detective Trotsky from the zone two police, miss. I'm trying to reach Gerald Brinker. Is he there, please?"

"Um, police? Mr. Brinker is, he's not available right now."

"Is he in your office, miss?"

"No, he's not here. He left for a meeting, um, at three-thirty."

And maybe not coming back. In the offices I usually visit—corporate and Wall Street—people are at their desks until long after dinner. I guess not everyone works like that. "It's important we talk to him as soon as possible."

"Yes, um, I'll tell him as soon as I see him. Just like the other detective asked me to."

"Other detective?" I realized Brinker might have called the police after all, after the attack at his barn. It might come in handy if I could find out who the investigating officer was. "Was that Harrison, miss? He and I have been working separate today, and I apologize if we crossed wires on you."

"Um, no, it was a lady officer, she said her name was Short, maybe?"

"Of course, Detective Short. I'll check in with her right now."

"Like I told her, Mr. Brinker did say he was planning to return to the office, but I don't know."

"I'll try later, then, but have him call me as soon as possible." I gave some imaginary contact details and hung up.

Then I called zone two. This one I routed through the Canadian proxy, for obvious reasons.

"Pittsburgh Police Department, you're being recorded."

"Detective Short, please."

"Do you know which station he works from?"

"She, and I think she's in your zone two."

"There's no detective by that name here. May I ask your reason for calling?"

"I'll try later, thanks." I hung up.

Well, well, well. Harmony and I seemed to be on the same trail.

I hadn't seen any obvious stakeouts when I circled the company thirty minutes earlier, but that didn't mean much. I started to feel paranoid and exposed.

But wait. Harmony was looking for Brinker—not *me*?

Or was she following Brinker in the hope that he'd lead her *to* me? I closed my eyes for a moment. Too many possibilities here.

I had the advantage, having stumbled into someone else's surveillance, but I wasn't sure what to do with it. Harmony was better than the Russians—at least we spoke the same language—but for all I knew they were here, too.

I looked around quickly, but still didn't see anyone. What the hell—I could give it another thirty or forty minutes. If everyone showed up again, we could continue the discussion that had been cut short at Brinker's barn.

The time dragged slowly past. Now and then a vehicle drove down one side of the canal or the other, heavy trucks mostly. Clay Micro sat blank and silent until five-thirty, when a woman came out. Through the binoculars I confirmed it was Sharon, and she went straight to a small silver car, got in and drove away.

I was hungry. The sun set and dusk settled in. I didn't have any better ideas, so I continued to sit there, watching security lights buzz on as darkness fell. Finally, around seven-fifteen, I'd truly had enough. I checked my phone once more, put it away and turned the ignition.

Clay Micro's CFO walked out the front door.

I didn't need the binoculars—Nabors's slicked-back hair was clear, even in the sodium glare of the parking lot lights. He was wearing a dark sport coat over a white shirt. I watched him walk to the Porsche, taillights blinking as he beeped it on from thirty feet away.

As long as I was leaving, I could see where Nabors might be going. Also, he might attract the attention of any other surveillants, and bring them out where I could see them.

I started the car and waited while the Porsche eased through the exit. Then I waited longer, as long as I could without losing Nabors completely.

Nothing else happened. No cars, no vehicle sounds, no lights clicking on or off in nearby windows.

I saw Nabors's turn signal at the far end of the block, and moved out to follow.

A complete mismatch, you'd be thinking, and you'd be right. Nabors was driving a machine German engineered to go seventy mph in first gear, and I had a six-year-old economy car with a hinky transmission. Also, I had to keep an eye not just on him but behind me, too, in case another team dropped into the train. But Nabors stayed well under the speed limit. The roads were cracked and pot-holed and generally of post-deindustrialization vintage, true, but he was being even more cautious.

We crawled along, past raggedy commercial buildings and un-developed land run to seed, stopping at every yellow light, pausing before every turn. Even after we'd got on the Parkway, busy with homebound commuters, the Porsche stayed in the far right lane. Not too slow, not too fast.

People have criticized my audit methods, but one thing for sure:

you don't see this kind of deep, newfound respect for the law after PricewaterhouseCoopers walks out the door.

It was like tailing a driving-school student. I kept a hundred yards back, occasionally switching lanes and drifting closer or farther—the best you can do solo. But if Nabors noticed, he didn't let on, just maintained a nice grandmotherly pace.

At the Canfield exit he pulled off the highway, waited through a red light at the ramp's end, and turned right onto a wide avenue. Then the turn blinker came on again, he slowed, and we entered a strip mall.

"Mall" might be generous. A badly paved parking lot fronted a row of small stores bookmarked by Frank's Discount Liquors at one end and Mighty Dollar at the other. Night had fully overtaken day while we were driving, and of three light poles in the lot, only one was working. Fluorescent tubes under an overhang illuminated the sidewalk in front of the store. The Toyota dealership across the street, already closed for the day, was better lit than the mall.

The lot was maybe one-tenth full but Nabors, a busy man with important things to do, parked on the fire lane directly in front of Frank's and got out, leaving the engine running. He was inside only for two or three minutes and came out with a clinking paper sack in one hand and a six-pack in the other.

Then he drove the Porsche about fifty feet to stop again, this time in front of a dry cleaner's. Inside, engine running.

The laundry had sheet-glass windows covered in painted signs—SHIRTS IRONED NO CHARGE, DOWN COAT SPECIAL, and so forth. The view was further obscured by racks of clothing inside. I could barely see the top of Nabors's head.

Hmm.

When Nabors emerged two minutes later, he held a stack of

plastic-sheathed suits and shirts by their hangers, using both hands. He strode to the sidewalk's edge, stopped abruptly and stared around, mouth open.

The Porsche was gone.

I coasted the Aveo to a stop in front of him. The passenger window was rolled down, Nabors about two feet away. I leaned over the seat so he could see me.

"Yo, Nabors, need a lift?"

"Wha—you! Y-y-you . . . where's my fucking *car*?" So angry he was tripping over the words.

"Hop in." I pointed the Sig at him. "Get in right now, or I'll shoot you and drive away."

He hesitated. Still keeping the pistol aimed at his face, I used my left hand to yank the door handle and shove it open.

"You're not a runner, Nabors. Try it and die, or get in."

He did as told. I switched the pistol to my left hand and held it cross-body—I'm not a lefty, but you don't need precision aiming from three feet away, and I didn't want the handgun so close he could think about grabbing for it.

"Close the door." The pile of clothing was slippery in the flimsy plastic bags, sliding around on Nabors's lap, which kept his hands occupied.

"What do you want?" he said.

I drove slowly away, one hand on the wheel, one holding the gun. Really, this was about as stupid a position to put myself in you could imagine—a professional would have either killed me or bailed in about two seconds.

Fortunately, Nabors was no professional.

"Follow-up interview," I said. "Dotting the i's, crossing the t's."

"I don't know anything."

Of course not. As we exited the lot I glanced across the street toward the Toyota dealership—the Porsche was parked at the end of one row, close to the showroom, nearly invisible among all the other shiny cars. It was still running, because I couldn't figure out how to turn it off with no key in the ignition—those all-electronic remotes make things complicated. But I'd left the lights off, and the slight exhalation of exhaust from its tailpipe was unnoticeable.

Nabors didn't even look in that direction, instead hypnotized by the barrel of the 226.

"When we talked earlier," I said, "you forgot to mention something."

"No, I didn't."

"The acquisition?"

"That's secret!" He actually looked shocked.

"Secret? *Secret?*" I shook my head. "Nabors, I'm your *auditor.* I'm like a doctor. You have to tell me everything."

"You're not—"

"Or the relationship just doesn't work."

I drove back the way we'd come, toward the highway. Halfway there I'd noticed an out-of-business car wash, weeds in the paving, fixtures stripped from the vacant bays. The only light came from a street lamp across the road, leaving plenty of shadow. I killed the headlights and drove around back. I didn't switch off the engine.

"I know, I know—*Consumer Reports* says you shouldn't idle more than thirty seconds." I twisted around to face him directly. "A waste of gas. Not to mention kind of foolish if you get out of the car. Anyone could come along and steal it."

"I don't know what you *want.*" His voice was strained.

"Aren't you listening? I'm the auditor, and that's all. I don't even work for Clayco. This should have been a simple little job."

"You got what you needed."

"That's what I thought, too. But suddenly people are pulling out automatic weapons and RPGs." I lowered the pistol and pointed it at Nabors's groin. "Tell me about the fucking acquisition."

He caved immediately, just like our last interview. "I don't know! Brinker never lets us in on anything—I might as well be an invoice clerk, for all the responsibility I have."

"You must have heard you were on the block. Not even the Chinese would buy a company without talking to the chief financial officer."

"Chinese?" He looked puzzled. "They weren't Chinese."

The oldest trick in the interrogator's book. "You *did* meet them."

"Only for an hour. They wanted to go over the statements. Especially cash flow—they were real interested in cash flow."

That didn't necessarily mean anything. The income statement is notoriously easy to rig, and even the balance sheet can be less than useful if someone's playing games. If you really want to understand a company's books, cash is king. As always. But there are reasons other than fundamental stock analysis to be primarily interested in cash flow.

Tax avoidance, for example. Money laundering. Misappropriation. Absconsion.

"Did they notice your missing seven mil?"

"No." Disdain mixed with defensiveness in Nabors's expression. "They walked right over it. Never saw a thing."

Kind of suspicious that Clayco headquarters hadn't noticed either—not until the serious due diligence was queued up. But that happens in private companies. Without the sunshine of public-market oversight, as flawed and compromised as the regulators are, the corporate chiefs can run their fiefdoms any way they want.

"So who were they?"

"I don't—" His voice squeaked and cut short when I shoved the pistol barrel into his lap. "Two accountants, that's all! We sat down, went through some ledgers, I showed them some reports. Like any inspection."

"How good was their English?"

"What?" His mouth opened.

"They were Russian, right?"

"I don't think so." Either he was a far better actor than he looked, or my question had truly come out of the blue. "Russian? They were as American as you and me. We talked about the playoffs. One guy had a Carnegie Mellon ring."

I didn't say anything for a moment. If secretive and mysterious Russians weren't trying to buy Clay Micro's seismographic technology . . . then why were secretive and mysterious Russians trying to kill me?

"Are you sure?"

Nabors must have sensed my uncertainty, for his own self-assurance began to return. "Yes, I'm sure. When we were finishing up, one said something like, hurry up, we've got a long drive back. And the other was like, just throw everything in the briefcase, we can sort it out on the road, Cheryl's gonna be pissed if I'm late again."

"Cheryl?"

"Whatever. His girlfriend." Nabors shrugged.

Zeke and I had come to Pittsburgh by car, but we had reason to avoid airplanes. Anyone else would fly—unless they were within a hundred miles.

Maybe a hundred fifty.

"Were they independent?" I asked.

"Huh?"

I raised the pistol to his nose—just a little reminder. Nabors swallowed hard.

"Were they company employees? Or outside accountants, hired for one task?"

"I don't know! We just talked about the statements, they asked some questions."

"But they *were* CPAs?"

"They knew what they were talking about, sure."

Another ten minutes, but I couldn't get anything else useful out of him. Deliberately or not, Brinker's fault or otherwise, Nabors really was a mushroom.

My hand had tired, holding the pistol. The Aveo's interior smelled of Nabors's sweat. Time to move on.

"Give me your phone," I said.

"Wha—?"

"Now." I prodded him in the sternum. He quickly reached inside his jacket and handed over a smartphone of some sort. I glanced down long enough to power it off and put it in my own pocket. "Can't have you calling 911 two seconds after you get out of the truck, that's all."

He breathed out abruptly, relief obvious. "You're letting me go?"

"Sure." I switched the pistol to my left hand again and shifted into drive. "I'm even going to take you back."

Yes, it would have been better to leave him behind as quickly as possible, but wandering down the avenue on foot he might attract attention. As carefully as before, I turned out of the car wash and drove back to the strip mall. Inside the parking lot I stayed at the edge, near the exit, ready to depart.

"Out you go." I watched Nabors scrabble for the door handle, not looking away from my face as he pushed the door open and scooted onto the pavement. The pile of dry cleaning fell in a tangled mess to the ground. "Nabors!"

He paused, about to slam the door and, probably, run.

"Go back to one of these stores," I said. "Borrow a phone, call a cab. Keep it simple."

"Yeah, right, good idea."

"Keep me *out* of it." I paused. "Or we'll be talking again. In person. Understand?"

"Uh-huh."

I put the Sig away, finally. Nabors swung the door closed and bent to pick up his shirts. I put the car in gear, and when Nabors stood up, the clothing a heap over both arms, I looked through the window.

"I really don't want to see you again," I said.

"No sir."

I exited onto the avenue. Nabors stood and watched me go. His plastic dry cleaning bags reflected the streetlights, flickering in my rearview mirror.

CHAPTER NINETEEN

S omeone else *was* watching the Clay Micro offices.

I'd driven back, the same route Nabors had led me out on, figuring I'd give it one more try. Maybe Brinker would have returned. I could do one more interview and still get dinner before midnight.

The parking lot was emptier now, maybe five vehicles left. Security lights were on at the corners of the building. Small floodlights illuminated the sign at the lot's entrance. I continued along the canal, past the lot, headed for my spot opposite the iron bridge. With the windows down, I could smell the canal's dank, brackish water.

But the spot was occupied.

I didn't notice until I was almost there—the new vehicle was as small as the Aveo, and concealed behind the half wall. Four doors, light-colored, not too old. Only one person visible inside, a shadow in the driver's seat.

I kept the car's speed steady and drove past. At the end of the industrial row, where windows were broken and dock bays boarded over, their renovation still long in the future, the canal road ended in a T with another street. I stopped, signaled and turned right, around the corner and out of sight.

Now what?

Whoever was in the sedan had chosen the spot same as I had—for covert surveillance. They couldn't be responding to a report from Nabors. It was too soon, and in any event he didn't know I'd picked him up here. So whoever it was, they were watching Clay Micro for some other reason.

It wasn't the Russian's panel van. Odds were running strong on Harmony's team.

No reason they'd have recognized the Aveo, which Dave and I had bought six hours ago, and I'd kept my face turned away after the first glimpse. Their attention would have been on the Clay Micro doors anyway. I could assume I was unnoticed.

No reason to go rushing in. I turned the car around, crossed a bridge farther down and drove back on a parallel road, one block away from the canal. Low buildings—empty garages, deserted warehouses, decrepit light industry—blocked my view across to Clay Micro's mill block. When it felt like the right place I parked, rolled the windows up and locked the car, then continued on foot.

I came to the canal's edge between a chain-link fence and a blank cinderblock wall, dark and unlit. The iron bridge was in front of me. Two hundred yards right, Clay Micro's few lit windows shone over the lot. Across the bridge I could just make out the mystery car, sitting still and quiet in its own shadows.

Not perfect, mostly because I'd had to leave the Aveo. But I couldn't see anywhere else to park that the new stakeout wouldn't notice—the canal's service roads were empty, the parking lot lit. I was confident of my own invisibility, and if either Brinker or the sedan drove away, I could probably get back to my own car quickly enough to follow.

The night had cooled and dampness drifted off the canal. Grime crusted the rough brick wall beside me. I checked my handgun once more, kept it out and sat on a rusted metal box at the base of the fence. It might have housed a transformer or some electrical connection once, for two heavy conduits ran from it into the ground. But that was decades ago.

A flash of light in the sedan caught my eye. Behind the windshield, something glowed before the driver's face, then winked out.

A phone?

I stood up. A minute passed, then another. A tractor trailer drove past, somewhere behind us, its diesel engine echoing off the deserted buildings.

Brinker walked out, pushing through both glass doors and letting them swing shut behind him.

Either he'd returned, or he'd been there the entire time. I patted myself on the back for not having given up the surveillance too soon.

Brinker strode across the parking lot, out the exit and—without hesitation—along the canal toward the sedan. Whoever was in the car, they expected him.

I needed a shotgun mic. A better vehicle, parked closer. More weapons.

I needed a fucking *team*. I wished Zeke had been able to come sooner.

Instead, I holstered the Sig, crouched and moved onto the bridge.

And when I say "onto," I don't mean the road deck. The box trestle was riveted together from twelve-inch iron beams, a broad trapezoid that bent to the top height from either side of the canal.

By grabbing either side of the beam slanting upward in front of me, I was able to climb it like a monkey—or rather, like one of those machete-wielding island natives who zip up palm trees to drop coconuts to the tourists. Fifteen feet to the top, and my hands began to hurt from the rough metal edges.

The bridge's open top was a framework of girders crossed from side to side. I kept low and moved as quietly as I could, along the beam until I was at the far end. I stopped and squatted there, a new gargoyle crouched at the top corner of the trapezoid.

It was dark, almost misty, and street lamps cast dim pools of light. I hoped that Brinker's attention was on the car, and the driver's on him. He didn't look up and nothing happened in the car, so perhaps I remained unseen.

Twenty feet from the car Brinker stopped abruptly. He stared at the windshield for a moment and backed away, starting to move fast.

Harmony swung her door open and stepped out, pistol raised in an easy two-handed grip. Shielded by the door she called out in a clear voice.

"Brinker! Stop there!"

"You're not—" He bit off the word. "Who are you?"

"Get over here. Keep your hands where I can see them."

This was fun. I shifted my weight a fraction, getting comfortable.

Brinker didn't move, except for his head, turning slightly this way and that as he looked for help.

"Your pals aren't here," said Harmony. "Just me."

Was she serious? If it was me I'd have said "us" even if I *was* alone, to intimidate Brinker as thoroughly as possible.

Maybe Harmony didn't play that kind of game.

"But I got a call." Brinker was almost plaintive. Looking more closely I could see a bandage on his hand, and his other arm seemed unusually stiff. "I was supposed to come out here . . ."

"A ten-dollar children's toy can change anyone's voice," Harmony said.

Ha! I've done that myself. But I probably wouldn't have boasted about it.

"What's going on?" she said, raising the handgun enough to catch Brinker's attention.

He shook his head. "I don't know anything."

"On the phone, you said there was a problem."

"Yeah, but I thought—"

"Tell it, Brinker." Her voice sharpened. "Or I'll fucking shoot you. I'm *really* tired of not knowing what's going on, and if you can't help me out, then fuck it, you might as well have a few more holes in your head."

He didn't think about it long.

"Nabors just called me. His car got stolen out from under him."

"Really?" Harmony became more alert, straightening into a quick left-right scan. "He got jacked?"

"No. From in front of a store or something—he went inside to get his dry cleaning, he came out, it was gone."

"What about him?"

"Nabors?"

"Yes, Nabors." Maybe a little impatience there. "Anyone threaten him? Point a gun? Did he *see* anything?"

"Nothing." Brinker laughed, too high-pitched. "Literally nothing— just an empty space where the car used to be."

"What about police?"

"Police? You don't want us to call *them*, do you?"

"He didn't, did he?"

"No. I told him to find a taxi and go home."

Pause. Harmony seemed to be thinking. I tried to see her shoes, but it was too dark at the ground. The plain black windbreaker and dark pants carried no message.

"All right." Harmony had apparently come to a decision, her voice sharp. "You're coming with me."

"What? No, I'm not!"

She raised the pistol. I couldn't see the make. "Yes. Silas was smart enough to pick off your CFO. He must be looking for you, too."

"Silas? He's here?" Brinker's head twitched side to side. I hunched involuntarily.

"Of course not. He's driving Nabors's Porsche. Or searching it, more likely—I bet Nabors left his laptop inside, full of all kinds of evidence."

Shit. I didn't even think of that.

"In any event, I want to talk to him, and he probably wants to talk to you. We'll have a nice little sit-down."

"Uh-uh." Brinker shook his head. "That's not part of the deal."

"Deal? There is no *deal*. Get in the car, asshole."

"You think you can fuck with me?" Brinker was back to his old self. "I'm *protected,* you dumb bitch. Do anything to me—anything at all—and the Russians will tear you into shreds."

Ah-hah! Russians.

"You're leaving, and I'm going back inside."

He turned away. Harmony raised her handgun—a nice two-handed Weaver stance, steady and unhurried.

"Brinker." Her voice still calm, but with an absolute edge. "Get in the *car.*"

Decision time.

She appeared ready to shoot him if he didn't turn around. I

didn't want Brinker dead until I understood what was going on. I didn't want him disappeared, either—he might never come back, no matter what she said about using him to draw me in.

And, okay fine, I admit it, I wanted to talk to Harmony directly.

I raised the Sig—slowly, still trying to avoid attention—aimed and fired at her car's front tire.

BAANG!

The gunshot was stunningly loud. I missed the tire, but a cloud of steam jetted from the grille—guess I hit the radiator instead. Harmony dropped immediately, seeking cover behind her car door. I could see her scanning the area, rapidly, efficiently.

Brinker went to the ground and stayed there, curled into a ball.

I ran down the beam, firing three more times as I went. Because the beam was at about seventy-five degrees, "fell" or "skidded" might be more accurate, but I managed to land on my feet and keep going. Harmony, undeterred by my wild aim, raised up just enough to shoot back. I dove for the other side of the car, fired twice more underneath it, then jumped up, bringing the Sig into line—

—and stared into the barrel of Harmony's pistol, pointed straight back at me.

We both froze.

She was still behind her open door, aiming down over the corner of the windshield. I crouched behind the tire, my head exposed and both arms just above the hood, holding my handgun in a range grip.

If we fired simultaneously, the bullets would probably collide. Just like in *Wanted*.

"Hi, Silas." If there was stress in her voice I couldn't hear it.

"Hey, Harmony."

"Sorry I missed you last time."

I paused. "That's pretty good."

"You going to pull that trigger?"

"I hope not." If either of us fired, an involuntary muscle spasm in the other would bring a return shot. Even unaimed, we were so close that the odds were good of mutual, possibly lethal, injury.

Steam hissed from the radiator. Something pinged inside the engine. My senses were on overload, hearing every little rustle, seeing every little movement.

"How are the horses?" I said.

"Horses?"

"His." I kept my eyes and aim at Harmony but tipped my head toward Brinker.

"They were fine when we left. I gave them some fodder."

"Glad to hear it. I felt bad about them. All that gunfire."

Brinker stirred on the ground. "What the fuck are you *doing*?" he said.

"Is he yours?" I asked.

"No." She glanced over his way, utterly disdainful. "What's your interest?"

That was a good question. "I'm not . . . hmm. Staying alive, I think."

"Somebody wants to talk to you."

"I heard."

"In person."

My hand trembled slightly. You try holding two pounds of metal at arm's length, motionless—it's not so easy. Harmony was able to brace her forearms on the car frame.

"Not today."

She nodded slightly. "What are we going to do here?"

"I was hired for a job. You were hired for a job. Mine's done."

Another pause. From the corner of my eye I noticed Brinker start to slide backward, out of the way.

"Shifting terrain," Harmony said. "Not quite sure where I stand."

"How about you go find out? We'll set something up later."

"Uh-huh."

"Starbucks?"

"I'm going to down weapons," she said. "I'd rather you didn't shoot me."

I stared into her eyes. They were dark and unblinking. "Okay."

I moved the pistol sideways and down. Harmony lowered hers. We both straightened up.

"Your vehicle's shot," I said.

"Yeah." Her gaze flicked to the engine compartment, then back to mine. "More than once, in fact."

"Sorry." I paused. "You know, Nabors isn't using his right now."

"Oh?"

"It's in a lot on Canfield Avenue. Engine's running. Hitchhike up there, it's all yours."

"You're serious, aren't you?"

Brinker stood and ran. Harmony and I swung toward him in unison, both weapons up again. He sprinted across the road—four, five steps—and dove unhesitatingly into the canal.

The splash was loud, and I thought I saw drops glittering briefly in the air, reflecting the street lamp's dim light. More splashing as Brinker paddled away.

"Ah, fuck." Harmony walked over and looked at the water. "Brinker! Brinker, you dumbshit, get back here!"

No response. He'd already flailed to the other side, and we could see him pulling himself up the canal's rock wall. In a moment he was over the top and running down the same alley I'd come through. The squelching of his shoes echoed slightly.

I glanced sideways. Light from the parking lot outlined Harmony's profile, making her hair glow with a sort of halo.

Halo? Jesus.

"I have to go," I said. "We good?"

"No." She still held the pistol in a movement ready. "I don't know."

I thought about offering her a ride, but managed to suppress myself. "You have a number?"

She looked directly at me, frowning, though the handgun stayed down. "What?"

"You know." I made a phone pantomime with my free hand by my ear.

She laughed. "Get out of here."

"Sure." I backed toward the bridge. Once I was a little farther away and moving, she probably couldn't hit me except by luck. We watched each other the whole way, until I scuffed the main beam with one heel. "Later," I said, and started jogging.

I didn't look back. She didn't shoot me. Good enough.

CHAPTER TWENTY

Harmony reminded me of someone.

Showing up to brace Brinker all by herself—that wasn't so smart, especially if she had backup available. He was a civilian, sure, but he'd already proven to have dangerous associates. The firefight at the barn was adequate demonstration of that. A lone gun for hire, prone to unnecessary risks . . . oh, right, that's *me*.

Anyone else on the other side of our standoff, I probably would have kept firing, the hell with the risks. But Harmony struck a chord.

So to speak.

I bet she hated that sort of pun.

Meanwhile, a more immediate question: where could I sleep tonight? Dave wasn't answering. I didn't want to drive all the way down to the cabin in West Virgina, especially with the bedbug problem there. Moncy was low but hadn't run out yet, so I found a motel not far from downtown, a five-story granite building with a façade from the nineteenth century. It still had "Fur Exchange" carved into stone above the second story, but now it seemed to house mostly homeless families, not trappers and traders.

I took a shower so long and hot it was a wonder the boiler didn't run out.

The night wasn't restful.

I was out at dawn, hauling my satchel of guns down to the car— no way would I have left it in the trunk overnight. Breakfast was coffee, "cheese" Danish and a jar of peanuts from a gas station. Then I drove out of the city. Back to horse country.

Brinker had left home.

No lights, no cars. I waited two hours, sitting in the Aveo a quarter mile up the road, the estate just visible. Commuter traffic started early: pickups mostly, at first—the hard-used vehicles of people who work for a living. Then more cars, newer and shinier as the clock ticked through rush hour. Around eight-thirty the volume slowed again. I ate peanuts and tried not to yawn too much.

An hour after that I emerged from the cab, stiff and tired. But the day was beautiful, sunshine burning off the dew and birds in the air. I pissed against the rear tire, checked the Sig, got back in and drove straight to the barn.

All the way in I kept scanning the grounds. Nothing suggested habitation. The windows were blank and still, the doors all closed up tight. The gravel drive was gouged and the lawn torn where my Lincoln had been flipped over, but no other sign of the events two nights ago was visible.

The barn was empty. It smelled of horses and feed and shit, but the animals themselves were gone. I walked back to the house and tried the bell, then pounded the door. Nothing.

I could have broken in, but Brinker didn't seem like the kind of wrongdoer to leave evidence lying around in plain view. After another minute I gave up and returned to the car.

Down the road I called Clara.

"Kind of busy right now," she said.

"What's going on?"

"Deadlines. Server crashing my last post. Twitter queues. The usual. Hey, how's Harmony?"

What is it about women? "We're not completely trying to kill each other anymore."

"That's progress."

I pulled off the road at a wide patch of gravel—the kind of place hunters might park for a few hours of deerstalking. Trees shaded the ground. A pair of cars went by in the other direction, one tailgating the other, clearly impatient.

"Give me a minute?" I said. "I was hoping you'd found something on Clayco's mystery buyer."

"They're selling the Micro division, all right."

Nabors had confirmed as much, but it was nice to hear it from outside. "I thought so."

"This guy I know, he's an analyst at Wetherell Stark."

The name was familiar. "Hedge fund?"

"Private equity, mostly. It's been a bad few years—they're trying to move into distressed debt."

"An evergreen market, the way the world is now. What about them?"

"So he pays attention to subgrade issues, and Clayco's barely treading water. It's a lot worse than it looked when I first checked. You know the story—borrowed way too much when the money was easy, and now they can barely roll it over every quarter."

"Liquidity crunch?"

"Serious. Selling Pittsburgh will keep the wolves away for . . . let's see, he gave me some cash flow numbers . . . nine months."

I found myself nodding. "Clayco really needs the deal."

"Nine months takes us just through next bonus season. What do you bet the CEO's rewriting his retirement provisions as we speak?"

"No bet." I got out and leaned on the car's door, stretching my legs. "Okay, I get it. Clayco is a motivated seller. Who's the buyer?"

"Ah." Clara sounded disappointed. "Not so much progress there. The entity's name is Dagger Light Holdings, but it's just a shell. Montserrat incorporation and the directors are names from the same local law firm that set it up."

"Can your friend track them down?"

"He's busy. Wetherell Stark looked at Clayco, decided against it and moved on. Probably why he was willing to tell me anything—it's just an anecdote now, impress the crowd at the bar."

"Was that you? A face at the bar?"

Clara laughed. "I bought him some drinks, yeah, so what?"

"Uh-*huh*." I let it go. "Know anyone else you can throw at Dagger Light? Which, by the way, that's a pretty good name."

"For a throwaway." She paused. "Sorry, had to check . . . um . . . oh, right. Montserrat. Yeah, I'll ask a Scottish contact I know. She's got some connections at HMR." Her Majesty's revenue service, that is—Montserrat is a British territory.

"Maybe you could talk to Johnny, too."

"Why, is he in on this?"

"No, but he might be able to help out. He knows everybody."

"I'll call him." She might have anyway—he really was good for gossip, and always willing to listen to Clara. I know he fed her storylines occasionally, hoping to spin the market one way or another. They could be remarkably useful to each other.

"Nothing about Russians?" I said.

"No." Clara paused a moment. "Though, I wonder . . ."

"What?"

"Want me to plant something?"

"Try to flush them out?" I thought about it. "No, not yet. Might be useful later."

"Whatever you do, you're going to let me know, right?"

So she could beat the other newshawks into print. "I don't think there's anything in it for you."

"There's always *something*."

A beep. "Hey, I got another call."

"See you." She hung up.

I looked at the phone, pressed a couple of buttons and lost the call waiting. That's what happens—I'm always buying new crappy phones, and they're all a little different.

The incoming number read as "unavailable."

I tapped the steering wheel for a few moments. I'd tried Dave earlier, and he still wasn't picking up.

The phone rang again. This time I got it.

"Where are you?" said a familiar cranky voice. "I've been on the road all night."

———

I don't know what it is about Zeke.

He's no more than average height, kind of stringy, wears plain cotton shirts, talks quiet and—mostly—polite. Nothing particular to see, unless you study his hands, or maybe watch him move, and those are the sorts of clues that only people in the business pay attention to. But somehow, there's a feral, lethal aura that even children and dogs notice.

Which is just to explain why there were three empty seats next to him at the Stanwood Road coffee shop. He'd been working on a large cup of something—black coffee, no doubt—and watching the street, while businesspeople and slackers and poseurs flowed in and out and around his invisible force field.

"Thanks for coming," I said.

"You're late." He didn't shake hands, just got to his feet like smoke rising from a fire.

"I had to drive back into the city." I looked at the line of people waiting. Some damp croissants and vastly oversized muffins sat un-invitingly on a tray behind the counter. I thought I heard a percolator—a *percolator*!—bubble somewhere.

I missed New York.

"Let's get out of here."

"Let me finish my coffee."

Zeke had taken a bus to Pittsburgh, which is a truly pathetic way to travel, but safer and more anonymous than driving. Over one shoulder he had his own go bag—stiff waxed canvas, faded with age and neatly strapped shut.

He must have left long before dawn. Maybe he slept on the bus.

We walked along the sidewalk, which felt empty compared to Manhattan's constant throngs. For three blocks the downtown was a metropolis, skyscrapers and reflective glass and office workers smoking outside revolving doors. Then it all stopped. We crossed a four-lane avenue and landed in a scrabbly little park running along the bank of the Monongahela.

Zeke looked up and down the river. The sun was bright enough to be painful. A powerboat motored past. Traffic noise drifted steadily down from the span of the Fort Pitt Bridge.

"Ryan's still missing," Zeke said.

"Nothing?"

"He's not answering calls and no one's seen him." Zeke started walking. "I mentioned to a couple of people."

"That he was missing?"

"Yeah."

"And now they're looking for him, too?"

"Exactly. Wide attention, in fact."

Of course. Not because Ryan had a lot of friends worrying about him, but because he'd worked with many of us, here and there, different jobs over the last two or three years. If something had gone wrong and he'd been killed, well, that's sad, but it happens and life goes on. On the other hand, if he was sitting in an interrogation room at the Federal Building, that was an altogether different matter.

Most of Ryan's acquaintances would surely prefer him dead.

My world. Zeke's world.

"Hope they find him," I said.

"Yup." Zeke shifted his shoulder bag. "So tell me a story."

I ran through it again, the detailed version. It took some time.

We walked along the bridge to the water, the cars above us banging over expansion joints. I could smell exhaust and diesel.

"Russians," said Zeke when I'd finished.

"Yup."

"Mafiya?"

"Probably. Regular business doesn't usually come to the table with light artillery."

"I thought the mafiya *was* regular business over there."

"Less so than ten years ago, according to the State Department."

"Not sure why they're interested in seismographs . . ." He left the thought hanging.

"Could be a natural gas company. Maybe the money angle is more important. Or some gang might be working for the government. Hell, in Russia now the gangs *are* the government, only they came out of the security forces."

"No need to make it complicated. If mystery Russians are shooting up America's heartland—one phone call and the U.S. government will be all over this. That's what the FBI's hotline is for. Solve your problem for you."

We stopped on some wide stone steps leading down to the fountain at the end of the park. Water jetted fifty feet in the air. A light breeze blew the fountain's steady mist away from us. It was warm enough to remove my jacket, but the world didn't need to see the holster I had underneath.

"The U.S. government might already *be* involved," I said. "You don't get a ghost plate at the DMV."

"Maybe. Maybe not. There's a market."

"Really?" I looked at Zeke. "I didn't know that. Who's selling?"

"Something I heard once." He made a who-knows gesture with one hand. "Could have been nothing but bar talk."

"I'd like to follow that up."

"I'll try to remember who it was."

We watched a power yacht sail past, cutting a steady rumbling wake on the river.

"This should have been a simple audit," I said. "One little company fiddling the books. You know what the problem is?"

Zeke shrugged.

"Firearms," I said. "There're too damn many of them. People are always trying to fix things with guns."

"That's funny, coming from you."

"Yeah, but I'm careful, well trained and respectful."

My phone rang. I pulled it out.

"Yeah?"

"This is Brinker."

I wasn't sure I heard right. "What?"

"Brinker. Remember? You've almost gotten me killed twice now?"

I gestured at Zeke, tipped the phone out so he could lean in and listen.

"How did you get this number?"

"You're Silas Cade, aren't you? That's what that woman was hollering at my barn. I made some calls."

"Mistaken identity."

"I don't think so. You still in town?"

It sounded like him. The attitude was right. Brinker had an exceptionally generous allowance of self-confidence, even for a one-percenter executive.

"Not sure what town you—"

"We need to talk. You and me, in person."

"You're talking to me now."

"Not on the phone. It's possible you're not who I think, right? Not likely, but possible."

I raised my eyebrow at Zeke. He shook his head.

"What do you want?" I said.

"Two o'clock. Versailles Road between Leechburg and Freeport." He pronounced it ver-SALES. "Be there, and we can have a civilized conversation."

"Where?"

"Right on the river." He repeated the address. "Go in the second gate. The lock's broken. I'll be near the foundry."

"Foundry," I said. "You want to meet at a steel mill?"

"It's been shut down for thirty years. Kids and scavengers get inside now and then, but that's it."

"You're setting up a meet . . . in an abandoned steel mill." The conversation was going south.

"It's safe, and private, and I can see you coming from a mile away."

"You think we're in some Jerry Bruckheimer movie? This is fucking stupid."

"No more ambushes. Two o'clock." He hung up.

Zeke straightened, a smile glinting. "*That's* more like it," he said.

CHAPTER TWENTY-ONE

We could see the plant before we arrived, stained smokestacks and a massive, rusting gantry rising above the wooded hill. The mill had been built on a fork of the Kiskiminetas River, near where it enters the Allegheny. A double-tracked rail line led in along the banks. On a rise overlooking the site I turned off the blacktop, following a dirt road marked PRIVATE—NO HUNTING. Once we were hidden from traffic I killed the engine and we both got out.

Dave pulled in right behind us, bouncing the Charger over the rocky trail.

We'd met for a brief lunch after he finally called me later in the morning. Packaged burritos and bottles of juice from a convenience store, eaten off the road outside Clabbton. Zeke and I didn't need any more public face time. Surprisingly, he and Dave got along like peas and carrots. At heart, perhaps, their life philosophies weren't that different—*live for the moment, the hell with the rest.*

Unlike me, always worrying.

"You stay here," I said as Dave stepped from his car. "That's the deal, right? Zeke and I have years of experience in this sort of thing."

"Sure, whatever."

We were next to a stream picking its way down the hollow. The water was stained dark red, striking against the green leaves around it.

"Iron in the water," Dave said, noticing me looking. "Maybe some oil, too. See the sheen? This is mineral country."

"Guess we can't drink it, then."

"No."

Zeke glanced at it. "I've had worse."

No doubt.

Dave watched with open curiosity as Zeke opened his satchel, withdrew two handguns and checked the magazines and action. Laying the weapons on the hood, he removed his belt and re-threaded it with two holsters, one behind each hip.

We both preferred thigh holsters, but even in NRA heartland, it wasn't a good idea to go running through the woods looking all Ghost Recon. Zeke's jacket covered up the weapons well enough.

"You should load up, too," he said. He took out an M500 combat shotgun—it had a fourteen-inch barrel, the shortest stock model— broke it open and started pushing in shells. A yellow one, a red one, another yellow. Six, altogether.

"Sabot rounds?" I asked.

"Fléchettes alternating with unjacketed slugs."

I nodded. He wasn't fucking around—that was a seriously illegal, seriously room-clearing load.

"That's awesome, man," Dave said. Zeke rolled his eyes.

Meanwhile, I'd opened my own bag and removed the MP5.

"Maybe you should take this," I said. "I don't want to scare Brinker, walking up with it."

"He'll expect you to show up armed."

"Maybe."

"You're going to be drawing fire, not me. You should have it."
Zeke added a combat knife to his belt. "What I'd really like is a
long gun."

"Sorry."

"They *will* be in ambush, you know."

"Of course."

The forest smelled of new growth and dampness. Leaves rustled
in the trees.

The Sig was still at my back. I pocketed some extra magazines.
Zeke put on a pair of shooting glasses—clear lenses and metal
frames.

"Give me a quarter hour," he said. To Dave: "You *stay* here, right?
I'm not kidding."

"Sure."

"Have a drink before you go." I handed him a water bottle from
a crate we'd picked up the same time I filled the car's tank on the
way here. I'd also bought some blueberry energy bars and, finally, a
toothbrush.

"Right." He drank, tossed the bottle back into the car and left.
No wave, no goodbye.

No need. We'd done this before.

Dave and I waited, not saying much, listening to the quiet
sounds of the forest. A bird called in the distance. Cars drove past,
not frequently. An airplane buzzed overhead, then faded away.

Half an hour. No need to rush Zeke, and showing up exactly on
time would only empower Brinker.

At two-twenty I policed the area, finding a paper insert that had
fallen from one of the ammo boxes and a Mylar wrapper I'd dropped
during snack time.

"Is it really a trap?" said Dave.

"Probably." I checked the weapons once more. "Can't think of any other reason he wants to meet way out here. But even if not, best to prepare like it is."

"I'll be watching."

"Use these." I ducked down to reach through the Aveo's window and handed him the binoculars. "You should take them back anyway—they came from your friend's cabin."

"Okay."

A moment's awkwardness, not looking at each other. Finally I kind of tapped him on the arm. "Something goes wrong, find Chief Gator and tell him everything. Do that before you talk to anyone else—especially any federal agent."

"He's a good guy."

"That's why." I got in the car. "See you back here in a few."

I put the MP5 in my lap and drove down to the mill.

I crossed a small, heavy bridge that led to the Kiskiminetas, then turned onto a gravel road that led around the perimeter of the plant.

A chain-link fence encircled the site, newer than the decades-old buildings inside, with coils of razor wire along the top. Probably put up when it closed, to keep people out—or to demonstrate a good faith effort, at least. No fence would deter the metal thieves and thrill seekers, but leaving the place wide open would only invite lawsuits.

I paused at the main entrance, pulling up to look through the gate. It was secured with a heavy chain wrapped around the galvanized posts, held tight by a huge padlock. Weeds had grown up through the pavement, including shoots where the gate would scrape along when opened.

No one had come in this way for weeks.

The service road continued around the side, following railroad tracks. These too were long out of use, overgrown and rusty. A switch point had been tagged with an illegible spray of dirty paint, the red-green signal light smashed years ago. A few wrecked train cars sat abandoned on the sidings—two tankers, a sagging boxcar near the next gate. The boxcar's doors hung open, and I could see scorch marks on its walls.

The side entrance was where Brinker had said: a single gate big enough for only one vehicle, entering between a metal-walled out-building and a huge gantry crane. The gate was pushed open wide enough for someone to walk through, but there it had jammed, stuck against rubble inside.

I wished we had tactical radios. Once the shooting started—if it started—constant contact was critical. But cellphones would have to do. We'd turned off the ringers.

I dialed, listened to it buzz once and then heard nothing.

"Zeke?" I whispered.

Two loud clicks. *Yes.* He tapped his phone's case, not talking.

"You see me?"

One click.

"Okay, I'm at the gate, I assume that big shed's in the way. You in position?"

Two clicks.

"Good. I'm going in now, unless you say different."

Three clicks, pause, one more. The security phrase we'd set, thirty minutes ago. A one-off. Impossible to imagine that this simple communication could be compromised, but one last redundancy always makes you feel better.

"Okay. See you inside."

Click click, then silence. I replaced the phone in my pocket.

I looked at the debris that had blocked the chain-link gate. Chunks of concrete, some metal scrap.

If someone wanted me to *walk* in, unprotected, they might have rigged it that way.

The car was still running, the engine humming quietly. Pootie really had tuned it up. I backed up, diagonally across the service road, until its rear bumper tapped the boxcar's frame. About fifteen feet, nose to gate—good enough.

I engaged the clutch, moved the shift from reverse to first and put the accelerator all the way to the mat. The engine redlined, suddenly screaming loud, and I let the clutch go.

The Aveo jolted, rear wheels spinning and throwing dirt before catching traction. Then they caught. The vehicle exploded forward.

SMASH!

The gate flew out of the way, slammed aside. The car bucked as it hit the rubble, almost grounding before banging over. A long scrape on the underside. I lost some control and skidded sideways, striking the metal shed. For an instant I was out of focus, bouncing around, head whipsawed from one side to the other at impact.

No airbags. Pootie had skipped something after all.

I seized back the wheel, which had been yanked from my grip, and swerved back onto the pavement.

A horn blared behind me. I twisted around—

Dave's Charger was on the service road, roaring up at a hundred miles an hour. Just as I looked he turned *right,* away from the gate, and an instant later his front wheel clipped the railroad track.

The car immediately spun, 180 degrees in a half second of flying dirt and screaming metal. Coming around, the spin halted abruptly when the same right wheel slammed into the fence curb. The Charger bounced violently, now skidding straight backward, the rotational velocity somehow exactly canceled by the two collisions.

"Noooo!" Dave yelled through his window. "Don't!" He continued to slide, finally coming to a halt mostly behind the boxcar.

And that's when the ambushers engaged.

Gunfire hammered into the Aveo. Both forward tires immediately blew—I could feel the front sag and rims grind into the paving. Holes appeared in the hood, dozens all at once. The windshield starred across its entire surface. I ducked, abandoning the wheel to put my arms over my face, and shoved myself down.

The car crashed into something and slewed to a halt. I lay over the central hump, legs driver's side and my torso under the passenger's dash. The gearshift stabbed my abdomen painfully. Bullets tore into the entire car body, an unremitting fusillade. Through half-open eyes I felt the light increase—so many holes were drilled into the roof and side panels, it was like new windows.

The car was a death trap. I had a little protection, the engine block and the firewall between me and the ambushers, but that wouldn't last long. Meanwhile I couldn't see anything, couldn't fire back, couldn't do anything but huddle on the floor.

I somehow got my phone out, stabbed the buttons blindly. Redial.

"Silas!" Zeke's voice, barely audible over the waterfall roar of incoming fire. I guess we didn't need the tap code anymore.

"Which way?" I yelled back.

"Out the right side. *Starboard*. On three, okay?"

"Go!"

He counted it off. I reached up, twisting like a contortionist to pull the door handle, and shoved forward with both feet. My head, a battering ram, forced the door open in a squeal of ruined metal. I kept moving, rolling out, dragging the MP5 by its shoulder strap.

The hail of fire slowed. Now that I was outside, in the open air, I got a quick placement—gunshots from left and front, in the foundry, other shots from somewhere right. Zeke was doing his best to put down suppressing fire, though he'd now exposed his own position.

I got out and half ran, half dove for the side of the shed. I collided with the dark wall, hitting my head again, and collapsed behind a metal drum holed with rust.

BL-A-A-MM!

An explosion rocked the Aveo, punching it into the air, then dropping it back. A cloud of dust bloomed. Debris battered my face and the wall behind me.

RPG? A planted charge? It didn't matter. I wouldn't be driving away.

Manic laughter. For a moment I couldn't tell from where, then realized it was Zeke, yelling incomprehensibly, coming through the cellphone, which apparently I hadn't switched off.

Dave's horn blared again. I turned around to see him through the chain-link—he'd backed fully into the lee of the railcar, sheltered from the attack.

"Come on, get out of there!" Dave yelled through the boxcar's open doors, from the other side. I could just see his head, and nothing of the Charger. He had to be standing right outside it.

"Zeke?" I spoke directly into the phone. "*Fuck* this. Time to go."

"Who's in the car? Good guy? Bad guy?"

"It's Dave. Didn't you see him?"

"Other things happening. *Your* car's wrecked."

"I know. We'll take the Charger."

I finally got my shit together. Lots of scrapes and bangs, no serious injuries. I untwisted the MP5's strap, cleared the Sig in its holster and stood up.

"Where are you?"

"Up on the gantry."

I went to the other end of the shed, knelt to put my head at ground level and looked around the corner. The traveling crane's near end rose from a pad of cracked concrete about ten yards away, up into the air and then stretched across the ground, a massive frame of rusting girders and drooping cable. Three rail spurs ran underneath, their connection to the main line now interrupted by the chain-link fence.

A small controller's compartment was bolted onto the middle of the gantry—a little steel shed, empty window frames. Through the door, which faced back toward my way, I could see someone's dim form.

Gunfire had picked up from the foundry. Shots banged into the shed, puffing dirt on both sides. I heard a bullet crack past my head, then another. I ducked back.

"How you getting *down*?" I yelled into the phone.

"Hang on." Two shots—I heard them in slight echo, both through the air and the phone, as Zeke fired at someone. "They're not showing themselves."

"Silas!" Dave, calling again. I glanced over. He made a *let's-go* gesture, beckoning with his arm. I waved back, then held up one finger.

"Ten seconds," said Zeke.

"Ready." I raised the submachine gun. "You call it."

A long pause. The ambushers' fire slackened. I smelled dirt and sweat and gunsmoke.

"Now!"

I kicked the oil drum just past the corner, dove behind it, and fired the MP5. Three-round bursts, placing them into the windows I thought our attackers might be hiding behind.

Return fire immediately blasted my way, tearing into the barrel and the shed and the ground. Bullets and metal shards and dust everywhere.

From the corner of my vision I saw Zeke emerge from the control house and run along the topmost beam of the gantry. A hundred feet in the air, the beam maybe six inches wide. Jesus. Something loose— his jacket?—flapped from one hand.

"Silas!" Dave, again. Gunfire came in even stronger.

An electrical cable extended from the crane's end to the shed roof, clamped to insulating posts. Zeke didn't stop, just threw his jacket around the cable, grabbed on with both hands and jumped.

We all stopped shooting simultaneously, equally stunned by the move. For a full second nothing but silence, as Zeke slid down the cable like it was some Delta Force zipline.

Then everyone lit up again.

CHAPTER TWENTY-TWO

Zeke crashed onto the roof, rolled off and fell to the ground just behind me. I ducked back, gunfire following.

He was hurt. Blood on his head and all over his shirt, arms held across his chest in that way meaning *pain*. He'd lost one pistol, but the other was holstered and the shotgun was jammed barrel-first into his belt.

"Shit," he muttered hoarsely. "Just when I hit the roof."

No time for triage. "Can you move?"

"Have to."

I lifted him up. He groaned, teeth clenched.

"Dave?" I shouted. "Ready to go?"

As an answer, I heard the Charger's engine roar to life.

But the chain-link fence was still between us and him.

I grabbed the shotgun from Zeke, held him up with one arm and aimed with the other.

BLAM!

The first round was fléchettes and didn't do anything to the fence. We hobbled forward, still protected from the ambushers by the bulk of the shed, until I could hold the barrel a foot from the fence post.

I fired, and the slug round cut the pole off at its base.

"Awesome." The fence sagged. We staggered six feet to the next pole, I fired twice, and it went down too.

One more and then the chain-link drooped enough that I could haul Zeke right over, dragging him like we were trampling a field tent.

The Charger appeared in a spray of gravel, wheels skidding. Dave jumped out and helped me pull Zeke into the rear seat. He slammed the door and slid into his harness while I got into the back. We took off so fast my door was still open, but it banged shut as the car swerved back onto the service road.

"Hospital!"

"Already called," Dave said. I raised up enough to look out. Puffs and smoke, nothing else—they were probably still firing, but Dave got us out of there in about four seconds.

"They can't follow," I said. "Not through the gate, with the Aveo in the way."

We crossed the bridge and hit the blacktop, bouncing hard across the edge of paving. Zeke winced and moaned. He was almost unconscious.

"Sorry." Dave shifted, the car flying but more smoothly now on the blacktop.

"How'd you end up down here?" I was working on Zeke, but talking to Dave.

"I was watching through the binocs—saw gun barrels in the windows. Had to warn you."

"I told you to stay out."

"Well, fuck that."

"Yeah." I glanced at the back of his head. "Thanks."

Chest wound. Bad. Air bubbled in and out. I ripped off my jacket, folded it with the nylon shell on the outside and pressed the pad hard onto the torn bloody mess.

"Ambulance'll meet us at Route 509," Dave said.

"How far?"

"Five miles. Maybe . . . three minutes."

It was an empty crossroads, two state routes meeting in the woods, a yellow blinker hung in the middle. One verge was wider, with some gravel—just a place for cars to pull over for a moment, maybe turn around. Dave brought us in nice and gentle, despite the long deceleration, stopping at the edge of the ditch.

"They're coming from Leechburg." He pointed down the left road. "Dispatch probably has police and fire from Freeport, too, but the medics'll be here first."

"Help me get him out."

"What?"

"We'll wait here. You take off."

The roads were deserted. A light breeze carried the smell of brush and asphalt.

"I can't just *leave* you like this."

Zeke was as stable as he'd get for the next few minutes, so long as I kept the lung puncture closed and an eye on his circulation. "We'll be fine. If it makes you feel better, drive a half mile down and pull off. If you don't see the ambulance go by real soon, come back and you can drive us in." I watched Zeke's breathing—short and labored. "No offense, but he'll be a lot better off on a paramedic's gurney than your backseat."

"All right." It bothered Dave, but he could see the point.

"Take the weapons." I pulled the Sig out one-handed, keeping my other on the improvised chest pad, and passed it over. Then the extra magazines. The MP5 was in the car.

"What about you?"

"What's . . . if I walk straight through there, where do I come out?" I pointed into the forest, directly away from the road.

"There?" He frowned. "Nowhere. The Allegheny, eventually. Farms? I don't know."

"Okay, I'll wing it—hike until I find another road, then I'll call."

"Yeah, okay, shit." He didn't like it. "You need another car already, you know."

The Charger vanished around the bend about half a minute before the ambulance appeared. It was an advanced life support vehicle, one paramedic inside and another right behind in his own vehicle, a private Blazer with a rooftop blue light flashing. One paid, one volunteer—typical for a small-town department.

"What the *fuck*," said the volunteer, staring at Zeke's bloody torso, but the professional got to work.

"Two rounds through the chest," I said.

"I see that." He lifted my ruined jacket to see the wound. "Hunting accident?"

"Sort of."

He glanced up. "Anything you need to tell me?"

"Keep him alive. Everything else is for the cops."

"Right."

They were putting Zeke on a backboard, getting ready to strap him to the gurney, when the law finally showed up—county police, one officer in a dusty cruiser.

He nodded at me, then looked at the paramedic. "How's he doing?"

"Stable. Shooting incident."

"Is he conscious?"

"No."

They loaded him up. Zeke looked small and helpless—oxygen mask, two IV lines, bloody white gauze crisscrossed over his chest. "We're taking him to St. Joe's if that's okay." A half question, directed to me.

"He's not local. That the best choice for trauma?"

"Around here?" The medic shrugged. "Without driving all the way into Pittsburgh, yeah. Saturday nights are busier than you'd think."

His volunteer partner closed the door on him and Zeke, then jogged around to the driver's door. "Have somebody drive my truck back to the station," he hollered at the police officer. "The keys are on the seat." And then they were gone.

I should have left too, right then, but I was staring at the bloody dust where Zeke had been lying on the ground. The adrenaline of the last thirty minutes had ebbed away. I felt leaden and inert.

The policeman stepped up. "So what happened?"

I noticed his holster was unsnapped. Both hands were free, and he stood ten feet away, sideways to me, feet angled, knees slightly bent.

He knew what he was doing. He was, reasonably enough, suspicious of me. I had no weapons, no energy and no desire to start shooting it out with the law anyway.

What the hell. This had gone too far. Multiple running firefights were out of my league. Not to mention seriously out of proportion to a little accounting fraud—even if Russian gangsters *were* involved. I was over my head, and this seemed like a good time to turn it over to the authorities.

"I think it was a meth gang," I said.

"That right?"

"Yes. So here's—"

That's when I noticed a white panel van approaching, the same way Dave and I had come.

It had a roof rack, and indistinct lettering on the side—and it was moving about ninety miles an hour.

"Shit!" Why had I assumed they wouldn't try to finish the job?

The officer turned, frowning, and drew his service weapon—some sort of 9mm—pointing at the ground but looking at the oncoming truck.

"Who's that?"

I was already running, diving into the ditch at the edge of the turnout.

BRRR-R-R-R-R-A-A-A-PPP!

Automatic gunfire stuttered across the ground, somehow missing both of us. The van braked hard, screaming through a long skid that took it sideways into the intersection. A barrel pointed out one window, muzzle flashing, but the vehicle's motion made aiming impossible.

Fortunately.

I scrabbled at the ground, seeking a rock, a stick, *anything*. Before the van stopped fully the side doors swung open. Two men leaped out, assault rifles in hand.

And fell immediately.

Two gunshots. My brain was a little behind. I looked over and saw the officer, standing in an old Chapman stance, two hands holding his pistol. He'd dropped both assailants, one shot each, like they were no more threatening than paper targets at the range.

Clint Eastwood was in town, apparently.

"Hands on the dashboard!" he shouted at the truck, fully in control. "Anyone else in back, stay there!"

For a long moment, no one stirred.

The van's engine was running, a low grumble and exhaust visible from the pipe. I could see a figure at the wheel, through glare on the windshield—too blurry to recognize, but surely he was one of the Russians.

"*Ubey etih vybliadkov!*" Faint, from inside the truck, but audible.

Clint glanced my way. "Whose side are you on?"

Just my own, but that seemed like the wrong answer. "Yours."

"Stay dow—"

Then everyone exploded into motion.

The policeman broke for his car. The driver gunned the van forward. One of his pals in the back leaned out the open door holding a Vikhr, and fired a long, wild blast.

I tried to burrow into the dirt, arms over my head. Bullets nicked the ground and cracked overhead. More shots—at least two weapons, maybe three. Someone screamed, abruptly cut off.

WHOO-O-O-M-M-P!

The explosion sent a fireball over me, hot enough to scorch for an instant. A millisecond later shrapnel rained down. Something struck my back, burning through my shirt. I jerked in pain, grabbing at it, and came up with a long, jagged piece of metal.

I risked a look.

The officer was down, bloody in the gravel. His car burned, huge gouts of black smoke pouring out of its blasted frame. Another Russian lay slumped from the truck's passenger door, and as I watched the driver pulled him inside.

Was he going to leave?

No. Christ.

The driver swung down from his own door—the seven-foot motherfucker, in body armor, carrying a shotgun in one hand and a pistol in the other. He stood, head moving side to side, surveying the scene. Smoke billowed from the burning car, thick and acrid. A gust of wind pushed it down and across the turnout, obscuring him for a moment.

I rolled to a crouch and sprinted toward the flames.

No other voices. I had to assume the driver was the last Russian standing—otherwise they'd be yelling at each other, coordinating. No one can survive this kind of action—watch their teammates killed, blow shit up—without shouting.

Not exactly even odds, though.

BLA-A-A-M!

The shotgun blast peppered the police car, which I'd now taken shelter behind—I figured the smoke and flame would make me harder to see. I could barely make him out, a dark figure shimmering indistinctly through the inferno. He raised the shotgun and fired again.

And then he drove away.

I mean, he picked up his two *tovarishi,* slung them into the truck, slammed the doors and *then* drove away.

He was the worst kind of enemy. Not just armed, armored and shooting to kill . . . but sensible.

He didn't know what kind of weapons I might have. He'd lost three fourths of his team. Other police and fire volunteers were probably already on their way, responding to the first call, and the scene could quickly get crowded and messy. He wanted me dead, clearly, but he was willing to make smart choices along the way.

The truck disappeared. I stood up and ran around the burning vehicle, but it was too late—the officer had died immediately, his head shattered by the bullets.

So much for going to the authorities.

Plan B. Or C or D, maybe. I looked at Clint's pistol, still in his hand, but that was too much risk—steal a dead hero's gun, and you're as good as dead yourself when his fellow officers catch up.

Instead I brushed myself off, looked around, didn't see any obvious clues to pick up and headed for the volunteer's Blazer.

Keys on the seat, just like he'd said.

CHAPTER TWENTY-THREE

RT @lcPDept: Squatters in violent gun battle at old steel mill—2 dead, 5 wounded http://bit.ly/z8gtCW #leechburg #crime

@shootmaven: serious shit they blew up 2 cars, police say 5000 bullets found

RT @ctymoose: #scanner 123.65 hz—heard #fire response, recording online here http://bit.ly/z8gtCW

@blt33: musta been drugs—fuckin gangstAZ send em all back 2 NYC

@anarchyn0w: yr asshol @blt33 all that crack comin from Pitt u know it

@blt33: @anarchyn0w you lv in NY dont you? no crack here its just getto gangz

@anarchyn0w: @blt33 Id rather lv here thn fuck sheep like u do u crackhd

@SidewalkRepairCheap: Cracks in your driveway or sidewalk? We're the EXPERTS!!! http://bit.ly/H7qxBl

"Anything about me?"

"No."

"Really?" Dave sounded disappointed.

"Don't worry—someone figures out you were involved, first you'll hear will be when SWAT comes through the door with a battering ram."

"Huh."

We were in the Charger, headed back to Clabbton on small side roads. I'd driven the volunteer's Blazer to Leechburg, wiped it clean and walked away. Dave picked me up fifteen minutes later—he really had been just down the road, waiting for my call.

"How's Zeke doing?"

"Alive." I'd called, but of course they wouldn't say anything. Total news lockdown. All we had was some skimpy journalism and a thousand online rumors. "I assume."

"Soon as he wakes up, they'll start asking questions."

"He won't say anything."

"Nothing?" Dave sounded skeptical.

"Zeke's been there before. Even if they prove he was at the mill, so what? The bad guys aren't going to the police, and they'll have removed any bodies. The prosecutor might get frustrated and file a few nuisance misdemeanors—discharge of unlicensed firearms, that sort of thing—but he'll be fine."

"Anyway," Dave said. "I mean, I wish Zeke hadn't got shot, but you know . . ."

"What?"

"Really." He slowed, went through a turn, shifted back up. "When I wrote that letter I thought you might—well, I dunno what I thought. But this is a goddamn *adventure*." He grinned.

Gunfights. Explosions. Men dead and hospitalized. Those kill-joys always criticizing modern entertainment for brutalizing the culture—they might have a point.

"I don't like to mention it," I said. "But I need another vehicle."

"What is this, number four?" Dave sat on the passenger side for a change, while I tried to slide the bench seat farther back. No luck, it was jammed in place.

"Five, if you count borrowing the Blazer."

"You're hard on cars, man."

"I'm a very safe driver."

He laughed. "Me too."

It was an old Chevrolet single-cab pickup with a cracked wind-shield, no tailgate and a pronounced list to the right side. Reverse didn't seem to engage, and smoke coughed from the pipe whenever I accelerated. None of the interior lights worked.

"This can't be legal," I said. "And I don't see an inspection sticker."

"Naw, you're good."

"Nice of him to leave the temporary plate on."

"Yeah." Dave grinned. "I think he done forgot, actually."

I didn't have enough money to buy another used car. But Dave, ever resourceful, knew a teacher who ran the high school's voca-tional auto repair course. They always had a couple of vehicles to work on, given to the school by other charities.

Someone donates a clunker to Goodwill to get the tax deduction. Goodwill, not in the used-car business, simply sells it on. Sometimes the car is so pitiful that even bottom-feeding chop shops won't take it, so Goodwill trailers it to the school for students to practice on.

Some money changed hands, but not much. I had a new ride, the teacher could buy a few tools the next time the Snap-on truck stopped by, and it was all subsidized by the federal tax code. Win-win.

"I know he's your friend and all," I said. "But it's a school day, and it sure smelled like weed when he came out of the break room."

"Probably."

"Uh-huh." I slowed for a traffic light, pedal all the way to the floor before the brakes grudgingly took hold. "I hope the kids *learned* something, putting this bucket of bolts back together."

I wasn't convinced the truck wouldn't fall apart at about fifty miles an hour, but Dave said he was satisfied, so I drove back to the high school. I pulled up alongside the playing field, where we'd left the Charger. The truck's engine promptly died.

"I need to end this," I said.

"We can figure something out, though, right?"

I wasn't sure what he meant by that, but I didn't feel like more get-rich-quick schemes. "How'd it go with the chief last night?"

"Gator? Aw, he was fine. Don't worry, I ain't mixing you into it. Far as he knows, complete strangers drove up to my garage and shot it up for no reason in the world. Since nobody got hurt, for Gator it's the insurance company's problem."

The mill near Leechburg was out of local jurisdiction. The staties might put two and two together, but they were stretched as thin as anyone else nowadays. I figured the CSI van was the last official contact they'd have with Barktree.

Dave might actually be in the clear.

If I could finish off the Russians, that is. And Harmony, whatever *she* wanted.

"Wait a second," he said, getting out. The door took a couple of tries to latch shut.

"What?"

He walked to the Charger, opened the truck and pulled out the plastic bucket that had carried his tools to the furnace demolition.

I turned the ignition while I was waiting.

Rrr-rrr-rrr-rrr-click.

Rrr-rrr-rrr-rrr-click.

"You should hold on to this," Dave said. "Brendt didn't want it in his car no more."

"Is the dynamite still in there?"

"Yeah." He put the bucket in the truck bed. "Don't give it so much gas, you're gonna flood it."

"I don't want the dynamite either!"

"Well, we can't just leave it on the street for some kids to find."

A reasonable point. "Yes, but—"

"Look, if anyone's gonna need some unstable high explosive, it's you, right? Keep it out of the hands of careless civilians."

The engine finally turned over and caught, sputtering.

"This junker's too unreliable," I said.

"White smoke's better than black."

"It could break down and crash any minute, and then what? You're the one with the tuned automobile and the high-end driving skills."

We argued another minute before Dave grudgingly returned the bucket to the Charger.

"If there's a bridge over a nice deep river, we can drop it in," I said.

"Okay, I guess." He closed the trunk. "I'll catch you later."

"Where will you be?"

He grinned. "Elsie said her car was all banged up, needs some repair. I thought I'd see what I can do for her."

I shook my head. "She's Brendt's girl."

The grin disappeared.

"Now, Silas, that ain't your business."

"You ought to think it through."

"*You* got no right telling me what to do."

"Maybe not, but——"

"Don't be acting like my fucking case officer."

Dave turned away and got in the Charger. The engine roared to life with more gas than seemed necessary.

I watched him go, the wheels spinning just enough to throw sand in my direction.

Being someone's sibling was harder than it looked.

———

Zeke had a double room to himself, which was kind of nice except maybe he still should have been in the ICU. I looked at him through the room's window to the hallway before I entered—the blinds were slanted open. Bandages across his chest, tubes and wires, the bed at a slight angle. The overhead fluorescents were off, illumination coming from cove lights along the wall.

His eyes were open and alert when I came in. Fortunately, the TV was silent.

"You look great," I said.

"Fuck off." His voice was attenuated and whispery, hard to hear. I guess you can't put much air through with half your chest caved in.

"Okay, you look like shit." I gripped one of his hands for a moment. "I'm sorry, Zeke."

"Not your fault."

He was hooked up to oxygen from a freestanding green tank on the floor. Old-fashioned—most hospitals have stopcocks right in the wall, connected to a central supply. No mask, just a nasal cannula, so he could speak okay.

I sat in the bedside vinyl chair. A meal appeared untouched on the little swing table, now pushed toward the monitor rack.

"There's no recording," he whispered.

"What?"

"I've been staring at the walls for four hours. Can't see any microphone, or any obvious place to hide one."

"How come everyone says I'm so paranoid, but they never talk about you?"

He ghosted a smile. "They didn't handcuff me to the bedrail, either."

"I noticed that. No restrictions on visitors, for that matter." I'd left my weapons in the truck, expecting a police guard or at least private security, but the only barrier to entry was a harried triage nurse who just pointed me at the elevator.

"They let *you* in."

At least his spirits were up. "I would have called, but I figured they wouldn't let you have a cellphone in here."

"Nah." Zeke pushed down the sheet by his side, revealing his phone. "They don't care. I'm keeping it for when I call a lawyer."

"You haven't yet?"

"No need."

I wasn't sure about that. "What do the police say?"

"They're having trouble with the hunting-accident story."

"I can see their point. Whatever's in season now, I don't think mortars and automatic weapons are on the permit."

He started to shrug, then grimaced and went motionless for a long moment. When he started breathing again it was slow and labored.

"You shouldn't be here," he said finally, his voice even hoarser.

"Don't be ridic—"

"No." Pause to breathe. "Serious."

"What?"

"Been thinking, drugs make it hard. How'd they know where you were?"

"At the mill? Brinker *called* me, remember?"

"No." Some color in his cheeks now. "At your brother's garage. You lost the tail the night before. You didn't do anything to surface, right? Cash, no bars, all that?"

"Yes."

"So how'd they know you were at the shop the next morning?"

I opened my mouth, then closed it.

"That's a good question."

"Phone? GPS?"

"The phone's not traceable. The GPS I turned off. No reason to let Alamo follow me around."

A cart rattled down the hallway outside. Muffled alert tones beeped steadily from the nurse's station. We could hear voices as people walked past, but the words were indistinct.

"You want that juice?" I took the pint serving of OJ from the dinner tray and stripped off the foil lid. "Been a while since I ate."

Zeke shook his head slightly on the pillow. "Dumb."

"What?"

"A rental? And they followed you in it?"

"I told you, I lost them. Checked about three times, too."

"But they got the license plate. Easy."

Oh. "Um, maybe."

"Then they bribed someone at Alamo. GPS doesn't matter. The big fleet companies, they've installed tracking in all their cars now. Saw it in the news."

"Shit." The juice stopped halfway to my mouth.

"Not LoJack but like that. Satellite transponders. Whatever. They always know where you are."

"Okay, I fucked up." My fault Dave's life got blown to hell after all. "But at least they wrecked that car when they attacked us. They haven't been able to follow me since then."

"Don't have to." Zeke's eyes were bright, and he lifted his head a little to stare at me. "Don't you get it? They know where *I* am."

I realized the hallway had gone silent. I turned, starting to rise, looking at the door.

It crashed open, kicked to the wall and bounced back.

"*Umri, huesos!*"

The seven-foot Russian came in hard, both hands inside his leather jacket.

Drawing weapons now because he had to keep them hidden in the corridor.

I flung the orange juice into his face, let the cup go, and dove forward. My head and left elbow struck his legs. He fell back, banging the door, and we collapsed onto the floor.

He brought one hand out empty and punched at my head. I ducked enough to take it on the skull, then jabbed him as hard as I could in the privates. A grunt, but now he had a gun in the other hand, bringing it around.

BLAAM!

The shot went into the monitor rack, smashing it against the wall. Sparks and pops. Zeke groaned and alarm beeps went off everywhere.

Another shot. Glass shattered into the hallway. Screaming.

I had to control his gun hand.

He brought his knee up. Weak leverage but it still almost broke ribs. I grunted, punched again and used the motion to rise up a bit. He twisted, swung his other arm—

—and I trapped it with my own, bringing my forearm under and locking his elbow. The pistol fired again, deafeningly loud. With a surge of terror and desperation I twisted, jamming his arm and trying to break the elbow.

No go, but it must have hurt. He dropped the gun. It clattered to the floor, knocked sideways by our struggles, and went skidding under Zeke's bed.

He clouted me on the head and I rolled away. A split second to make a decision—fight or run?

As if. I pushed myself through the doorway. He must have gotten his other gun out because another shot smashed the wall above me, then two more. I kept rolling, scrabbling on the tile to get farther from the door.

A real alarm went off, fire maybe, a painfully loud blare synchronized with on-off red lights along the corridor. Nurses in scrubs and doctors in white jackets ran this way and that, mostly away from us. A patient down the hall peeked out a doorway, leaning on a walker.

"*Gondon!*" he roared, coming through the doorway. Good—to the extent I had any strategy, it was to draw him away from Zeke. I sprinted down the corridor, knocking a gurney into his path, dumping a rack of linens.

BANG! BANG!

Shots followed me. He wasn't aiming high, either—another patient's window shattered on one side, and the other bullet cracked so close to my head I could hear it pass. I grabbed the corner of the nurses' station, almost tearing my arm off but using the pivot to fling myself around and into another corridor.

"Get down! Get down!" I yelled as I went, not that it did any good. Some people are drawn to explosions, some freeze in terror and only a few have the sense to cower. I ran square into a doctor coming through a door, knocked her flat and kept going.

Where was the fucking *exit?* I needed a fire door, an exterior window, a stairwell—anything. But there were just more blue cement walls and equipment carts and empty wheelchairs.

The fire alarm made it hard to hear anything, or even to think.

I turned another corner. Crashing behind me, and another shot.

I didn't have my own pistol. The Russian was stronger, far better armed and either insane or fearless or both. *"Fu-u-u-u-u-u-ck!"* I let out a long wail of frustration and rage as I ran.

And then I saw my chance.

A steel cart against the wall held five oxygen tanks, just like the one in Zeke's room. Green, three feet long, neatly racked on low, horizontal shelves.

No time to think it through. I grabbed the cart, my momentum spinning it around and into the center of the hallway as I slammed to a halt. I grabbed one tank—it was heavy, at least fifteen pounds—and pulled it out.

Empty, full? Probably there was a dial or something, but I couldn't waste time checking. I hoped for full and raised the tank above my head.

The Russian turned the corner after me, thirty feet down the corridor. The rack was dead center in the hallway, the blunt bottoms of the tanks pointed directly at him.

He fired and I swung the tank down simultaneously. The bullet missed.

My tank struck the stopcock of the first bottle, knocking the valve clean off.

SS-S-S-SH-O-O-O-SHHH!

The tank exploded out like a rocket, propelled by two thousand PSI of pure, compressed oxygen. It shot down the corridor too fast to see and slammed into the opposite end. The wall disintegrated, blueboard and aluminum framing blown to pieces by the impact.

"Motherfucker!"

Missed, though.

I swung again and struck the second bottle, which launched with equal flare. This time the flight path was crooked, too high. It went into the ceiling tiles, tearing a vast gash before banging into something and crashing to the floor. Shredded acoustic insulation and wires and a fat pipe fell from the ceiling, followed a moment later by a gush of water.

Oops.

The Russian crouched behind the far corner, leaning out to fire twice. Both shots went wide, so he wasn't aiming very well. Between us the spray of water increased, cascading down.

Then I saw sparks. Some of those wires might have been 220 or even 440 volts. A hospital wasn't a factory, but it had plenty of big equipment, like full-body scanners.

The sparks were closer to the Russian than me, on the far side of the waterfall. He had to be worried about that, but he showed no sign of retreat.

Hopefully all the patients had fled. I lifted my tank once more.

The next bottle struck the corner right above the Russian's

head—wish I could take credit, but it was dumb luck. He ducked out of sight. One tank remained on the cart.

What the hell. I smashed the last stopcock.

WH-O-O-O-M-M-PPP!

A fireball filled the entire end of the corridor, blasting in all directions. I heard a yell under the noise—the Russian, with luck. The explosion rolled forward and even pushed through the cataract coming from the ceiling, but the water diminished its force and I felt only a brief flash of heat as the compression wave blew past.

Pure oxygen + electrical sparks. There's a reason those tanks had DANGER and NO SMOKING stenciled in big bright letters.

Debris continued to fall along the corridor, but I didn't see any other motion.

Time to go.

CHAPTER TWENTY-FOUR

O utside was confusion and crying and sirens and chaos. Emergency vehicles were just arriving, screaming up with lights and sirens. Not just regular police and fire but the volunteers, too—I thought I recognized the Blazer I'd borrowed, and there were others. I had no trouble slipping through the crowd.

I had to assume the Russian was alive. My improvised rockets had done some damage, but he seemed like the kind of *spetsnaz* ironman who'd shrug it off and come walking out through the flames, guns in both hands.

The hospital had two parking lots and a third area in front of the emergency entrance for ambulances and drop-offs. Lots of exits—and there was no reason to think the Russian had parked in any of them. I hadn't; my rattleback pickup was by the side of the road, on a turnaround opposite a T-junction.

But there was only one *main* road. St. Joseph's Hospital was in a rural county, a small town around it, and when the Russian made his departure, he really had only two choices of direction.

If it was me, I'd head west, back toward Pittsburgh. That's where his colleagues were, that's where all this started, that's probably where he was more comfortable. I'd pointed my truck in that direction on the same reasoning.

So I slipped into the cab, using the passenger door and thankful for the broken dome light, and sat to wait.

Plenty of traffic continued toward the hospital. Not so much in the other direction. Two news vans appeared, going about ninety miles an hour, and I thought I heard a helicopter, too. Some local TV anchor just got the résumé opportunity of his or her career.

A few minutes went by. I checked my phone—still powered, no messages. On the off chance, I dialed Zeke's number.

"What?"

Faint and weak, but it was him.

"Hey," I said. "You okay?"

A raspy noise came over the wire, which I realized was Zeke laughing. "Shit, that hurts. What the fuck did you do in here?"

"Self-defense. You saw the guy come in, right? I had to drop half the building on him to make him stop."

"Guess I appreciate it."

"Where are you?"

"Cafeteria. They moved out the chairs and shoved us all in. About twenty-five patients in here, beds all every which way."

He *really* didn't sound good now. "I hope this didn't set you back too far."

"Just glad to be alive."

"Yeah." I watched a pair of motorcycle officers go by, sirens loud and lights flashing fore and aft. "Me too."

"You waiting for him?"

Shot up, half dead and full of painkillers, Zeke was still sharper than anyone. "A quarter mile away. Kind of a long shot."

"Luck."

"You sure you're safe?"

"Way too many people around. Have to knock past ten crash carts to get close. Don't worry—he's gone."

I thought so, too. Coming into the hospital in the first place was an aggressive move, but assuming Zeke was right, the Russian had been on surveillance outside, waiting for me. When I walked up, he must have worried he might not see me on the way out—a person on foot would have far more options on leaving than a driver. So he'd risked a quick entry.

But same as after he'd shot the lawman near the mill, he was too careful to stick around once things went pear-shaped. Far, far too many people were involved at the hospital now, including probably every law enforcement official in a fifty-mile radius. He had to be on his way out.

And son of a *bitch*, there he was.

"Got to go," I said and hung up.

How many white contractor's vans could there be in Allegheny County? I saw it coming down the road, waited just long enough to confirm and ducked below the window level. It passed without slowing, ten feet away, the sound of its wheels and engine loud. A few seconds later I sat up and saw the taillights following the curve of the road ahead.

I started the truck—first try, amazingly, maybe it was getting used to me—left the headlights off and pulled onto the road.

And lost him in about one minute.

He wasn't even trying. My truck was just too slow. The road away from the hospital entered the hills, made some turns, bumped over a decaying concrete bridge. By the time I reached a more open space, dashed line again and some clear vision, the taillights were gone.

I stopped.

With the window rolled down, cooling night air drifted through the cab. A small mobile home park sat off the road ahead, maybe five older trailers in a flat, mowed field. Three were occupied—the usual blue glow—and one still had Christmas decorations up, four months late. Icicle lights dangled from its roof edge.

I was mad as hell at the Russian, by the absurd madhouse at the hospital, by the lousy vehicle I'd been reduced to. I wanted to get out of this stupid backward countryside and go home. How had such a simple job gone so far off the rails?

Not to mention I was hungry. I checked my pockets, hoping for an overlooked granola bar. No luck.

But I did find Nabors's phone. I'd forgotten all about it, ever since taking it from him after our little interview.

Hmm.

A smartphone of some kind. I turned it on, and didn't recognize the icon set—Christ, was he using Windows Mobile? My estimation of Nabors, already scraping the bottom of the mine shaft, dropped further.

I poked around, trying to find recent calls and messages. Nothing interesting. He didn't text, he didn't seem to use the browser, and a skim through the contact list seemed to be all business numbers.

There might be more useful data lurking in the cache. I didn't feel like excavating it now. But just before turning it off again—he might have reported it stolen, and for all I knew wireless triangulation was flashing my location—I paused.

Then I dialed 911.

"Hey, police?" I pitched my voice high, put in some tremolo. "Some crazy driver just about drove me off the road! You got to stop this guy, he's gonna cause a huge accident."

"Your name and location, sir?"

"I'm on Tuppers Road right outside town. Minding the speed limit, right about thirty-five—and suddenly this van is in my rearview, flashing his high beams, tailgating. Then he actually *bumps* me! Jams his bumper right into mine! About drove me straight off the road. And he's honking his horn the whole time."

"Any injuries?"

"No, no, thank goodness, I kind of skidded and turned all the way totally around, but still on the road somehow. He roared past without even stopping!"

"What's your name, sir?"

"It was a white panel van," I said. "Had ladders or something on the roof. I got a good look."

"Is this your phone number?" She read off ten digits, presumably Nabors's. Even if he'd blocked Caller ID, E911 services have automatic overrides.

"I don't want any trouble. Just catch that jerk. He's probably drunk, and he's headed for Leechburg. The way he's driving, you'll have all sorts of reasons to pull him over."

I hung up and powered down the phone.

Now I felt a *little* better.

I slept in the truck that night.

Cash was running low, I didn't feel like driving all the way back to Pittsburgh, and I'd started to worry about what other methods the Russians could have for tracking me down. That I'd missed the rental-fleet LoJack was bad enough. What else might I have overlooked?

I used to be able to sleep wrapped in a poncho on snow-dusted hard rock with nothing but cold MREs and eighty pounds of kit for company. Maybe I'd gone a little soft since those happy days, but one night of car camping was hardly roughing it.

Especially after I stopped at a Walmart for supplies. The superstore was unexpected, vast and windowless and brightly lit, the parking lot half filled even this late at night. I guess we were near I-76. Even so it had the same feel as one of the U.S. military's prefab bases, a fully functioning community airlifted into the wilderness. At the edge of the lot three RVs were parked for the night, awnings unrolled and lawn chairs out, folks drinking beer and eating from a huge box of pretzels they'd probably bought inside.

A camo sleeping bag, a change of socks and shirt and a loaf of bread plus cheese cost less than one night at the Clabbton Motor Inn. Maybe those RVers knew what they were doing.

Not that I wanted to stay there. I drove on, the megastore's bright lights fading in the rearview like I was driving away from Vegas into the desert.

Eventually I found a deserted state road-maintenance facility. A plastic awning, open at both ends, covered a twenty-foot pile of sand—for the winter plows—and two hard-used dump trucks were parked next to a small brick building. The asphalt lot was otherwise empty, and though the whole thing was fenced in with chain-link and a roll of razor wire, a dirt path led around the perimeter to a pair of dumpsters.

I killed the headlights and bumped to a stop.

Silence. The sand pile stood between me and the road, blocking casual notice, and the dumpsters were empty. No bad smells, just light wind in the trees. After I'd pissed against the fence, I noticed a faint sound of running water, and followed a footpath down to a creek. I had to use my phone's display as a flashlight in the woods.

The stream descended from a fold in the hill, burbled through some rounded stones, and disappeared into a culvert under the road. I sat on a rock by the rill—not the first to do so, judging by the soda cans and cigarette butts I saw now that I was closer to the ground. Probably where the maintenance guys took their breaks.

After a while I went back to the truck for the bread and cheese. I'd hardly started when the phone rang, startlingly loud in the night's stillness.

"Silas, it's Johnny."

"Hey."

"Where are you—still in Philly?"

"*Pitts*burgh."

"Whatever. Say hi to the flyover people."

Maybe I'd been feeling a little sorry for myself, stranded in the middle of nowhere, guilt about Zeke pressing, assassins trying to kill me for unknown reasons. It was nice to hear a voice from home.

"What's up?"

"I just got served."

Huh? It was ten-thirty, late for dinner even by Johnny's careless standards. "Why?"

"Ah, just bullshit. The U.S. attorney is looking for headlines again, so every small-fry hedge fund in Manhattan is getting subpoenaed."

Oh. "For what?"

"Insider trading, to judge from the discovery request. We're pure as driven snow, of course. They're just fishing."

"Phone calls, contacts . . . ?"

"Exactly. On specific dates. I put one of my guys on it."

"You keep your own phone records?"

"What? No, not *that*. I'm having him look up the market data."

It took me a moment, then I laughed. "Why bother? Whatever happened, it's done and gone."

"Yeah, but if we can identify the trades, maybe we can guess at who was involved." Johnny's voice lowered. "And then we can . . . *hammer* them."

The USA was giving too much away. By indicating when the insider contacts might have taken place, she'd more or less told Johnny where to look for the suspicious activity. It wasn't completely obvious—serious violators had moved away from public markets to things like debt derivatives or credit default swaps, precisely to better conceal their activity—but some twenty-five-year-old could stay up all night and figure it out.

Once Johnny knew roughly what had happened, he might be able to determine the prosecutor's actual targets. And then he could go after them full bore: shorting their positions, getting into their deals on the other side, whatever opportunity might arise.

"The USA knows all that," I said.

"Sure." I could almost hear Johnny shrug. "It's probably deliberate."

"What? No. You think?" Even jaded as I'd become, this seemed over the line. "She's *using* you?"

"Everyone who got paper today, we're all doing exactly the same thing." Johnny laughed. "Whoever the prosecutors are targeting, they've just ridden into the Valley of Death."

"But why—?"

"To force a settlement, probably. At this point the guy's roadkill. Even if the suspicious trades turn out to be nothing but innocent coincidence, he's staring into the massed cannon bores of every soulless trader on the Street."

"Soulless?" Sometimes Johnny was almost poetic. "That would be, let's see, *all* of them."

"Exactly."

"It's self-fulfilling."

"A perfect trade," Johnny said. "Can't lose. So I have to be in."

"And the USA—"

"Like I said, she gets the settlement. Publicity. Another inside-trading criminal goes to jail—well, probably not jail, but probation and a revoked license. Public confidence in our free-market system is restored. It's morning in America."

I worked on a chunk of cheese, leaning against the truck's hood.

"Is that *all* she gets out of it?" I asked.

It took Johnny a half second—but that's a half second longer than usual. "Shit. I can't *believe* I didn't think of that."

"I mean, she knows the target is going down. And she knows before absolutely anyone else because she's pulling the trigger."

"Son of a bitch. She's in the game!"

"Yeah." I gave him a moment. "Or maybe not. She's an upright public official. Spotless."

"If you read the *Times*. The *Journal* seems to have a different opinion."

Well, that right there told you all you needed to know, but Johnny and I didn't need to get into another argument about the Foxification of the *Wall Street Journal*'s coverage. "Honestly, if she was in it for the money, there are many, many easier ways of doing it. Without even breaking the law, the way the revolving door's been spinning lately."

I finished the bread and wrapped the remaining cheese in the plastic bag. I wished I'd gotten some fruit, too, but nothing had looked particularly fresh in the produce aisle.

"Fuck, forgot why I called," Johnny said. "I found out something about Dagger Light."

"Dagger . . . ? Oh." The Montserrat holding company fronting for Clay Micro's potential buyer. "Clara called you."

"You haven't been keeping me in the loop," he admonished.

"Haven't had time. Pittsburgh's more exciting than you might think."

"That's okay. She brought me up to date."

"Good. So did you track down Dagger Light's real owners?"

"No. I don't think so. But there's a connection—you know how these things work, fifty-one-percent ownership by a law firm in the Caymans, which is in a joint investment with another brass plate in the Bahamas, which has nonvoting stock in an Isle of Man SIV that controls sixty percent of Dagger Light's other primary investor, and that's just getting started. The ownership diagram already looks like a plate of spaghetti."

Typical money laundering—nothing complicated in concept, just layer upon layer of interlocking relationships, impossible to pull together coherently. "Okay."

"So that Bahamas nominee company? I found the incorporation papers. There are more entities in between, but ultimately one of the beneficial owners seems to be Sweetwater Institutional Investors."

That took a moment to sink in.

"Holy batfuck." I couldn't believe it.

"That's right."

"Sweetwater owns Clayco. Sweetwater also owns Dagger Light. Wilbur Markson is selling Clay Micro to *himself.*"

"Looks that way."

"That's just . . . fucked up."

"It explains one thing." Johnny paused a moment, then came back. "Sorry, had a message there. What was I—? Clayco, right. With Markson involved on both sides, you can see why they're desperate to clean up a mucky spot on the books."

"By clean up, you mean obliterate." A few reversed journal entries wouldn't do it. The beauty of double-entry bookkeeping—properly done—is that everything is transparent, all history right out in plain sight, even after you've swept up. Clayco had taken more extreme measures—Ryan and me and maybe Harmony—because they wanted the dirt *gone*.

"They're going after this problem with an acid bath," I said.

"I've seen Sweetwater at work. They're altar boys. No, priests. No, wait, not like that—you know what I mean."

The Catholic Church isn't exactly a good metaphor for moral behavior anymore, but I followed Johnny's point. "Sweetwater can't allow even the slightest hint of impropriety to slip out."

"Of course, the whole deal feels improper. If nothing else it's self-dealing, but the way they're trying to keep it secret—something's wronger than that."

I walked away from the truck, pacing along the fence.

"Unbelievable."

"I've got to go, but one other thing to think about."

"Yeah?"

"The Russians."

Oh. Indeed, them. "How do they fit in?"

"If they're mixed up in Dagger Light somehow . . ." Johnny's voice trailed off. "I can't see it. Markson wouldn't ever get in bed with the mafiya."

"If he's pulling shit like this with Clayco, he might be doing anything. He could certainly be working with Russian money. It's nice and clean and legitimate, up in the stratosphere. Hell, they own the Nets."

"All the more reason they'll want to sweep everything under the rug."

"Yeah, you're right."

"Everything," said Johnny. "Including you."

"Good point."

"I'll keep my guy on the research."

"You know, it may not matter." I ran my hand along the chain-link, looking up at the night sky. "They're Russian. I don't know what they want but they're sure as hell motivated, judging by the number of firefights they've started out here. I don't think I care exactly *which* Russian oligarch is involved, I just want to get out."

"Firefights?"

"Put a Google alert on 'Pittsburgh' plus 'unexplained shooting.' I don't think it's over."

"I'll let you know."

"I'll say it again, Johnny—stay away. I really appreciate the research, but you don't want to be transacting *anything* with this crew."

"I got it."

We hung up. I finished my dinner, brushed my teeth at the creek and unrolled the sleeping bag in the bed of the truck.

The night was perfectly clear overhead. I looked up again, noticing how many stars there were in the sky away from the city. I could even make out the Milky Way.

It was like the sky when I was a kid.

Comforting to think about all the other worlds out there, all the distance, the impossible light-years. Some people are disquieted by the realization of earth's ultimate insignificance, our vanishingly small place in the universe. But I've always liked it.

We're so damn petty down here—maybe somewhere else they've gotten it right.

CHAPTER TWENTY-FIVE

slept in. Birdsong woke me long after the sun had come up. In the daylight I could see trash on the ground and blown into the chain-link, but the trees rustled gently in the breeze. Best night I'd had yet—there's nothing like open air for sleeping.

I spent a half hour cleaning the weapons.

Breakfast came from a catering truck, of all things. Several miles down the road I came across a fracking site: a barren acre of mud with a fifty-foot derrick in the middle, lopsided construction trailers and a dark, shiny, plastic-lined flowback pond. Stained shipping containers near the road were labeled RESIDUAL WASTE. A row of pickups sat parked along the verge. At the end, an old Chevy with a stamped-aluminum silver shell had pulled in, awning flaps up to display racks of packaged sandwiches and soda. Laborers stood around, waiting for hamburgers and chicken from a propane grill set in the rear. Others sat here and there, on barrels and the fence, eating from paper plates. The proprietor looked like he'd retired from the oil fields, a good-sized belly under his red apron and a Pirates cap on his graying head.

Several of the workers wore white hazmat outfits, hoods back and respirators dangling from their necks.

I stopped at the end of the row, my battered vehicle fitting right in. The men looked at me with some wariness as I walked up.

"Morning." I nodded in a general way.

One of the men standing nodded back. "They're not hiring here," he said. "Got a full crew."

"I'm not looking." I ordered a chicken sandwich and the proprietor pulled a frozen cutlet from a cooler. He'd rigged up a deep fryer next to the grill, which seemed awfully dangerous to be driving around with. "Not for work, not here. Just breakfast."

"Come to the right place, then."

"Really?" I glanced at the hazmat suits.

The supervisor laughed. "Bobby's food ain't the problem."

"Good to know."

They took me for one of them, like everyone else seemed to. Sleeping rough hadn't left me looking sharp—I needed a shave and some clean clothes—but that was hardly an issue. Some of the drillers were muddy to their waists, and all were stained from oil and those toxic fracturing fluids.

When I was done I thanked the caterer, started to leave, then turned back. "Hey, I just realized something. Where are the tanks?"

"Tanks?"

"For the gas. That's what you're doing, right? Bringing natural gas up? Where does it go?"

The supervisor grinned. "You really ain't a rigger, are you?"

"Like I said. Just driving past."

"We're still drilling. If we hit a good pocket, we'll install a permanent wellhead. Then they can run a pipeline, or just truck it away. There's a compressor station ten miles from here."

"Oh." All this mess and just for a test bore?

"The carpenters might have work." The supervisor seemed like a nice guy. "I heard something. Try the union hall."

"Thanks. You all have a good day."

"You too." I walked back to my truck, past the flowback pond and the sealed containers. The frack water gleamed evilly in the morning sun. It was driven in clean and fresh, deep into the earth, then came out saturated with a toxic stew of hydrocarbons, heavy metals and radioactive minerals.

Way I felt this morning, it seemed like an exact metaphor for my line of work.

As I was climbing into the cab, my phone rang.

"Yeah?"

"Silas Cade." A woman's voice.

"Who's calling?"

"I think we should talk."

I couldn't believe it. "Harmony?"

"Right."

"How did you get this number?"

"Dave gave it to me."

A cold feeling spread from my stomach. "Don't—"

"He's here with me right now, in fact."

I had to force myself to ease my grip on the phone before it broke. "Put him on."

"Is that necessary?"

"Put him on the line!"

A pause. Scratchy thumping, indistinct background noise for a moment.

"Silas?"

I breathed again. "Are you okay?"

"Sure. We're having lunch. You ought to come over."

Wait, what? "Having *lunch*?"

"At Sully's. Hey, you didn't *tell* me you had friends in town. Harmony—" his voice lowered, and the background faded, like he'd covered the lower part of the phone with his hand. "She's *hot*, man."

I'd mentioned the people looking for me, but not her name. "How did she find you?"

"I dunno. Just walked in and saw us here and introduced herself. Listen, I understand maybe you didn't want to let on, but I got to say—"

"Who's Sully?"

"Sully? Don't know if it's anyone, not anymore. Just the name of the pool hall. Right across from the monument, you know, on the Clabbton green?"

"Stay there."

"Well, okay—"

"I mean it. I'll be there soon as I can." What could I say—*she's a fucking contract assassin*? "Harmony isn't . . . what she seems."

"She seems okay to me."

Jesus Christ. I put the phone in my shirt pocket and slammed the truck door.

Rrr-rrr-rrr-rrr-click.

Rrr-rrr-rrr-rrr-click.

And then it caught, coughing to life. I tore out as fast as the old truck would go.

They were just sitting there. Talking. Eating. Laughing even, now and then.

I got to Clabbton in less than thirty minutes, drove across the railroad bridge and parked by the green. Sully's was a first-floor storefront on the other side, facing the statue, just as Dave had said. A bank on the left, a vacant space to the right. The broken sign above it read SHOES.

Dave had given me back the binoculars when we got the truck. I pulled them out and focused on the windows. They were dusty but large, and I could see some booths, a twenty-foot bar and the billiards tables farther back. Each had a light with a broad conical shade hanging directly above. Hazy smoke drifted among the tables. Racks on the walls held dozens of cues.

Dave, Harmony, Elsie and Brendt sat in the front-most booth, near the plate-glass window by the door. A couple of pitchers, some stuff on the table I couldn't make out—dishes, probably.

I could have shot Harmony from here. Double tap right through the window. Traumatic for the other three, yes. But she had made no defensive arrangements at all that I could see—both hands were in the open, one holding a mug.

Of course she *knew* all that. It was an invitation, or a trap.

Or both.

I considered the MP5, but dismissed the idea. Too many innocents around, waiting to be caught in a crossfire. They always stand up at exactly the wrong moment.

Finally I just checked the pistol, seated it back in the holster and walked over to join the party.

"Hey."

"Silas!"

The booth was an L-shape, Dave inside, Harmony at the end— back to the wall, naturally, with a clear view of both entrance and windows. Brendt and Elsie were across the table, his bulk taking up most of the space, leaving a chair for me. I stood looking down.

"Good to see you again, Harmony."

"Nice day, isn't it?"

"Can we talk for a minute?"

Plates on the table held the crust ends of sandwiches and left-over curly fries. The pitcher seemed to be soda. Harmony sat still, hands flat on the table, smiling a little.

"Pull up a chair."

"Outside." I saw Dave start to speak. "Business," I said to him. "Boring. We'll be right back."

Elsie tipped her head with a knowing smile. Brendt had a hamburger half stuffed into his face, watching the television over the bar.

Harmony shrugged a little. "Sure."

I stepped back as she slid out, keeping my jacket loose. She wore an unstructured vest over a white shirt and dark pants that narrowed at the ankle. Running shoes.

The handgun was probably in an IWB holster at her back, with a backup or a knife on the other side. No purse. She paused in a way that I had to go first or look like an idiot, so I looked like an idiot and waved her forward. In the end we walked to the door side by side. I held it open and she stepped through.

"Over there." I pointed to the Civil War cavalryman, on his plinth in the patch of green lawn across the street. As she stepped off the curb I took her arm, gentleman that I am, assisting the lady through dangerous traffic.

She twisted slightly, bent her elbow and broke the come-along in an instant.

"Oops," she said, pretending to stumble, and made to grasp my hand instead. I was a second late, and she almost had my thumb in a pain lock before I clenched my fist hard to prevent it. As we moved another step I came down sharply, trying to kick her inside foot, but she was too quick.

God knows what we looked like from the window. Halfway across the street we separated, about two feet, then came back together as I tried to hook her elbow again, to walk arm in arm like old friends. She let me, then reached across with her other hand and caught my wrist. As she started to twist I did the same with my right hand.

We were now inseparable: arms intertwined, all four hands seized together, muscles straining as we shifted for advantage—all the while trying not to be so obvious.

She was strong and almost my height, but come on, I have the Y chromosome.

"Stay calm," I said through clenched teeth. "Around back of the monument. I'm sure they're watching us."

"Your lead." Harmony's voice displayed no hint of stress.

We shuffled around to the rear of the granite base. Sully's was out of sight, but we were still in the open, visible to passing cars, pedestrians and old farts on benches in every direction. For a small town, Clabbton sure seemed to have a lot of people with time on their hands.

"You can let go," she said.

"You first."

Neither of us moved. We'd pulled close enough together it was almost an embrace. I slipped my shoulder slightly, and now my face was about six inches from hers.

We looked at each other.

"Feeling kind of stupid?" I said.

"Not exactly." That damn half smile again.

"How about . . . on three."

"Sure." Her hands were warm, tight on mine.

"One two three!" I said, fast—but she was faster, already letting go and twisting forward. A little off-balance, I went right an instant sooner than I'd planned. Harmony caught me, one arm around my torso, enough to shove me into the fall. I went with it, down to one knee and immediately back up, spinning back to face her.

I stopped cold. She held my Sig Sauer in one hand, at her waist, pointed down. It was good placement—she stood close to the monument, the pistol shielded from view but ready for use.

Long pause. A church bell started to ring—it sounded like a real carillon, a few blocks away.

The sun was overhead, casting almost no shadow.

"That's mine," I said.

"You can have it back when we're done."

"You assumed I'd be carrying, figured out where it had to be and guessed that I'd have loosed it in the holster on the way in."

"Don't tell me you didn't do the same."

"Uh, yeah, sure."

Harmony laughed. "You men are so *easy.*"

Ha-ha. "Maybe I underestimated you a little."

She moved suddenly, two hands on the pistol, ejecting the magazine and glancing inside.

"At least you didn't leave a round chambered." She tossed me the magazine. "Put that away."

I caught it automatically, like a cat that can't control its reactions. It would have been the obvious moment for her to steamroll me, but she just stood there. I rolled my eyes and put the magazine into my jacket's slash pocket.

"I'll hand you the gun but keep it discreet, okay?" She held it forward slightly. I stepped up and took it with my left hand.

That would have been the obvious moment for *me* to steamroll *her*. But I just holstered the now-empty weapon and stepped back.

"I'm off the contract," Harmony said.

"What?"

"Got the call last night. All done, thank you, the payment's wired, fuck off."

I stayed sideways to her, rear leg grounded, front leg bent just a bit, hands at my side. "Is Brinker dead?"

"Of course not." She shrugged. "Unless he swallowed some of that canal water."

"You let him go."

"Yes."

"And you're letting me go."

"The parameters changed."

"So why are you still here?"

"Ah," she said. "That's why we need to talk."

CHAPTER TWENTY-SIX

Elsie had to go to work. Brendt needed his car. Dave offered to drive Elsie to the Super Duper, but Brendt wasn't having any of that.

We stood on the sidewalk outside Sully's, watching Brendt drive off in his car, Elsie in the passenger seat. Dave sighed.

"She's breaking my heart," he said. Then he turned to Harmony and grinned. "*You* wouldn't do that to me, would you?"

"Dunno. You drive a better car?"

"A better *car*? Do you know what I *do*?"

"Barista?"

"What?"

"No, that's not right . . . nursing home attendant?"

Dave frowned. "Of course not!"

"She's kidding you," I said. "I think."

Harmony patted Dave on the shoulder. "You're just like your brother."

His frown deepened. "What does that mean?"

"It means you'd have better luck with Elsie," I said.

Dave finally went off, something about fixing someone's boat rack. Before he got in the Charger he handed me a small paper sack.

"Elsie gave me this," he said. "Take a look."

"What is it?"

"She found it in Brendt's car." He looked sideways at Harmony, not sure where she fit in.

"Like, it didn't belong there? After a more thorough search later?"

"I think she was finally cleaning out all of Brendt's trash, but yeah, that's the idea."

"Good." I put it in my jacket pocket. "I'll call you, okay?"

No need to set specific plans while Harmony was listening. Dave waved once, gunned the engine and took off.

The day had warmed considerably. I wasn't hungry—the pipe-fitter chicken had been huge and generously seasoned with mayonnaise.

"Let's go sit on a bench." The town green was emptier now. Maybe everyone had gone back to work after lunch.

"Sure."

This time we walked across the street like proper citizens. I saw a Clabbton police cruiser three blocks down, so I steered us down the slope, toward some towering spruce at the lower end of the park. Neither of us spoke while the patrol car drove past, both of us watching it in peripheral vision.

We sat on a weathered slat bench under the evergreen. A faint smell of needles drifted past. Neither of us relaxed particularly. Harmony sat straight, her back not even touching the wood, hands on her thighs. I was angled sideways at my end. Either of us could have leaped into death-dealing action in an instant.

"Funny," I said.

"What?"

"How the first part of your name is *harm*."

"Gee, I never heard that before."

Oh, well. "What are you doing here?"

"I was hired to find you," Harmony said. "Only that."

"When?"

"Last Friday night." The same day I'd done my audit at Clay Micro. "You know, they wake you up at midnight, they want it done by breakfast. I was on a plane an hour later."

"Commercial?"

She looked at me. "Are we in the same business?"

"You know all about me," I said. "I don't know anything about you."

"You knew my name by the time we, uh, met at Brinker's barn. Either I've been sold or you got some research done. Either way . . ."

I nodded. "They wanted immediate results, but you're based three time zones away. What does that tell you?"

"They weren't risking us being acquainted."

"Right."

Conflict-of-interest problems arise all the time in the business world, but those are usually handled with contractual provisions. When you're hiring mercenaries, the issues are more vexing. Even the most coldhearted ex-paras can have trouble shooting their former comrades in arms. I've turned down a few offers after I found out who might be on the other side.

Life's too short, and friends are scarce enough in our profession.

"Who are the Russians?" I asked.

"Russians?"

Uh-oh. "Aren't you on the same team? I thought they might have hired you, actually."

"Maybe. All I had was one contact, but he could have been from anywhere."

"No accent?"

"Midwest generic."

I leaned back on the bench, relaxing one notch. "How'd you find me?"

She nodded. "They'd given me a picture. Service record, maybe. I started showing it around town yesterday, and most everyone knew who it was."

My jaw dropped, but a moment later I figured it out. "Dave. They thought you were looking for *him*."

"That's right. You don't live here? No one even mentioned he had a brother, but you two really do look alike."

"Long story."

"I told them I was tracing a paternity skip."

I laughed. "Really?"

"Which they all thought was totally credible." She glinted a smile. "I kinda see why."

A trio of Harleys rumbled past, keeping it slow through town. Each had the leathers and the vest and the Afrika Korps helmet, but also the gut, plus about twenty years on me.

All the same, I wouldn't want to tangle with them.

"You haven't said why you're still in town."

Harmony nodded and eased her own posture slightly. "Talking to people like I was, they kept telling me how nice and quiet Clabbton is. Small town, peaceful. Everybody knows everybody."

"That's my impression. More or less."

"But the county—Dave's welding shop, what happened out there? Sounds like someone drove a tank through. Then something out at an abandoned steel mill, which the news is talking up like a drug war. And last night an armed gang stormed a hospital. A hospital! It's like we're in Ciudad Juarez."

"All since you came to town."

"Uh-uh." She shook her head. "You were here first."

I noticed a news van parked up by town hall. It was around the side, half hidden, which was why I'd missed it earlier. The telescoping antenna was fully raised, cables spilling out the open rear doors, but no one was visible.

"The Russians are out of control," I said. "If this is Chihuahua, then they're the Zetas. They'll be stringing bodies from that railroad bridge there soon enough."

"Exactly."

I studied her posture. "You're worried about them coming after *you*."

"Yes."

"My friend who looked you up—you have a reputation of your own." I crossed my arms. "Yeah, the guy I've seen is a monster, but I think you could take him."

"Aw, that's sweet."

"But if you're concerned, just fly home to LA. No one's going to follow you there. You're just a hired hand, same as me. No one cares."

"Clay Micro." Harmony finally sat back. I felt some tension go out of my own muscles. "This is some bullshit commercial dispute. I've done corporate work before. At the end of the day, it's just another deal."

My interest sharpened. "You know the details? Because I sure don't."

Harmony shrugged. "Someone's buying, someone's selling, who

cares? Whatever Clayco is up to, it's *not* the sort of thing they start killing civilians for all over the gameboard."

"So?"

"So if they're willing to shoot up hospitals and welding shops and horse barns just to make a point, then either they're not rational or the stakes are way higher than anyone's bothered to tell me. See?" She frowned. "Either way, I'm still in it."

"Maybe."

"And so are you."

I started to get the picture. "You want an entente here, is that it?"

"My enemy's enemy." She opened her hands. "We share some intelligence, we're both safer, we both live another day."

I thought about it. Ryan, missing. Russian killers, trying to kill me. Mysterious shell company surreptitiously buying out the American heartland, possibly with the assistance of the most famous billionaire in the country. Zeke, badly wounded.

Blond assassin, asking for help.

I hadn't exactly signed a nondisclosure agreement.

"All right," I said.

We walked to the railroad bridge. Just a pair of tourists in charming Clabbton, viewing its picturesque sights—anything not to stand around on the sidewalk, drawing attention from locals.

"First thing, more background," I said. "Some people I know have been looking into this. The paperwork's murky, but Clayco is owned by Wilbur Markson."

"The Buddha?"

Again? Whoever did Markson's image management deserved a

big bonus. "Yeah, the teddy-bear savior of capitalism. What's peculiar is, he *also* owns Clay Micro's buyer—a shell company called Dagger Light."

"Huh? That doesn't make sense."

"Markson's not looking too clean on this."

Harmony frowned slightly, thinking. A light breeze lifted the hair from her forehead. I was a little taller, and I noticed the top buttons of her shirt were undone, pushed by the vest.

"Brinker's working with the Russians," she said, glancing up. I quickly moved my eyes to safer territory. "And they seem most interested in eliminating a potential roadblock to closing the sale."

"Namely me. Yes."

"But they could be on *either* side of the deal. The contact that hired me—"

"Midwest generic." I repeated the phrase she'd used.

"Yeah. Like, maybe, Ohio."

We thought about that.

"I'm not sure where to go with this," Harmony said finally.

"Me neither."

We leaned on the bridge rail, looking down the cut. Tracks curved around a long bend, trees in spring bloom overhanging the right-of-way.

I wondered how much of what Harmony told me was true. Part of me said *everything, you suspicious cretin!* And I sure wanted to think so.

But that particular part of me was also the part keenly interested in looking down her shirt. Untrustworthy, perhaps, in some matters.

"Okay," I said, pulling out the paper sack Dave had given me. "Here's our new clue."

"What's that?"

"The Russians borrowed Brendt's car when they attacked the welding shop." I held up my other hand. "I know, I know, but I really think it was coincidence."

"Uh-huh."

"We checked the car that morning, but there was so much crap lying around Elsie didn't see anything unusual. I guess she found this later."

"Doesn't look like much of a clue," Harmony said, shaking the paper sack open to peer inside.

"The best ones never do."

"What?"

"Because if they were obvious, they'd have been noticed already."

She gave me a look. "That's like a detective koan."

"Don't touch anything in there." With a *may I?* gesture I took the bag and set it on a waist-high girder in the middle of the bridge. "Might be prints."

"Got a dusting kit?"

"No."

"Friends at the FBI lab?" Harmony was off and running. "Think the locals have a forensic team waiting to go? We're not quite CSI Pittsburgh here."

"Yeah—"

"Not to mention I don't think brown paper even picks up fingerprints."

She had a point but I was too far in to concede. "Are we going to do this right or wrong?"

"Fine." Harmony walked to the end of the bridge, studying the ground, then picked up a small stick and returned.

"Let me." She used the twig to poke around in the bag. "Okay, *Murder She Wrote*, here we go. Ready to bust the case wide open?"

She withdrew a roll of duct tape. It was clearly new, the edges of the roll still sharp and clean, but a jagged tear indicated at least some had been used.

We looked at it.

"Lots of uses for that," I said. "Friction grips. Taping magazines. Covering gun ports."

"Uh-huh."

I sighed. "Or possibly taping up boxes for the post office. I know."

"Yeah." She let the roll slide off onto the girder. "On the other hand . . ."

She abandoned the stick, reached in and came out with a scrap of white paper.

"No way. A *receipt*?"

"Maybe they're not so smart after all."

We looked at the thermal-printed strip. Duct tape, "Misc Hardwr" and "Snack Item" for a total of $18.37. Paid in cash of course, off a twenty.

And the name of the store: "Rankin Avenue Hardware."

"It can't be this easy." Even Harmony was skeptical.

"Where's Rankin Avenue?"

"Let's find out." She handed me the receipt and pulled a slick-looking smartphone from somewhere inside her vest.

"You have the internet on that thing?"

"Well, duh." Typing away already, two thumbs flashing.

I thought about my crummy, prepaid basic service. "Is that safe?"

"What?"

"Don't you worry about being tracked? The government listening in? The permanent data trail?"

Harmony stopped long enough to give me a you're-not-serious look. "Type 1 encryption tunneled through either local wifi, packet radio or, if necessary, public GSM. The gateway's proprietary and offshore—I buy time from some Ukrainian hackers. How do *you* do it?"

"Never mind. What's the number?"

"Why?"

"I won't write it down, I promise."

She thought for a moment. Cautious.

"All right." She read it off.

"Thanks."

Harmony went back to the search, which took only another fifteen seconds. Less time than I probably would have needed at home, on Verizon FIOS.

"Eight miles south of Pittsburgh." She showed me the screen, with a map displayed. "What do you think?"

We took two vehicles.

"We're partners now, aren't we?" Harmony said. We stood beside my hand-me-down pickup. "You should ride with me. I'm not sure you'll even make it to the city—that tire looks halfway flat."

"Nah, it's fine." I hoped. "But I was followed at least once already. With two cars, we can keep an eye on each other, see if either of us picks up a tail."

"You just don't trust me."

"Of course I do." Not. "But the point stands—we're safer in two cars than one."

"Think you can keep up?"

"Stay under forty and we'll be fine."

She had an Escalade around the corner—a monster. Oversize spoked wheels, blackout glass, chrome racks on the roof, rear *and* front ends. The paint was dark gray with a silver lightning bolt down each side.

"Holy shit," I said.

"Like it?"

"You damn well better stay under the speed limit—that thing will draw police attention from every jurisdiction in the state."

"After you shot my car, I decided, no more fucking around."

"Is it armored?"

"Well, no." She shook her head. "Some people I know, they lent it to me. I'd have preferred something more discreet, but this is what they had."

People? "The M1 Abrams was already checked out?"

"I had some work in Youngstown a while ago." Harmony tapped a keypad on the door and beeped the monster open. "Squared away a problem, totally unrelated, but it solved some issues for a guy here. You know, interstate commerce stuff."

"Sure." Presumably the kind of commerce that federal task forces were established to combat, but whatever.

"So he thinks he owes me a favor, and I'm collecting."

I looked over her shoulder as she climbed in. In the driver's seat her head was a good foot higher than mine. "He didn't offer anything else, did he? An antitank gun? Maybe a rocket launcher?"

"No, but the tank was full."

"Which is probably, like, five hundred dollars worth of gas." I stepped back. "Keep your phone on."

"If we have an encounter, you draw their fire, and I'll do mop-up."

"Sure."

The afternoon was still clear and bright. Driving northwest, glare quickly became a problem. I found some sunglasses on the dash—not too scratched, so I left them on.

We didn't have to coordinate the driving patterns. Harmony knew what she was doing. Once on the highway, twenty-five miles of open road, we slowed and sped up, switched off point and pace, drifted farther apart and closer together. A good team with several cars could have stayed with us, but it seemed unlikely.

Of course, they could also just wait. We weren't exactly under the radar—Harmony's absurd penis mobile drew even more attention than the Charger.

My phone rang. The incoming number didn't mean anything. At this point I was in front, so I glanced in the rearview and saw the Escalade's massive grille five cars back. No obvious problem.

"Yeah?"

It was Johnny. "I'll keep it quick. Just wanted to let you know we've got confirmation on Sweetwater."

"Wow." I still hadn't quite believed Wilbur Markson could be in. "How much?"

"They own fifty-one percent of Dagger Light, which is buying Clay Micro."

"You told me that. Who's got the forty-nine?"

"Rockwire Industries. They're a gas industry supplier—pipe, drills, vehicles. All kinds of equipment. Not exactly consistent with Markson's pledge never to invest in nonrenewable energy."

"How big?"

"Midsize. And they're local—not far from Pittsburgh. Clay Micro's practically a neighbor."

Now *that* was interesting.

"But that's not the interesting thing," Johnny continued.

The Escalade switched lanes, came up on my left, passed and dropped into place a hundred yards ahead. Traffic slowed, thickening as we neared the I-376 junction.

"What?"

"Somebody bought Rockwire. Last year. More offshore-entity bullshit, but they seem to be coming out of Cyprus."

"Russians, all right."

"Looks that way."

Ever since the chaotic nineties, Cyprus had been a favorite destination for Russian flight capital—to the point, now, of so dominating the island's economy it might be considered a fully held subsidiary of Putin's oligarchs.

"And Markson is mixed up in this."

"Controlling interest on both sides of the table. You think the Russians know?"

"Shit."

"That's sure what it feels like."

"How public is this?"

"Not very. And not provable. Any lawyer could throw up a blizzard of objections and counterarguments. But it's good enough for me."

Me too, if Johnny said so. "Why do you think he's in?"

"Markson?"

"It totally undercuts his entire image. Thirty years of financial probity and ethical investing! Why would he even *talk* to mafiya money?"

"I don't know." Johnny paused. "But I'll tell you this—I've just started building a short position on Sweetwater."

"Whoa." I thought about that. "You think Markson's in trouble?"

"It's one explanation. You said it yourself—thirty years. Most fund managers haven't been *alive* that long, let alone beating the S&P every damn year. What if the long glorious run's finally ending?"

It made sense. Markson was almost sixty and had more money

than God. At this point he was playing for his immortal reputation—and if results started to slip? He'd lose the aura.

"This could get Clara a Pulitzer," I said.

"Let's wait awhile."

Meaning he hadn't been able to lay down a big enough bet yet.

"Okay." I needed to extricate myself first anyway. "But give her the background. You can trust her not to publish until it's safe."

"I know."

"Let me know if you find out more."

"And you," said Johnny. "Like, if you happen to find yourself pointing a gun at the man himself—you absolutely must call me before you pull the trigger."

It'd be the inside trade of a lifetime. "That's not going to happen, and even if it did, remember all those subpoenas you just got?"

He made a dismissive snorting noise. "Yeah, yeah."

Some debris in the road—it looked like a tire had blown, leaving scraps of rubber and some long skid marks. I swerved to avoid the biggest, and the truck shuddered. For a moment it felt like it was going out of control, but I held the wheel and got back into the lane. Harmony drifted back during the few seconds this took, let me pass her on the left. I glanced over, saw her frowning at me, but I gestured with the phone and she nodded.

"That's great work, Johnny," I said.

CHAPTER TWENTY-SEVEN

Rankin Avenue Hardware was a shabby building on a commercial strip in one of the hollowed-out zones around Pittsburgh, the kind of neighborhood with more buildings boarded up than occupied. At five P.M. a couple of contractors' trucks were parked out front, one sagging under a bed full of old junk—probably a trash-out. Harmony drove past slowly, nodded at me through the windshield and kept going around the block.

I couldn't interpret the nod, but I didn't want to be anywhere near her rolling arrest-me-now billboard, so I pulled over across the street and waited. She walked up a minute later and I got out.

Traffic was sporadic in both directions. We could see the front of the hardware store, though its broad windows had stock piled against them inside, blocking the view.

"Before we go in," I said. "I was just talking to someone."

"Me too." She looked at me. "You first."

"Clay Micro's buyer is definitely owned half and half by Markson and the Russians. They've partnered up."

"Markson and the mafiya." She shook her head. "That's a hard sell."

276

"Johnny thinks maybe Markson's finally hit the skids, and he had to scout the only kind of money that won't talk about it. He can't go to a bank or the markets or any kind of legitimate investor—it'd be all over the internet in five minutes. But criminals know how to keep their mouths shut."

"But why would he sell to himself?"

"Well, he can't just hand over assets to the Russians. Clayco is a well-known U.S. company. Doing it this way, he can start shifting ownership without people noticing. Remember, he only has half of Dagger Light—the other owners get the rest. The Russians are probably happy to keep it sub rosa for now, too—the government is worried about investment coming in from dubious regimes abroad."

"Okay . . ." She sounded doubtful.

"And it's just Markson's bad luck that Clay Micro turned out to be one big septic tank."

"Why would the Russians be hooked up with Brinker, though?"

"I don't know. But Brinker probably met them early on—he'd have had to, even if the deal was totally nonpublic. Nabors, the Clay Micro CFO, knew about it, right? So I'd guess that Brinker and the Russian team met and sized each other up, and each realized they'd found a soul mate." I shook my head. "Brinker's just as bad as them, certainly."

A woman pushing a jogging stroller went past on the sidewalk, a toddler dozing in the seat. There was a can in the cupholder on the stroller's handle, and the green band on the aluminum looked familiar—Dave's favorite beer.

Harmony put her hand on my arm.

"It's a good thing we're on the same side," she said.

I couldn't look away from her eyes. "Uh, yeah. A real . . . good thing. Good."

"I'm not sure anyone else could have figured this out."

"No, it's—I mean, ah. Never mind." I cast around for a reciprocal compliment. "You're one hell of a shooter."

She took her hand away. "Uh-huh."

Shit, wrong thing to say. "Because, you know, I've seen a lot of gunnery, and . . ." I gave up, and the moment slipped away. Harmony sighed and crossed her arms.

I looked at the hardware store, then up the street. A long pause. I was pretty sure Dave wouldn't have screwed that up.

"How about you?" I said, finally.

"What?"

"Your call?"

"Oh." Harmony nodded, and we were back to business. "The guy who hired me. And fired me, for that matter. He seemed upset I hadn't left town yet."

"How did he know?"

"Yeah, that's a good question, isn't it?"

Watching the airport. Visiting her home in LA. Having observers here in Clabbton who'd seen her. None of the obvious answers would make her feel better.

"It's all speculation," I said. "There's no proof for any of this—Markson, the Russians, whatever."

"It's good enough for me."

She wasn't flustered, but her hair seemed looser, her hands a little more in motion. The vest hung open, obviously to keep free access to whatever cannon she had holstered in the small of her back. Another button seemed to have come undone at the top of the white shirt.

"What?" she said again.

"Huh?"

"You're staring."

"Oh." Nothing to do but brazen it out. "What kind of holster do you use?"

"Sam Andrews. You?"

"Nothing that fancy." A custom Andrews could cost three hundred dollars. "Sometimes I just push it into my belt."

She shook her head. "Not worried about shooting your willy off, huh?"

"Nice." If casual razzing was all that was on offer, I'd just have to be happy with that.

A van pulled up next to the hardware store, and the panel door slid open. Four men emerged—dirty, cement dust on their jeans and hair. They gestured brief goodbyes, and the van drove off.

All were short and dark-skinned. Their voices were inaudible from this far, but I'd have bet they were speaking Spanish. Day labor, earning their forty or fifty dollars.

Not so much difference, me and them.

"Come on," I said. "Let's go conduct an investigation."

"I remember them."

The woman behind the counter was at least fifty or sixty, gray haired and short. She started to read the receipt, but when I said "duct tape" that was all it took.

"Two of them, and didn't they have trouble? Wandering around the aisles for ten minutes and never asked for help."

The store wasn't large—twenty feet this way, thirty that, every shelf and pegboard crammed. Heavy plastic bags of grass seed were piled at the front in what passed for a seasonal display with some hand trowels and spading forks by the register. At the end of the store, directly down the aisle from the door, a rack of color chips sat on a short bench over a paint-mixing machine. A wall of screws and bolts, a narrow trash can holding rakes and shovels upside down, sacks of charcoal.

"I thought they might be thinking about robbing the place." She didn't seem fazed by the possibility. "It's happened before. Not that I ever have much cash in the drawer. Everyone uses plastic nowadays."

"You've gotten held up?" Harmony looked interested.

"Once. And my husband one time—that was after closing, at eight o'clock. They pointed a gun right through the glass in the door."

"I'm sorry to hear it."

"No one hurt, thank God. It was kids both times. Drugs, I imagine. Not much younger than you two."

A man in overalls had been finishing his purchase when we came in, taking a plastic bag and a coil of hose. The door's spring was broken, and he had to stop to push it shut behind him, its bell jingling. We seemed to be the only other customers.

"What's your interest?" the woman said.

"Um." Maybe we should have thought about that *before*hand.

"Someone broke into my car," said Harmony, picking up the slack. "Smashed the passenger window and stole all the change from the pockets. Broad daylight, can you believe it? Like no one would notice them or care."

She was subtly imitating the woman's gestures and voice—a little broader, a little louder, a little more inflection. I moved back a half step, happy to cede the limelight.

"So of course the police are like, how much did they take? And when I told them maybe ten dollars, they wouldn't take a report.

Even for the insurance on the window. Now it's true I have a glass rider, but still."

The woman nodded. "There's plenty worse crimes they need to deal with, sorry to say."

"Well, I guess that's true. All the same. So we looked around, and this paper bag was sitting on the ground right next to my car. Like maybe they dropped it."

"Duct tape," the woman said. "Some candy and a Maglite. I remember."

"We found the duct tape. I saw on TV once, someone's breaking into a house, they put tape over the window so when they break the glass, it doesn't fall and make noise. Maybe that's what they were thinking."

"Was there tape on *your* car?" She leaned forward, keen.

"No. So maybe not. But we thought we'd follow up because it was only about a mile from here."

"I can't tell you anything about them, really." She straightened up. "Two men. Large. About your size." She nodded to me. "Dark hair? I don't know. Customers come and go all day."

"But you remember these two," said Harmony.

"Because they wandered around for so long. I was starting to wonder. But then they found their duct tape and flashlight, and one picked the bag of candy, and that was that." She gestured to a small display of candy on the counter. "Paid up and left."

What they looked like didn't matter so much—we'd seen them ourselves. Or some of them. For that matter, these particular two might even be dead. There'd been substantial attrition among the Russians at the mill.

"They didn't happen to say where they were going?" asked Harmony. "Or maybe where they were from?"

"No, they did not."

A few more questions, and no more information. Harmony glanced at me, offering the floor, but I couldn't think of anything to add.

"I guess we *should* just let it go," she said. "Maybe the police are right. Insurance covers the window, like I said."

"Not worth it," the woman agreed.

But on the way out, just as I'd pushed open the door, she called over the jingling of the bell, "Oh, one thing."

We stopped and looked back. "Yes?" Harmony said.

"They weren't driving."

"Driving?"

"They didn't have a car." The woman had a thought. "Maybe that's what they were really after. You're lucky—they could have been trying to steal yours!"

"How do you know?"

"After they left, I had to close the door. The mat had gotten wedged again—you saw the problem when you came in. But when I straightened it out, I happened to look up the street, and they were walking off." She pointed. "Down that way."

"Perhaps they parked over there."

"On this block? I don't know why—there are plenty of spaces much closer to us all day. Even at the busiest, on Saturday, you wouldn't have to go far. No." She shook her head. "The more I think on it, the more I think they were on foot."

"We should go back to the police," I suggested, feeling I ought to put in at least a few words. "Maybe a different car was stolen near ours."

"Yes!" But her excitement faded. "Not that it would matter. They've got too much else to do than worry about a couple of joy-riders. And that's what they'll call it, you know—just kids."

Outside I started to cross toward the truck, a little surprised to find Harmony right beside me.

"You should go get your car," I said. "She's probably watching us. We shouldn't hang around."

"All the more reason." Harmony checked the street in both directions. "What would she think if we split up?"

"Ah, right."

"We'll go around the block. You can drop me at mine."

But once I started up and pulled into the street, we decided to drive around a little. Dusk was falling, streetlights flickering on— every other one, I noticed—leaving the streets more shadowy than lit. Budget cuts, probably.

"How far would they walk?" Harmony said, eyes scanning every building we passed. "A hundred yards? A quarter mile? Unless they have good reason, even Russians would probably drive. Like the woman said, parking is certainly not a problem."

"And in this direction. You want to check a map online?"

"There's no guarantee every hotel would be listed. Or they might be in a regular house, or maybe they're not staying here at all—just happened to be in the neighborhood." Harmony shook her head. "Makes more sense to look and see. All the internet ever does is put your imagination in a box."

"A big box." But I agreed.

The district was older, with some run-down apartments and houses on the smaller streets, businesses and commercial property on the avenue. We passed a muffler shop and I thought of Brendt. Some kids—real kids, like twelve-year-olds—were standing in front of a taqueria. Next door was a freestanding hair salon in an ancient bungalow, with a huge window hacked into the front wall and the lawn paved into a parking lot.

"Over there." Harmony pointed to the right, as we came up on the Sleep Tite Motel. A few cars in the lot, none that I recognized.

"Maybe," I said. "Who knows?"

We slowed. No Russians loitering outside, cleaning their rifles and practicing Systema. Like all of Pittsburgh, the scene felt empty of people, almost postapocalyptic, but that was probably just me missing Manhattan.

"Keep going," Harmony said.

She seemed fully engaged in the mission. Her hands were nowhere near her weapons and her head was turned away from me. I could easily have seized physical advantage, especially because I'd shifted the Sig around to the front of my belt, at most a two-second draw. But she didn't seem to care.

It felt like we'd crossed a threshold, however modest.

Around the corner we passed a used-car lot, then a blocky two-story building with a faded, barely readable sign: BLANKENSHIP AUTO BODY.

"There!" Harmony pointed again. "The panel van."

She was right.

CHAPTER TWENTY-EIGHT

A 1960s motor inn—two stories in one long building, yellow-painted concrete and dark red railings on the balcony. Each unit had an identical door to the left of one square window. It was set back thirty feet from the avenue, just enough for a row of parking spaces and some turnaround pavement.

And at one end a white contractor's van was parked nose out. Its roof rack held a battered aluminum ladder and two PVC pipes, six inches wide and maybe eight feet long, bolted down. This close I could finally read the logo on the door—EZ-FLOW PLUMBING SERVICE.

I drove past, not changing speed. Harmony stared intently.

We circled the block, and I stopped well away, up a slight rise. We could look down the street and see the motel's sign, illuminated by one dim floodlight at the edge of the lot. The van and the building itself were concealed by the body shop between us.

"It wouldn't be good enough for any kind of warrant," said Harmony, "but I'm convinced."

"I agree." I switched off the pickup's headlights but let the engine run, thumpy and erratic in neutral. "Now what?"

Harmony pulled out her pistol, a Glock 19 compact. The same one she'd pointed at me three nights earlier. "What do you *think*? We go in."

I made no move toward my own weapons. "Why?"

"Why?" She glared. "Because they tried to kill me. Because they're private assassins involved in a secret takeover of an American manufacturer. Because they shot the hell out of a rural hospital and killed at least one policeman. Because they're fucking *bad guys* and they deserve it."

O-k-a-a-y. Always nice to see some honest enthusiasm in the troops.

"I get it," I said. "Totally with you, one hundred percent. But is this the *best* way of going about it?"

"What do you mean?" Harmony held the handgun casually, below the edge of the window, pointed at her door.

I crossed my arms and leaned back against the bench seat.

"Assume it's them. Assume they're all inside, playing cards and drinking vodka, as opposed to some of them out doing errands and buying more vodka. Assume that we could walk in and surprise them and achieve tactical superiority—*without* drawing any attention, like with a full-scale firefight, because we're going to want to talk with them for a while, and having SWAT surround the place with bullhorns and snipers would be a problem." I paused. "Assume all that, for the sake of argument . . . why in the world do you think they'd tell us anything?"

Harmony set her jaw. The block was poorly lit here—we were under one of the nonworking street lamps—but a globe light over a doorway twenty feet away illuminated her profile. She gestured slightly with the Glock.

"Because we'll *make* them talk," she said.

"Uh-huh. Look, it was me?—I'd tell you everything. Stare into your eyes, see the madness, I'd give it up straight away. But these are *Russians*. They probably got counterinterrogation instruction from ex-KGB torturers. They train by fighting bare-knuckled in the snow in Siberia. They're fucking inhuman killing machines, and they're just not going to be persuaded by you." I shook my head slowly. "Or even by you and me together."

Harmony actually ground her teeth. "I'll do this myself if you're backing out."

Where was this insane determination coming from? "I have a better idea," I said. "Let's at least sit and watch for an hour or two. See if anyone comes or goes. Maybe they've got another vehicle in the lot. Maybe they've been reinforced—to start with, I don't know that we've seen all of the team. They lost three guys on Leechburg Road, but who knows how many others there are? That'd be good to ascertain, right? Before breaking in the door?"

Another minute, but I finally wore her down.

"All right. That kind of makes sense." A grudging concession but good enough. "We'll surveil."

I let out a long breath. "Good decision."

Cars had been driving past, a few every minute. I hadn't noticed any pedestrians so far, but that didn't mean none would show up. Not to mention we couldn't even see the motel.

"Where do you want to set up?" I said.

Harmony moved her arm and the Glock disappeared. I blinked. That was a nice trick.

"Not here," she said. "Not in the Escalade, either. I'm not going to piss in a coffee can with you in the car."

I had to agree with her on that point. "A vehicle post doesn't make sense anyway. Too visible." The Russians could do it with their van—probably one reason they were driving it—but endless PI procedurals to the contrary, sitting in a parked car draws all kinds of attention. "One of these buildings might make sense. Maybe the garage."

"Yes," Harmony said. "The second floor."

I was looking there too. The body shop was dark, shuttered for the night. "I don't see any light in the windows up there. Could be an apartment—"

"Doesn't have that feel."

"No."

We drove back to Harmony's SUV and returned in caravan to park near the motel. After a small amount of argument we put hers on the street, and the truck right behind the body shop. In theory, if we needed to run down and follow someone leaving, our vehicles were situated to go either way.

In reality, we'd go for Harmony's no matter what, because in the pickup, every single mile was an adventure.

Harmony had returned from the Escalade with a dark nylon bag over one shoulder. "Tools," she said when I raised an eyebrow. "Plus some feminine hygiene products."

I let that go.

"Bring your phone," she added. "I had to leave mine to charge."

"Yes sir."

The back of the building had a small iron balcony with a metal door, fifteen feet from the ground. Probably a fire escape—no stairs or ladder to make it harder for burglars.

"Up there," Harmony said.

"Yup." I got back in the truck and advanced it to a stop just beneath the balcony. The engine sounded about to die. As I switched it off, there was a loud thump in the bed, then a bang on the metal cab roof above my head. When I got out, Harmony had already pulled herself onto the balcony. In a moment she was back down.

"Medeco deadbolt and a bar keyhole below it," she said. "How good are you with locks?"

"Excellent, if I can use C-4. Got any?"

We studied the building. The body shop had a row of opaque windows, their frames bricked in. The second floor had the same tall windows, most with original glass, some protected with iron grilles, some open.

"Must have been an old factory or something," I said. "Back when they needed lots of natural light."

"Spiderman could get in easy enough."

"That's not me. Let's check the roof."

We climbed up. At the landing I knelt, let Harmony clamber to my shoulders and stood up, raising her enough that she could pull herself over the roofline parapet. She disappeared for a moment, then came back and leaned over.

"It's good. Come on up."

"Catch." I heaved up her nylon kit—the damn thing must have weighed forty pounds, but she caught it easily. "Give me a hand."

"I can't pull you up."

"I know." I stepped on the guardrail encircling the landing, which got my hand to hers. We clasped wrists in a climber's grip, and I used that for balance while I got one foot onto the top edge of the door frame. Then it was an acrobat's move: swing up, other foot scrabbling on the brick, grab the underside of the pediment left-handed in a counterpressure hold, release Harmony's wrist and fling my right arm over the parapet. Another few seconds of scrambling and I was over the top.

"Smooth." She said it deadpan.

"I'm up, and that's what counts."

We took a minute to scan the streets below, looking for anyone who might have spotted us. Nothing happened. Harmony led us to the other side, about fifty feet across the flat roof. Two skylights jutted up from the tarred gravel, the seams patched and caulked. A headhouse at the end probably topped an interior stairwell, its sheet-metal walls rusting away at the base. Harmony knelt in its shadow.

"Good view from here," she said.

Indeed. We could see the motel easily, its upper level lower than ours because of lower ceilings and a natural gradient in the topography. The panel van was still there, along with the same cars. I could hear occasional traffic on the streets around us, the faint noise of a television or video somewhere, and a brief siren, blocks away.

"We can take shifts."

"No need." I was at the headhouse door. "You have a screwdriver in that bag? Or a pry bar?"

"Sure." She unzipped an outside pocket and handed me an eight-inch flathead.

"Perfect." As is so often the case, the nuclear-silo level of security on the first door we tried was belied by a totally pathetic fastener up here. A cheap padlock hung from a galvanized hasp. It looked like someone had tried to shove their way out, more than once, deforming the hinge. I couldn't quite reach the screws, but one quick yank levered them entirely out of the rotting wood. The lock flung free, clattering onto the roof.

"In we go."

"Give me the driver back."

Inside we didn't even need a flash. Enough light from the motel's parking lot came through the wall of windows facing it to illuminate most of the interior. I stepped carefully down the wooden stairs, Harmony five feet behind, and stopped on the floor.

"Wow."

"No shit."

The entire floor was open, like the industrial loft it must once have been. Brick pillars were spaced every fifteen feet or so. One wall had a row of benches, old scarred wood, with some scraps of packing and cardboard. In the middle a wooden rail surrounded descending stairs, and crates and cans and closed buckets had been piled carelessly nearby. It looked like the auto shop used this floor for materials storage. But the rest of it was empty, vast and echoing.

"Clean it up and this would sell for seven or eight million in Soho," I said.

"Not to point out the obvious, but this isn't Soho."

I examined the supplies in the middle of the floor. Solvents, paint, cans of filler. A faint, sweetly chemical smell came from below—the miasma of toxic solutions used on damaged cars.

"It's amazing they don't all get cancer and die," I said, studying one label. "Toluene, aliphatic polyisocyanate—it's like Love Canal here."

"This is ideal." Harmony stood a few feet back from the windows—careful, always careful—studying the motel. After a minute she opened up the carrier bag and started pulling out equipment.

I checked the parking lot outside. When I looked back, Harmony had assembled a tripod, mounted a video camera and run a cable from it to a microsized laptop. She adjusted the camera using the manual viewfinder while the computer booted, then made further adjustments until the picture on the screen was just right.

"I've got the van and the last five doors of the motel in the frame," she said.

"Okay." The rig was impressive, but I wasn't sure why we needed it. "Are you hoping to get pictures of them?"

"Of course—we can run them against the databases, see if they've been flagged anywhere."

"Databases?"

"CJIS. You don't have a contact there?"

I ducked that question. "Ah, I knew Justice had a photo repository, not just fingerprints. But I didn't think it had been digitized and indexed yet."

Harmony must have seen my expression. She laughed. "I'm kidding. Next Gen ID is the usual billion-dollar clusterfuck—they won't have a photo database worth using for years."

Good to know I wasn't totally behind the curve. "So what's the point?"

"Motion sensing." She knelt to the laptop and started tapping keys, opening menus and adjusting settings. "I'll set some baseline imagery—the doors and the van. Maybe the other vehicles, too. The computer will let us know if anything changes."

"Huh." Maybe I *did* need a technical upgrade.

"That way we don't need to watch the whole time. I don't know about you, but passive surveillance drives me nuts. I can't tolerate just sitting and waiting."

"Right." I looked at the laptop's screen, which was now window-paned into several different close-ups of the motel. "What happens if, I dunno, a pigeon flies by? Or someone goes down the sidewalk?"

"That's why the images are zoomed in on specific targets." She glanced up at me. "They use this in the black-ops community now. After your time, maybe?"

Ouch. "When did you take *your* discharge?"

"Who says I was in the service?"

"You weren't?"

"Maybe."

Almost anyone with her skill set acquires it in the defense of our country. There are plenty of training courses around—wannabes can spend thousands of dollars on anything from tactical shooting to combat driving. But nothing compares with actual experience in the field. There's a reason the merc firms like Academi hire guys out of the service, not certificate holders from Joe's School of Gunnery.

If she wasn't ex-military, her background was probably even scarier. *Spookier,* so to speak.

"Want to tell me about it?" I said.

Harmony looked at me and smiled. "No."

It was about six o'clock. Surveillance boredom began to set in. I watched the last of the sunset through the western windows, against Pittsburgh's skyline. The computer beeped occasionally, always a false alarm—someone passing too close, a car driving in. Once a dog loped across the lot, maybe feral, maybe just out for an after-dinner run. I started to get hungry.

"We should have picked up something to eat beforehand," I said. "Seems risky to go in and out now, just to get some hamburgers."

"Oh, sorry, forgot about that." Harmony went back to the carrier bag and tossed me a couple of granola bars. "I have a liter of water, too."

I'd found several broad pieces of thick, open-cell foam in the mechanics' heap of junk. From the cutouts it looked like packing material, something that had been wrapped around bumpers or body panels. Stacked by one of the pillars it made a sort of sofa for us to sit on—low to the floor, but we could still see through the windows, and almost comfortable.

Harmony finished her granola bar and crumpled the wrapper into her pocket. No clues to be left lying around. I drank from the Nalgene water bottle.

"How long you been doing this?" I asked.

"Long enough."

"Like it?"

"It's better than retail."

"Have many clients on the East Coast?"

"Why would you want to know that?"

I turned to look at her. "Is there *any* part of your personal history or outlook on life you'd care to share with me?"

"Why?"

"Ah . . . light conversation?"

"I used to play lead guitar in a South Central band. We opened for Against Me! once. It was great, but girl bands can attract some really scary groupies. So I decided to do this instead."

I nodded. "I don't believe that."

She smiled. "Good for you."

Light from the windows fell on her face, leaving the other side in shadow. Her eyes were clear and steady. The perfect haircut was soft and disordered.

Was there an invitation there or not?

"You know my history," I said. "Even about Dave. I don't think I have any secrets bigger than that, and he's really more in the way of a surprise than a secret."

Harmony nodded and her smile faded slowly away. She reached out and put a hand on my shoulder.

Then she took it back. I was having all *kinds* of trouble reading the signals.

"I had some trouble once." Her voice was so quiet I could barely hear it.

A long moment. That seemed to be it.

"Trouble," I said.

"When I was young. Seventeen."

"Okay."

Another spell of silence.

"I decided," said Harmony, then stopped.

"Yes?"

"That it would never happen to me again." Her face closed in, suddenly hard and impenetrable. "Never."

I kept still. "Got it."

"Ever."

Another siren went past outside. In New York I could have told you police, fire, maybe even which ambulance company. Here, out of place, I wasn't sure.

The foam was compressed to the concrete floor underneath me, not as comfortable as at first.

Some of the tension left Harmony's face. She looked away, and her shoulders relaxed.

"I don't take any shit," she said.

"I've noticed."

"It's mostly about attitude."

I'd noticed that, too.

"Sometimes . . ." she said, "sometimes it gets tiring. Carrying the attitude around."

She looked back at me and smiled.

CHAPTER TWENTY-NINE

reached forward, a little hesitant given the discussion to this point, and met her halfway. The foam squeaked beneath us. Harmony put her hands on each side of my face and drew me in, a long slow kiss that gradually opened up into more exploratory realms.

For the first minute it was gentle—slow and achingly gentle.

My arms went around her waist, under the jacket, and I felt her muscles flow and tighten as she shifted into me. One hand went round my neck. She grabbed the back of my head and pulled. We separated for air, then back in, deeper, more desperate.

I twisted, seeking leverage, and instead toppled over, pulling her with me. Her hands were all over my back and chest, tearing my shirt out of the way. I tried to slide my own hand into her pants and collided with the Glock.

"Ow!"

"Shit." Harmony reached back, drew the pistol and dropped it on the floor next to us.

"Yo, careful."

She slipped out of her jacket, started tugging my shirt over my head. I went for her belt, one-handed, tangled up.

And then it was a frenzy. We tore at the rest of our clothing, mouths together, on our faces, our necks and chests. Harmony wore a dark sports bra, a wide band of lycra. I pulled it up, trying not to claw at her breasts. An odd weight on its side . . .

A folding knife, in a nylon sheath.

She yanked at my pants. The Sig fell out, clunking to the concrete. I tried to pull one leg from my pants but it got hung up on my backup Taurus in the ankle holster. Standing on one leg, pants at my ankles, Harmony all over me.

"Don't—"

"Yes!"

"Oh . . ."

I had her panties down—more lycra, another hunk of heavy metal. A Kahr compact 9. I shoved it out of the way, grabbed her ass and pulled her close.

Something rough between our bellies. I felt around front.

"*Duct* tape?"

"Don't tear that off!"

"What . . ."

"There's a razor under it." She put her mouth on mine again, tongue reaching.

"Jesus."

Boots—hers slipped off and *another* hideout gun tumbled to the floor. Mine took some work, more wasted seconds sitting bare-assed on the foam with Harmony straddling my waist while I reached around and yanked at the laces.

Socks disappeared. Finally we were both almost naked, rolling on the foam. I hit my elbow on the floor and the pain almost distracted me for a second.

"Cold," Harmony gasped. The foam had slipped and her thigh was on the floor.

I pulled her sitting, grabbed for the foam, but it went every which way, skittering out of reach.

"Fuck," I said. "Up, up, up."

We stood, her leg wound around me, pulling me off-balance. I toppled, banged into the pillar, found my footing and straightened up. With my back against the brick I embraced Harmony, a great enveloping hug, running my hands and arms up and down her back, feeling the heat of her skin. Harmony's hair brushed across my face and I breathed it in. I found her ass, muscles dense and smooth and tight, then grasped it with both hands and lifted her up.

She helped, reaching down with one hand to make some room while pulling up with the other hand round my neck. One leg rose, hooking around both of mine.

I slid in, electric warmth and intensity. *Ohhhh* that felt good.

Harmony gasped.

We moved—the first moment out of sync, then finding the rhythm, gloriously.

"Don't . . . don't—" Her voice slipped into incoherence.

I felt the build and couldn't help a groan.

CRAAAASH—BAANNGG!

An explosion shattered the room. I jerked in shock. Harmony screamed, eyes shut, head thrown back.

Fireworks in my brain. The loft was filled with gunshots, smashing glass, yelling. Synesthetic overload—I smelled gold bursts, saw screams, heard gunsmoke.

Two figures had crashed through one skylight, jumping in even as a third provided covering fire from above. In the fractured instant, I saw rifles and goggles, body armor and muzzle flash.

Harmony and I fell, landing on enough foam. I threw out an arm, found a pistol by sheer luck and fired without aiming.

I was still inside Harmony and the lizard brain had its way—I came in a great heaving spasm. I jerked the handgun's trigger repeatedly, no more control over my fingers than I had over any other part of my body.

A few seconds. An eternity.

The pillar provided some cover, in particular from the man still at the skylight. One of the jumpers remained on the ground. Bad landing.

The other was on his feet, a dazzling beam from a superbright LED mounted under-barrel swinging through the haze.

Two Russians remaining, one below and one above. Reinforcements, sure enough.

I fired once more, then the slide locked open. Empty.

Harmony shoved at me. "Go! Go!"

I rolled out and off, skin shocked by the freezing concrete. The handgun—Harmony's Glock—was empty. I dropped it.

She went the other way. I had a flashing glimpse of leg and back and golden hair, then she tipped the bench up and over and slid into cover behind the heavy wood.

A burst of automatic fire cut through the air above my head, chips spattering from the wall and pillar. I lunged, no plan—scraping my totally unprotected, still half-mast privates on the concrete. I screamed and curled up.

Gunfire from behind the overturned table. Harmony must have found a weapon, or maybe she'd had yet another holstered somewhere I didn't notice. The LED flash swung in her direction.

I saw the pile of auto shop materials, realized what Harmony was doing, and went to ground, wrapping my arms around my head.

KA-ROOONNNK!

The toluene detonated first. Not much explosive pressure but it immediately set the paint and solvents on fire. Pinpricks stung across my back as superheated shrapnel blasted through the room. Yelling—Harmony? The Russians?

No, me. I forced myself to shut up.

Rolling across the floor, I'd snagged the sports bra. Even as I stared wildly around, trying to locate our assailants, my hands were busy extracting the knife. I flipped it open with the thumb lock, shifted automatically to a saber grip.

Flames roared at the stairwell. Acrid smoke rapidly filled the entire room. The man at the skylight fired three-round bursts this way and that, randomly. I guess he couldn't see any better than I could. The LED beam shone at floor level, motionless in the fug— the attacker had either dropped the flashlight or was down himself, lying beside it.

"Silas!"

I looked over. The haze was just thin enough that I could see her emerge, standing from behind the table with guns raised in each hand, glaring at the ceiling.

Stark naked. Under close-quarters attack, probably about to die from gunfire, flames, smoke inhalation or all three—I still stopped for a moment, dumbstruck.

She fired two-handed, the pistols in exact parallel, rapidly alternating her shots.

The LED beam moved.

The attacker on the floor was back. He had the assault rifle.

I screamed and ran straight at him. The beam swung my way. A burst cut the air but I ignored it.

The man was an indistinct lump in the smoke, crouched in a kneeling stance. I leaped, crashed into him and punched as hard as I could with the knife.

It struck the ceramic plates in his chest armor, jarring my grip so hard I almost dropped it.

He grunted. I struck again, this time aiming for the gap between his helmet and chest armor. Missed again—the knife bounced off his neck guard.

If he was smarter, he'd have dropped the Vikhr—I was inside the radius, too close for him to do any immediate damage with it. But the noise and choking smoke and explosions had rattled him— he clung to the weapon, and that let me strike one more time.

Up, into his armpit, right between the side plates and the pauldron. The knife ripped straight through his jacket, into the shoulder. I'd put so much force into the blow that he stumbled left, knocked off-balance—even as blood gouted out, covering my hand and forearm.

The axillary artery is fatal. I snagged the rifle as he went down, blood spraying everywhere.

"Harmony!"

She'd exhausted both magazines but driven the rooftop sniper back. I coughed, choking and nearly blinded.

A hand on my arm and I almost lashed out—but it was Harmony, holding me up, eyes red and streaming like mine.

"We have to get out of here!"

I looked at the stairwell down—the epicenter of the inferno, a wall of flame and intense heat. Not that way.

"Up?"

She shook her head violently. "He's waiting—suicide."

That narrowed the options to one. I checked the Vikhr, pushed the selector to full auto and aimed at the window right next to the exterior door. I pulled the trigger and held it down, twitching the barrel right and left. The window glass blew out in a spray of shards.

Smoke and flame immediately billowed toward it—not quite a flashover but too damn much.

"Run!" I yelled in Harmony's ear, over the roar and crashing of the fire. "Truck's right underneath!"

She grabbed my hand and we sprinted for the window. I dropped the rifle—nothing but a hindrance now—and we hurdled the sill, still clutching hands, right into space.

An instant of clean cold air, the plummet, then we landed in the pickup's bed, hitting it simultaneously. I fell, Harmony on top of me. We tumbled around the plywood in an awkward, tangled mess.

The fall was only about twelve feet but we had no padding of any kind and nowhere to roll to absorb the shock. It hurt.

The truck sagged.

I breathed. A moment passed, then we both tried to move.

"You hurt?" I said.

"I can move."

"Check me."

I pulled her up and we did a quick, mutual exam, looking for broken bones and blood and spinal injury. Shock can leave you functional for a few minutes—better your buddy figures out you need immediate attention, before you collapse and die.

Lots of bruises, nothing permanent. Amazing.

"We have to go," I said. "The guy on the roof will figure it out any second."

But when we climbed from the bed, I saw that the rear tire had finally collapsed. Our combined impact must have popped the ancient radial like a balloon.

"Fucking Christ!" I started to kick the shreds of rubber on the rim, stopped myself just in time. No need for broken toes.

"The SUV," said Harmony. I glanced at her—naked, covered in soot and dirt, empty-handed. I was no better, especially with blood drying all up one arm and across my face.

"Just our luck someone will have a video camera." We started running—slowly and painfully on our bare feet—toward the next block.

I really hoped she had a spare key.

CHAPTER THIRTY

My go-bag burned up back there," Harmony said. "I didn't bring anything else."

"The floor mats are bolted down." I sat back up. "No seat covers. Think there's a horse blanket in the back?"

We had two handguns—the Kahr and my 226, both of which Harmony had scooped up on the way out. Fortunately the Escalade was locked with a keypad, so it wasn't a problem getting in. She drove one-handed, her left arm across her chest. Not so much for modesty, at least not from me, but to avoid drawing attention from other motorists.

Of course it was dark—night now—and the Escalade's cab was higher than most, making it harder to see in. But the last thing we needed was bystanders pointing and pulling out their cellphones and posting photos to Facebook.

We did have one more resource. Harmony had left her cellphone in the vehicle, plugged in to charge.

"I'll call Dave," I said. "He can meet us somewhere."

"I guess that's—I can't think of anyone else."

I lifted the phone from the cupholder, leaving it still wired to the cigarette lighter, and swiped the screen. The glass remained completely black but for a small white box in the center.

"How do I turn this on?"

"Biometric lock, plus a gestural password." Harmony started to reach for it. "No, forget it, I need two hands."

I hadn't gotten a good look at her phone earlier, and now I studied it more closely. "This doesn't look like an iPhone."

"Of course not. Apple collects every bit of your data and never lets go."

"So what is it?"

"Modified Chinese hardware, running a custom OS built on a mobile Linux kernel."

I thought about my twenty-dollar throwaway. "Guns, unarmed combat and dark-side hacking. Is there anything you can't do?"

"I know some guys, and I pay them very well. Right? Recognize your shortcomings and hire what you need." She glanced over. "You should try that."

"I'm more of a Renaissance man myself."

She slowed the SUV, studying the road. We were off the main avenue, driving through a semi-industrial area—low, dark buildings behind chain-link fences, a gas station, an equipment-rental lot with cherry pickers and excavators and minidozers lined up under sodium lamps.

"I'm going to stop over there." Harmony slowed, crossed the road left and pulled along a railroad siding. It wasn't a station or a stop, just a stretch of double track with some rusty signs and a pair of turnouts. The closest building was a hundred yards away. She killed the lights but left the engine running. "Switch seats. I'll call, you drive."

The Escalade might have been Humvee huge, but with the hump and the shift and the steering wheel, it was crowded in the front seat. Harmony slid right, I awkwardly tried to climb over her—and our lack of clothing was suddenly very obvious again. My knee came down between her legs for a moment, my chest brushed her head . . . she put a hand on my thigh for balance, looked up.

"Um—"

Our mouths met. I braced myself with one hand, ran my other across one breast. She gave me a squeeze and I was instantly ready to go, all other thoughts driven from my mind.

"No, wait." She pushed back. "This is stupid!"

"Yes. Right. Absolutely." I released her, twisted around and managed to fall into the seat beside her, more or less upright. For a moment we sat like lovebirds at the drive-in, side by side and pressed together.

My johnson was staying with its own program, straight up and waving around. Harmony looked at it and grinned. She turned to put both arms around my neck and snuggle in.

"Really . . . stupid . . ." she whispered. Then she threw her leg over and rolled on top of me.

We looked into each other's eyes. I couldn't move much, pressed into the seat with Harmony in my lap, but my hands were free to roam.

A vehicle drove past, fifty feet away. It didn't stop and we barely noticed. Harmony braced her knees on the seat on either side of me and lowered herself down.

"Oh, jeepers," I said.

Harmony started laughing. "Jeepers? *Jeepers?*" But then she gasped and stopped talking and that was all for a while.

———

At one point I thought the Escalade moved, bouncing and skidding on the gravel, but maybe it was just me.

———

We slumped, wrapped together. The seat fabric seemed damp everywhere, underneath, behind. I could feel Harmony's pulse, strong and rapid, where her chest was pressed against mine.

After a minute she eased back slightly, so she could look me in the face again. Dim light from down the road showed her eyes gleaming in the shadow.

"Jeepers?" she said.

Too embarrassing. "Something, you know, in high school the, uh, first time . . ." I tried a casual shrug. "It kind of got stuck in my brain, I guess."

She kissed my nose. "I got something stuck in my brain, all right."

And I think it reflected the tenderness of the moment that we both let the puns drop there.

Ten minutes later, back on the road. I drove carefully, getting the feel of the three-ton behemoth. Harmony hunched, keeping herself low in the cab, and tapped at the phone. When it began ringing, she handed it over and I lifted it to my ear.

"What do you *want?*" The voice raspy and muffled.

"Dave?"

"Yeah."

"It's me. We need some help."

"I'm in the middle of—oh, *man*." Indistinct noises.

"Dave. I said we need some *help*. Serious."

"Can I get back—?"

"We're in trouble!"

Click.

I glared at the phone, looked at Harmony. "He hung up."

"What's going on?"

"Dunno."

I came to a railroad crossing and bumped over the tracks without slowing, unwilling to linger under the gate's bright streetlights. Harmony took back the phone and redialed.

"Dave!" Pause. "It's Harmony. Don't hang—don't hang up on me! Look, if you drop us now, I will come over and—what? *Shoot* you?" She laughed, short and sharp and scary. "No, I won't shoot *you*. I'll take some Tovex and blast your Camaro into a pile of smoking junk so ruined and pulverized the insurance adjuster won't even recognize it as an automobile! Okay? Are you listening?"

She handed the phone back to me. "He's listening," she said.

I put the phone back to my ear.

"Silas, what the fuck?" Dave's voice was clearer now. "What's with her?"

"Don't worry, she was kidding—she knows it's really a Charger. Can you meet us?"

"This isn't a good time."

I couldn't help looking over at Harmony. We were covered in dirt and smoke and blood. The cab smelled of all that, plus the tang of sweat and coupling. We had one phone, two handguns and nothing else in the world.

"I'm sorry it's not a good time," I said. "But we need clothes, money and a ride."

"Uh, give me an hour?"

Noise in the background. A woman's voice.

"Who's there with you?"

"Well, you know——"

"Is that *Elsie*?"

Even through the crummy cellular transmission I could hear the satisfaction in his voice. "Yup. In fact."

I shook my head and glanced at Harmony again. "He's fucking Elsie."

"No I'm not!" Dave said. "We're, shit, talking and like that."

"Where's Brendt?"

"At Sully's."

"Where are *you*?"

Pause. "His and Elsie's house."

We came to a dark intersection. I looked left, right, saw no traffic and picked left arbitrarily.

"Okay," I said. "You're going to save us, and I'm going to save you from yourself. Like I said, we need some clothes."

"Clothes?"

"Yeah, clothes. Pants, shirts, socks—the whole bit. I'd say Harmony's close enough to Elsie's size, you can borrow some underwear from her."

Dave started laughing. "You two are buck naked somewhere, and you're giving *me* shit?"

"Long story."

When we hung up, I handed the phone back to Harmony. "Third Street and Dunbar in Clabbton. A church. He says he'll meet us behind it, half an hour. Can your phone get us directions?"

She nodded and tapped it into life. "This is total, gangster-on-the-run fucked up," she said.

"Oh, that reminds me. Call 911 first. I assume your geek-boys have rigged that to block any line trace."

"911?"

"Pretend you just fled the fire at the garage, and tell them it was a meth lab."

Harmony got it immediately. "They'll believe it, all those accelerants."

"If they think there's benzene and ether around, they'll be a lot slower going in and investigating. Plus the red herring should keep them busy for hours."

"That's good." She was already dialing.

"And after that, maybe one of the newspapers? Or TV stations? If we can get the idea out into the press that it was meth, that's like perfect cover. Everyone will believe it."

"Which might even buy us a day." Harmony lifted the phone. "You're kind of smart for a lunkhead."

"And you're a nice girl," I said. "For a ninja weapons master."

———

The Charger was already there when we arrived, parked in back. It was one of those newer churches, a wooden building with some metal siding and a cheap cross on the top. The sign out front had theater-marquee plastic letters: HAVE YOU "LIKED" JESUS THIS WEEK?

I pulled in alongside, closer to the building. A security light mounted on the corner pointed toward the road, leaving the back shadowed. The road was quiet. We were at the outskirts of Clabbton, where the cheap commercial strip gave way to open fields and third-growth forest.

Dave's door swung open. I got out, wincing as I stepped barefoot on the gravel. Harmony came around from her side, much less bothered—probably all that time in the dojo, kicking the hell out of the *makiwara*.

"Silas—" Dave stopped, gaping at Harmony.

"Eyes front, asshole," she snapped. "It's been a long night."

"What *happened* to you?"

"Those guys who blew up your shop," I said. "They seem to specialize. Another auto garage now lies in ruins."

"The Russians?"

"We didn't have a long discussion."

Dave pulled his gaze away from Harmony. He reached back into the car and handed me a big plastic bag. "Brendt's, mostly," he said. "Elsie threw a few things in there too."

"How about shoes?"

"Not sure if they'll fit." He retrieved a pair of workboots, heels worn down and laces frayed. "What size are you?"

"Eleven."

"I don't know what these are—they're his." He had a pair of running shoes for Harmony.

We dressed quickly. Brendt's clothes hung loose on me, no surprise considering his mass. Harmony's jeans and T-shirt were tight but at least long enough.

"That feels better," she said, threading a belt. "Much, much better."

"Thanks," I said to Dave.

He waved a hand. "I got to say, your phone call, you really killed the mood there."

I wasn't his keeper. "You left Elsie at home?"

"Sure. Brendt has the car."

But I *was* his brother. "You're not going back, are you?"

"I guess not."

"Where is Brendt, anyway? I thought you said he worked days."

"Got a temporary job, rigging out at Erlenton. There's a big press conference tomorrow and they're building a temporary stage."

For what I'd thought was a depressed, declining, Rust Belt dinosaur, Pittsburgh seemed to have a lot going on. "FerroCorp again?"

Dave looked puzzled for a moment. "The mill? Naw, this is different. It's one of the fracking companies."

"Oh."

"Someone's buying in. They want to make a big splash, I guess. Brendt has a friend in the carpenters. Cash, no bullshit."

Slapping together a temporary structure in the middle of the night—probably no permits, either.

Might be a little packet for the building inspector though.

Harmony had been checking her Kahr. Slapping the magazine back in, she said, "Want your pistol back?"

I nodded. "Thanks."

She passed me the Sig. I made sure it was decocked and slipped it into my back pocket.

"Eight rounds between us," she said.

Not much. "I know."

Dave watched. "You all gonna get into more shooting?"

"I hope not." Harmony had that steely look again. "But chasing Silas around—best be prepared."

"No shit." He nodded. "So . . . now what?"

A very good question.

"That thing's a liability," I said to Harmony, gesturing at the Escalade. "Maybe they saw it, maybe they didn't, but I don't think we can take the chance."

"I don't want to abandon it."

"Why not?"

"The guys who lent it to me—they're not exactly U-Haul. I ought to give it back."

I looked at Dave. "What do you say?"

"What?"

"Follow us into town, Harmony returns the Humvee, you drive us back?"

"Sure."

And that was that—we had a plan. Harmony rubbed some dirt onto the Escalade's rear license plate, while I fine-toothed it inside for anything we might have dropped.

"The seat," I said, scooting back out of the cab. "It's kind of, you know . . ."

She laughed.

Dave watched, leaning on the Charger, arms crossed.

"You two," he said. "Man."

CHAPTER THIRTY-ONE

Back into Pittsburgh. This had to be the tenth time I'd driven up or down the Parkway. At least now, long past rush hour, it was both dark and lightly traveled. Harmony put the Escalade in the center lane and kept it at a steady sixty the whole way.

We exited east of the city proper down a long ramp that seemed to get bumpier and more potholed every yard. The street at the bottom had been cut up and patched so many times that some of the metal road plates had been asphalted in place.

"Everyone tells me Pittsburgh's a beautiful city," Harmony said, fighting the wheel as the SUV bucked over the road's cratered surface. "But I haven't seen it yet."

"Depends on your business. Downtown looked nice."

"Maybe we'll get over there sometime."

She navigated without hesitation, taking several turns and a long, dark street past a fuel oil distributor. Behind a heavy fence we could see a row of tank trucks, parked for the night. The pump gantry sat near one huge tank, at least thirty feet tall, and others were visible under security lights farther in.

"Are we near the river?" I said.

"I don't know."

"They probably bring the oil in on barges."

"Does it matter?"

I glanced at her. "Tactical considerations? Maybe we'll have to leave in a hurry."

Harmony slowed, then nosed the Escalade off the road, toward another industrial parking lot. It was right up against the tank farm's fence. A number of small vans were parked in the lee of a prefab metal building—several truck bays, closed tight, but it wasn't a warehouse, because the doors went to ground level, not loading docks.

I could just read the sign mounted under the building's roofline: RED BALL DELIVERY.

"These guys are okay," she said.

"You know them." I shrugged. "Sure, it's low odds, but I'd hate to get in a shooting match next to a million gallons of high-test."

Stairs led to a low wooden landing at the end of the building, a few feet off the ground. The door was blank and closed, though the window next to it showed light through an opaque shade. Harmony parked at the end of the row of vans and we got out.

"Maybe we ought to clean the surfaces?" I said.

"They'll take care of it." She pushed the door shut without slamming it. "I told you, they know their business."

At the office door she knocked, waited, then stepped back when it opened and light spilled out.

"Come on in, honey." The guy was short and thick, in blue-twill work clothes. A patch above one pocket had "Red Ball" embroidered in red over white, barely readable for fading and grime.

Harmony gestured at me—an invitation to follow, and an introduction. "This is Silas," she said. "We're friends."

The office was small—desk, some chairs, a sprung couch. Curling safety posters and a calendar hung on the faux knotty paneling. The short man closed the door behind us, but Harmony had addressed the other occupant. He sat behind the desk, dark hair and reading glasses, papers stacked all around his laptop.

He didn't get up, or offer to shake hands.

"Rough day?" he said.

The borrowed clothes helped, but we were still dirty, bloody and probably reeking of chemical smoke. "Same old, same old," Harmony said.

"You're early. Thought you needed the car for a week."

"Sometimes it goes smooth."

"Uh-huh."

"You can keep the extra day's payment. I already billed my client."

The man studied me, looking over his glasses. "Silas?"

I didn't know him, but it didn't sound like an offer to introduce myself—he seemed to be talking to Harmony.

"I know," she said.

"Funny, him having the same name."

"It got complicated. Turns out we're on the same side."

I guess she'd mentioned what she was in town for.

"That's nice." He leaned back a bit, and I could see the shoulder holster, which was no doubt deliberate. "Good to find out who your friends are."

"I ought to tell you," said Harmony. "We happened to be nearby to some excitement."

"Nearby."

"In the general area. I don't think anyone was taking pictures or writing down plate numbers, but I can't swear to it. You might want to keep the Escalade out of the fleet for a few days."

"What kind of excitement?"

"You know, kids. Did the Steelers lose today? Maybe they were letting off steam."

"Football hasn't started yet. As a girl, you might not know that."

Delivery was a convenient business—a completely unremarkable excuse to have people driving all over the city, double-parked here, stopping there, visiting any company they liked, transporting anonymous boxes everywhere.

"It's been like Halloween this week," the man said. "Devil's Night, practically. Those kids must be serious."

"Serious?"

"Arson, explosives, shooting. Even went into a hospital, the news says. Firing at patients, blowing up the wards."

"Nothing to do with you."

"Course not. And you say you're done. But the ones looking for him"— he looked at me—"do they know that? Is there any chance they might get upset at *you*, for example, and end up here?"

Harmony shook her head. "None."

"Uh-huh."

A long pause. The short guy stood by the door, more or less blocking it, arms at his side. A game controller sat on the couch, and an LCD monitor atop a two-drawer file cabinet showed a silent, frozen, CGI image—smoke and dust and smudge. In the silence I thought I could hear the hum of a second computer.

"They're Russian," I said.

Attention swung my way. "Who?"

"Russian speaking, anyway. The ones who've been shooting up your city."

"Not *my* city." He sat forward again. "And it seemed to be all out in the suburbs. Clackton."

"Clabbton."

"Right."

"So I was wondering," I said, "whether maybe you heard any-thing."

"About Russians?"

"Anything helpful."

The man pushed his chair back, its plastic rollers scraping on the linoleum floor, and stood up. The reading glasses deceived. He was wiry and muscled, not some potbellied middle-aged manager. Another stretch, showing off the holster again—looked like serious hardware in there, an FN maybe—and he opened a door behind him. It led to a small alcove with a sink and counter, where a coffee machine had a pot half full.

"Want a cup?" he said, over his shoulder.

"No thanks." Harmony took the opportunity to move sideways, still between the short guy and his boss, but enough that he was no longer at her back. "It would only keep me up all night."

The man came back, mug in his left hand. It had some sort of cartoon on it. I squinted.

"Polacks, we got," he said. "Been here for a hundred years, work-ing the mills. Indians—they're *buying* the mills. FerroCorp just sold themselves to some Indian steel company. And the Chinese, they're all over the place, looking for God knows what. Scrap metal, maybe." He swirled the mug. "It's like we're the third world now, you know? Sell raw material to China, buy back televisions and iPhones."

It seemed like an odd place for a discussion of international competitive advantage. "Funny," I said.

"But Russians, they're thin on the ground."

"Just a thought."

"When are you leaving?"

The question was unexpected. He was looking at Harmony.

"Soon as we're done."

"I thought you already were."

"Someone's trying to kill me." She said it like it was just another of life's minor irritations—*the toaster broke, I ran out of oatmeal, and, oh yeah, a hunter-killer team is shooting the hell out of Pittsburgh.* "Have to take care of that first."

He drank some coffee, watching us. "Oh?"

"You know me."

"Unfortunately."

She let a smile go by, almost too fast to catch. "I'm here until it's done."

"Yes."

"But," she added, "the sooner, the better."

"And you think I might share that perspective."

"You don't?"

It was a Garfield cartoon. His hand covered the punch line.

"The only Russians I know of are the ones who bought into Rockwire a year or two ago," he said. "Over in Fellsville."

"Rockwire." Harmony didn't react. "I've heard of them."

"Russian money saved that company. There'd be two, three hundred guys out of work if the plant had gone under."

"Rockwire's bigger than Fellsville. They have operations all over the Midwest."

"Could be."

The short man shifted on his feet, not impatiently, just keeping the blood moving. His gaze traveled a steady circuit: me, Harmony, his boss. Me, Harmony . . . I caught his eye, but he just glanced at my hands and my feet, then on to Harmony.

"You do any business with them?" she asked.

"Rockwire? Nah. Some parts deliveries, maybe, but I'd have to look at the books to be sure."

"They're probably not connected."

"Don't see how they could be." The man finished his coffee and set down the mug. "They make pipeline equipment."

On the way out the short man finally stepped away from the door, nodding at Harmony. "See you around, honey."

"Sure."

"You need a ride? You only drove the one car here."

"A friend's waiting for us."

She held the door for me, and we clumped down the wooden steps. They watched us go, the door not closing completely until we reached the gate and stepped out of the lot.

No sidewalk. It wasn't a pedestrian neighborhood. We walked on a gravel verge between the road's paving and the tank farm fence.

As soon as the Red Ball warehouse was no longer visible I borrowed Harmony's phone.

"We need to know more about Rockwire," I said.

"They make pipes, right? Like he said."

"But they own half of Dagger Light—and Markson has the other half."

"You know how to use the browser on there?" She gestured to the phone in my hand. "It's custom as well, but I think they started with Mozilla's code—"

"Not necessary." I finished dialing and raised the phone. "Johnny's looking in to it."

CHAPTER THIRTY-TWO

Dave stood outside the Charger, tossing a rock from hand to hand, at the far end of the tank farm. He'd parked for a rapid getaway, next to a heap of dirty sand as tall as him. As we walked up I half waved—*no rush, no problem.*

"All set?"

"We're good." Harmony and I both reached for the passenger door handle at the same time. "Hey."

"I'm not riding in back—there's no seat."

Dave seemed offended. "Of *course* there's a seat."

"That's a piece of wood!"

The car's rear held a plank—precisely cut and fitted, and varnished to a smooth gloss—but Harmony was right. The Charger was built to go around a track very fast, not to carry passengers.

"Also," she said, looking through a rear side window, "is that the *gas* tank underneath it?"

"Yeah." Dave nodded. "Taking out the upholstery frees up some weight. The tank's always been there, but now you can see it. That's all."

"I am *not* sitting on top of a petrol bomb."

I could see her point.

In the end she took the front and I perched rather uncomfortably on the hard wood. After some complaining, Dave held the speed down and tried to ease over the bumps for my sake.

With the windows open, cool night air flowed through the car. The engine rumbled like the well-tuned, barely restrained jet turbine it was. Dave kept two hands on the wheel, posture as correct as one of the mannequins in a driver's-ed video, the same ingrained and professional habits I'm sure he used on the track.

"Where to, then?" he said.

"The airport."

"What?" Harmony and Dave reacted simultaneously. "You're leaving?"

"No," I said. "But we can't have you driving us around. I hate to do it, but we're going to have to collect my car from the parking lot there."

"Car?" He seemed confused. "Didn't you fly in?"

"Oh." I forgot I hadn't explained and gave the short version.

Dave laughed. "So that's like, what, five vehicles you've destroyed?"

"Only four, but now I'm down to the last one."

Transportation resolved, we still had the question of where to stay.

"I don't think Brendt would mind," Dave said. "The basement's got carpet. It's not too bad down there—it only flooded once last year, and he dried everything out with one of those big fans."

"Gosh, that sounds perfect." Harmony patted him on the shoulder. "But Silas and I shouldn't attract any more attention. We'll find a hotel or something."

I started to say that I didn't have the cash for that, then realized that we could travel on *her* credit card for a while. "Good idea."

"When is Brendt coming home?"

"He said they're going to finish tonight no matter what—the ceremony is tomorrow."

"Ceremony? At a fracking site?"

"I dunno. Sounded like PR—they have to clean up all the crap lying around, too. Make it look nice and clean for the reporters."

"You still don't have a place of your own, do you?" I said.

Dave downshifted, slowing through a blinking yellow light. A few blocks ahead a long bridge crossed the avenue, and as we approached I saw it was a highway viaduct. Dave got into the left lane, signaling onto the on-ramp.

"I'm trying to work it out with Elsie," he said.

I considered that. "She doesn't have a place of her own, either."

"Yeah."

"And if I were Brendt, I probably wouldn't be very accommodating."

"That's the problem, all right."

At the airport Dave dropped us at Departures. Not many people around at nine-thirty P.M.—a few taxis, some grim-looking businessmen headed for red-eyes, a state trooper parked and staring at his inboard computer. We got out and shook hands, just like real passengers. "Call me," Dave said.

"We're close." Harmony gave him a quick hug, like she was his sister. "I can feel it. We're almost there."

"See you tomorrow."

He drove off. The trooper watched him go with a frown, but the Charger attracted that sort of attention all the time. Harmony and

I passed through the wide doors into the terminal, walked all the way down the row, and descended to Arrivals. Past the baggage claim, across the roadway and into the garage. A brisk climb up the stairwell took us to level three, where I'd parked a week earlier.

It seemed like a month.

"What did Johnny say?" Harmony asked as I recovered the spare key from its little holder magnetized to the underbody. Bad security, but awfully convenient. "About Rockwire?"

"I left a message. He'll get back to me." I settled into the driver's seat. "Look under the seat. There's a map folder."

Harmony pulled out a dusty plastic case. "The phone has GPS, you know."

"No. I keep some extra cash inside there. We'll need it to get through the gate."

We drove out of the garage. Harmony leaned back in the seat and closed her eyes. "I'm crashing."

"Me too." Long day.

"Go to . . . let's see, the Marriott on University Boulevard, right outside the airport."

"You know it?"

"Checked in when I arrived. Room 242. Second floor—the card key's buried in the planter holding a plastic-looking shrub to the left of the elevator."

I slowed, stuck behind a taxi entering the exit road. It felt good to be in my own car for once. "You know, I'm paranoid, but even I'll carry my hotel key around with me."

"I have rooms at three different places." Harmony yawned. "Paid a week at each one when I arrived, mussed the bed and hung out the do-not-disturb."

"Three?"

"Be prepared. That's all. When you need a bolt-hole, having to talk to the desk clerk in a public lobby may be a problem."

Three rooms, one week each—more than two thousand dollars, probably.

Just *in case*.

"You run a nice budget," I said.

"Expenses." She opened her eyes to glance at me. "Charged to the client."

"Of course."

"Drop me first, come in five minutes later. Okay?"

"Yeah, yeah, I know."

I followed the airport exit road. Harmony seemed to doze off, but a minute later she spoke again. "I can't figure who hired me."

The question had been nagging at me also. "Not the Russians."

"Not considering how they faced both of us off at Brinker's farm. I suppose someone could have sent them and me on the same mission—but why? The Russian team was already here tearing up the place. They wouldn't need me dogging you in New York."

"What exactly was your assignment?"

"To find you."

"That's all?" I rested my hand on her shoulder briefly. "It's okay, you can tell me if there was more to it."

"Terminate with extreme prejudice? Wetwork? Like that?" Her eyes were still closed. "No, that really wasn't part of the RFP. Just to collect you for an interview."

"Interview. I've had some clients use that word."

"By phone. I was supposed to sit you down somewhere and put you on speaker. There'd be a discussion, and then we'd let you go."

"Hmm." But one more question nagged. "They didn't ask you to look for someone else first, did they?"

"Someone else?"

"Maybe named Ryan?"

"No." She opened her eyes. "Who is he?"

"The guy who subcontracted me." I explained. "I have to assume the Russians got to him first—and then turned up my name."

No trouble when we arrived. The Marriott was the usual cheap cube, a circle drive and portico in front and plain windows on the sides. The parking lot was reasonably lit, and street lamps illuminated the roadway as well. I stopped around back, near an exit—we could see the hallway inside, through the glass door. A status LED glowed on a card reader alongside. Harmony waited a few minutes until someone approached the door from inside, then hopped out and arrived just as the guest was pushing through. She held the door for him, stepping back in a way that facilitated his departure and kept her face turned aside.

I parked the car—nose out, pointed directly at the lot's exit—and went in the same door. Harmony had slipped a bit of paper into the jamb, holding the latch back just enough that I could fake a card swipe and pull it open. The paper scrap fluttered away.

Room 242 had two double beds, a narrow desk and a chair, plus a three-foot flat-screen TV above the credenza. No lights were on. Harmony stood at the window, the blackout curtain held open a few inches, studying the view.

"Backup gear bag's on the dresser," she said. "I left it here when I checked in. There's an extra phone you can have, some money. Toothbrush in the bathroom."

"Okay."

"You can take either bed," she said, not looking around.

I parsed that statement for a few seconds. "I thought we, well . . ."

"Sorry." She let the curtain drop and turned back. I could barely see her in the bit of light that made it past the curtains. "I need a bed to myself."

"All right." I scratched my head.

After a moment she sighed and came over to me. The room was barely larger than the furniture—a foot or two of carpet around the edges.

Harmony pulled me into an embrace. I could feel the muscles in her arms and legs. She was only an inch or two shorter than me.

"I told you," she said quietly. Almost a whisper. "Stuff happened. I can't—it's hard to sleep if there's anyone next to me."

"That's okay."

"I'm working on it."

I rubbed my hand slowly up and down her back. "I guess I could sleep in the car."

"I thought about it, but you'd attract attention."

Through the wall we could hear muffled music and shouting—the next room's television. Down the hall a door slammed.

"What about before you go to sleep?" I said.

Harmony lifted her face, and in the dark I sensed, rather than saw, the smile. "That's a different matter," she said.

CHAPTER THIRTY-THREE

I n the morning we had some trouble.

"Ouch!"

"Sorry, didn't mean to kick you."

"Why don't you do your kata over there?"

"I *tried* shoving the bed but it won't move. There's no room."

Light streamed through the east-facing window's gauze privacy curtain—Harmony had pulled the drapes open when she woke. We were both trying to run through our dawn exercise routines.

"Do some isometrics or something. I can't even stretch."

"Okay, okay." I gave up and pulled on Brendt's pants. "I saw a Waffle House when we drove in. I'll get some coffee and pastry."

"Black. See if they'll give you some oatmeal to go."

I picked up her card key from the credenza. Its white plastic was stained from dirt.

"Is it okay if they cut your melon, or do you need little round balls?"

Harmony had one leg raised above her head, leaning against the wall in a ballerina's vertical split. She looked over at me. "I'm sorry," she said. "Hungry. Bad mood."

"I know. Me too."

Outside the air was cool, dawn broken but not yet warming things up. Cars hummed along the airport road, and a jet rose, shining gold in the sunrise. The Waffle House was only a few hundred yards down the road, but I drove anyway—pedestrians were the exception here, and I don't like being an exception.

Coming out of the restaurant with a paper sack and two cardboard cups, I bought a copy of the *Tribune-Review* from a vending box. It seemed like a good idea to allow Harmony some additional time to herself. Back in the car I powered all the windows open, clicked the ignition back to off and pulled out the phone she'd given me last night. It was nothing fancy—another throwaway, in fact. I dialed Clara's number.

"About time I heard from you," she said.

"Sorry about that. Busy down here."

"Harmony, huh?"

I paused a half second too long. "There's lots going on—"

Clara laughed. "Good for you. She coming back to New York?"

"No, and we haven't picked out a china pattern either. Can we talk about this some other time?"

"Sure." The flippancy departed. "I saw Zeke in the hospital last night."

I knew he'd planned to get a medflight back to New York. Zeke lives cheap in many ways, but he has the best medical insurance private money can buy. "He doing any better?"

"Stronger every day, he says. He didn't look too bad, actually. Doctors wouldn't mind keeping him, but you know Zeke—more worried about iatrogenic infection than a bullet through his lung. He's going home later today."

"I'll check in as soon as I'm back."

I pulled the tab off my coffee cup and drank. The sun was just up, and in the dawn's long shadows the car was still cold.

"Zeke couldn't tell me much about what's going on, though," Clara said. "Johnny had some bizarre story—Markson selling one of his companies to himself, in partnership with Russian energy money. What the hell are you doing down there?"

"I think that's right," I said. "It doesn't reflect very well on Markson, but I wasn't hired to enforce an ethics code. The real villain here—actually, 'villain' is too strong. The real *idiot* here is Brinker. If he hadn't totally corrupted Clay Micro, Markson's scheme would have gone off without a hiccup. He'd get his money, the Russians would get a half share of a drilling tech company, and they'd be on to the next deal. I'm sure Clay Micro is just one small step in a long chain of interlocked acquisitions, facilitated by Markson to keep his empire afloat a few more years."

"But Brinker screwed it up?" I could hear her taking notes on her computer.

"This is all deep background, right?"

"Sure. Until you tell me different."

"Brinker might have skated through, despite all the money he'd stolen, but he tried to shut down the investigation. Unfortunately, he used the crudest method available—his new drinking buddies, the Russians. They went and started a range war just to put a few curious accountants off the trail."

"That's how Johnny told it." She stopped typing. "So . . . is it over?"

"Starting to feel that way." I wasn't sure, though. "I'm just not sure what to do about Markson."

"Why do you have to do anything?"

"Harmony's worried someone might come after her. Or me. Just to keep the story buttoned up."

"That doesn't sound like anything Markson would do. I mean, come on, the Buddha? He was on the cover of *The Economist* like two months ago!"

"I don't know," I said. "Maybe I'll write him a letter."

After we hung up, I started to call Johnny, then reconsidered. He'd already said he was trading against Markson, but that wasn't going to get anyone in trouble. Maybe he'd even put a little aside for me, throw a little friends-and-family into my beneficial account.

I flipped through the newspaper while I finished my coffee. God knows why anyone wants to know what's going on in the world anymore. I looked for the sports pages.

I almost missed the article, buried on page five of the third section.

―――――――

"It must be the same site Brendt and his buddies were working on." I talked through a mouthful of muffin, checking both mirrors before I bumped the car out of the parking lot. Harmony studied the paper folded in her lap, spooning oatmeal rapidly from a plastic container. "How many fracking press events can there be today? With a celebrity like him coming?"

"There's no address. Just says Erlenton."

"We'll go over to Brendt's house. He can tell us."

"If he's back yet."

"If he isn't—I hate to say it, but Dave will probably be there. He might know."

I'd already tried Dave's phone, and it had gone to voicemail twice in a row.

"Too much sugar." Harmony finished her oatmeal. "But, you know, thanks."

The article was short, with no photo:

WILBUR MARKSON TO VISIT NEW NATURAL GAS PROJECT

The man himself, come to cut the ribbon at the biggest well-head yet drilled in western Pennsylvania. The reporter hadn't done much more than retype a press release, quoting company executives talking about millions of cubic feet per day, tax dollars, clean fuel and energy independence.

"Looks like he's okay with nonrenewables after all," I said.

"But fracking?"

"Not so much, but if there's money in it, I imagine he'll bear up." Having his smiling, cherubic face at a well-manicured well, nothing but a quiet pipe about the size of a fire hydrant, was just believable.

"He's not too far away, either."

"What do you mean?"

"Doesn't Markson live in Ohio? That's right across the state line."

"It's a big state." But she had a point.

"What do you expect to do?" Harmony asked.

"Confront him?"

"That's dumb. And pointless. Markson won't talk to you—his people won't let you get near him."

"I know." I jammed the rest of the muffin into my mouth and

mumbled around it. "It's what you said. 'His people.' That might include the Russians."

"So?"

"So I'm tired. I want to go home. A conversation with Markson directly might be the easiest way to convince him we're done."

"What if he doesn't believe you?"

"Then I threaten to go public. Can't hurt."

Harmony drank off her coffee. "Okay. Why not?"

Coming up to Brendt's house, the first thing I saw was the Charger, gleaming in the early sun.

"Dave's here," I said, pulling into the driveway behind it. "And Brendt's Saturn isn't. He must not have come home yet."

"Overnight." Harmony got out, shaking her head. "That's not going to end well."

We walked up. The wooden steps creaked once, but the house stood silent, windows closed. After a moment I knocked.

The door swung open beneath my hand.

Fuck.

Harmony went sideways immediately, the Kahr appearing in her hand.

"Elsie?" I called into the darkness inside. "Dave?"

Nothing. Harmony and I glanced at each other.

"They could still be asleep," I said in a low voice.

"Uh-huh."

We went in like it was hostile—me first and immediately left, Harmony next and right. I shoved the door back with my shoulder, making sure no one was hiding behind it, while Harmony swept the room then moved to the next door.

Still nobody, but I caught a smell coming from the kitchen.

"Aw, *shit*."

Harmony was already there, peering around the door frame. She straightened and turned back to me, raising her free hand slightly.

"It's bad," she said.

We cleared the house first. Protocol. Harmony went point, pistol at ready, room to room, then the basement. It took less than a minute—the bungalow couldn't have been more than a thousand square feet. No one else was there.

I stood in the kitchen doorway.

Elsie slumped in a chair, half fallen onto the table, one arm dangling to the side. Blood ran underneath her, over the table, dripped onto the floor. It looked sticky already. I could see an exit wound at the back of her head, and there was enough mess in the back of her T-shirt to suggest another one there.

Rage coursed through me, stiffening my muscles. A keening, wordless sound came out for a moment before I realized and bit it off.

Flies buzzed.

The other body had fallen in front of the stove, curled onto the floor. He held a pistol, and the side of his head facing up was nothing but gore.

For all the violence I've seen, it never gets easier.

"It's *Brendt*," I said finally. My jaw hurt. "I thought, for sure—"

Harmony knelt, not touching anything, studying angles.

"Looks like a murder-suicide," she said. "He killed her first, then put the gun to his head."

I was wrenched two ways—horror at the deaths, relief that Dave wasn't one of them. The emotions didn't sit well together, and I forced them down, forced myself to concentrate.

"No." I said. A scrap of white on the floor caught my attention.

"*Looks* like."

"He didn't do it."

She stood up, holstering her own weapon. "It could be a setup. Forensics might find some clues. Main thing is, situations like this, the murderer usually doesn't kill himself in front of the victim. He goes somewhere else."

I didn't answer, but bent to the floor and picked up the bit of paper I'd noticed. No—not paper, a cigarette.

Filterless. Just like the one from Brendt's car.

"On the statistics," Harmony said. "Like he can't look at what he's done."

"Whatever. I know *this* one's a frame."

"We have to get out of here."

We stepped through the living room, more carefully this time.

"I think you're right," said Harmony quietly, as we paused by the front door. "And we have to think about who might have done it."

"The Russians." I didn't like how cold and certain my voice was coming out, though I couldn't control it.

"Maybe." Harmony put her hand on my arm. "But you have to consider—it could have been Dave, too."

"No."

"Why would the Russians care about Elsie? Dave's the only one with *motive*. It's the oldest triangle in the world."

"Brendt's left-handed," I said. "Dave knew that—he's been friends with the guy since they were eight years old."

"Oh."

"Yeah." I looked out. The neighborhood was quiet. No sirens. "Whoever arranged the scene in there, they put the gun in the wrong fucking hand."

Harmony went straight for the car, but I angled across the lawn, headed for the neighbor's house. It was the same vintage as Brendt's, though more nicely kept.

"What are you doing?" Harmony called.

"Just a minute." I pressed the bungalow's bell, setting off chimes inside. A baby began to cry. After a half minute a drawn woman in sweats opened the door.

"What's so goddamned important you had to go and wake her up for!" she demanded, rocking an infant in a stained onesie over her shoulder.

"Sorry," I said. "I'm looking for Dave Ellins. My brother? Have you seen him?"

"What?" Her mouth opened.

"Dave Ellins? That's his car over there."

"I know Dave." She squinted. "You look just like him!"

"Yeah. Listen, you hear anything earlier this morning? Shouting, like that?"

"What are you talking about?"

"I'm just trying to find Dave." That didn't make much sense, but the woman looked too tired for logical reasoning.

"Dunno." She stared at Brendt's house. "The way Carly cries, I could of missed a bomb going off. Up half the night."

"Okay, thanks." I turned to go.

"Wait—where's Brendt?"

I didn't reply, just gestured vaguely with one hand and kept going.

Harmony was sitting in the driver's seat, but slid over when I opened the door.

"I was getting ready to wire it," she said.

I paused. "Can you do that?"

She rolled her eyes. "How do you *manage*?"

I ignored the comment. "There's only one way to figure this. Dave came over in the Charger, then left again. Brendt must have lent him *his* car. The killing happened after."

"How—?"

"If Dave found them like that, and decided to run, he'd have taken the Charger—it's faster and it's his. Even more so if the Russians were chasing him."

"What if they caught him already?"

I didn't want to think about that. "Let's assume not."

Harmony still didn't seem convinced. "We don't *know* it was them."

I showed her the cigarette I'd picked up from the floor. "It's the same as we found in Brendt's car after they used it to attack the garage."

"Well . . ."

"There's no one else involved." I said it with utter finality. "You, me and them are the only players on the field right now."

She nodded slowly. "Okay."

"Look up Rockwire. On that fancy phone of yours? That's where the Russians came from. So we'll go there and ask where they went."

"What about Dave?"

"He could be anywhere. I don't *know*." Frustration raised my voice. "Rockwire is our only lead."

"Yeah." Harmony didn't like it any more than I did, but she saw the logic—and she had the address in twenty seconds. She could thumb as fast as a twelve-year-old on the phone's virtual keyboard.

"Let's go. Fellsville is west and south—head for 119."

"Hang on." I looked once more at Brendt's house, the neighbor, the trees, a truck on the road, downshifting at the grade. "Let's do this smart. Can you hotwire the Charger?"

"Easy."

"You take it, then. I'll drive this one. We're too vulnerable in one vehicle."

"Right." She nodded. "In that case." She rummaged in the backup gear bag and came up with a bluetooth earpiece—her "Be Prepared" approach was really making me look bad—then a moment later a second identical one.

"Synch this to your phone," she said. "You need to be hands-free if we're going in hard."

"Far as I know, we're going in to ask a receptionist some questions." But I took the earpiece. While I fiddled, getting them talking to each other, Harmony went over to Dave's car.

I'd just gotten the blue indicator to glow steady when the Charger rumbled to life. I glanced up, saw Harmony strapped in, pointing at her own head. After a moment I realized what she meant, slipped the earpiece into place and dialed her number.

"You hear me okay?"

"We're good." Her voice, traveling through multiple wireless connections, was a little buzzy but clear enough. "Ready?"

"Wait." I got out of the car once more, ran over and banged on the neighbor's door again. The baby howled inside. The mother came out furious.

"I *told* you, don't fucking make so much fucking *noise*!"

"Call the police," I said.

"What?"

"Elsie and Brendt are dead."

Her mouth fell open.

"Just call 911!" I sprinted back to my car, checked the rearview and accelerated backward into the road, gravel spraying, Harmony right behind. As I backed up, the engine whining in reverse, Harmony got in front and took off.

"What was that about?" she said over the phone.

"Someone might have seen us, right? This way, telling her to call the police, we don't look so much like murderers."

"Huh." She sped up, almost leaving me behind.

"Slow down!" I shouted.

"This machine is a *beauty*."

We decelerated for a red light, but it turned green and the Charger rabbited forward. I put the accelerator to the floor and strained to keep up.

"Just . . . drive it like you *own* it," I said into the phone. "Dave will never forgive me if you total his car."

CHAPTER THIRTY-FOUR

Rockwire sprawled over several acres, from what I could tell driving past. A bit of shrubbery and a large wooden sign at the front gate, and chain-link stretching off in either direction down the road. Behind the fence a large muddy lot held an open-pit mine's worth of heavy equipment: trucks, tankers, bulldozers and excavators, specialized drilling rigs and stacks of pipe. A pile of gravel at one end, stacked barrels with hazmat labels at the other. A long metal building had most of its bay doors open to the sun, mechanics and welders visible inside.

Not far from the front gate was what was obviously the administration building—two stories of brick and glass with a neatly kept lawn and blacktop for executive parking. Several large American cars in the front rank, and some older econoboxes at the back, presumably owned by secretaries and junior accountants.

And a Saturn, empty, in one of three visitor spots closest to the front entrance. Fear stabbed me in the gut.

"The car's there," I said.

"I saw it." Harmony's voice in the earpiece, flattened by the connection. She was a quarter mile ahead of me. "You sure it's Brendt's?"

"Long scratch down the side and a cracked windshield. Dave must be here."

"What's he *doing*?"

"Same as us, has to be." I realized I'd clenched the steering wheel so tightly my hands hurt.

"Maybe." Other possibilities were on the table, but she didn't need to mention them. "Look, keep driving. There's a farm stand down the road. I'll wait for you there."

We were off I-79, not far from the interchange, in rural countryside. I'd already gotten stuck behind a tractor towing a large, empty trailer—several minutes at ten miles an hour before the road opened up enough to pass. Low hills, fields and fencerows, patches of forest. Hand-painted signs were nailed to trees and fence posts here and there: MULCH, FRESH CORN, 45 ACRES FOR SALE—MAKE OFFER.

Harmony parked the Charger at the edge of a gravel lot. The barnlike wooden building behind it had some shaded tables with potted seedlings and sacks of compost and vermiculite. Two plastic-sheet greenhouses extended from the rear. No other customers—it was midmorning, early for business.

She got out as I drove up, and we stood in the sun.

"No time for recon," I said. "God knows what's happening in there."

"Yes." She nodded. "If they're killing civilians, either the clock is running or they don't fucking care."

"Brendt doesn't make sense. Still less Elsie. They didn't have anything to do with *anything*."

"You and Dave look so much alike." Harmony stood with her arms crossed. It was as if last night—everything between us—had never happened. "They might have mistaken him for you, somewhere along the line, and tracked him down."

"And interrogated Brendt and Elsie to find out where he went, then killed them to cover their tracks."

"Or just because they made a mistake and were pissed about it." Her voice was flat. "Assholes like this will do anything."

She knew it, same as me.

"Time to go," I said.

"Dave—no telling what he's doing in there."

"Nothing. If we're lucky."

"Yes."

"Are you . . . I mean, this isn't your fight."

"Don't be stupid."

We'd slipped a link, somehow, on the personal stuff. "Okay."

"I'll stay outside," she said.

"Mobile response." On the other hand, we were totally synchronized on the pragmatics. "Right."

"You bring him out, I'll follow, make sure there's no pursuit. Something goes wrong, blow the whistle and I'll come get both of you."

"That's a plan."

"No, it's not." But she wasn't arguing.

We checked weapons and double-checked comms. I switched the Sig to a shoulder holster. Harmony had the Kahr. Plenty of reloads, thanks again to her foresight in planting that kit at the hotel.

"Oh, by the way," I said. "Is the dynamite still in your trunk?"

"*What?*"

"Did I forget to mention that?"

She hit the release and we took a look. The bucket of explosive that Dave had been carrying around since the FerroCorp demolition sat next to a large toolbox and an oily blanket.

Harmony stepped back. "That's raw nitroglycerine! I can't believe you let me drive around like this!"

"Yeah, you might want to take it a little slower."

"Shit." She shook her head. "Leave it here. That stuff is contact sensitive—one stray bullet and it's game over. Get it *away*."

"Okay, okay, I'll keep it." She had a canvas athletic bag, and I dropped it in with the extra magazines. "We can't have some innocent gardener stumbling across it."

Finally packed, we got in our respective cars. Harmony hesitated.

"Nothing happens, we meet back here?"

"Sure."

"Be careful." And she was gone.

Huh.

An uneventful two minutes to drive back. Harmony went past. As I entered the plant I could just see her down the road, turning around.

The gate was open, both sides swung back, and not staffed. Mostly to keep thieves out at night, probably. I drove another hundred yards to the admin building and did a three-point turn, backing the car in right next to the Saturn.

I left the engine running, the driver's door almost closed but not quite latched, its window rolled down. Someone walking past might notice, but I was faced away from the building's windows and no one inside would see anything odd.

Distant noise from the shops—metal banging on metal, the squeal of an air wrench. A tanker truck drove out, the diesel engine blatting loudly enough to echo off the walls in front of me. The day was warming but still cool.

I shrugged to settle the holster, made sure my jacket still hung free and walked to the entrance.

Double glass doors, a reception area tiled in ceramic, wraparound desk at the other end, framed photos of drill rigs and pipelines on the wall. The woman behind the desk looked up as I came in—she was on the phone, talking into her headset. Two low couches with vinyl cushions faced each other, one person sitting.

Dave. A wave of relief, as overwhelming as the fear had been when I realized he was here.

He got up, eyes opening wide in surprise.

"Silas! What are you doing?"

"That's *my* question." I kept my voice low enough that the receptionist couldn't hear. "Why the fuck are you here?"

"Brendt and I were talking after he finished up that job last night. I asked about Russians, like has he seen any around, and he mentioned this place. I thought I could come check it out. Brendt lent me his car so I could be, like, undercover."

"We have to leave," I said.

Resignation flitted across his face like a shadow. "I was trying to help," he said.

"It's okay. I'm glad. Come *on*."

"What's—"

"Too dangerous here."

"Why?"

He couldn't know about Elsie and Brendt. No one was that good an actor.

"Can't explain now. Let's go."

He turned toward the receptionist, who was staring at us.

Maybe because I hadn't announced myself yet; maybe for the same reason everyone stared at Dave and me, because we looked so much alike.

Maybe because she'd just called the Russians.

"We have to go *now*." I grasped Dave's arm lightly, above the elbow, and pointed him to the door.

"Okay." He shrugged. "Back in a second," he called to the woman, whose response was lost as I pushed out the door.

I kept moving. "Come with me. You leave anything in Brendt's car?"

"Uh, nope. Like I said, he let me borrow it because, you know, it doesn't stand out like mine."

"I figured. Move."

"We're leaving?"

"As fast as possible."

Dave finally seemed to get the picture. "Okay then."

We approached the vehicles. "Can you drive?"

"Sure."

"No offense, but Brendt's car is both a pile of junk and known to the Russians." I gestured. "Known quite well . . . we'll take mine instead."

Dave looked. "That's a Toyota."

"That's right."

Dave shook his head but put out his hand. "Keys?"

"Inside. It's running."

I slid into the passenger seat as Dave slammed the driver's door. He quickly adjusted the seat and mirrors, lowered the steering wheel a notch and put it into drive.

All very competent, but the real reason I wanted him there was in case the Russians appeared. His competitive advantage was driving, and mine was shooting at bad guys. It'd be stupid to reverse that.

Five seconds after leaving the building we rolled toward the gate. Nothing happened.

Sunshine. A guy walking across the lot with a lunch box in one hand. I smelled exhaust and mud.

"We're clear," I said as we exited the gate.

"Got you." Harmony's voice. She'd heard everything I'd said, of course, and had the sense not to add unnecessary cross-talk while I was inside. I twisted my head around to see her behind us, swinging onto the road two hundred yards back.

"I have to tell you something," I said to Dave.

"What? What's going on?"

"Elsie is dead. Someone killed her this morning."

"Oh my God!" We lost some acceleration as he fell back in the seat. "Wha—what . . . ?"

"In Brendt's house."

I was ashamed of myself that moment, holding Brendt back to see if Dave made a mistake. More than ashamed.

But I wasn't taking chances.

"I can't believe—I was there an hour ago! Her and Brendt gave me some breakfast, you know, toast and corn flakes, after Brendt got back from his job." He stopped. "Wait, what about *Brendt?*"

"I'm sorry." I was. "Him too."

"Who *did* it?"

"I don't know."

"But . . . but, dead, killed—"

He was taking it about as well as anyone, which is to say not great.

"Silas!" Harmony shouted in my ear. "They're on you!"

I woke up and wrenched my attention back to the road. Nothing in front. I swung around and saw a truck roaring up on us.

Not a truck—a white panel van with a contractor's rack on top.

"Behind us!" I drew the pistol from under my jacket. "Watch out!"

Dave looked in the mirror, straightened up and jammed the accelerator to the floor. The Toyota sped up.

Far too sluggish compared to the Charger.

I felt a sudden rush of wind, and a second later realized the rear window had been shattered. Air noise roared through the car. Too loud to hear gunshots, but I saw a man leaning out the van's passenger window with a handgun.

"They're shooting," I yelled to Harmony and Dave both. He swerved right, then left, jinking across the blacktop, tires squealing.

"I'm on them." Harmony was calm, at least. "But I can't do much. They're right behind you."

"I know."

"Who *is* it?" Dave raised his voice over the road and wind noise.

"The Russians. The ones who killed Elsie and Brendt." Probably.

"Cocksu-u-u-u-u-ckers!"

The windshield starred in front of me—a bullet must have gone right through, between us. I pointed the Sig and fired once, twice. No effect. Impossible to aim from the moving car. The van closed, speeding up, but there was too much glare on its glass to get a clear view inside. Dave jerked our car to one side again, then back onto the straightaway. My eyes were tearing from the rush of wind through broken windows.

"This car's a piece of shit," he yelled. "We're losing to a fucking *minivan*."

Oncoming traffic—we shot past a row of cars trailing a slow flatbed in the other direction. A flashing glimpse of shocked faces, staring at our shattered windows and the van about two feet behind us.

"Anyone behind him?" Dave shouted.

"Uh—"

"*Fuck* them." And he suddenly yanked the parking brake, twisting the wheel hard left simultaneously.

"Harmony!" I realized what Dave was doing. "Drop back! Drop *back*!"

"What?"

The Toyota spun around, skidding down the road at sixty miles an hour as it slid through a one-eighty. Dave let it drift into the left lane and the van rocketed past us, unable to stop. He tapped the gas, flicked the wheel, then twisted it farther, and we stayed in the spin, coming all the way back around. I had a glimpse of the Charger, rubber smoking as Harmony jammed the brakes so she didn't slam into us. The handbrake released—a fishtail right, left, then Dave stomped the gas again and I was jolted back as the wheels bit.

Suddenly we were behind the van, coming up fast. Harmony accelerated into position, following.

"Hey, that's *my* car!" Dave said, checking the rearview. "Who's driving?"

"Harmony."

"Does she know what she's doing?"

"I hope so."

The van cut into the left lane, then back. We'd accelerated again, maybe sixty or seventy miles an hour. Dave was twenty feet behind. He floored it, and we rapidly closed the gap.

"No, wait—"

Too late. We struck the van's bumper. I was slung forward, the seatbelt cutting painfully across my shoulder and chest. The crash knocked the van hard, and it swerved back and forth before coming back into the lane.

I reached out the window and fired twice more, hoping the men inside would see me and think twice. A glance back confirmed that Harmony was still on our tail. The road curved and rose, fell, rose again. We flashed through a stand of trees, shade briefly dappling the vehicles.

"Don't do that again," I said. "Dumb."

"What?"

"Come up alongside, then tap their rear wheel well with the front of this car." I looked over at him. "Don't you know this?"

"Know what?"

"It's how you knock out a car in front of you. The police use it all the time. Hitting the back is stupid—*everyone* ends up in the ditch that way."

"I never did demolition derby."

"Trust me."

He moved right, and a second later the van moved in the same direction, to block us from passing. Dave smiled grimly.

"Harmony," I said. "Stand clear."

"Coming up on the interstate," she said.

What was she doing, watching her phone's GPS? "She says we're almost at the interchange," I told Dave.

"Whatever."

He lured the van a little farther right until all our passenger-side wheels were kicking gravel from the breakdown verge. Then he hit the gas. The Toyota leaped forward and left. In two seconds we'd cleared the rear bumper, coming up to pass the van on the left. It accelerated, trying to get away. Dave drifted a little farther left—

—then swung the wheel hard right. The car swerved and struck the van just behind the rear wheel. The collision thrust them into an immediate spin. We were past in an instant. I had a kaleido-scopic glimpse of the van's front, twisting around as we missed it by inches. Then we were clear.

Dave popped a second bootlegger's turn, to the right this time, and the Toyota screamed through the one-eighty, burning rubber down a hundred yards of asphalt.

We slid to a halt.

The van's wheels went into the ditch. The driver almost made it, but the skid took him just a little too far right. When the tires dipped and hit the soft mud of the verge, they seized up. Momentum threw the van over. It kept moving another several yards, tearing the hell out of the ground, sliding on its left side.

It finally stopped, a hundred yards behind us.

Harmony skidded to a stop too, right alongside Dave's door. She looked across.

"Nice one."

"Dave gets credit."

"Harmony." He sounded shaky.

Nothing moved at the van.

Dave reversed and swung the car around to face forward, then pulled to the side. Harmony followed. Vehicles approached from the other direction, slowed and stopped closer to the van. I could see an SUV on our side, also stopping. Doors swung open.

Harmony put her head out her window to talk to us. "Now what?"

"Authorities will be here any minute," I said. "Troopers first, probably, if we're that close to the highway."

She looked down—must have had her phone in her hand. "Markson's making his big speech in half an hour."

It wasn't a hard decision. "Let's go."

"Wait." Dave looked between us. "What's happening? Shouldn't we wait for the police?"

"Nah." Harmony grimaced. "That'll just waste everyone's time."

"Markson," I said.

"Right."

"What?" Dave, still confused.

"It's our chance," I said. "He'll be out, talking to the public, and if he hears anything about this cockup"—I gestured toward the wrecked van—"he might be a little off-balance. We'll probably get only one shot. This seems like the best time."

"*One* shot?" said Harmony. "You?"

"We're only going to talk," I said.

CHAPTER THIRTY-FIVE

Markson was guilty of *something*. I just wasn't sure how far he'd been involved.

True, he'd definitely gone into business with shady Russian money, and tried to keep it secret. Thirty years of ethical profit making, but when push came to shove, apparently the profits part was a lot more important to him than the ethics part. Selling Clay Micro was a way of shifting assets over to the Russian mafiya, in exchange for their money laundered through Dagger Light.

Furthermore, once I showed up at Clay Micro, Markson apparently hired Harmony and her crew to abduct me for an extended session of tea and interrogation. The Clayco board must have tied themselves in knots over that one—they'd contracted Ryan to hide a little problem from Markson, then it blew up and suddenly Markson himself swooped in with his own shut-it-down-*now* initiative, right over their heads.

But by that point Brinker had knocked everything truly to pieces by calling in the Russians. Unlike the refined *oligarkhi* Markson presumably dealt with, Dagger Light's street-level enforcers came after me the same way they'd probably once pacified Chechen villages. Now it was anarchy: everyone shooting at everyone else, innocents in the cross fire everywhere.

The question was, what did Markson know about Brinker? Were they aligned with each other somehow? They weren't consulting at the beginning—otherwise either Harmony or the Russians would have come knocking, but not *both*.

But Harmony got a cessation-of-contract notice and the Russians didn't.

In the end, Markson knew or didn't know. It wasn't more complicated than that.

We didn't have time to plod through a long, detailed investigation. For personal reasons, we couldn't hand it over to the real authorities—anything more than passing interest from the law would mean vast difficulty for Harmony and me. Dave's circumstances were no less muddled.

No, we needed a quick resolution. And by far the quickest I could think of was to confront Markson directly. Get it all out into the open, and see what happened.

He wouldn't confess, of course, if he was guilty. But maybe he'd have a convincing denial—and if not, he'd at least be on warning that we knew the story. Then Harmony and I could start negotiating a deal that let us walk away.

And Dave too, of course.

It was a tough ride. Harmony stayed in the Charger, but I took over the driving from Dave, who had begun falling apart when the adrenaline ran out and the fact of Brendt and Elsie's deaths sank in.

"All my fault."

"What?"

"If I hadn't been over at their house so long, no one would have looked for me there."

I had to concentrate on driving to keep the Charger in view. Harmony was way over the local speed limits.

"You didn't kill them," I said. "Hold on to that. Other people do bad things—it's nothing on you."

"How did they die?"

I shook my head. "Badly."

We arrived at the event site in twenty-five minutes. I had only a vague idea where we were—Harmony had the directions, and I was just following. Somewhere east of Clabbton and south of Pittsburgh, in a region of hills and woods and small farms. We'd been on I-79 for fifteen miles, then back onto state roads, then county blacktop. Not far past a one-stoplight town Harmony slowed, and I came up behind the Charger.

"Another mile," she said through the earpiece. "According to the online maps."

"Can you get satellite view?"

"Nothing useful. We're in low-res territory out here."

We passed a cemetery, stones and markers in the midday sun. Some had small American flags in front of them.

"We're almost there," I said to Dave.

"Okay."

Harmony's voice: "What's the plan?"

Good question. "Any ideas?"

"No."

"Well, then," I said. "The usual."

There weren't the crowds I'd been expecting. Two television trucks, a row of cars parked along the road, a small group of people around a small stage. The area wasn't anything like the fracking site where I'd had breakfast—here, the drilling had been completed, all the equipment removed, and the pipeline put in place. The ground had been resodded, the pits filled in, the slick-water catchment erased from the landscape.

A few pickups and one heavy truck had been relegated to the farthest parking. I didn't see a hard hat anywhere.

We parked at the end of the row. Harmony put the Charger between the last car and the mine, and I left plenty of room—the next latecomer wouldn't block it in.

"We're just going to talk?" Harmony said.

"Sure." I took the canvas bag with the extra magazines she'd given me and checked the Sig one more time. "But you never know. Maybe he'll have a lot to say."

The pipe came out of the ground in a small concrete pad. It gleamed with fresh green paint—subtle, that—an elbow and valve wheel at the top, another pipe leading away at ground level on a lightly graveled bed. The standpipe had been roped off with surveyor's twine tied to metal stakes, ten feet square.

Nearby, the stage was raised four feet above the turf, a plain affair of two-by-fours and planking, clearly knocked together with circular saws and screw drills. I thought of Brendt, feeling a pang I had to suppress. A podium with a microphone stood in the middle, flanked by two flagpoles. The Stars and Stripes, sure, but I didn't recognize the other, barely stirring in the breeze—Pennsylvania's state flag? Or did Markson have his own pennant?

We split up, to move in from different points and converge. Three people shoving their way through all at once would be too obvious.

I drifted along, examining the gas pipe at my feet, like I was pondering the vast amount of energy it promised to deliver. Less than a foot in diameter, but a million cubic feet per day—the disproportion was impressive.

"Sir?"

I looked up to discover two police officers. No, not police—private security, but with bloused combat boots, blue uniforms, badges and heavy sidearms. My mistake was probably common and surely intended.

"Yes?"

"You can't carry that bag up near the stage."

I glanced at it. "Just some books and stuff. A water bottle."

"All the same. Sorry, sir."

"I'll leave it here." I slid the bag off and set it on the ground.

The man started to speak, but someone tapped the microphone and an amplified voice boomed out. "Hello? Hello?"

"They're starting," I said. "I don't want to carry this all the way back to the car."

"Well, sir—"

I pushed the bag into the pipe's shadow, where it was barely visible. "Don't worry, I won't forget and leave it here."

"All right." The second guard spoke. I nodded thanks and they turned away.

"Thank you for coming." The amplification really was too loud. "It's a beautiful day for us here, for Pennsylvania, and for America's energy future!"

Brief applause. One TV crew was filming, the other still standing around, presumably waiting for the headliner. The guards moved off. I considered recovering the munitions bag, but it seemed too risky.

And I wasn't *completely* disarmed, after all.

Harmony was on the other side of the crowd—forty people, tops—and catching eyes. Even the man at the podium had a glance for her. Dave was in the middle somewhere, as anonymous as, hopefully, me.

"We are extremely fortunate to have Wilbur Markson joining us today. Wilbur needs no introduction, surely!" The speaker went on to introduce him. "America's most famous ethical investor, whose Sweetwater fund has returned twenty percent every year for thirty-*one* years now—an unequaled record, and he's done it entirely by focusing on good, honest American companies. Those are the kinds of businesses that create *real* value. Value for his investors, value for customers, value for the entire economy . . ."

The speech went on. I continued through the crowd, approaching the stage.

Markson was instantly recognizable: tuft of white hair, his plain farmer's face, a twinkle in his eye behind old-fashioned glasses. He sat between another man and a woman—executives, in suits much nicer than his.

Motion at the edge of the crowd caught my eye. Four men, jogging up from the row of cars.

One was a head taller than the others, and he looked seriously pissed.

"Yo," I said quietly into the earpiece, not moving my lips. "Trouble."

"I see." Harmony's voice.

"Have they seen *you?*"

"No."

No, because they'd seen me first. The big guy shouted something I didn't catch. The speaker on stage faltered. Markson frowned, looking out from the stage.

Private security flowed through the crowd—at least six in uniform, plus a couple of men in suit coats who were moving with too much purpose to be bystanders. All headed for the Russians.

They might not have coordinated cross-jurisdictional issues beforehand.

I stepped to the side of the platform, closer than I would have gotten had security not been distracted by the new arrivals.

"Markson." I said it quietly, just loud enough to carry. "Hey, Wilbur."

The five people on stage turned to look down at me. I heard voices in the crowd—something Russian, a response.

"Clay Micro," I said, more clearly. "What gives?"

Markson smoothed his frown away and looked puzzled, like your favorite cuddly uncle. "Excuse me?"

"That thoroughly corrupt pipeline supplier you're selling to your oligarch partners? Have you seen the financials yet?"

Markson pointed at me and looked behind him, saying something I couldn't catch to the woman. Her eyes widened, and she pulled out a cellphone.

"Silas Cade!" The voice was loud, heavily accented—and far too close. I spun around.

The seven-foot Russian was almost on me, bulling through the crowd. He strong-armed a man in a gray suit, who stumbled and fell, then pushed past a woman in a windbreaker. She squawked an objection. Three security men caught up with him, and he shook them off like gnats.

I went for my gun but he was too fast—leaping forward, he struck me hard in the center of my chest. I tumbled backward, breathing paralyzed from the blow, and fell gasping.

"*Mudak!*" He yanked me up by one arm. A moment later a second Russian arrived and grabbed my other.

They hyperextended my elbows with immobilization grips, one on each side. I couldn't do anything—the slightest pressure would break the joints. More blue-uniformed security arrived. The giant just growled at them.

Markson stepped to the edge of the stage and looked down at my face. His expression was no longer avuncular, but cold and thin lipped. He shook his head slightly.

"Mr. Markson? Sir?" One of the American guards tried to get his attention. "We'll convey him to the police—"

"That won't be necessary." Markson gestured. "Settle the audience."

"Yes sir, but—"

"*Thank* you, officer."

The man took a hint, perhaps flattered slightly by the honorific. Markson leaned in. "*Ubey ego i izbavsya ote tela,*" he said in a low voice.

He spoke Russian? Interesting, but even more so was the one phrase I'd caught: *Ubey ego.*

Kill him.

The seven-footer smiled slightly and started to pull me away. I couldn't do anything but try to stay on my feet and hope the ligaments didn't tear.

KA-BLAAAAM!

An explosion shattered the air, stunningly loud.

The pressure wave knocked people off their feet all around

me. Both my captors stumbled. Their holds faltered—and that was enough.

I went low, recovered one arm and struck backward as hard as I could with the elbow, catching the shorter Russian just below the belt buckle. He oofed and started to collapse.

A great huge *WHOOMP!* and the fireball expanded. I felt heat sear the side of my face. Screaming and terror all around.

Harmony had shot the dynamite, right under the pipeline.

The big guy clouted me on the shoulder. Probably trying for the neck and thank Christ he missed—as it was, my entire arm went numb. I pushed back, trying to get away from him, and banged into the wooden frame holding the stage. He swung again, I ducked.

His fist broke a two-by-four. The stage sagged. Markson and the woman fell atop each other, yelling.

I spun away again, managed to get some distance.

"Silas!"

Dave's voice. I glanced in that direction. So did the Russian. He grunted and slapped his hand backward, like he was shooing a dog. Dave took it in the face and collapsed.

I had my balance, so I snapped a kick at the giant's knee. I hit the patella dead on, and with all the force I could muster—but his leg was flexed, and so strong that my foot bounced off, not doing any apparent damage.

"Yobaniy v rot!"

Jesus Christ. I backed up again, deflected a blow, scrambled for room.

This wasn't going well.

The fireball subsided slightly, but the burn remained fierce, a hot flaming roar twenty feet high. The pipeline must have broken open, flaring all that high-pressure natural gas.

So much for energy freedom. If this got out of control, we'd probably burn down half of Pennsylvania.

The Russian came at me again, trying a kick of his own this time. He was so tall the mechanics slowed him down and I had a half second to twist away. He followed through easily, spun on his other foot, and kicked again. Missed me, hit the stage a second time. More wooden beams fractured.

It seemed to be personal. I would have gone for a gun.

Wait a minute—I *had* a gun. What was I thinking?

My right arm was still uselessly numb. I tried to draw left-handed, while still scuttling away. He sneered and followed, fast as a whip.

I gave up on the gun and ran—straight for the fireball.

He was two yards away. I turned, stumbled, started to fall.

A scream. Even through the chaos and fire I recognized Harmony. The giant was a blur, fists swinging in. I went to the ground hard, on my back—

And brought both legs up, curled and *kicked*. As hard as I could, every bit of strength and anger channeled into one strike.

I caught him square, at hip level. The combination of his momentum and my assist kept him in the air, flying right over me. Out of control.

Right into the inferno.

CHAPTER THIRTY-SIX

The Clabbton VFW wasn't much—one story, wood—and could have done with new paint years ago. But the gravel lot was filled, and more vehicles were parked down the road on both sides. Two guys in black suits pointed newcomers where to leave their cars, helped older folks through the door, murmured directions and condolences.

The morning sun was sharp and clear. Birds twittered in the trees behind the hall. It took a moment for my eyes to adjust when I stepped inside.

Closed caskets, of course, on a dais up front. Two, end to end so people could pay their respects in order. Some black bunting on one table with flowers. A slatted metal hatch had been rolled up over the pass-through counter to the hall's kitchen, and two women were serving coffee. Some trays of cookies and brownies, the plastic wrap just coming off. Nothing store-bought here.

There must have been a hundred people inside and with those numbers, even quiet and respectful chatting raised a din. But that was okay.

No one likes a silent wake. It really is for the living, not the dead.

Dave found me in the crush, coffee cup in one hand. People gave us room—or maybe it was just me. Him they knew and liked. I was a stranger, and maybe they could sense I'd brought this death into their community.

"Good turnout," I said, working on a plate-sized sugar cookie. "They had a lot of friends."

"Brendt grew up here, and Elsie one county over. Not everyone moves away."

"You doing okay?"

"Sure." But he didn't smile.

We hadn't talked much in the two days since ruining Markson's jamboree. Chief Gator had taken one look at the scene in Brendt's house and dismissed the suicide scenario, but he didn't get any further before federal agents airlifted in and claimed jurisdiction. Which was reasonable enough, given the numerous SEC violations, environmental and commercial lawbreaking on a wide scale and apparent involvement of Russian criminal elements.

Remarkably, Wilbur Markson was staying afloat—a victim, like everyone else. The Russians were either dead or had disappeared, conveniently, on nonstop flights back to the motherland.

"The CEO who started all this, Brinker, he's not even in jail," Dave said. "He's been getting pizza deliveries out at his mansion."

"How do you know that?"

"Heard it down at Sully's." He shrugged. "It was him and the Russkies all along."

"He was just an opportunist." When Clayco's board let Brinker know his division might be on the block, he must have gotten worried—and rightly so because even a blind-and-deaf auditor couldn't miss the games they were playing. "I think every single person at Clay Micro was stealing from the company, and only the fact that they were making so much profit let them get away with it."

"So why'd the Russians still want to buy in, if it was that raggedy?"

"My guess? Someone like Brinker they could understand. Just another amoral *biznesman* on the make. It was probably oligarch money at the top, looking for investments in America—lots of natural gas in Russia, not to mention other resource extraction, so it makes sense they were starting with a business they knew. And because you apparently can't make an honest dollar in Russia nowadays, the mafiya were in, which meant they had their crew of enforcers handy to smooth the deals."

"Well, they're out of it now."

And indeed, Dagger Light's acquisition of Clay Micro had been stopped dead. Rockwire, Dagger Light's part owner, was "under investigation." Markson had already started to extricate himself and his money, claiming no knowledge of what such small and obscure holdings in his vast empire might have been up to. Throwing the Russians under the bus, of course, but that was okay. They'd find other opportunities later, other chances for synergistic cooperation.

People Dave knew came over, shook hands, said what you say in circumstances like these. They generally had an eye for me, too, but I didn't offer much, kept quiet and let Dave send them on.

"What are you going to do now?" he asked me, in between.

"I don't know."

I really didn't. Zeke was on the mend, back in New York, but I was responsible for getting him so badly hurt in the first place. Brendt and Elsie were dead. I didn't feel bad about the Russians, but only psychopaths can kill so many people and not be affected.

Well, soldiers, maybe, but that's a different story and even there the PTSD numbers are stunning.

Considering how murderous mankind has been through history, you'd think we might have gotten better at dealing with the consequences.

"I might take a sabbatical," I said. "Visit some friends in quiet, sunny parts of the world. Sit on the beach."

Dave grinned, a flash of his old self. "Friends like, I dunno . . . Harmony?"

"Harmony." I smiled back, but it faded quickly. "She left."

"Really? Man, I thought you two were, shit, like totally *made* for each other."

"Maybe that's the problem."

At least we'd kept her out of the clutches of the law. Dave and I didn't lie or make stuff up during the many interviews we'd had with law enforcement, but I know I committed numerous sins of omission. They had Harmony's name, and some useless eyewitness descriptions, and that wouldn't get them anywhere. If she didn't want to be found, she wouldn't be found.

"That's too bad." Dave shook his head. "I'm sorry."

"Nah." I finished the cookie. "Or maybe yes. I don't know."

Later I found the bank officer, Vanderalt, standing to one side. He was almost as busy as Dave, a steady flow of people offering greetings, nods, brief conversations. Like I said, a pillar of the community, beloved by all.

"Silas." He shook my hand. "An eventful visit you've had."

"I'm sorry it happened." I nodded toward the caskets. "Too many bad actors in the world."

"So not meth gangs after all."

I squinted for a moment, then remembered Dave's speculation about the destroyed garage. "The Russian gangsters. Yes, they cut quite a path of destruction."

"I'm glad no one got hurt, that time."

"No one got shot. Dave lost his business."

"Didn't he tell you?" Vanderalt looked surprised.

"What?"

"The mineral rights. Turns out he might be sitting on a nice clean patch of Marcellus shale."

"Natural gas." I nodded slowly. "No way."

"I was trying to think of anything he might get out of the land, and I called some of the other landholders nearby. Scouts have been around, offering contracts. It's not lottery money by any means, but it could pay off the mortgage and maybe turn into some cash flow, over time."

"Didn't he *know* that?"

"I gather they'd been trying to talk to him, and he just kept sending them away."

Figures. I looked at Dave across the room. Two women were speaking to him, close in, and I saw that amazing grin appear for a moment. "That's too ironic for words."

"Isn't it though?" Vanderalt was probably one of the few people in Clabbton to appreciate that sort of thing.

"But fracking—" I thought of the drilling site I'd seen, the swath of destruction, the hammering so loud it made your eyeballs hurt. "Is he going to take it?"

"Ah." Vanderalt paused. "That's the question. With Dave, you never know."

The wake thinned out after an hour or two, people drifting away. Dave and I left, stepping back into the sunshine outside, past the funeral home guy still murmuring his words of comfort. We stood by the Charger, which Dave had finally waxed to a brilliant, blinding sheen.

"You're leaving, aren't you?" he said while we waited for the parking lot to empty further.

"Yeah."

"Back to Vegas?"

"No, I told you—" But I saw him grinning. "No, not Vegas."

"Maybe I'll come see you, up there in the city."

"Do that."

"Well, I . . ." He hesitated. "You know. Hope you stay in touch, that's all."

"How could I not?" I turned my face to the sun, feeling its warmth. "We're brothers."

CHAPTER THIRTY-SEVEN

The cornfields stretched as far as we could see in front of us.

Which was far, because the land was flat as a pool table, and this early in the season the corn was no more than shoots poking from the dark harrowed rows.

"How do you even know it's corn?"

"Because we're in Ohio. What else do they grow here?"

"Soybeans. Beets." Harmony shook her head. "Rye. Lots of cash crops."

Yes. Harmony. I hadn't explained everything to Dave.

She and I had one last piece of business to see through.

"What do you think?"

I looked at the distant house, by itself on the plain, surrounded by a white painted fence. In addition to the usual outbuildings—two barns, a roof with some trucks underneath, hayricks, utility sheds—there was a big, old-fashioned satellite dish and several antennas, one at least thirty feet high. A single road led up to the estate. We'd watched for several hours, and a steady flow of vehicles had gone in and out: FedEx, town cars, a limousine and even a police cruiser, though he only drove through, waved to someone on the porch and reversed out.

"I think Camp David would be easier."

"He always says how he lives in the same house he grew up in."

"So maybe his parents were paranoid, right-wing millionaires."

"Right-wing?"

"Look at the bumper of the SUV by the house." She handed me the binoculars. "That's a Ron Paul sticker."

I couldn't get a clear focus. We were a half mile away, at a picnic table by the side of the road. You don't usually see rest areas on two-lane county backroads, but we weren't the first ones to stop here. A trash barrel was full of Styrofoam takeout containers and soda cans, and the rutted spring mud was completely torn up by tire tracks.

"Ron Paul's a libertarian."

"That's not right-wing?"

"They're prepared to argue the point." I handed back the binoculars. "Very well prepared."

An RV pulled in, trundling off the road and sighing to a halt. After a few moments the side door opened and a woman in jeans stepped out, followed by a white-haired man in a Hawaiian shirt. Husband-and-wife retirees, surely.

Harmony had already disappeared her binocs.

"Afternoon," the man said, nodding to us. "This here's the spot, ain't it?"

"It's not bad, I guess." I made room at the picnic table. "We just stopped to eat our lunch."

"You know whose house that is over there?" He pointed. "Wilbur Markson."

"Oh?"

"A billionaire, and he lives like plain folks."

"How about that."

"Uh-huh. Smartest investor ever. Smarter than those idiots in Washington, for sure."

His wife put two bottles of energy water on the table and sat down. "We stop here every time we pass through," she said.

"Uh-huh."

She looked over at us as her husband joined her at the table. "On vacation?"

"A working vacation, I suppose." I noticed some road dust in the distance. "You know how it goes, always a few loose ends."

"You said it."

We sat for another minute. The tourists murmured to themselves as they ate chips. The dust drew closer, then resolved into several vehicles, pacing each other at high speed toward Markson's compound.

"Look there." The husband stopped eating.

"What's going on?"

It wasn't police or emergency—no lights, no official markings. One truck with equipment on its roof, a van, and several smaller, anonymous cars.

The first vehicle made it through the gate and most of the way up the drive, but guards appeared and waved the others to a halt at the entrance. Even from the distance it looked like shouting and arguments.

"They're armed." Harmony had the binoculars out again, ignoring the tourists.

"What?"

"The guards. But they haven't drawn weapons."

And why would they? The arrivals were all news reporters.

Which we knew because twenty-seven minutes earlier Clara had posted her first story about Markson's desperate and colossal fraud.

Once she'd started digging, evidence piled up fast—so fast you had to wonder why the regulators hadn't opened enforcement hearings long ago. That would happen soon enough now, though, no matter who'd been taking payoffs.

Markson had indeed lost his golden touch. Probably the worldwide economic collapse hit him just like everyone else, but he tried to make it back before anyone noticed—he was Wilbur Markson, by God, and he had that three-decade record to uphold. Hubris? Panic? The first soft tendrils of senility?

It didn't matter. He needed money, he needed results and he needed them fast. He'd been doing business in Eastern Europe for a long time—some buyout equity, some utility privatization, some straight stock investment—and it was easy to start dealmaking further and further into the gray zones.

Clay Micro turned out to be the loose thread that unraveled the whole mess. Once it snagged, his new Russian partners reverted to old ways of solving problems, and then it was only a matter of time. Markson could neither suppress the collapse nor continue funding his losses.

And now, finally, the entire world was getting the story.

The RV driver was on his phone.

"No, we're right here, seeing it for real . . . outside his farm, you bet. In Ohio. Can you believe it? There's a downright *mob* in front now!" He listened. "No, that's impossible. Russians, you say? What are you watching, Fox News? No, I don't . . . never . . . he was ordering people *killed*?"

The man turned to his wife. "They're saying he's worse than Goldman Sachs!"

Harmony handed me the binoculars. The driver was right, the reporters *were* a mob, gesturing and yelling at the guards. They'd closed the gate and started to spread out along the fence, positioning themselves to prevent the more enterprising journalists from trying to climb over.

A flash of sunlight reflected off a window on the second floor, across the empty fields. Perhaps Wilbur Markson was up there this very moment, in his home office. A few minutes ago he could have been setting up another megadeal, earning another billion dollars, toying with the fate of millions as he talked on speakerphone to plutocrats all over the world.

Not now.

My own phone buzzed once, and I saw a new text.

SWTR.A -115.83 (-12.4%) haha awesome

"What?" said Harmony.

"Johnny's making good on his short." We stepped away from the tourists, who were still staring at Markson's estate and talking in low voices to each other.

"How much did he commit?"

"No idea. But I think the year's bonus season might just be looking up."

"I love seeing the free market at work."

Before we got in the car, I glanced back once more. The TV truck had extended its aerial antenna. More cars were arriving—the police, finally, and a pair of shiny black SUVs. Damage control. The fight had only begun, and Markson had billions of dollars to defend himself with. He might never go to jail, but his reputation was burned to ash.

The Buddha had just retired in disgrace.

I closed the door and started the car. Harmony smiled, resting one hand on my shoulder. We drove out of the turnout, bouncing over ruts, and turned east.

It was time to go home.

COOPE
Cooper, Mike,
Full ratchet /

LOOSCAN
09/14

LOO